THERE
WILL BE
KILLING

THERE
WILL BE
KILLING

A Novel of War and Murder

John L. Hart
and Olivia Rupprecht

THE
STORY PLANT

THERE
WILL BE
KILLING

A Novel of War and Murder

John L. Hart
and Olivia Rupprecht

The Story Plant
Studio Digital CT, LLC
P.O. Box 4331
Stamford, CT 06907

Copyright © 2014 by John L. Hart and Olivia Rupprecht
Jacket design by Barbara Aronica Buck
Interior illustrations by John L. Hart

Print ISBN-13: 978-1-61188-166-0
E-book ISBN: 978-1-61188-167-7

Visit our website at www.TheStoryPlant.com

First Story Plant paperback printing: October 2014

Printed in the United States of America
0 9 8 7 6 5 4 3 2 1

For those who were there
Those who wrote
For those who welcomed me home

Those who know do not talk
Those who talk do not know.
—Lao Tzu, Tao Te Ching

The Nightbird and Morning Glory

If you flew like a Nightbird up over the mountains and into the dark of the jungle and then sat on a limb above a small animal trail and waited. . . .

You would see the point man. His growing anxiety is becoming palpable. He thinks he can feel someone or something trailing him.

He whispers. "Shep, that you? Quit fucking around."

There is no response.

Panicked, Point Man heads out again. The Nightbird's eyes follow him. Point Man's breathing is gasping and scared. He tries to move quietly but everything he steps on crackles and pops, and that just adds to his panic. He thinks he hears something off to his left and, startled, starts moving to his right. He is disoriented and becoming exhausted from his own adrenaline. He slows down. His stuff weighs the world on his back and he wants to drop it all and just run. Instead, he turns.

Point Man can't stop his smile or his near sob of relief as he steps forward, says, "Oh God, I'm glad it is you."

The Ranger Lieutenant punches his shoulder. "Get a grip, Stanley."

"Yeah, yes sir."

Suddenly the M16s open up behind them. They hear shouts and yelling from their guys on patrol until the Ranger Lieutenant shouts back.

"Cease fire, knock it off!"

The shooting stops and then it is very quiet, very tense.

Back down the path a short distance, imagine the deep bass of Graveyard Train. Up in the tree is a predator. He looks down at the last three men of the patrol and isolates the last man by shooting the two men in front of him. The last man standing is frozen, doesn't know where the deadly fire has come from. The predator drops out of the tree right behind him. The terrified young soldier whirls around to shoot, only to have both of his hands cut off by a blade in a glinting blur. He turns to run with stumps of his wrists spraying his life out but drops and screams as he bleeds out.

Ranger Lieutenant and Point Man carefully make their way back to the too silent patrol. They come upon the bodies of the men who were shot. All of their hands have been cut off at the wrists. The Ranger Lieutenant and Point Man come upon one bloodless hand after another, all pointing ahead to a body sitting up against a tree. His severed head in his lap, the startled eyes that saw the predator stare straight at them as the Nightbird watches, then flies away again.

1

NHA TRANG
THE REPUBLIC OF VIETNAM
MAY, 1969

It was shortly after dawn, a brilliant clear day, and yet Israel Moskowitz could only wonder what he had done to land in the hot stinking bowels of a dead animal. Sure, the charter TWA flight from the states to the Tan Son Nhut Air Base had been pleasant enough, but from there he had been shuttled onto a no-frills military transport and disgorged *here*. A tarmac within spitting distance of the South China Sea where he stood sucker-punched by what had to be one hundred and fifteen degrees of scorch and simmer heat spiked with ninety-nine percent humidity.

Something had gone terribly wrong.

For twenty-nine years, the cosmic planes of destiny had been in perfect alignment with the whole summa cum laude package of what had been Israel Moskowitz's preordained right to a glorious, successful life. Sweaty, steaming stench and rot and rice paddies had not been part of the deal.

Yes, the war was escalating. But what country in its right mind would draft a child psychiatrist fresh out of his residency from Columbia University Med School and send him to Vietnam? He'd been told not to worry, the situation was a screw up and would get fixed. His father had contacts in high places and favors to cash in, namely with New York's 2nd congressional district's highest elected official. Israel could still hear Congressman Atkinson's assurances: *At worst, you will be serving your obligation to your country at an army hospital child guidance clinic in Washington, D.C. You'll love being in the nation's capital, in the heart of the action, so to speak.*

Oh, he was in the heart of the action all right. Only it was in the war ravaged armpit of Southeast Asia, a mere 8,761 miles from D.C.

Now Israel Moskowitz, with his brilliant MD in child psychiatry, was in some very deep shit. Heat radiated up through the soles of his boots and beat down on his head, doing its best to turn him into a melted puddle of nothing but a fifty pound duffel bag and the fogged up horn-rimmed glasses that kept sliding down his distinctively Jewish nose.

Some fellow psych officer was supposed to meet him here but hadn't shown up yet. So Israel shuffled forward, wondering if he could make it to the nearest building before he passed out—or, threw up. Ever since opening the mailbox to find a REPORT FOR DUTY notice instead of brochures for a honeymoon in Spain, he had battled the threat of nausea. Even worse was the slight but deeply troubling tremor he had recently developed in his once steady hands.

Israel sucked in a deep breath that felt like swallowing a soaked pillow, shoved up his horn rims, and was re-hoisting his duffel, when a jeep rounded the corner and came to a rubber-burning halt a few feet away.

The sandaled feet that swung out belonged to a male about his own age and pinch above average height, but their similarities stopped there. No way had this guy spent a Saturday studying the Torah or living in the shadow of skyscrapers. Dressed in surfer shorts and a faded USC Trojans Tennis Dept. tee, a booney hat topped off sun bleached hair. Athletic build; all-American good looks. He should have been selling ad copy for Coppertone.

"Captain Moskowitz? Israel Moskowitz?" A lazy good vibrations smile and a tip of the hat to Israel's nod. "I'm Gregg. Captain Gregg Kelly, clinical psychologist at the 99KO."

Israel was immediately struck by two things: He had never before heard such a beautiful voice emerge from a woman or a man. And: "You, uh. . .you don't look like you belong here."

Gregg threw back his head and let out a big belly laugh, so infectious that Israel smiled. It had been awhile.

"And you do?" Gregg's eyes were a deep blue. They sparkled like the waves he probably caught on a surfboard. "Hell man, none of us belong here. We're all just counting our days."

"Days?"

"Until you go home."

"How many do you have?"

"One-twenty-six and a wake up," no pause. "Less than a month and I'm hitting the magic number."

"What number is that?"

"Ninety-nine. Two-digit midget. If anyone asks, you're counting down as of today from three-sixty-four."

"Three. Sixty. Four." His voice a croak, Israel couldn't fathom spending three hundred and sixty-four days and nights in this hell hole. Yet Gregg had somehow gotten this far and still seemed mentally sound. At least he had maintained the ability to laugh. And his hands weren't shaking as they reached for the duffel bag that had dropped to Israel's feet.

"Hop in and we'll drop off your stuff at the officers' quarters before I take you to meet Lieutenant Colonel Kohn and the rest of the crew."

Gregg no sooner hit the gas than it seemed he was pointing out the 8th Field Hospital compound where their psychiatric unit—the 99KO— was located amidst a small grid of wood framed buildings surrounded by high green walls of sandbags. A few more turns outside the hospital compound and Gregg was pulling up to an old villa that could have come out of Les Misérables, with its cracked stucco walls covered in wild bougainvillea, the psychedelic color of Tang. In short, Israel had his new room, up on the second floor next to Gregg's, and across from a shared bathroom, where Gregg was taking a quick shower.

Before Israel could switch into a fresh shirt or peel off the sweat soaked underwear that clung to his nuts that were itching like crazy, another voice called from below:

"Hello! Anybody here?"

Because the other medical officers who lived at the villa were already at the unit, Israel forced himself to emerge from the privacy of his room—a room equipped with the cooling breeze of an overhead fan.

"Up here," he called back, pausing at the top of the stairs.

There was something he couldn't explain, something instinctive that made him want to keep his distance from anyone who projected...Israel wasn't sure what the guy was projecting but even with a flight of stairs between them he gave off a vibe like a switchblade stashed inside a tuxedo.

Or in this case, a crisp, laundered Tiger camo shirt emblazoned with whatever insignia gave him the latitude to wear nonissue silver bracelets on one dark arm. And, what looked like some skin damage on the other; aviator shades pushed over a widow's peak, hair straight and black as a raven's wing. He smiled to reveal even, white teeth as he bounded up the stairs with a duffel bag in each hand and a rucksack on his back.

Up close, too close, Israel could not see a single bead of sweat pop from a single pore of his smooth, olive skin from the exertion. Penetrating eyes locked on Israel like radar zooming in on a target. Those eyes, a *7up* bottle green, were made even more striking by their slight almond shape, suggesting the new house guest had inherited some exotic DNA. But the uniform, nose, and cheekbones that could have been engineered by NASA all coincided with a pitch-perfect voice that could have come from Anywhere, USA.

"Let me guess, you're the other new shrink." His duffels landed with a *clank* and a *thud*. The right hand he extended sported an expensive looking watch, and those were definitely scars, not only on his right arm but also the left. There was also a fine line of white scar tissue that ran from below his left ear and disappeared into a black T-shirt beneath the jungle fatigues.

As for his rank, the insignia declared him a major and, therefore, a senior officer who was offering a handshake instead of a salute after making a mockery of professional protocol by referring to them both as "shrinks."

Israel awkwardly cleared his throat. Swiped his sweaty palm on his sweaty jungle fatigues and hesitantly accepted the handshake.

"Israel Moskowitz, MD Columbia University. Three hundred and sixty four days."

The other new shrink's hand was cool, dry, and just the right firmness in grip as he responded, "J.D. Mikel. Call me J.D. I was going to be the new shrink in Da Nang, but got sent here on special duty instead. Great to meet you, Izzy."

2

"There are many kinds of casualties in wars," the Colonel began. "Psychiatric casualties, of course, have been around since the beginning of warfare. Human beings, although an aggressive, brutal, and vicious species, are not well designed for long-term combat stress...."

Israel stared at his new Chief of Psychiatry and CO, Lt. Colonel Kohn, a kindly middle-aged career officer from the Midwest, and tried to focus on his little welcome speech. The other medical personnel, including Gregg, were busy with morning rounds, so just three of them were gathered at the table that doubled as a nurses station: Colonel Kohn, him, and the other new shrink, Dr. J.D. Mikel, who had called him by an old nickname, Izzy. He said it so slap-to-the-back familiar it felt déjà vu weird. Only his best friend Morrie could still get away with calling him that. And that was only because Morrie had been confined to a wheelchair since seventh grade after trying to save Israel's dog from getting hit by a speeding cab on their way to play ball in a park.

The unit's mascot, a mutt Gregg had called "K.O.," parked her rump by Israel's chair, which directly faced the air conditioner unit blasting cold air for the entire room, and its marching line of beds filled with psychiatric casualties. If the random tremor in his hands and constant urge to puke were any indicator, Israel feared it wouldn't be long before he was a candidate for one of those beds himself.

Mikel caught his line of vision, gave a slight conspiratorial smile, and then covered his mouth for a little yawn as Colonel Kohn went on about earlier American wars, when soldiers would return with "the shakes," or people would say that old Sam had lost his nerve, but how, by the beginning of the Vietnam War, Pentagon researchers had scientifically determined that nearly everyone in a combat situation was slowly breaking down the entire time that they were exposed to war.

"Basically, it is just a matter of time." Colonel Kohn gestured toward a thrashing patient in full restraints. "Everyone's psyche, they realized, was slowly eroding. Some faster, due to earlier childhood and life traumas, and others perhaps from too much, too soon in the war zone, with quick and repeated exposure to horrors moving up the erosion—"

"Help me! HELP ME!" screamed the patient, jerking against the restraints with such force his spine arched off the mattress, causing the metal headboard to slam against the wall. The head nurse, a luscious redhead in jungle fatigues Israel had briefly met, Capt. Margie Kennedy, broke from the morning rounds entourage and moved in that direction.

"True, some humans are slower to wear down," Colonel Kohn sonorously intoned, "perhaps due to their fortunate genetics and upbringing. And in rare cases, a few individuals actually seem to thrive. . . ." He glanced at Mikel before looking again directly at Israel. "But by the time we got to this war, here in Vietnam, the Pentagon was anticipating these kinds of mental casualties. This is why *we* are all *here*."

Here. As in the 99th KO. The 8th Field Hospital's psychiatric unit conveniently placed in a combat zone. We. As in the psychiatrists, psychologists, psychiatric social workers, psychiatric nurses, and enlisted psychiatric techs who are doing the good work for our brave fellow men in uniform, serving on the front lines of Vietnam....

Finally, Colonel Kohn wound it all up with, "The rate of psychiatric casualties is huge and basically unknown to the general population back home. But really, there is one thing, and one thing only, that matters and you can never forget. The patients here are very dangerous. Every minute, every hour and day that you are here, never forget that these patients were trained to kill people. There is no locked ward. Forget, even for a second, that you are treating trained killers who have been pushed over the edge, and you could be the one going back home in a body bag. Any questions?" was clearly directed at Israel who stared numbly back at Colonel Kohn while the loud drone of the air conditioner blended with another shriek of "HELP ME!"

"Okay then, we have an interesting catatonic patient with Dr. Thibeaux to discuss, along with our rather vocal Sergeant Waters in the restraints over there. Dr. Mikel, Dr. Moskowitz?" The colonel got up, his attention carefully trained on the new child psychiatrist. "After you."

As they moved toward the mind-blasted Sergeant Waters, Israel tried to wrap his brain around what he'd been repeatedly told in officer's training: His first priority was to "preserve the fighting force," which meant *not* getting damaged soldiers like these home. No, his job was to get them back to their units and the same combat zones that had landed them in this front line mental hospital that made Bellevue look like Club Med.

"As you can see, we have fourteen beds here," Colonel Kohn was saying. "These patients have been brought in from the field or came through our Camp McDermott outpatient clinic. It's just a short drive and for now the two of you will be accompanying Dr. Kelly out there every day directly after rounds." Having caught up with the group, Kohn addressed the leader, mid-thirties at most, with thinning brown hair spared from a comb-over. "This is our chief psychiatrist, Dr. Robert David Thibeaux. Robert David, I believe you were on call last night. Would you care to fill us in on the situation here with Sergeant Waters?"

"Well, now thank you Dr. Kohn, it would surely be my pleasure." Robert David Thibeaux's refined southern accent and aristocratic bearing struck Israel as absurd in this setting as the military making attempted suicide a punishable, criminal offense because it damaged government property. "It was a quiet night except for Waters. The Sergeant has been agitated, and ranting and hallucinating constantly about this so-called Boogeyman story that got started a few weeks ago and seems to be spreading like a bad case of VD."

"And what has the Sergeant said about this Boogeyman?" Mikel asked.

Waters cried out a terrible sound, a keening wail punctuated by "Ghost Soldier! He gets you in the dark. Shep's dead, everyone's dead. Oh god, please," he gasped, pleaded, *"Help me!"*

For a blessed moment Israel was able to completely detach, to step outside his body and observe the macabre scene like he was back home in the movie theater, watching the horror film he'd seen last year, *Night of the Living Dead*. Only now starring in the show was Sergeant Waters, eyes bulging, panting, and sobbing; writhing in restraints on the mattress like he was being attacked by ghouls. And Mikel, he could be the director, stroking his chin and strangely untouched by the riveting performance. The surrounding audience, all dressed in mottled green, zoomed in and out, then *snap*.

A SLAM of metal bed to steel Quonset wall coincided with the sudden shriek of "STOP"—Slam—"STOP"—Slam—"STOP!" Waters' earlier shrieking and writhing violently escalated, accompanied now by terrible grimaces and facial tics that were hideous to watch.

Thibeaux urgently tried to calm him with that low, soothing voice that dripped culture from somewhere down south, an assurance of "Shh, nothing will hurt you here. All the bad things have gone away." Then, to Margie asked, "How much Thorazine did you give him before?"

"Two hundred and fifty milligrams. He gets it b.i.d."

"My god," Israel blurted, disbelief overtaking his horror of the whole scene. "Two-fifty twice a day? That is a ton. He shouldn't even be conscious."

"But as you can see, it is not even touching him," responded Thibeaux. "More Margie, up it stat to three hundred fifty q.i.d. The hallucinations are driving his agitation towards burning him up in his own skin."

As Margie saw to the injection, Thibeaux continued to soothe Waters in a lullaby voice until the drugs kicked in, mercifully quick, then promptly ushered the group "right this way" as if they were being led to a cotillion ball rather than another hospital bed, fully occupied, eerily silent.

"We have here Lieutenant Bill Wilson. Just brought in two days ago from Pleiku." Solicitously, "How are you, Lieutenant?"

Wilson stared up at the ceiling, unblinking, his eyes fixed on something no one else could see.

Clap, clap! The sharp strike of Thibeaux' palms next to Wilson's ear produced nothing, not even a flinch. Next Thibeaux shouted, "Look out!"

Israel ducked, covering his head with the hands he struggled to get under control.

Someone softly touched his shoulder. "It's okay." Gregg's voice.

Israel forced his hands from his head and behind his back, the substance of jelly. Then Margie caught his gaze. She was looking at him with a kind of knowing look. Even if he couldn't force more than a grimace in response to her little smile, Israel was grateful. *Thank god*, he thought, *there is someone else here as scared as me.*

"Observe." Thibeaux gently lifted Wilson's arm high into the air, released. It stayed there, a mannequin pose.

"As you can see, Lieutenant Wilson exhibits classic catatonic features. The waxy flexibility of his limbs and the nonresponsiveness to sensory stimulation confirms this diagnosis. Lieutenant Wilson was found in the field, sitting there, just like this. He has yet to speak. Every man around him in the field had been killed. Clearly, they are not speaking either regarding what happened to instigate this extraordinary condition."

"Wilson is our newest arrival and will likely be sent out within a week, Dr. Moskowitz," explained Colonel Kohn. "We have only seven days or less with the patients. If they are admitted here, they are almost always acute and severe and if we do not think that we can get them back to duty within seven days then they are sent out to Japan."

Thibeaux lowered Wilson's arm, touched him warmly on his shoulder, a sincere "thank you, Bill," and he moved on to the next bed where another poor soul, in full leather restraints on his wrists and ankles, slept heavily. His face was calm, at peace, and Israel could see that he was just a big boy.

"Corporal Kim Sellers," Margie announced, handing Thibeaux another metal clad chart.

"Corporal Sellers is completely restrained and heavily sedated with good cause," Thibeaux continued, as though lectures in catatonia and demonstration lessons of deep compassion were just a typical day's work. "This man is extremely agitated. He is paranoid and he is violent. We have dangerous jobs here, Dr. Moskowitz. The KO down in Saigon lost their psychiatrist, a social worker and a specialist six months ago. They weren't the first and they won't be the last."

"Lost?" Israel noticed the group was very quiet. "How were they lost?"

"They were killed by a patient. And unless we want to risk the same fate, we must all be most careful with our Corporal here. He is quite dangerous to himself—and to you. And you ... and you." Thibeaux' finger pointing down the line ended with Israel, before Thibeaux jabbed the air a good distance from the unconscious Sellers, as if he didn't trust the corporal's teeth from taking a body part while the rest of him slept. "Watch him. We will keep him heavily sedated, but do not turn your backs to him if you get him up to the toilet or you are feeding him or bathing him. The medication will slow him but he is a tied up tiger. And he will not hesitate to take you down."

Israel willed himself to detach again, but he couldn't. His head was buzzing and his stomach churned bile, produced by the dawning realization that he was in a war zone where the patients were murdering their doctors. This was worse than anything in a horror movie. He was trapped in a ghastly prison sentence and had a year of his life to spend in this kind of special hell. Why, *why,* hadn't he followed in his father's footsteps and gone to law school instead?

"Good work, Robert David." Colonel Kohn congratulated Thibeaux with a salute. "Okay folks, that's it. Clinic people, move out." Then, privately, "Dr. Moskowitz, as you can see we keep some formality in rounds, trying of course to remember we are doctors here in this place."

Israel swallowed. His throat was sandpaper. He felt numb all over, except his fingers, toes were tingling. He didn't trust his voice but he had to say something. "Yes, sir. Where—where is the clinic again?"

The Colonel came in closer, put a steadying hand on his shoulder. "Take it easy, Izzy," he said quietly. "It's your first day. Don't worry, we will get you through this."

For the second time today someone had called him Izzy. It took Israel back to more innocent times. It took him back to Morrie who would roar at the irony of his best pal getting saddled with a dorky nickname he'd ditched at the onset of pubescent acne when *Iz ze da pits or what?* threatened to stick like gum to a shoe.

What Morrie got stuck with was worse. Much worse. He would trade in his wheelchair for combat boots and jungle fatigues in a heartbeat. And because Israel needed to find some dark humor in something, do a little more penance for the accident no one had ever blamed him for but himself, "Izzy" managed a nod.

"That's it," said Kohn, sounding like a proud coach whose best player hadn't let a little rough sacking take him out of the game. He even threw in a back slap as he called, "Hey, Gregg, would you be so kind as to take Izzy and Dr. Mikel for the usual introductions at headquarters with The Emperor, then show them the ropes at the clinic?"

"My pleasure, sir," Gregg called back and promptly steered his charges out of the air conditioned unit and into the sweltering heat.

The effect was immediate and intense. Izzy felt like he'd slammed into an invisible forest fire while the humidity simultaneously plunged him under boiling water. He struggled to breathe. Sweat moved down his back and his thighs.

"It's hot," he gasped, and felt so damn stupid. *You're in a war. If you aren't careful, the patients are going to kill you, and here you are whining about the weather?*

"Oh yeah, it's hot at first, but then..." Gregg gave him a sympathetic look, "...it can get even worse if you're not careful. You're not wearing underwear are you?"

"Uh..."

"Because you can get a bad rash if you do."

"Yeah, crotch rot is bad," agreed Mikel, who must not be human because he was not sweating, panting, or showing any signs of physical distress. "Guys bleed down there if it gets bad and if they get infected, it's worse than bad. You hanging in there, Izzy?"

"Yeah, yeah. Fine, fine," he lied, knowing if this cool cat Mikel in his aviator shades was showing concern, he must look like road kill. Izzy half expected to see buzzards circling overhead while they continued to traipse across the metal tracks that covered the sand and mud stretching to the headquarters it was taking them forever to reach.

The many different buildings serving various hospital functions that Gregg pointed out en route had a temporary yet somehow established feel—like the Red Cross building that looked a bit like a tropical lounge with a bunch of soldiers hanging around on a thatched roof porch where a stunning brunette suddenly emerged.

Spying Gregg, she gave a whistle and waved.

"Hey, Nikki!" Gregg stopped in mid-step and motioned her over. "Got a couple of new docs in town for you to meet."

As the prettier than pretty Red Cross girl *in a dress* bounded their way, every eyeball still on the porch ate up her tracks. With a dazzling smile spiked with a twang, Nikki said, "Well, welcome to Vietnam, Doctors. Come on over and get some cold lemonade. Make a phone call while you're at it."

"That's a very kind offer," responded Mikel. "But Gregg's taking us to headquarters."

"Yeah, thanks a lot, Nikki," Gregg agreed before Izzy could protest, "but I promised Colonel Kohn I'd get them introduced to Colonel Kellogg, then out to the Camp McDermott clinic. Maybe later?"

"You just come when you can, Gregg, and I'll make y'all some fresh lemonade. And remember, I've got the phone if you want to call home. Even if it's not Wednesday." A wink and Nikki was gone.

Gregg and Mikel were already several paces ahead when Gregg stopped and pointed to the space between them. "Hey, Iz, if you want to know all there is to know about Nikki, ya gotta come and get it."

Izzy caught up in the hope there might be some cold air at headquarters to compensate for the phone call he was dying to make to his fiancé. The letters Rachel had sent to officer's training were already falling apart from his constant folding and unfolding to read and re-read what he had already committed to memory.

"Nikki is Margie's roommate." Gregg's voice had some kind of soothing magic to it, like they were chumming around the water cooler for some hospital gossip. "Nikki is a really fine woman—they both are—but while Margie's available, Nikki has something going with a strange one that was fortunately elsewhere this morning. Peck, you'll meet him soon enough. He's the other psychiatrist besides Robert David."

"What makes Peck so strange?" Mikel sounded curious. Izzy didn't care if this Peck ate lab rats for breakfast as long as he could get his hands on that phone and chug a gallon of the lemonade Nikki had offered.

"Well ... I don't like to badmouth anyone, but let's just say he's a real piece of work. One day he's Mr. Nice Guy, the next he's filing a report because some captain passed him on the highway. *Oops.* Guess I did cut that one a little close. He left some candy out on the table at our quarters, and then got all pissed off because Robert David ate a piece while he was gone. Petty things like that, plus some other stuff you'll hear about that gets a little disturbing. Peck has a room at the villa, doesn't use it much, which suits

the rest of us fine." Gregg shrugged. "You can draw your own conclusions when you meet him, but beats me what Nikki sees in the
man. Especially, because she's a 'Dolly.'"

"A what?"

"He means a Red Cross Dolly," Mikel explained. "They got the
nickname Donut Dollies because of all the donuts they gave out to
the troops in World War II."

"Donuts sound good." Izzy wondered if he could keep one down
if Nikki offered one along with the lemonade. How he had loved the
donuts that were always around the hospital break room. A little too
much perhaps, though no one would guess it now. He had already
dropped twenty pounds and was on track to lose another five in
water weight before they made it to the stupid headquarters.

"They do a lot of other work to support our men. Like having a
shoulder to spare when 'Dear Johns' get delivered, and that's a huge
help for sure with morale," Gregg said. "Except for the nurses, the
Dollies are the only round eyes around here."

"Round eyes?"

"The women who aren't Asian." Mikel again.

"She, uh...she said something about a call?"

"Sure, let's come back after lunch. It is Big Wednesday, phone
call day." Gregg thumbed back at the line of soldiers on the porch
that was now behind them. "You can call home, back to the world.
It's a big deal."

Home. Izzy nodded, unable to get another word past the lump in
his throat. Calling home would be a very big deal right now, bigger
than any deal he could think of. Because he felt like an eight year old
sent off to camp—

A camp so far away it was no longer considered to be in the world.

3

They continued to walk on, passing some surgical units, a mess hall, the officer's mess. Gregg knew Colonel Kohn was worried about Izzy and there was ample cause for that. Everything about their new Dr. Israel Moskowitz suggested a classic intellectual who'd get shell-shocked by stumbling into a strip joint. His bottom lip gnawing, probably to stop it from quivering, did not bode well. The erratic tremor in his hands bode even worse. Doctors were scarce and the 99KO needed him. Just like they needed their other new psychiatrist, Dr. J.D. Mikel.

Gregg wasn't yet sure what to make of him. While most everyone was not there voluntarily—him included with the ink barely dry on his PhD from USC when he got served—Mikel came across as an organic anomaly in his element, owning every room he walked into. Fine, let him have the whole continent of Asia if he wanted it. Guys like Gregg Kelly were perfectly content with a surfboard, a tenure-track professorship, and a little bungalow off the Ventura Highway—especially if it came with the dream girl next door he hadn't given up on yet.

"So, what can you tell me about the CO you're taking us to meet?" Mikel asked, as if he was just making small talk. Gregg knew better. This was not a personality type to make small talk about anything or anyone. Everything that came out of his mouth had some purpose behind it. Even if it was to distract a colleague like Izzy from the urge to go crazy or start crying for mommy.

"The CO's not a bad guy. He's a career medical officer, and that's cool, but we call him The Emperor because Colonel Kellogg really, *really* wants to be 'General Kellogg' and rumor has it he was recently passed over for his promotion again which might explain why he's been dressing like Patton lately. I think the idea is to make sure everyone sees him as the true warrior he is. . . ." Gregg negated that with a loud cough into his fist as they finally reached the building known as headquarters, "But the unfortunate outcome is that he looks more like—"

"Motherfuck, goddamn motherfuck!" coincided with the hard *BANG* of the entry door that flew open and hit the exterior wall. An enlisted man stormed out, his face contorted with rage.

"Hey, hey, Derek, slow down man." Gregg stepped in the path Derek was cutting, did the job he was here to do. "Cool down, buddy."

"A motherfuckin haircut my ass!" Derek shouted in Gregg's face. "No shit, no shit, Doc. I am done with this shit. I do not fuckin' care!"

Gregg ignored the spittle that hit his skin and just tried harder, voice calm. "Come on now, Derek. Come on man, be cool. You got less than thirty and you'll be home, all done. This will be a bad dream, and you'll be back in the world in a month."

Derek pushed Gregg's hand off his arm, then pushed past Izzy and Mikel, furiously waving his arms in the air, yelling, "Fuck, y'all!"

Gregg stared after Derek. He didn't have a good feeling about this. Derek had always been quiet and restrained, but things had a way of building up when suppressed.

"What was that about?" Mikel asked.

"I saw him at the clinic a couple of times. His wife is real sick at home. We tried to get him a compassionate, and it was turned down. We wrote his unit and told them to get him out of here, but that was turned down, too. He is ready to blow."

Izzy made a sound of distress. Now that Derek had stalked off there was nothing Gregg could immediately do to get the soldier's head in a better place, but at least he could get poor Izzy out of this ungodly heat.

"C'mon, let's help ourselves to some air." He didn't have to make the invitation twice. Izzy made a bee-line to the window unit blowing marvelously cold air into the reception area that was standard military, clean and unfussy, but with nice decor in a 60s Winnebago kind of way.

While Izzy draped himself over the vents, Mikel stood off to the side, allowing Gregg to approach the desk of Master Sergeant Reginald Jackson. The Top Sergeant was a professional soldier; everything about the desk and his uniform and the way he held his body said so. He was by the book. But he was also fair and good humored and Gregg admired him for all that, but chiefly for being a devoted family man, as evidenced on his desk by the framed photos of his wife and five children he would gaze at with pride.

"Good morning, Top. What's up with Derek? He looked like hell coming out of here."

The Sergeant came to his feet, bringing his full 6'4" to attention. "Morning yourself, Doctah Kelly, sir. Damn kid, all I told him was to get himself a damn haircut. His ass and his hair belong to the US Army for thirty more days and he is not going to have any damn afro on my grounds. By the way you need a haircut yourself, Captain."

"Okay, Top, right away."

"The sooner the better. I do not want any goddamn surfer hippies on my grounds. You got me? You are an example."

"Right away, Top."

"No, you won't." Top called him on it every time and as usual he sighed a grudging defeat. "You just all talk, no walk, Gregg. I hate to see you in a uniform."

"I know, Top, I feel just the same as you do."

The Sergeant looked over at Izzy.

"Who the hell you got with you? He think he own that air conditioner? That is *my* air coming out of there, Captain." At Top's claim of ownership Izzy jumped to the side, eyes big as Jiffy Pop pans. Top chuckled. "He kind of jumpy, ain't he, Gregg? My god, Captain, I have not seen a newer new guy since you got here."

Gregg gestured Izzy over to join them. "Top, this is Dr. Moskowitz. Just in this morning. Izzy, this is Master Sergeant Jackson. He runs everything here, and as long as he is here, everything is fine."

"Pile it on Gregg, you still should go get that haircut." The Master Sergeant engulfed Izzy's hand in his own. "My pleasure, Doctah Moskowitz, and it is certainly a treat to have a man like yourself who clearly loves the climate and knows how to wear the uniform."

"Nice to—" a visible swallow. "Meet you." Izzy looked as lost as Gregg had felt when he was the newest new guy around. Top had given him some much needed grounding while he found his inner compass, and Top would do the same for Izzy.

As for Mikel, the way he stood completely still in the room, aviators hiding whatever his eyes took in, agreed with the vibe that he *was* the compass and just maybe the whole damn ship he was guiding, too. Still, introductions were in order.

"And, this is Dr. J.D. Mikel, our other new psychiatrist just moved down from Da Nang."

Top looked Mikel over for several long seconds. "Welcome to the 8th, Doctah."

"Thank you, Sergeant. And please, just J.D."

"Hey, is the CO in?" Gregg pretended not to notice Kellogg posturing just inside his office at the farthest end of the corridor.

"Captain, do I look like the secretary?" Top signaled them to another desk about ten paces away from the CO's office.

First Lieutenant Terry Carver, fresh out of West Point, had the bad luck to be assigned desk duty for the 8th but it hadn't dampened the enthusiasm with which he greeted them.

"Hi Gregg, what's up?"

"Got some new guys to meet the CO. Is he available?"

"Yes, but only briefly. He's flying up to Cam Rahn."

"Glad to be brief," Gregg assured Terry, then made the intros all over again.

"This is a really great place," Terry told them. "You are lucky to be here."

Izzy gave Gregg a look that said, *how can anyone be enthusiastic about anything here except leaving?*

Gregg gave Izzy an encouraging smile. One that grew broader at the sight of Colonel Alistair Kellogg. Posing beside a bookcase, dressed in full combat regalia and wearing a double holstered gun belt, he looked more like Hopalong Cassidy in the jungle than General George Patton.

Gregg rapped sharply on the open door. "Excuse us, sir, do you have a minute?"

"Hello. . ." The Colonel paused to artificially deepen his voice. "Well, hello there soldiers, of course I do. You shrinks saving the war for us?"

"Sir, we are trying, and the good news is that we have reinforcements." Gregg nodded to his companions. "I'd like you to meet the good news that arrived this morning."

Kellogg threw his arms open wide. "Welcome, welcome gentlemen. Do a good job, as I expect you will and no less. You both are new to the military, I presume?"

Izzy found his voice again, stronger now. "Yes, sir."

"Good, good. There is no greater service for the country than being men in arms." Kellogg adjusted his gun belt. "I'm heading up to Cam Rahn, inspecting the troops, keeping the morale up, you know. The men need to see me there."

Casually Gregg asked, "Are you golfing, sir?"

"Well. . ." Kellogg gave a little shrug. "I may be taking the clubs in case the General is there, of course. But this is essentially a combat mission." Acknowledging Mikel for the first time he asked, "Do you golf?"

Mikel closed the door. He then deposited himself in the closest chair facing Kellogg's desk and extended an invitational hand to the other side of the polished oak.

"Sit down, Colonel." When the ranking officer didn't immediately respond to his directive, Mikel reiterated, "Please, have a seat. You have golf, I have work. Time is short."

"Have you gone nuts?" Gregg wasn't too high on ranking systems in or out of the military, but you could get in a lot of trouble for insubordination, especially in uniform. "I'm sorry Colonel, he just got here and must be a little disoriented. You know the heat and all. I'm sure no disrespect is intended."

"I should say so," blustered the Colonel, his voice rising to its higher pitch. "Get out of my chair. You are in my army now, soldier!"

Mikel tossed an envelope marked TOP SECRET onto the clear, flat surface of his desk.

"No, not really, Colonel," he said evenly. "These documents are for your eyes only. It's an official introduction, but I believe that General Glen Claiborne at MACV headquarters has contacted you already—and you in turn must have prepared Col. Kohn given his appropriate response to my arrival."

"Then you're CIA? The spook?"

"Boo."

Kellogg made tracks in the direction Mikel had indicated and eagerly tore open the envelope. Mumbling as we went, he devoured more than read the contents. Eyes alight, Kellogg possessively gripped the official documents, flashed a gleeful smile that was at odds with his suitable chagrin.

"My apologies Agent Mikel, I wasn't expecting you just yet."

"Given the severity of the situation, I expedited my arrival prior to speaking with the General again. Do you mind telling him I'm here when you see him later today?"

"Of course, my pleasure, and. . .did the General mention me to you by name?"

Gregg was wondering what shifty mental calculations were going on behind the cool shades that gave Mikel the unfair advantage of looking out without others looking in, when he removed the aviators and hung them from his shirt front, just like a regular guy. His face was an open book, pleasant as his reassurance.

"Of course he did, Colonel." Just J.D.—oh yeah, he was definitely playing that good buddy calling card now—clasped his hands on the desk, leaned forward. So earnest, no one could doubt it, especially an ambitious officer whose time to make general was running out. "In fact, *Glen* suggested we choose this hospital because you are in charge."

Kellogg's beaming smile said he'd just had his highest hopes confirmed.

"All right, all right, very good then. Now, what is our mission?"

"It seems, Colonel, that someone out there is killing our soldiers."

Gregg nearly choked on a laugh. At least the guy had an appreciation for the absurd. "Excuse me, but wouldn't that be the enemy, the VC?"

Mikel cut his attention to Gregg. "Not exactly."

"Boogeyman," Izzy blurted. "The Ghost Soldier."

"Very good, Dr. Moskowitz. No wonder you were top of your class."

"I don't believe this," was all Gregg could say. The whole thing was just too crazy. And boy, did he know crazy. "This is not for real."

"I can assure you, Dr. Kelly, it is indeed for real. Otherwise, I would not be here. The government does not assign me to bogus missions."

Gregg pressed a hand over his eyes. He removed it and Mikel was still there.

"In that case. . .this is going to make a big difference in how we"—he pointed to Izzy, clearly leaving the bogus amongst them out—"and the other doctors handle our previously considered delusional patients."

Mikel stood. He was a little taller than Gregg but not by much, and yet he projected a Jolly Green Giant stature, only not nearly so jolly or green. "You will *not* be telling anyone about any of this. None of you will. We can't risk anything getting back to the nightly news back home."

The sound of a second hand on a clock somewhere in the silent room measured off several *ticks* before Kellogg got up to speed.

"Actually, I think being on TV might be just the ticket, I could put out some interviews and—" Kellogg suddenly stopped as Mikel stared him down with those emerald eyes that could slice diamonds.

"Of course," Kellogg mumbled, "not a word leaves this room." He gazed at the top secret documents as if his hopes for an exclusive with Walter Cronkite had just kissed a landmine goodbye—then pushed the papers back into the envelope.

Kellogg wore the look of a man who had lost some of his pride and felt naked without it. "Why are you here?" he asked briskly, then quickly followed up with a disdainful sweep of his hand toward Gregg and Izzy. "And what are you doing with these people?"

"The thinking is Colonel, as you probably would have concluded yourself with the appropriate information, is that this 'Ghost Soldier' is either part of a successful Russian or Chinese psyops maneuver, or one of our own gone rogue. Unfortunately, there is the possibility the killer belongs to us due to a disturbingly similar pattern of violence that previously occurred."

"When?" Kellogg demanded. "Why didn't I hear about it?"

"Because it never happened—just as this will never have happened. But I will tell you in strictest confidence that a man was removed from the field five years ago, placed in the Madigan General psychiatric lockdown unit, and apparently being both brilliant and dangerous, he somehow managed to disappear with his charts, leaving behind several dead bodies and not much else. The army has given Intelligence precious little to work with beyond the recent emergence of a so-called Ghost Soldier, and some similar activity five years ago that got buried so deep the paper trail was extinguished. Whatever the case, my people figure your mental people here are central clearing for this sort of thing. It's my job to pick a couple of your men to help me while I work undercover as one of them. They are to provide the professional guidance I require to find whoever is doing this if it's coming from behind, or determine if we're dealing with another form of psychological warfare that will be dealt with as swiftly and severely as possible. Case solved, I disappear. That's it."

Kellogg nodded slowly. A little smile now befitting an Emperor restored to his cloak and crown. "I would like to volunteer. I'm a trained physician, and I am perfectly ready to go out after any sick bastard killing our troops."

"And that's exactly what I was told to expect an officer of your caliber to say." Mikel said this so sincerely Gregg half believed it himself, until he smoothly tacked on, "But Colonel, you have too high a profile. I mean, everybody knows who you are and we have to be incredibly discreet. Besides, it's dangerous. The army does not want to risk losing you. I was told."

"Oh! Well right, of course, I understand the General's thinking on this."

"He knew you would, Colonel. He only requests your complete support, which he felt confident you would gladly provide to me as well."

"Of course I am here to help in any way I can. Do you have anyone in mind yet to help you?"

Mikel gestured to either side, to Izzy and Gregg. "These two."

"What?" Gregg was sure if he looked on the ground he would see his stomach flopping around his feet. "What, are you kidding? No way!"

"You don't even know us!" Izzy had definitely found his voice. It was the loudest in the room. "I just got here!"

"Sorry." Mikel shrugged. "Too late. I checked everyone out. You guys drew the lucky straws. And Izzy, I am sorry about what happened to Morrie."

Frantic, Gregg appealed to Kellogg. "Sir, we can't do this. We are just drafted shrinks, we—"

"And Captain, you have been drafted again," Kellogg decreed. "Is that clear? Do you hear me loud and clear? This is a direct order from command. We—that is I and YOU—will cooperate fully. Am I clear soldiers!"

Gregg looked at Izzy who looked back at Gregg and they both just started shaking their heads when a loud commotion could be heard from the outer office.

Sergeant Jackson yelling: "PUT DOWN THAT WEAPON AND GET THE HELL OUT OF HERE, RIGHT NOW!"

Then Derek's voice: "NOW IT IS YOUR TURN, MOTHERFUCK."

Gregg raced for the door. Mikel and Izzy were right behind him, racing into the main area. There was Derek. Holding an M16.

He brandished the rifle at Top. "How do you like being yelled at, huh? Like being scared? You like it, motherfuck?"

Gregg knew he had a gift and that gift was his voice. He had never needed it more than now.

"Hey, Derek," he said softly, reasonably. "Hey man, just easy huh?"

"Stay back! I got no quarrel with you, Doc."

Gregg took a step closer to Derek, still talking really calm and quiet. "Come on, Derek, come on man, you'll be home by—"

Sergeant Jackson stood up. "You will put that weapon down and come to attention soldierrrrrr. . . ."

The concuss of the M16 fire shredded the room as Derek opened up and exploded Top's skull, then tore holes through Top's chest, blowing him across the room and slamming him into the wall where he slowly and wetly slid down to the floor, joined by shards of glass and the remains of family photographs.

There was only silence and Derek's ragged breathing.

"Fuck you all!" he screamed. He fired another burst into Top's body.

It seemed like slow motion as Gregg saw Derek bring the barrel of the rifle up toward them, everyone frozen in shock and horror.

Except Mikel, leaping horizontally into the air, knocking Izzy, and then Gregg to the floor. Then somehow Mikel was fluidly ripping Terry's pistol from its holster and was rolling and firing in return as Derek's M16 rounds ripped over their heads.

On the ground Gregg felt very far away as he watched the slow rolling of volumes of blood, flowing over the floor. Top was down and dead on one side. Derek down and very dead on the other. Gregg turned his head to another angle and stared into Izzy's unblinking gaze, glasses knocked off, brown irises swallowed by his pupils, huge inky pools of black. Gregg's ears were ringing and then he heard choking moans and turned his head yet another way. Terry was on the floor with a chunk of an upper arm blown out, pumping even more blood from one of Derek's M16 rounds.

Mikel was already using his own belt as a tourniquet to bind Terry up when Izzy began to retch.

"Shouldn't he be accustomed to blood?" Mikel asked Gregg. "I thought psychiatrists were supposed to be medically trained."

Gregg couldn't get his vocal chords to move. He stared dumbly at Mikel, whose serene expression was jarring in the sea of carnage.

"Never mind, almost done here," Mikel said. Then to Izzy, "Welcome to Vietnam."

If you realize that all things change,
There is nothing you will try to hold on to.
If you are not afraid of dying,
There is nothing you cannot achieve.
—Lao Tzu

The Death of Flowers in Spring

KILLERS

Everywhere war happens there are casualties and sometimes those who die in them are as close as home. I know this because I was the only kid in my freshman class to have had a war at home and kill my father. He wasn't really my father, he was my stepfather, but I never knew my father and Burt had been there for as long as I remembered and was the real father of my two sisters. I remember killing him. I felt pretty good when I did it. I cried, but more from relief than anything else. It certainly wasn't grief.

He was a beater. He beat me, he beat my sisters, and he beat my mom. Anything pissed him off, he would just whack you right in the face, hard, really hard, and if you looked at him wrong or anything else, he whacked you again and again. When he was officially punishing he used a whip. He would use ropes or willow branches, but his favorite was a telephone line. Not the telephone line from the phone, no that wasn't very heavy or whippy. He used the telephone line from the overhead lines off the poles. This he could put some bite into when he wanted to make you scream.

Once I tried being clever and stuffed my undershorts with comics. I knew it was coming but he liked to put it off until dinner was over. That way my sisters or me or sometimes all of us would be sucking up and being "Daddy would you like this, can I bring you this. . ." hoping to nice him into forgetting about it. He rarely forgot about it, and the time with the comics he certainly didn't. I was so scared that I put in too many. As soon as he put the whip on my butt I started to scream and cry like crazy. The sound of the whip on the comics was way too loud. He got mad. I had to take my pants down and then he really laid into me. I rolled and writhed on the ground, screaming for real, and he just kept on. He thought I was trying to be smarter than he was, although I already knew I was that, but it didn't make me less afraid.

One night he was really mad. He whacked me when I dropped my cup. My mom started to say something to stop him and he whacked her and for some reason she stood up and told him to *stop it, stop it, stop it, stop it, and every time she said it he just hit her again, slap, slap, slap. Then she did it, she pushed him and said stop it and this time he punched her and her nose broke and blood sprayed and he punched her again. My sisters were screaming, mom shut up, and then just like I knew just what to do, I got up and went into the closet and got out the shotgun. I just said stop it. "You don't have the guts," he said. He should have looked at my eyes. I pulled both barrels, and the kick blew me across the room and into the wall. The blast cut him in half. I was glad. I knew then it was something I was good at.*

I got sent to juvie for a year. It was OK, and there were not any killers there but me. Nobody touched me. Nobody even looked at me. When I got out I went back to high school, but for awhile I kept expecting to wake up and be in juvie again.

4

The night of the same day in downtown Nha Trang, Izzy kept wondering when he would wake up. Soaked in sweat, his nerves like bees inside his body, he hadn't wanted to come here, but Gregg and Robert David and Mikel had insisted. They didn't want him staying at the villa alone and Izzy didn't make them ask twice.

He was too afraid to be alone. Even now he wanted to hold onto their hands like a child. If they left him, he would collapse right here, enveloped in the soft warmth of a tropical night that saturated his nostrils with the scents of flowers, spices, food, shit, beer, and marijuana. His vision felt assaulted by neon and a moving carnival of cars, jeeps, and bicycles. Vespas and three-wheeled cycles swirled amidst constant honking while Magical Mystery Tour blared in the background. The streets were full of GIs in jungle fatigues and men in gaudy aloha shirts openly soliciting baby girl prostitutes dressed in barely anything.

"Nha Trang is where the troops and contractors come to avail themselves of some in-country R&R, Izzy." Robert David was talking to him now, acting as tour guide and his cultured Southern accent, with the way his R&R came out soft like "Aah" and "Aah," seemed even more preposterous than it had during rounds before the world fell apart and Top got murdered and Mikel killed Derek before Derek could kill him and Gregg.

He should be dead right now, his first day in Vietnam. He should be in a body bag while his fiancé sang "Where Have All the Flowers Gone" and lit candles. If it wasn't for Mikel, his blood would be all over the floor instead of the vomit that got cleaned up with Top's brains and—

Izzy lurched to the side and started dry heaving into the street. There was nothing left to throw up. He hadn't been able to eat all day. He didn't think he could ever eat again.

"C'mon." It was Mikel, his hand on Izzy's shoulder. "Let's get you drunk."

"I don't think. . .Agent Mikel, I don't think—"

"That's a very good idea. *Don't. Think.*" Then next to Izzy's ear he whispered sharply, "And for Chrissakes, don't call me `Agent' again and make me regret getting in the way of that gun. It's J.D., okay? Just J.D." A slap on the back and Just J.D. announced to Gregg and Robert David, "I say we could all use a drink."

"I concur," announced Robert David as he grabbed Izzy by one arm and Gregg took the other, moving him out of the flow of traffic and with a quick turn, down a back alley street. That's when Izzy noticed that Gregg's hand was trembling, and so was his go-easy voice, as he picked up with the travelogue.

"Troops come in from all over and try to forget where they are and what they are going back to out there. You can buy anything and anyone you want on this street, and it's what, five minutes from our quarters?"

The street was packed on both sides with small shacks made of tin cans and cardboard and plywood. Izzy numbly watched a couple of men who could have been at a stateside barbeque with their tropical Hawaiian shirts stretched across big bellies and big gold watches that yelled Jersey, held up on each side by two little Vietnamese girls. Even made up like whores with little pushed up breasts and tiny skirts they couldn't have been more than eleven or twelve years old.

"This is a nightmare." Izzy closed his eyes tight, willing the grotesque vision to go away. It did, only to be replaced by the sight of a little boy, also made up to look pretty, leading another fat middle-aged pleasure seeker past a shack's door. They disappeared, to do only God knew what.

God could know. Izzy didn't want to know. And then J.D. apparently thought a little history lesson was in order, as if that put it all into some kind of perspective.

"This old alley has existed since the Indochina War when the French were here. The visitors that look like they should be roasting on a spit are mostly civilian contractors behaving badly away from their own homes. Money is precious. They have it. The families do what they must to survive."

"I want that drink," Izzy told J.D., told them all. He honestly didn't give a rat's ass if he threw it up immediately as long as it bought him even a moment's respite from this. . . this. . .

He couldn't even give this a name.

The bar they entered was full of drunken soldiers and more prostitutes. Izzy never thought he'd be grateful to see girls who were closer to twenty than ten selling themselves on a very open market. "B girls," J.D. explained, as if that explained anything about the inflated cheap boob jobs that made Izzy wish he could do a lobotomy on the plastic surgeons responsible—though he'd lay dollars to every Red Cross Dolly Donut not one board certified plastic surgeon had performed a single one of the surgeries.

A terrible really loud band played "Proud Mary," and that's when Izzy was jostled by some drunks, got turned around, and was suddenly lost in the smoke and neon.

Frantically he scanned the room for J.D., Gregg, Robert David. No luck. Everyone around him was in the same green uniform or garish aloha shirt and he didn't recognize even one face from the hospital. His nausea, momentarily forgotten, courtesy of the "Scotch rocks, make it a triple, and make it your best" J.D. had ordered for him, returned with a vengeance. And it wasn't from the few sips consumed. Homesick, that's what he was; literally physically sick with his longing for home. He would easily give up all the years of his later life just to be home right now. No wonder everyone was obsessed with counting the days.

"Three hundred and sixty-four days and a wake up," Izzy said aloud, wondering if crazy people talked to themselves because it made their alternate realities more real. Perhaps this would make a nice clinical trial test at the end of the impossible tunnel of days where reality glittered so wonderful and precious Izzy could not believe he ever took it for granted as he muttered the first of ten thousand small prayers to whatever, or whoever to just let him live, make it home, and he would do anything in gratitude.

The bodies pressing all around him took on the substance of quicksand, and then the quicksand became like fluctuating concrete that jostled Izzy one way then another. The bass of the band thundered into his brain until he found himself standing in front of a ridiculously big and very drunken warrant officer, shouting at him.

"What, what? I beg your pardon," Izzy shouted back above the din. "I'm lost. Did you say you could help me find my friends?"

"I *said* Welcome to the Nam, you fuckin idiot new guy!"

And then J.D. was dragging the fuckin idiot new guy away, shouting, "Try not to antagonize the animals," as he plowed a path to the relative safety of a back exit door.

Outside it was hot but thankfully quieter and Izzy wanted to apologize, though for what he didn't know. "I wasn't, wasn't, I did not say. . ."

J.D. silenced him with a glare that had the effect of a double slap.

"Listen up and listen up good because I need you and you are no good to me dead," he said bluntly. "Wake up, quit whining and feeling sorry for yourself. Nobody here gives a shit where you come from, or where you are going. Nobody. What will get you killed faster than anything is pretending you are still what and who you were in the world. You are *not* in the world anymore. You are *not* anywhere near where there are rules you can still live by. So I am telling you: Wake the fuck up. Are you with me so far?"

Izzy managed a creaky up and down movement of his head.

"Now, the second most dangerous thing besides the danger you pose to yourself are the other fucking idiots who were sent over here. If you were not a shrink and an officer, if you were just some grunt in the field, your own guys might have shot you already because your head is so far up your ass it's still in New York and that makes you too dangerous to be around. If you don't wake up soon, one of ours is far more likely to kill you than Charlie. Just about every third guy here is ready to snap, lose it, go psycho. You got a real life introduction to it this afternoon. This is one giant insane asylum, the whole place. Take note, Dr. Moskowitz, because this is your first, last, and only reality orientation that just might keep you alive long enough to help me out and get you home." J.D. gave him a little thumb to forefinger *ping* on the bridge of his black horn rims. The ones J.D. had fished out of the blood and brains and puke, then cleaned off with his shirt before perching back on Izzy's nose. "Now tell me, Doc: What's The Big Message?"

"Wake the fuck up."

"That's right. Now follow me."

J.D. took off down the alley, no backward glance. Izzy followed as instructed, muttering robotically, "Wake the fuck up, wake the fuck up. . ." while he tried to wake the fuck back up in New York City where everything and everyone he'd ever cared about existed on some alternate plane.

But they still hadn't materialized as the officer's quarters came into view. Or even by the time he laid in bed listening to the fan turning overhead, the sounds of a Vietnamese family sitting on the porch of their house in back of the villa. He imagined their voices belonging to his mother and father, aunt and uncle, and grandparents; imagined them all sitting together on the porch at their summer cottage while he and Rachel snuck away to make out under the stars, and he imagined all that gloriousness until he fell asleep.

Suddenly the sensation of some invisible hand yanking the sheet out from under him and throwing him to the floor jarred him awake. There were shadows of racing feet in the hallway, accompanied by shouts of "INCOMING! INCOMING!"

Before Izzy could pick himself up another concussive blast sounded, followed by screams outside the villa, then another explosion even closer that coincided with a loud *bang* as his door flew open and Gregg raced inside.

"Come on, get out!" Gregg was hauling him to his feet before the command could register, then together they scrambled down the stairs and out the front door, just in time to see another mortar blast hit. They both dropped to the ground, next to another young man Izzy didn't recognize.

"C'mon, c'mon!" he urged them, "Get up! We need to get to the bunker!"

Gregg grabbed Izzy's arm to go, but Izzy couldn't move. He was paralyzed. Something warm and wet drizzled down his leg. His muscles were like water, his eyes felt like they were spinning in their sockets. He was dizzy, hyperventilating, and he couldn't stop it, couldn't even control his own bladder while Gregg shouted:

"Let's go, let's go!" Gregg and the other man were up and running. Even if his own life depended on it, Izzy could not follow. All he could do was look at Gregg's back—which suddenly stopped its retreat as Gregg glanced over his shoulder, saw Izzy still down on the ground where they had left him.

"Izzy!" Gregg raced back to help him up and had him halfway to his feet when the high pitch of another mortar shrilly screamed and they both dove back to the ground, and watched the burning, white phosphorous mortar hit almost directly in front of where they were going to run for the safety of the bunker.

Their companion, the one who had urged them to run with him, turned into a gory cartoon character. For a moment, his legs seemed to be moving from his severed upper body and Izzy could smell seared flesh. He wasn't cognizant of crying, but it felt like hot tears were racing down his cheeks while he tried not to choke on his own vomit as some important part of him, a part of his self since boyhood that had been raised on Disney movies and Cub Scout meetings departed, never to return again.

Covered in every conceivable bodily fluid except blood, Izzy knew a terrible truth that would forever haunt him: what saved his life that day was that he was not brave; he was too scared to move. The brave man, the man doing the smart thing of getting to the safety of the bunker, was cut down by a random and malicious darkness of fate that cared not a whit for right or wrong. And if right or wrong didn't matter, what did?

Survival.

Gregg's chest was shaking from holding in his silent sobs. Izzy would have offered him a tissue if he'd had one handy like shrinks always did back in the world. But they were no longer in the world and he was no longer the Israel Moskowitz who had arrived in Vietnam just that morning. Izzy really didn't know who he was anymore and he had no idea who or what he might become. He only knew that if he was going to survive and get the hell out of this hell-hole, he had to be smarter than the smartest guy he'd once been in the Columbia University med school.

"Wake the fuck up," Izzy whispered as he wiped the snot from his nose with the end of a military-issue tee that smelled like piss and stomach juices minus any solid bits from breakfast, lunch or dinner. In order to survive you had to eat and so he would eat in the morning whether he was hungry or not. He had to eat and he had to remember his first, last, and only orientation, which defined this new reality that came down to four simple words.

Izzy said them once more, only this time like he meant it:

"Wake the fuck up."

❋

The Nightbird takes flight to distance itself from the piercing whistle of mortars. The feathers of the bird make no sound as it swiftly moves through the sultry evening towards the jungle, then lights in the branches of a tree and watches.

The LRRP team moves quickly and efficiently. Several of them are new but they are highly trained and this is what they do well.

Their leader is confident.

"OK, let's hump it out there, one more click. Set up a perimeter, get ready to ambush and hurt some people. Move it! It's getting dark soon."

And soon it is dark and quiet.

The men are spread out just the way they have been trained to do. They wait in the gathering silence. It is in the silence of the night that the predator kills, moving with the soft silence of the panther, the quiet slither of the cobra.

The Nightbird watches one man sitting in his place just before the day dawns.

"Hey, hey, where are you guys, where are you?"

As the light comes up and he can finally see, he begins to shriek.

All the men are sitting around him and have their bloody cut off heads sitting in their laps.

5

It was nearing dawn and J.D. Mikel had yet to sleep. He didn't require a lot, which was fortunate, because he had been summoned to the MACV headquarters in Saigon, three days earlier. As his spine settled into the hammock where no one would find him—god, he hoped not—he ran through the details again that had called him from the jungle and literally landed him in a nut ward.

When the summons came he had been dressed in black silk pajamas, Vietnamese Highlands style, and flip-flop sandals, just as he was now. And just as now the sky was still and shadowed—only then he had been sitting in the back of a jeep, driven by a Special Forces Officer.

As they rolled up to the entrance of the sprawling fortress in Saigon known as Pentagon East, they were joined almost immediately by a black late 60s Cadillac limousine. Another Special Forces Officer opened the door, then out stepped a man in an elegant English cut suit and highly polished shoes.

He greeted J.D. with their customary exchange, "And how are you, my young friend?"

The man's voice, high and a bit squeaky, in no way matched his attire or his bearing, or the worldly position such attire and bearing would dictate. J.D. bowed his customary bow.

"Not as young as I once was, Mr. Ambassador."

"And thank goodness for that." A beat. "J.D."

They laughed as they always did at their private little joke, then slipped into the professional faces they were there to put on.

Flanked by the two Special Forces Officers, their shiny shoes, flip-flops and green nylon combat boots echoed down a long, gleaming corridor until the officers opened a pair of French doors, revealing a tasteful office where a much decorated general rose quickly from his desk.

"Good evening, Mr. Ambassador." General Glen Claymore gave a sharp salute. He had bulldog jowls, BB pellet eyeballs, and a Yul

Brenner globe you could spin on its axis. "It's a long flight from Paris. Please, have a seat, and may I offer either of you coffee, tea?"

The Ambassador, a title he retained despite the less than diplomatic purposes he now served, gave a dismissive wave and didn't bother to sit. J.D. flip-flopped over to the silver service before settling into the chair facing Claymore's desk where he placed the tea cup to steep.

"Agent Mikel, we have a dark one. I would not have brought you out of the current operation, but this is urgent."

Claymore slid a file across the desk. J.D. briskly thumbed through the surprisingly thin stack of pages while Claymore filled them in. He wound up his briefing with a fist to desk thump, growling, "We need this thing stopped *now*. Before the press catches so much as a whiff of this garbage. Sentiments back home are bad enough as it is."

Sentiments "back home" were not J.D.'s problem. He was a US citizen by birth but any real sense of affiliation didn't extend much beyond his employer. "You have confirmed kills?"

"We have bodies, yes. Dismembered in such a way that. . ." Claymore shot a look of distaste at the file. "We think this may have happened before."

"Explain."

More briefing, more desk thumping, then, "For all we know the crazy who escaped the nut ward at Madigan General is dead or doing his killing in some Iowa cornfield, but we can't discount the possibility that he's managed to pick up where he left off on the front lines." Claymore glanced uneasily at the Ambassador. "This is, of course, the worst case scenario from a public relations position and purely speculation on our part."

At yet another mention of public relations, J.D.'s annoyance rose to the level of flicking lint off a dark suit. The suit in the room, however, parked a well-tailored hip against the desk, got down to the nasty end of the stick.

"You find whatever this is, Mikel, and he—or, they—disappear. Personally I think it is the goddamn Russians. It stinks like them. Either way if it is one of theirs, a damned Chinaman or some psycho of our own, this cannot ever have happened. Understood?"

"Of course. But strategically speaking, there are over 500,000 troops here, not to mention the contractors, the civilians. If you want this on the fast track then I at least need a ground zero to start looking on the inside and more than this so-called report. Sure, it says he's insane, but who isn't some kind of crazy around here?"

"Maybe the shrinks who treat the crazies?" Claymore's jowls lifted like he had just pulled an ace out of his ass. He shoved a thicker file J.D.'s way. "Take your pick."

J.D. ignored the file, took a sip of his tea. Nothing special. He preferred a Longjing, just as he preferred to work alone. Especially if it involved some academic eggheads he didn't have the time to babysit. The fact they were mental specialists didn't particularly agree with him either. They probably tried to psycho-analyze everyone they came into contact with and he didn't want anyone snooping under his hood.

"What if they talk while I still need them?"

"They can't because of that oath they have to take. As for once they've served their purpose and are no longer required. . . ." Claymore shrugged, opened his hands. "If the good of the many has to take precedence over the good of the few that is the sacrifice all soldiers may have to make. They're no different."

J.D. didn't bother to say "understood" because such things were always understood when people were merely tools for some higher good—or not such higher good. "Anything else?"

"Happy hunting."

"It's time to go." The Ambassador nodded to J.D.

J.D. tossed back the tea. He decided he didn't like it any more than the files he picked up as they left.

"I have something I would ask you to do for me personally while you're in Nha Trang," the Ambassador confided en route.

Speaking in conspiratorial tones they retraced their steps in reverse. Shiny shoes then flip-flops, escorted by two pair of green combat boots, footfalls echoing down the gleaming corridor. Suit into the limousine. J.D. in black pajamas back into the jeep, where he checked his watch, tic-tic-ticking.

✳

Twelve hours later and two hundred miles swept north of Saigon, it was just getting dark in Nha Trang. Considering his present objectives in a city he knew better than the back of his neck, J.D. dressed accordingly before making his way down an alley to pass the open doorways of a long line of shacks where preparations went on for the evening ahead.

The smells of the street vendors' spicy offerings flavored the humid air as Vietnamese music competed with the sounds of Jimi Hendrix. The air smelled, tasted, sounded like home. At least as much of a home as he or any other Boogeyman who frightened grown men might claim.

Stopping just outside a familiar back door, in fluent Vietnamese he respectfully greeted the elderly woman known to all as "Grandmother" sitting on the stoop, silently chewing and enjoying the betel quid stuffed in her cheek. J.D. knew the psychoactive buzz in the leaf, nut and lime substance was a comfort to her and her old body. She looked up at him, frowning. Then she saw through the cleverly done disguise: The burnt out, drug-addled GI with dirty faded Tiger fatigues and booney hat and peace signs and beads around his neck was a friend.

Her bloody red smile and blackened teeth greeted him with a pleasurable laugh of recognition. "Ah! Ma Quý!"

J.D. crouched down Asian style and engaged her in their typical conversation regarding the weather, her businesses along the alley; catching up on the activities in the neighborhood. A cup of tea was brought for him by one of her many granddaughters. She didn't try to entice him with one since she loved her own too much to wish him onto even the most troublesome.

As they shared a small silence, J.D. realized he had missed a detail. The fatigues were dirty; his fingernails too clean. Scratching at the dirt, he casually asked, "Do you know anything about the stories of the Ghost Soldier, the Boogeyman?"

Her hand shook just a small ripple. She spat a bloody stream of betel juice. "Not story. Real." She said the word for demon in Vietnamese, "*Con Quý*. Truly *Con Quý*. Stay away."

J.D. didn't want to show disrespect and laugh inappropriately but the urge was there. The irony of it all was just too much. He had spent the better part of his thirty-two years trying to escape the nightmare of a moment's insanity, only to get railroaded into a psych ward. Now Grandmother was trying to warn him away with the very nickname she had given him years ago—only there was a big difference between a fond "you little devil" and some supernatural overtones no Asian would ignore.

When Grandmother wasn't more forthcoming than another "Bad. Very bad. *Con quy*," he asked, "Is An still selling the good stuff?"

A nod, a bow, and J.D. moved down the alley to buy three packs of mj from An. He then walked another short distance, passed a sign announcing 8th Field Hospital, deliberately avoided the 99KO's self-contained building and headed for the hooch—a screened-in, long, wood framed military dwelling where the enlisted men of the 99th resided.

J.D. opened the hooch door. As he had hoped, at the far end a group of the mostly too young enlisted men were gathered, listening to music, drinking beer, and hiding joints behind their backs as though the clouds of dope smoke were somehow invisible.

J.D. flashed a peace sign and dopily moved forward, smiling stupidly. In his blond wig and mustache and aviator specs and raggedy Tiger fatigues, he could pass for any other burnt out grunt.

"Peace, brothers," he called out, a fellow pilgrim. "I smelled something good and liked the sounds."

The guys were a little wary, but pretty stoned and when they saw he had the packs of nicely rolled Js things warmed up quickly, and then he pulled out a brand new cassette of Creedence. Soon they were passing the new Js around and he was able to move from guy to guy, rapping and gossiping and joking. Just like anywhere it was the guys on the ground who knew the dirt, and it didn't take long before J.D. knew some things the "take your pick" files hadn't dished up. Like a certain psychiatrist named Peck who had quite the reputation for some off-the-record Jeckle/Hyde behavior, so Major Donald Peck went to the top of his "Watch Him" list.

Once J.D. got all the stuff floating around about the Ghost Soldier who was apparently doing a kick ass job of heightening their collective paranoia, he disappeared himself with the stealth of. . . . Well, took one to find one.

✳

And now here it was a day, make it three, late and a dollar short as those yanks liked to say. They certainly paid him well enough, not that money was his only incentive, as the Ambassador knew. They had a history and J.D. had a past that had been as carefully obscured as the joy he took in shitting on his father's grave.

No doubt his two new recruits, Kelly and Moskowitz, would have a field day with that. He sort of liked them anyway. And that wasn't good.

Guys like him couldn't afford to have friends. He was as much a potential liability to them as they were to him. And if the liability should become too much to risk. . .

Bang, bang.

J.D. flipped out of his hammock and landed on all fours—only to realize the culprit was the alarm on his Jaeger-LeCoultre watch, and good thing he had set it. Presuming the 8th Field Hospital was still standing and the 99KO hadn't been blown to bits with the freaked out head cases strapped to their beds, what the shrinks called "morning rounds" would be over before he could get there.

Fine, he'd rather avoid the psych unit anyway, see what they had going at the Camp McDermott clinic instead. And, if Kelly and Moskowitz weren't there due to some early deployment in body bags, compliments of last night's fireworks from the VC?

Such was the way of the Tao. Death, like life, was the natural order of the universe. And, even if he discounted the ancient Chinese philosophy he'd studied for years in confines fit for a priest, The Byrds said as much in the lyrics they lifted from a biblical passage that his mother had read to him once.

J.D. let himself remember her for a moment. Then he let her go, free as the owls they had hooted back at one hot summer night.

Turn. Turn. Turn.

That's how it worked no matter where you came from, no matter when you went.

6

The sun threw glitter off the crystal blue sea and the asphalt shimmied up heat waves as Gregg steered the jeep down Highway One towards the out-patient clinic at Camp McDermott.

Izzy glanced over at Gregg. "You doing okay?"

"Hanging in there, thanks. How about you?"

"I ate breakfast and didn't throw it up."

"That's good, Izzy. Real good."

"So was not seeing J.D. this morning. Maybe he decided he didn't need us."

"That would be even better than waking up between Raquel Welch and Ann Margret."

"Throw all the Bond girls in there, too."

The normalcy of their conversation seemed so bizarre after the horrors of the past twenty-four hours Izzy wondered if they were both having some kind of delayed reaction to trauma.

Even if delayed, he would take it. Besides keeping breakfast down his hands had only acted up once all morning, and that was owed to a certain head nurse—the stunning Captain Margie Kennedy—who had made it her business to take him aside before morning rounds. Her quick visual inspection felt like a strip search and her voice slid over him like hot honey saying, "Don't bullshit me, I'll know if you do. I heard what happened at HQ yesterday. Are you all right?"

Despite near perfect recall, he didn't specifically remember what he said to Margie, mostly because his attention was on the sensory domino fall from her palms to his shoulders to south of that, but his response made her smile, and her smile—just this beautiful, transcendent smile she had—made him think of sex and thinking about sex made him feel better about life in general. At least until he thought of Rachel and her precious letters, and then the guilt kicked in. He probably should have felt even guiltier but he was just so damn grateful to still be alive with all his essential body parts intact and a hard-on to prove it.

It went away soon enough, though. All it took was a single introduction to Major Donald Peck, the other psychiatrist Gregg had warned him about.

Gregg turned the wheel and what must be Camp McDermott came into sight down the road.

"You said that Nikki is Margie's roommate, and Peck is seeing Nikki?" Izzy just wanted the Nikki-Peck thing confirmed again. *Uh-huh.*

"Yeah, who needs General Hospital back home when we have our own soap here?"

"We had plenty of drama going on behind the scenes at Columbia, too. Peck actually reminds me of one of the doctors on the Board of Directors." Izzy never thought he would miss that prima donna bastard but . . . nah, he still didn't. "Really nice guy," he deadpanned.

"A paragon of compassion, just like our dear Doctor Peck, huh?"

"Oh, absolutely, though I have to say today was the first time I ever saw a doctor try not to snicker while a patient was being strapped down. What is he, some kind of sadist?"

"Passive-aggressive for sure. But a sadist, like textbook?" Gregg shook his head. "Let's hope not. At least for Nikki's sake."

An ugly sprawling mishmash of every kind of military building imaginable signaled their arrival at Camp McDermott. The jeep wound through the base that was spread out over the coastal plain and sand like an instant military strip town. But instead of 7-Elevens and KFCs, there were artillery and communications companies, fuel dumps and motor pools and company headquarters and mess halls and PXs—all of which remained unscathed, unlike the 8th Field Hospital grounds that had taken a pretty hard hit.

Except for the 99KO. Like their villa, it looked like some patron saint of mental health decided the damage inside was bad enough.

Gregg pulled up to the back of the outpatient clinic, a generic, low-rise wood frame building with about four feet of concrete rising from the ground and GI green sandbags stacked against the concrete to meet the fly screen walls that supported a steel sheet roof.

"Nice." Izzy's assessment came out with the kind of New Yorker sarcasm he had never wanted to acquire and considering how fortunate he was to still be breathing, he wasn't starting now. "Sorry, I mean—"

"Just wait until you see the inside. You'll wonder why you ever wanted that Park Avenue office instead."

Izzy followed as Gregg led the way through the back door. The two clinic techs that had beat them there—Specialists Hertz and Bayer—were going about their everyday tasks of opening the clinic, making coffee, getting the waiting room in order. Highly efficient, even cheerful, it made Izzy wonder if mortar attacks and flying body parts were considered part of the daily grind.

As if reading his mind, Gregg confirmed, "Yep, the worse things get out there, the better business is for us in here. C'mon, let me show you to your office."

The new office basically consisted of four walls, a desk and three chairs, no couch.

"And now here we are at the Mayo Clinic of South East Asia," Gregg announced. "This plush setting will be yours. It is just as nice as mine except you get some nicer afternoon sun through that window, which means you can keep cozy and warm—say, about 130 degrees—so turn on your fan."

Izzy plopped into the regulation chair behind the regulation desk and promptly put his face mere inches from the fan generated air that began to evaporate the beading sweat on his brow. For a moment he drifted away, imagined he was below ground waiting for a subway where the heat couldn't completely reach—

Then he blinked. Shook the image out of his head and silently recited the one thing he could not forget as long as he was here: *Wake the fuck up.*

"We mostly have walk-ins during the morning," Gregg continued. "Sometimes they're brought in because their units or buddies are worried about them, or it could be they had an incident and got sent here to be checked out. We see other guys on a regular outpatient basis just to medicate and help them get through. Hertz and Bayer will be screening the walk-ins for us, do the basic work-ups with a mental status exam and a psycho-social interview, before passing them on to us. They've both been in-country over six months and have good training, absolutely know their stuff, so you can ask them what is up if there's anything you need to know." Gregg paused. "Also, be sure to ask one of them to sit in if anybody looks dicey."

"Dicey?"

"Yeah, it is a very special diagnostic category here. Remember a lot of these guys' jobs is full time killing and they are good at it and they are usually carrying some kind of weapon. If someone looks like they could go off on you, you know a bit agitated—"

"Like Derek."

"Oh man, he was beyond that, even before. . . "

They shared a moment that filled in the blank of their silence: They had a job to do and patients to see and unless Derek got out of the room and out of their heads they would lose even more men. They needed to save the ones they could, and that included themselves.

"Listen," Gregg told him, "even if you only have a creepy or bad feeling, get one of us. Guys can freak on all different levels without much warning, and when it happens, you do not want to be all alone. We watch each other's backs. If you hear one of us yelling just drop whatever you're doing and run to help. Same with you; you need help, just yell and we will be there. I'm not trying to scare you, just letting you know how it works."

"Scare me?" Izzy wasn't sure if he should laugh at the preposterousness of anything ever frightening him again, or duck under the desk with his fan and hide for the remainder of his tour because he was in a perpetual state of terror. Instead he settled for the reminder of what just might keep him alive long enough to get home, and he didn't care who heard him say, "Wake the fuck up."

"Did you just say—?"

"It's my new mantra."

"Can I borrow it?"

"Fine with me, but you may want to ask J.D. since he gave it to me."

As if on cue, the bad news with the good advice was standing in the doorway.

"Hey, you guys left without me this morning. After all the bonding we did yesterday, my feelings are hurt."

The awkward, momentary silence was bridged by Gregg's easy-going smile and that voice that would suit a minister or rabbi if he wasn't a shrink—or, maybe belonged on stage, given his smooth lie.

"Sorry, J.D. When you weren't at rounds this morning we thought something important must have come up—at least that's what we told everyone else when they asked why you weren't there. Good to see you. Care for some coffee?" Gregg hitchhiked his thumb in its aromatic direction. "We have all the bells and whistles so you can even have it Vietnamese-style."

"Then all is forgiven and now I don't have to blow out your kneecaps."

J.D. chuckled at their frozen reactions. Izzy felt that sense of detaching again but didn't much care for the view. What he saw were two well-educated civilians in uniform who were way out of their league. He and Gregg stood a better chance of taking on an entire gang in Little Italy than this enigma who could drop a room full of wise guys over their pasta before jetting to the Casino Royale for a dry martini.

A switchblade stashed inside a tuxedo. First impressions counted and Izzy's gut check insisted he'd gotten this one right. No matter J.D.'s assurance, "Oh c'mon, guys, I'm just pulling your chains. Now where's that coffee?"

As everyone gathered around the coffee pot, the powerful, dark roasted aroma hung in the air while Gregg showed Izzy how the French and Vietnamese did it up right with a generous portion of the super-sweet condensed milk over ice, followed by the extra strong brew, then the nice clatter of ice to glass as he stirred it up with a long spoon.

"This is delicious!" Izzy took another deep sip. "Thanks, Gregg."

"Hey it's tradition, as long as we keep bribing mess hall with sleeping pills," said Gregg, clinking his glass with Izzy's. "Here's to 125 and a wakeup."

"Hell yeah!" Hertz and the rest all clinked their glasses in a toast to Gregg's one-day-closer to home, then Hertz and Bayer added in their numbers, with group *clinks* to their own days remaining.

When Izzy announced: "Three hundred and sixty-three and a wake-up," the tapping of glasses was drowned out by loud hoots and groans over Izzy's misfortune.

J.D. took his turn last and shrugged. "Oh, who's counting?"

Bayer heartily toasted the jokester. "Good one, Doc, good one!"

"Yeah, we should keep him around." Hertz quickly fixed a second glass with the works as time was just about up. "By the way, sir, what is your specialty?"

"Excuse me?"

"You know. Your area of expertise?"

"Dr. Mikel specializes in delusion and hysteria," Gregg quickly answered on behalf of J.D.

"Yes, that is it exactly," J.D. agreed. "This is a nice iced coffee, thank you Hertz."

"Okay, we've got our customers lining up out there," said Gregg, hurrying things along. "Let's get going."

The techs took off and Gregg told Izzy, "Okay, you've got your first customer coming. Pretend this is a patient like anyone you'd treat back home, just dealing with an out of body experience on another planet, and you'll be fine. I'll be in my office and like I said, yell if you need me."

7

"Thanks, man." J.D. tapped his glass to Gregg's. "I owe you for covering my ass."

"We're hardly even since I'm still here to say as much."

"Then perhaps you wouldn't mind if I sat in on any cases where my specialty with delusions and hysteria might suggest a good match? At least until I get my office, too."

Rather than savor another swallow of his iced coffee, Gregg put down his glass. He liked J.D., but he didn't trust him, and if you couldn't trust the person who saved your life, then who could you trust? He was caught in the same damned if you do/damned if you don't dilemma of knowing if something twisted was going after the troops it had to be stopped, but his responsibility as a psychologist was to treat these messed up soldiers with kindness, dignity, compassion, while J.D. was there to get answers by any means necessary, even if it meant messing the poor guys up even more than they already were.

Before Gregg could respond, and the hell if he knew what to say, Hertz reappeared and in an urgent whisper reported, "Dr. Kelly, we've got an escorted Special Ops NCO out there who's not in good shape at all. I pushed him to the front, and you'll want this one, Sir. You know we usually never get Special Forces, even less Special Ops, but your friend Captain Galt sent him over."

That's all Gregg needed to hear. Rick Galt was tough as nails but he would do anything for his soldiers, and to be sure, they would do anything for a commanding officer like him. Galt was like a larger-than-life Special Ops version of....

Gregg wished he hadn't thought of Top. His throat got really tight and the coffee didn't sit well on his stomach. But since Top would be the first to tell him to get his shit together and a haircut while he was at it, Gregg took a deep breath and said, "Sure, get him to my office."

J.D. quickly followed up with, "And be sure to bring anything he came in with, Hertz."

"That would be his gun, sir, and his buddy. He's not letting the first one go and the second is propping him up."

Gregg no sooner got into his office, reluctantly bringing J.D. along, than Hertz escorted the staff sergeant and a corporal in, and immediately left to get something cold that tasted of home.

The obvious new patient slumped against the other soldier who'd brought him in from the field on Galt's orders. They both looked worse than hell—haggard and worn out, dirty with red mud caked all over them—but the similarities ended there. While the corporal was amply functional to bring his buddy in for help, the other man was closer to an unblinking zombie.

Gregg quickly stepped forward to greet them. "I'm Dr. Kelly. I appreciate Captain Galt sending you here with . . ." Reading the name tag, "Romero." Then to the escort, "Okay, now you want to take his weapon and hold it for him."

At first touch, Romero seized the gun closer. The corporal persisted and one-by-one pried Romero's fingers off the M16 while he filled Gregg in. "We were up near Dalat. Out on the wire all night and when we came back in Lieutenant Jones—he was Romero's long time LT—was sitting there at our meet-up point with his own head cut off and sitting in his lap. Romero freaked out about the Boogeyman story that's been making the rounds and...and we just didn't know what to do." Finally, the corporal extricated the weapon from Romero's possession. Gregg exhaled the breath he'd been holding as the corporal set the gun a safe distance aside and put a supportive arm around his comrade.

"You did the right thing coming here." Even though Romero showed no signs of comprehension or ability to engage in conversation, Gregg hoped on some level he still had the ability to respond. Gently, Gregg assured him, "You are okay and safe with us. I'm Dr. Kelly, let me talk with you for a little bit while your friend waits outside."

The friend took his cue to exit, Romero's M16 in hand.

"All right Sergeant Romero," Gregg said gently, "come on over here and have a seat in this chair . . . right there, that's good. Make yourself comfortable. How about a cold can of Coke?"

Romero, having mechanically followed instructions to sit in a chair beside the desk, looked up at Gregg. "Coke?"

"Got one on the way," Gregg assured him, keeping his voice real nice, soft, easy like the calm lap of a wave. "So, Romero, could you tell me your first name?"

"Mike?"

"Mike, good to meet you. And where do you come from?"

Hertz appeared with soda in hand. He held out the can but Romero's gaze didn't move.

"The Coke is here whenever you want it, Mike." In the few seconds Gregg took to reframe his question, J.D. pulled up the extra chair and jumped in.

"Hey Mike, it's Dr. Mikel, and I'm just here to help Dr. Kelly, and you know, Dr. Kelly is here to help you. But we can't help you much without knowing more about your situation. Did you get a 'Dear John?'"

Romero slightly shook his head.

"That's good, glad to hear. Have you got someone waiting back home?"

Romero nodded, just barely. "New baby."

"Congratulations! What's your baby's name?"

Romero stared blankly ahead, suddenly blinked. For a moment his eyes seemed to come into focus. He almost smiled. "Judy."

"Judy will be really happy to see her daddy come home. But you have to help us by answering a few questions." Gregg cut J.D. with a censoring glare but J.D. ignored him, continued to hijack the session. "Mike, can you remember being out in the field and seeing or hearing anything strange or unusual? Think hard and—"

"That's enough," Gregg sharply whispered when Romero's inhale/exhale became so rapid he was panting like a dog that had chased down a rabbit—no, more like the rabbit being chased.

"Take it easy, Mike," Gregg told him in the gentle, quieter voice he used when a situation was getting dicey. "You don't have to remember anything right now. Mike look right at me now, focus on me and know that you are safe here and—"

"NOOO!" Romero surged from the chair, his eyes bulging at something in some other place that only he could see. He started to run and Gregg leaped in front of him, arms splayed to block the exit.

"IM STAT! STAT!" While Gregg yelled for the sedative, J.D. calmly stood, applied some form of pressure to Romero's throat with a single hand, and within seconds Romero's eyes rolled up and he collapsed in J.D.'s arms.

"Sleep tight, sweetheart," J.D. muttered, and laid him on the floor.

"What the *hell* did you just do to my patient?"

"Nothing that will last as long as the sedative you should probably give him before he comes to." As if J.D. had the authority to issue the instruction, Hertz saw to the injection as J.D. explained, "It's just an acupunctural technique with the carotid artery. Dim Mak."

"Dim what?"

"Touch of death. Just a touch, though. He'll be fine."

"Wow," Hertz exclaimed. "What med school did you go to?"

"I'm here!" It was Izzy, racing into the room with Bayer. "I heard yelling so I came the way you told me to. . . Gregg? What happened?"

Gregg could only shake his head. "Later. Let's carry this guy out and have him taken over to the 99th. We'll ask the buddy who brought him in to let Captain Galt know what's up."

"I'll talk to the corporal now." J.D. stepped over Romero. "See if he has some information that might be useful—for diagnostic purposes, of course." He slapped a high five to both techs. "Fine work, Bayer. Hertz? Right on."

"Wow," Hertz said again with something akin to awe as J.D. strode out the door. "Dr. Mikel is cool."

"Hell yeah," Bayer agreed. "We sure are lucky to have him."

✳

After a lunch break, more hot sweaty hours, and more than a few patients later, it was time to end the day. Everyone except J.D. sat in the front office while they put away files and locked cabinets. Bayer and Hertz had their shirts off it was so hot. Gregg was glad J.D. was still gone, and yet he felt like he needed to keep an eye on him so he didn't improperly mess with any of their patients. Everything about J.D. seemed to challenge his inner equilibrium, like this see-saw between gratitude and resentment that the episode with Romero had ratcheted up another notch.

"So what's with all this Ghost Soldier stuff that's floating around, Dr. Kelly? The stories are getting really creepy." Hertz gave a slight shiver and Gregg knew it wasn't from the 100-plus degree air blowing dust through the windows.

"Well, what it comes down to is fear," Gregg ad-libbed in his best clinical voice, hoping to downplay the situation he wasn't at liberty to discuss. "You know bad things happen up there, it's scary and stories get started, so the mind thinks it's better to come up with a story to explain the bad stuff away rather than just accept how awful the war is."

"I don't know, Doc," Bayer interjected. "These guys this morning were Special Ops steel balls guys. They don't get afraid of the dark, or anything else. Everybody is afraid of *them*."

"True," Gregg agreed while shooting a quick glance at Izzy. "But you have to remember these guys are patrolling long range for days, they're isolated and stressed with their buddies getting shot, sometimes friendly fire. Nobody wants to admit to that, shooting someone in front of them by accident, but it happens and it's easier to believe it was some monster or ghost than deal with the guilt. Right, Dr. Moskowitz?"

"Right. Absolutely."

"But that still doesn't explain everything." Hertz made a slice at his throat with his finger. "What about the beheadings? Even if you accidentally shoot someone, you don't turn around and cut off his head."

"Of course not," Gregg quickly agreed and silently damned J.D. for putting them in this position. "Look, that's the rumor going around, but it's just a rumor. Have you seen any of these guys with their heads cut off?"

"Hands, too," Bayer reminded him before admitting, "But, no, we haven't seen any of that. Sure don't want to either."

"None of us do." Izzy got up to the plate, took a load off Gregg. "And none of us wants to be responsible for contributing to any kind of mass hysteria. This is a natural breeding ground for fear. Fear breeds hysteria, and the problem with hysteria is that it's infectious—especially where everyone's afraid at some level, no matter how well they may hide it. Wouldn't you agree, Dr. Kelly?"

"Completely. It's like Colonel Kohn was just telling me, that once a ghost story like this gets started, it spreads like measles, and if it keeps spreading, you think this morning was busy? It will look like Disneyland lines out there. The Colonel said we needed to put the kibosh on any rumors and I couldn't agree more."

"So what are we supposed to say?" Hertz asked Gregg. "I mean, when other guys ask us about it, because they know we hear things."

"The reason we are seeing more blow outs is that we have been here longer, and that means they have been out there longer and had more time and opportunity to lose it. And that's what you tell anyone who asks, then go back to reading your Batman comics or change the subject. Okay? We don't want to spread rumors or have people thinking the men in the field are seeing things that are not there."

Suddenly, Hertz and Bayer stood up so fast they nearly knocked over their chairs. They were both staring at the door maybe ten feet away, their mouths slack.

"I don't believe what I see," whispered Bayer.

"Me either," echoed Hertz.

Gregg turned. And just like that *he* was the one who must be hallucinating and delusional.

Backlit from the open door stood a drop-dead gorgeous blonde that belonged in a wet dream wrapped in a centerfold and you'd still want to take her home to mom. A sky blue sundress showcased creamy bare shoulders, all the right curves, and a shapely pair of legs that were made for walking all over a man's heart as she strapped them around his waist.

"Kate?" Gregg got up slowly because his own legs felt like rubber. And he felt a little dizzy, the way he always had, always would, with no more than a glimpse of, *"Kate!"*

8

Katherine Lynn Morningside knew she was beautiful and she knew what it meant. Her mother, who was also beautiful, had told her: *It means honey that you can get what you want from them when you want it, at least while you have it; then, it's gone. But being smart and being tough means you have a chance to get it for yourself and keep it. . . Be beautiful honey, and work it, but be my smart girl.*

And just how smart was she to be sitting on the patio of a scrumptious French restaurant on a beachside oasis half the globe away from where she once played a little "beach blanket bingo" with Gregg?

How smart she was to have taken the bait that landed her here remained to be seen. As for working it, Gregg deserved better than all the little torture treatments she had so generously dished out on a deserted sand dune once in high school. She had felt safe enough to practice on him and poor Gregg, always the deep thinker, thought it meant more than it really did.

Here, Gregg, put a little of this baby oil on my back? Oh yes, that's nice. Uh huh, get under the strap, that's good. Would you mind doing my legs, too? Hey, you must have had some practice at that. Now the other side. Mmm, that feels soo good. Want me to rub some on your chest? No? But why not? Come on, my turn. Just lay on your back and. . .Wow. That's amazing. Can I look at it? Please? I mean, I've never seen one before. . . .

She still remembered the snap of his grip to her wrist, stopping her in mid-exploratory plunge beneath his swim trunks, the way he was almost gasping for air while he squeezed out a pitiful, "wait." But like everything else, there was no stopping her once she knew what she wanted and she wanted to see what she could do to the boy next door who was the closest thing she had to a brother.

It should have felt incestuous. It didn't. It felt like raw, intoxicating power erupting in her hands. Like Charlton Heston throwing down his rod that turned into a snake at Pharaoh's feet, only this was her staff to command. And still was, judging from Gregg's glazed expression as he continued to stare at her the way he had the day she "took his virginity," as he insisted she had.

"What are you doing here, Kate?" The white dress shirt accentuated his deep blue eyes, golden skin, golden hair. If Dr. Kildare ever needed a stand-in, all Gregg needed were some scrubs and a screenplay. Even their voices were similar. No wonder he made all the other girls melt.

"Would you believe me if I said I was a spy?"

"Ha. Ha."

Gregg's besotted gaze migrated into a grimace. He masked it with a sip of the wine he had ordered. A very nice Bordeaux that he remembered was her favorite. He was always doing thoughtful things like that. If there was a perfect guy to settle down with it would be Gregg, and in a perfect world she would be in love with him.

The world simply was not perfect.

"Okay then, let's try this." Kate took a sip from her glass. The Bordeaux was perfect at least. "I'm a missionary."

Gregg practically spewed the wine out of his nose.

"It's true!" she insisted, glad this much of her well-rehearsed story was honest. Kate knew she should be a better liar considering how much she loved to bend the rules. "Mom's church put out a call to help staff their Vietnamese hospital ministry so I signed up for a year as a surgical nurse. It's not like I'm going door-to-door delivering Bibles, more like the Peace Corps, only with the Peace Mission Hospital, just down the road."

Gregg didn't look any happier than her mother had about the news. And both of them would be unhappier still if they knew Phillip was involved. Call it karmic justice: what she had done to Gregg in high school, and on some level continued to do to him now, Phillip had performed with fluent grace and charm on her in one fateful college semester studying abroad.

It was quite an education in love and sex, abandonment and adulthood. That's when she learned there are philharmonic level gifted players and then there are the gifted virtuosos. And no one played people better than Phillip. He made you helplessly enjoy it even while he was taking you apart. Kate supposed that's how he had convinced her it was her own brilliant idea to go to South East Asia in the middle of a dirty, bloody war to be his "spy"—oh, she knew she wasn't really a "spy" but that's how Phillip worked. He knew she was bored and would love the idea of being a spy, so he arranged through the State Department to have her signed with the mission as a surgical nurse and made an anonymous "gift" to the mission to increase their staff which somehow ensured she was immediately selected and assigned over another candidate. In exchange, she received several photos with instructions to report back on any unusual activity. So, she supposed, that made her more of a "mole" than a "spy" but semantics aside, it was all very exciting, which Phillip knew she simply could not resist.

Gregg regarded her for a moment, making her squirm. So Kate pretended to suddenly be captivated by the carp gliding in the lotus pond near their beautiful long teak table, set for six, room for eight. What she admired most about the man sitting directly across from her, and what she really didn't like about him either, was his uncanny ability to see what others did not. She always felt like he could look through her eyes and read her mind, which would not do at all and especially not now. If Gregg had any idea she and Phillip were still in touch, had even recently slept together again, he would be furious.

"Oh, no."

"What?" Kate dared a glance, studiously innocent.

"I know that look on your face. You're up to something."

With just the right hint of piousness, she informed him, "I am here to serve my fellow man and try to do some good where it's needed the most." When he dramatically rolled his eyes, she conceded, "Okay, I was bored. The opportunity came along and I grabbed it before someone else beat me to it. Happy, Kemosabe?"

"Only if I had something to do with the decision, Tonto."

He gave her a little smile. Perfect. She had always insisted on him being Tonto, her Kemosabe, and finally she let him pull rank. That should amply appease him to drop it.

Or not. The upgrade in position only netted her a shake of his finger. "Even then you have no business being here. It's a damn war zone, Kate. Nha Trang is a beautiful city, but people get killed here for no reason. I watched a guy get blown apart just last night, and he wasn't the first. You need to go home. Or back to France. Just go be anywhere but here."

"People get hit by busses and die in cars every day, too, Gregg." She left it at that. There would be no debate. She would, however, touch that dial and reach across the table for his hand while she was at it. "C'mon, pal, admit it. You're glad to see me."

Something shifted in his eyes then. A dark something she hadn't expected. He suddenly gripped her tip-toeing fingers and was leaning over, as if he meant to kiss her, only to...snarl?

It was some expression she had never associated with Gregg, his upper lip curling in distaste, his eyes narrowed to slit windows, and his voice, usually like something out of a fairy tale, consolidated into the nasty whisper, "And just what the *hell* is he doing here?"

Kate tracked Gregg's line of vision that had shifted from her to two other men approaching the table. She recognized one as the new doctor she'd met earlier at the clinic who went by Izzy. Like Gregg he was dressed nicely except in a frumpy, wrinkled kind of way that at least provided some relief from those redundant military fatigues. As for Izzy's companion...

Kate stopped breathing.

He moved with the lithe kind of natural grace only found in the wild, but stylishly well adapted to the animal of man in an old elegant ivory colored dinner jacket, white linen tailored slacks and sandals. He hadn't shaved for the occasion. His hair was straight, long, almost black. It matched the Aviator sunglasses he took off. His eyes belonged to an animal species: large variety, cat—that rare, sea glass color of a *7up* bottle. He had to be the most divine man she had ever seen in person or in print, and her hunger for all things risky, dark and unknown arose with jaws wide and insatiable.

Kate wanted to devour him on sight.

"J.D." Gregg said tightly as he stood to greet them. He had managed to rearrange his snarl into something a little less antagonistic. "I didn't realize you would be joining us."

J.D. initiated a handshake that Gregg hesitated to accept. In that moment's hesitation Kate noticed J.D. had two round white gold bracelets on his extended right wrist that had some small inscription she couldn't make out. On his left wrist was a stainless steel and gold watch she recognized as a Jaeger-LeCoultre. Design she knew; the bracelets were a mystery.

"Robert David asked me to bring Izzy over since he was picking up the rest of the party. I hoped you might have room for an extra—especially since Henri's has the best cassoulet in town."

"Cassoulet!" And now Kate was hungry for the rich, slow cooked casserole of meats and white beans, topped with fried bread cubes, confit duck legs, pork cracklings. She had fallen in love with the savory dish upon first bite from Phillip's own fork. And so began his tasteful seduction.

J.D.'s answering "Magnifique" kiss of bronze fingertips to sky and rich, articulate voice matched everything else about this rare animal that kicked her pulse into overdrive. Kate told herself to start breathing again, to just act normal while he spoke to Gregg. But his eyes were resting on her and the impact was exhilarating, a giddy kind of high like the time she hotwired a car on a dare—a cop car that she drove like a bat out of hell with strobing lights and siren full blast, then abandoned at the nearest Orange Julius.

"Of course we have room," Kate said brightly. "Don't we, Gregg?"

"Sure." Gregg's introductions were as curt as his agreement before he concluded with, "Or you can just call him Doctor Mikel."

"Enchanté." J.D.'s sea glass gaze continued to hold hers as he indicated the empty seat to her left. "May I?"

"S'il vous plait." Having consented with a "please" Kate asked, "You speak French?"

"La nourriture est spectaculaire et l'ambiance est rendue parfaite par votre présence."

The food is spectacular and the ambience is made perfect by your presence. It wasn't the sort of compliment that was easily pulled off, but slid off his tongue like clarified butter.

"And you?" he asked.

"A little." Kate preferred to be underestimated and found it amusing when people thought beauty precluded brilliance. She had a natural affinity for foreign languages, and though she was just getting started with Vietnamese, she did speak fluent French. It was the second language of the country, which Phillip had pointed out would work to both her advantage and his.

A quick glance at Gregg and she saw the tic in his cheek, the sharp, silent warning he shot her.

"Wow, this place is wonderful!" Izzy made himself at home on the table's other side, sitting in the chair next to Gregg and across from the apparent no-no sitting beside her. "Just look at this. A tropical sunset, French restaurant, everyone's dressed in real clothes, all these different accents—my god, are these people actually tourists?"

"Believe it or not, people do come here to vacation." It was her off-limits dining companion, J.D., who answered. "A lot of Australians, but even more French, because of their earlier occupation here."

"This is amazing," Izzy raved, oblivious to the tension bouncing from one side of the table to the other as Gregg shot her eye signals. "And here I thought nothing could beat the car J.D. drove us over in."

"Wine, Izzy?" Gregg abruptly offered.

Before Izzy could reply, J.D. signaled their waiter, whose earlier effusive demeanor turned palpably guarded as J.D. spoke to him in Vietnamese.

The brief exchange ended with their waiter asking in English, "And what would you like to drink, Dr. Mikel?"

"The usual, please. And one for our new friend Dr. Moskowitz here if he would like one. Kate, maybe try something a little exciting, too?"

"I'm *always* ready to try something exciting," Kate confessed.

"Gregg?" J.D. asked.

"No. Thanks."

"In that case—" J.D. placed his order with the eloquence Gregg's refusal had lacked: "Three *Soixante Quinzes*, please."

"Of course." Their waiter left. Quickly.

Kate stared at J.D. "Well, that was interesting. Do you always make such an impression?"

"I would think that making an impression is something you're quite familiar with."

Gregg's wine glass landed on the table with a *thud* and coincided with Izzy announcing, "Here they come."

Kate turned to see a pair of women, both in white sundresses, one wholesomely pretty with brown hair, one a glamorous, statuesque redhead—Ginger and Maryann off their island and bookending their attractive escort who bowed to Kate upon reaching the table.

"Ma'am, my apologies for your having to spend such an inordinately long time in the company of these ruffians and horrible examples of gentlemanly virtue. You are saved."

"You must be Robert David." Kate dimmed the wattage of her camera ready smile. She needed to make some girlfriends and being the center of attention was not the way to do it.

"An honor, ma'am, and I can certainly see why Gregg was actually shouting and screaming about his lovely friend from back home who was here for a visit."

"A long visit," Kate emphatically told them all. "I'm signed on for the next year at the Peace Mission Hospital as a surgical nurse."

The redhead extended her hand. "I'm Margie, the only female nurse on the unit so I'm thrilled to meet you, just promise me we won't talk shop for the rest of the night."

"Lady, I like your style." And Kate did. She liked Margie's forthrightness, the honesty of her grip, the way she looked you in the eyes and smiled right at you. "Besides, I'd rather talk about the city, the people, and all the places I need to see while I'm here."

"Then we will have a lot to talk about." The brunette gave her a quick hug. "It is really nice to meet you. I'm Nikki. Red Cross and Margie's room-mate."

"Not to mention newly broken up—but not too broken up about it—and now available."

"Margie. . ." Nikki warned. "Let's just enjoy this fine night amongst friends and keep my squirmy, wormy stuff as far away from our dinner plates as possible. Gregg, you got some more wine in that bottle to share?"

"Come right over here, darlin', where the Doctor of Love awaits." Gregg poured a generous amount of the remaining Bordeaux into his own glass and extended it to Nikki.

The sound she made was between a squeal of delight and a laugh as generous as Gregg's offering.

As for Gregg's behavior, the boy next door had changed somehow in the year since Kate had last seen him. She hadn't made it to his going away party or even his latest graduation. They just had a way of immediately reconnecting between her moves and trips abroad while Gregg remained steady as a barge plowing the ocean to its predetermined destination—at least until the blip with an unexpected draft notice.

There were seven of them at the rectangular table for eight and as the night progressed it reminded Kate of the childhood game musical chairs when Gregg would lose his own chair so she could have it. Only tonight he kept tracking her like a moving target and was bending over her seat, his palm possessively cupping her left shoulder—conveniently separating it from J.D.'s—as Nikki tipsily giggled in their midst, "Float like a butterfly, sting like a bee!"

Kate was feeling amply loose herself to cheer, "Ali! Ali! You gotta respect him, anyone really, who's not afraid of bucking the system to adhere to their own moral principles."

Kate felt a hot whisper of breath behind her ear, mocking her with, "Moral principles? Isn't that a new one for you, Tonto?"

As subtly as possible, Kate shrugged away from Gregg's palm and muttered, "Shut up, Gregg, and don't spoil the party just because you probably need to get laid by someone besides me."

Then to Nikki, loud enough to be heard over the convivial table chatter, Kate inquired, "And what do you think of Ali?"

"Well, my daddy like a lot of folks back where I come from in Tennessee hate him, still call him Cassius Clay and say he's a coward hiding behind some religion he doesn't even believe in to shirk his patriotic duty."

"But what do *you* think?" Kate persisted, curious, and more than a little annoyed with Gregg's hovering.

"Honestly?" Nikki put a secretive finger to her lips. "I think he's brave. And I think he's said a lot of things other people are thinking but might be afraid to say themselves."

Kate thought of her own liberal upbringing, how her lawyer mom had applauded Ali's interview when he said the US government could arrest him if they wanted to but he was not going 10,000 miles to go kill innocent people he had no quarrel with, that "No Viet Cong ever called me nigger" and much of the real enemy was right at home.

Clearly she and Nikki had different backgrounds but she respected Nikki for thinking beyond the narrow mindedness that was unfortunately shared by the cattle mentality comprising much of the homeland's population.

"I agree with you, Nikki. But it makes me wonder why you're here if you're more inclined to side with Ali than your dad. I mean, we are the only two people at this table in the country of our own accord."

"Let's just say even Vietnam could seem like a vacation from a less than peaceful household, a third cousin who wants to marry you, and has your family's blessing to do it. What about you?"

"Would you believe me if I said I'm just a good Christian girl pitching in to make the world a better place?"

"Not really." Nikki grinned.

"Why not?"

"Because you wouldn't attract *that* guy if you were." Nikki had enough booze in her to point to J.D. But then she pointed to Gregg and decreed, "However, I think this guy likes you just fine any which way you're inclined to be." *Hic.* "And, of course, any girl with a brain in her head would grab him if she had the chance, so you'd better get to it before somebody else does."

Gregg blew Nikki a kiss just as two palms came down on Nikki's shoulders and a pair of lips planted themselves on her neck.

"Hey, baby." A good looking Kennedy-esque guy intercepted Nikki's hand to the current glass she was working on. Except for the military buzz cut everything about him screamed pedigreed-don't-fuck-with-me-or-my-daddy-will-grind-you-to-dirt American. "Let's go finish business."

Nikki shook her head. "Go away, Donald. You weren't invited to this party and any unfinished business between us can wait till I'm ready."

"Major Peck!" Gregg sloppily saluted him. "To what do we owe this honor of your presence?"

"Fuck you, Kelly. I know sarcasm when I hear it and you're dripping it like diarrhea."

"With all due respect, Major Doctor Peck, Nikki is with us, so if she doesn't want to hear whatever you have to say, then I highly suggest you go away and not further intrude upon the good time we were having before you showed up. Sir!"

"It's okay, Gregg." Nikki laid a conciliatory hand upon his better intentions. "Don's right. We have some things to discuss privately so I'll be saying goodnight to the rest of y'all now."

J.D. stood up, followed by everyone else in various degrees of inebriation, ensuring nobody was getting to Nikki without plowing through their collective drunken asses first.

"Actually, Nikki," said J.D., clearly the most sober amongst them, or at least the one with the highest tolerance, "you don't have to go anywhere you don't want to go. Major Peck? Why don't you and I step away from the table and have a word together alone? I think we should get better acquainted."

Now Nikki was on her feet and ever the gracious southern girl insisted, "Now, now, that's just not necessary but I'm much obliged to you all and look forward to getting together again soon at that big beach party Gregg has planned for next week."

"Beach party?" Peck steered Nikki away from her chair, clamped an arm around her waist. "Why didn't I hear about a beach party?"

Silence. Then Margie whispered something to Izzy, who nodded, and she came over to join Nikki and Peck. "You don't mind if I catch a ride back with you two, do you, Don?"

"Of course he doesn't mind," Nikki quickly answered for him. "Do you, Donny?"

Peck's stony expression went soft. The rapidity of the change made Kate wonder if he could go off the other way, too, if Margie was insinuating herself as protection.

They said their good-byes then, left without fanfare, and took most of the steam of the party with them.

Now it was just Kate and the four men and only one of them she wanted to be alone with.

It was not Gregg.

But he had brought her here and she was not going to embarrass him by leaving with J.D. in a hot set of wheels that Izzy had described with such exacting detail she asked him if he had a photographic memory. His response was a muttered, "Eidetic, actually."

So there they were, all standing up and just sort of looking at each other, except for J.D. who nodded toward the dance floor.

Several couples swayed intimately to the smooth jazz band that announced it was their last set.

"Kate, care to dance?"

"Love to." She knew she didn't have to, didn't want to for sure, but still she made it a point to ask, "You don't mind, do you, Gregg?"

"I do," he said softly, just so she could hear, "But that won't stop you, will it? Never has before."

9

Gregg watched Kate and J.D. moving like twin shadows on the dance floor and thought his skull might hemorrhage from the primal spike of his blood pressure.

Desperate guys never had a chance with women like Kate and he knew anyone within ten feet could smell the desperation on him like stink on shit.

You could tell a lot about a man by looking in his wallet. And if you looked inside Gregg Kelly's wallet, what would you see? The epitome of desperation. He had been twelve when his obsession with the girl next door started. He was now twenty-nine. That made him a desperate guy who hadn't had a chance with her for well over half his life and he was still carrying around the snapshot of him and Kate that day on the beach. That amazing, miraculous day when she put a hand between his legs and, smiling with a giddy kind of high, watched him spurt what felt like a gallon of liquid lava onto the sand.

It was, by far, the most memorable orgasm of his life.

Sometimes Gregg wondered how much Kate had to do with his chosen profession just so he could figure out for himself what the hell she had done to his head, not to mention the rest.

Izzy and Robert David wove their way over and pulled up chairs on either side.

Robert David asked, "Are you up to driving the divine Miz Kate back to the mission?"

Gregg took stock of his inebriation quotient: He was just about drunk enough to put his fist through J.D.'s shiny, white front teeth before pouncing on Kate to molest her in a public place.

Translation: "I probably should have stopped at that last shot of tequila two shots ago."

"I'm not in much better shape," Izzy slurred. "And even if I was, I don't drive."

"What? Are you kidding? Everybody drives." But clearly not him tonight. J.D. and Kate had doubled into two of each of them. Great, just what he needed. Twice the competition.

"A lot of New Yorkers don"t drive." Izzy pulled out a picture of a girl with strong Jewish features and a stylish bob. "My fiancé Rachel does. See?" He teetered on his chair while trying to produce the evidence, then waved several ragged pages in the air. "She says so right here—that she's driving some friends to a concert. It's a few months away but everyone's already talking about it, so she's going to drive. But that's driving upstate, not in the city. Nobody wants to drive in the city. That's why we have cabs and subways and hired cars."

"I do declare," Robert David drawled, "that seems to leave me as chauffeur and I should be fine to get us back to the villa. But I am in no condition to be driving Kate to the mission when even Camp McDermott would not be wise given my cognitive impairment."

"Unh-unh." Gregg adamantly shook his head. Then he wished he hadn't. It felt like the South China Sea was swishing between his temples. "I am not about to let Captain Hook drive Wendy home."

Robert David looked out at the dance floor, then back at Gregg with great sympathy. "I'm afraid she's taken a liking to our other new doctor, and I wouldn't care a whit for that either if I were you. But Gregg, as much as you want to protect your dear Kate, she strikes me as the kind of woman a man is far more likely to need protection from than she is of him."

"She's not like that," Gregg protested.

"Perhaps not, but a word of advice? Be magnanimous. Leave with your dignity intact. You may hate the very idea at the moment, but you will marvel at your wisdom tomorrow."

"Really?" Gregg scrawled a note to leave with the stack of bills they all threw in to cover the tab. "Because I already know I'm going to be hurting like hell in the morning."

*

Kate could not believe her good fortune. Gregg had taken off without creating a scene, and actually left a note asking J.D. to see her home. So what if it came with some threat of "eunichism" if she didn't arrive safely or—and that's where the note ended, as if Izzy or Robert David had relieved Gregg of his pen-mightier-than-the-sword diatribe.

It didn't dilute her exhilaration, the sense of being enveloped by a fantasy. In another world called Nha Trang, where the wind whipped through her hair and kissed her senseless along the South China Beach Highway in a turquoise 57 Chevy. White ragtop accordianed down, a vista of stars glittered above her and J.D. who sveltely guided the wheel with his left hand, his right arm draped around the seat, fingertips flirting with her bare shoulder.

"Stop here," she told him, pointing to the roadside pull off with a view of the sea and half a mile before they arrived at the mission.

He removed his arm to shift the three on the tree and parked as instructed.

"You have three wishes," he told her. "That was the first. What about the other two?"

"I wish for a book of matches." Kate fished out a pack of French Gauloises. She loved to smoke and she especially loved to smoke these. Just one of her vices Gregg didn't approve of. He could be such a goddam prude. She didn't think J.D. was anything close, but to be polite she asked, "Mind if I smoke?"

"Only if you mind me joining you." J.D. plucked the filter from her lips and lit up. He took a puff to get it started, passed the cig to Kate, blew a smoke ring into the air.

She inhaled deeply, likewise blew a ring towards the moon to make a wish on.

"Jesus, I've been craving that puff all night."

"Yeah, I hear ya," J.D. agreed.

"Gregg's a great guy."

"The best," J.D. readily agreed again.

"I've known him most of my life."

"Wish I was that lucky."

"Do you?" Kate transferred the cigarette to J.D.'s incredibly kiss-able lips. She was glad neither of them would taste like an ashtray to the other after they finished business. The password was: "Phillip sends his regards."

Kate reclaimed their shared guilty pleasure, took another puff that tasted even better with J.D.'s mouth on it.

"He asked me to keep an eye on you."

"Yes, I noticed you were doing a very good job at that tonight." Kate laughed up at the stars, laughed at the craziness of this whole preposterous set-up.

"Do you think this is a joke, a game?" There was no humor in his voice.

"Everything is a game to Phillip, and the rest of us are pawns to be maneuvered for either his advancement or his amusement."

"You know him well." JD leaned over, slid a fingertip from her cleavage to her chin. The catch of her breath was hardly a gasp of offense. "And I want to know you much better."

"I like a man who knows what he wants."

He plucked the Gauloises from her lips, flicked it. The red ember rotated in the air and out of the car.

"I want to kiss you."

"Are you a mind reader, Agent Mikel?" Kate rolled past the leather and into his arms, undid the top button then the next of his shirt to get her hands on his chest, her nails into his skin. "How did you know that was my wish number three?"

"Better be careful what you wish for," he told her—then turned the tables so fast her head was literally spinning as it softly landed on the front seat.

She felt a whisper of wind hit the wet path he left up her neck, the scrape of his teeth at her jugular, then his shadowed face loomed above hers just before his mouth came down and his fingertips slid up and up. . . .

And that's when Kate understood how Gregg must have felt that day on the beach. She was in helpless surrender as her body convulsed into spasms against the hand responsible. As helpless to stop it as the moon's gravitational pull of waves to shore, licking the sand like a tongue culling salt from slick, sweaty flesh. Or, a pair of French silk panties drenched in 98.6 degrees of humidity.

They were still steaming when J.D. pulled into the mission's circular drive. Dimly lit, he cut the engine, kissed her again. Hard and deep, her heart had never pounded so hard. But then it pounded harder, faster, with his whispered warning, "It's not a game. Be a smart girl and get out. Before it's too late."

He sank his mouth into the thrum of her pulse for an interminable moment. Then left her at the sanctuary door and disappeared into the night as she watched the Chevy's taillights transform into red demon eyes glowing between two sweeping wings.

*

Everywhere there is sanctuary. Even here there were many different kinds in many places but when you needed to find some kind of peace, Camp McDermott had The Court. There were hoops and cement slabs anywhere there was a permanent base, but The Court had Rep. It was a place you could find Game. The city kind. The game here on any given night was a blend of NY and Philly and Memphis and Houston and LA. There were Indiana guys, and Seattle, and Iowa. Guys would show up from the rez in Navajo country. The players were black, white, brown, but the game was mostly all black. It was a city game. Other places there were games and players, but this court had become a place to come to Play. Guys on R&R, with anything and everything to do to get crazy and doped and fucked and stoned on these sacred blessed days of in-country R&R, where they knew they were maybe going back out to die, would take time to come play.

That was a part of it, they played like they knew they might die and they gave the game that kind of respect, and if you played like that, you earned that kind of respect. Any less, any kind of bullshit, grabass fuckoff stuff that you might find on other courts, was not tolerated here.

For most, the game was played in jungle boots but sometimes some guys would give another guy "shoes." Converse. No way of even describing changing from your boots to a pair of "shoes." You got Wings. For someone going home to leave you their shoes was a priceless gift. The game was a priceless gift. Outside the light of the courts the night was a black, humid, hot combat zone. Inside it was home. You forgot everyone was wearing dog tags, that everyone looked haggard and messed up in some way. As they started to play and got into the game they transformed so you saw their real faces and sometimes when the game was done and the soul shake was there someone would look you in the eye and you could really see him.

There were nights when men who had been pushing and shoving and banging, really banging just to that edge where any further meant a fight, would stop when that last shot went through and slap some skin, say "good game, man, good game, thank you man." Then you forgot where you were going to be tomorrow, where you were going tonight. There was just the sound of the ball, the rim, the boards, the net, the grunts, curses, the sounds from the ones waiting their turn mixed with the boom-box music of Marvin Gaye. . . .

And life for a moment was what you had always known. Life was not about counting the days or praying to whatever god you prayed to that a Boogeyman wouldn't come and take you apart or follow you home and hide under your bed just so you could shriek yourself awake.

The Game. The Court. The Boogeyman wanted to Play.

10

Izzy could not believe he had made it to "three fifty-seven and a wake up" in one piece and was sitting through yet another of Colonel Kohn's morning reports. Margie hit him with a knock-out smile that should be illegal for making him want something he could but absolutely could not have. He had already lost too much to sacrifice the better part of his character, the best part of his life.

Two letters from Rachel, his first in Vietnam, had arrived yesterday. Just touching them had been like fingering precious jewels. He was beyond excited but had made himself wait to open them, savoring the anticipation. Then he decided to forego dinner at the officer's mess, make a date out of it. He showered, shaved, put on some Coppertone Suntan Lotion because it smelled of Coney Island. Then all he had to do was go to the beach and the picnic came to him. A succession of vendors were always plying the area, so he brought a couple of icy cold Cokes, fresh pineapple from the mama-san selling fruit, a beautiful baguette sandwich. He settled in for his little beach picnic in a special spot he found under some ironwood pines. The setting was so perfect—except for Rachel not actually being there—that he decided this would become his ritual whenever a new letter arrived.

The two from yesterday were folded up now, stashed inside the pocket of his jungle fatigues, along with the new picture Rachel had sent. With her dark curly hair straightened and a kind of leather Indian headband across her forehead, he wasn't wild about the new look. Probably because he wasn't there to see how her new straight hair felt between his fingers. That and her mention of "hanging out with some new friends in the Village."

New. The reference had never bothered him before. And, he certainly liked new letters, so he told himself again to let it go and discreetly touched them, parked safely in his back pants pocket—yet another reminder of where his true affections belonged despite the residual effects of Margie's smile, her proximity.

How much was owed to Rachel's reassurances, how much to Margie's attention, and how much to just getting his bearings after a really rough start with a lot of help from his own new friends, Izzy wasn't sure. But amazingly, he had begun to feel like he actually knew what he was doing. Maybe the military brass knew what they were doing, too, because most of his patients were all young, and in their anguish and trauma, like big kids anyway. He loathed admitting it, but drafting a child psychiatrist had perhaps not been a bad call on the US Draft Board's end. They were bastards anyway, the whole filthy lot of them.

Not the patients though. They were as innocent in all this as him, Gregg, the psych techs, just about everyone at the table except J.D. and career officers like Peck who seemed to have some kind of control over Nikki, and wouldn't understand the concept of nobility if it bit him in his ass.

Nobility aside, in the past week it had dawned on Izzy that not only could he help these mentally messed up soldiers, he *wanted* to help them. He just had to get his own stuff together to do it.

Izzy felt the unit's mascot K.O. push her snout against his hip and gave her an appreciative scratch behind the ears before picking up his coffee—then almost immediately put the cup down before he spilled it into his lap. Quickly clasping his hands under the table, he frantically held onto his mantra: *Wake the fuck up.*

"Dr. Moskowitz?"

"Yes sir, Colonel Kohn."

"Well good, thank you, I was just saying that if you didn't want to lead on the sodium pentothal procedure with our catatonic Lieutenant Wilson, you can assist Dr. Peck. I leave the choice to you. Sergeant Washington, will you stand in for the procedure with us? I don't expect Wilson to get agitated but good to have you there, just in case."

"No problem, sir," said the hugely muscled specialist Sgt. Washington.

Oh shit, what had he missed? Izzy darted a glance at his hands. Steady now, maybe they hadn't been shaking as bad as he thought; maybe he had them under control. *Sodium pentothal procedure.* Top of his residency on those kinds of procedures, if he could do it back home in the hospital, surely he could do it here, spare the already damaged soldier from whatever Peck might dole out. Izzy subscribed to the basic goodness in man, but Peck seemed to have been short-changed when those particular goods were being distributed. At last week's crazy dinner party, Margie had confirmed as much with the whisper *I'd better drive along with Nikki to make sure he doesn't mess with her.*

"Absolutely, Colonel. I can lead." The words were out before Izzy could stop them.

Kohn looked pleased. Peck, not at all.

"Margie, could you prep the examining room for us?" requested Colonel Kohn.

Izzy glanced at Gregg for support. He was too busy machine-gunning eye darts into J.D. to notice. J.D., having just resurfaced after several days' absence, could have patented Teflon. He gave Izzy an encouraging nod.

K.O. wagged her tail and Izzy took further comfort in patting her head—until the growing sound of converging helicopters coincided with the shrill ring of the unit's phone.

Margie grabbed the receiver en route to the examining room. For several moments her anxious expression did all the talking until she announced, "Big casualties coming in, you can hear them already, and they need extra help on the pads and extra docs for triage."

Kohn sprang into immediate action: "Doctors Kelly and Mikel you two stay with me. Dr. Moskowitz, you go with Sergeant Washington and Specialist Bayer out to the pads—"

Izzy didn't wait to hear more. It was blindingly bright and ungodly hot as their team raced toward the huge sound of choppers coming down, their exhaust mixed with shouting and screaming and crying of wounded men coming in directly from a battle. Medics hurried from all directions to the stretchers to get the bloody, wounded, and burned off the helicopters so the next aircraft already hovering overhead could descend and unload more.

Gregg and J.D. grabbed a stretcher, headed toward surgery with Kohn. Robert David joined a triage team while Sergeant Washington, built like an NFL linebacker, grabbed the end of yet another stretcher with a soldier close to his own size, and yelled for Bayer and Izzy to grab the other end together.

Izzy did as instructed, grateful to have someone tell him what to do in this frenzy that had them rushing to the ER with a kid who couldn't be more than twenty, and so horribly burnt his lips looked like melted puddles of wax that semi-intelligibly moaned, "Please, man, help me, please I can't see, do I still have my eyes?"

"Talk to him, Doc, talk to him," urged Washington.

Izzy made himself look down at the oozing place where eyes were meant to be and choked back breakfast as he told the young soldier, "I'm here, right here with you, and I'm a doctor so you can trust me. You made it, you are at the hospital, and you are going to be okay."

Izzy could only pray the kid believed the lie. If by some cursed miracle he lived, the only visible thing that wasn't burned or disfigured was the left hand he somehow found the fortitude to lift, begging, "Hold my hand, Doc? I'm so scared. I don't want to die, but I'm more afraid of the news killing my ma if I do."

Izzy took his hand, held it, and the moment slowed for Izzy as he realized they were joined in some sort of tenderness, the young man holding his hand as he'd once held his own father's as he crossed a street as a young child, full of belief and confidence that whatever was hurtling towards them or swirling around them was halted by the sanctuary of their joined grip.

"I got the stretcher, Doc." Hertz suddenly showed up and grabbed the other handle Izzy was still holding onto, allowing him to free up both hands. "You bring him in, keep talking."

Izzy moved to the side, never letting go of the hand he covered protectively now with both of his. "We've got you. I am right here with you. We are taking you right through this, son. You are going to make it. We have you."

And then they were in the receiving area of the hospital. White light and a blast of cool air from real air conditioning, it felt almost like a real hospital, but then the reality of the scene hit Izzy. It was a painting of a white hell splashed with blood and green jungle fatigues being cut off the bodies of black and red burnt men who were screaming and sobbing and crying. The decibel level of suffering so stunned him that Izzy could feel himself splitting off to some safe place of numbness—but then he felt again the hand he was holding, gently squeezed back and leaned over the young soldier and promised:

"I am right here, right here with you, and you are going to make it."

✳

Almost exactly twenty-four hours later the catatonic patient lay on his side on the treatment table. He was naked to the waist and now his blue hospital pajamas were being pulled down to his knees to expose and prep his lower spine.

Izzy struggled to focus. He had to keep reminding himself they weren't in a bloodbath room; that at least he didn't have to break the news to a heartbroken mother who would never know her son had died holding the hand of a doctor who didn't even know his name. Or the name of the one after that or after that. . .

"Izzy?" It was Gregg, sitting between J.D. and Colonel Kohn in front of the patient, gently calling Izzy back to the present with that quiet, comforting voice he should be hoarse from using that endless day before.

Izzy nodded, letting Gregg know he was functional.

J.D. gave him a discreet thumb up sign of encouragement.

Although J.D. was about as much a real doctor as Betty Crocker was a cook, he had a way of imparting confidence. Izzy appreciated that as a particular kind of gift, even knowing J.D.'s presence was owed to hoping the catatonic Lt. Wilson might reveal something to assist in the case once the sodium pentothal procedure commenced. As for how things were commencing on J.D.'s end, who knew? Besides a fleeting mention of bringing them along to an area called the Highlands, thus far he had only asked his two recruits to generate some character sketches for prolific killers into mutilation and slipped Izzy a list of questions since the colonel had forbade J.D. from speaking during the procedure.

Izzy was about to look at his hands again from his position of privacy behind the examining table, when the exam room door opened. Robert David, Peck, Margie, and the techs lined up behind the front row to observe. Sergeant Washington came in last and Izzy welcomed the large man's presence beside him. They had worked side-by-side throughout yesterday's endless nightmare and Izzy couldn't imagine anyone he would rather have as a cellmate in hell. Even with the Sergeant holding steady by his side, the room felt crowded and hot and a lot like a make-it-or-break-it test of some kind that Izzy had a gut deep terror of failing.

He could feel the critical eyes of Peck looking at him. He remembered Margie telling him that Nikki had several bruises she tried to pass off as bumping into a filing cabinet at the Red Cross a few days before. Margie wasn't buying it. Neither was Izzy.

Yeah. He was glad Peck wasn't doing the procedure. He just wished he could get his nerves to settle down so he wasn't gripping the examination table like a man clinging to a ledge. Maybe he could get amply calm by narrating the steps, verbally remind himself he had the A-B-Cs of the procedure down as he went.

Sergeant Washington extended surgical gloves and Izzy put them on as best he could while he tried to stay focused on keeping his voice steady, not rushing his words as he typically did when he got nervous.

"Thank you, Sergeant Washington," Izzy began, and immediately wondered what puppet master was controlling his vocal chords because he sounded perfectly normal, even pleasant. "And a big welcome to the gallery. Lieutenant Wilson is prepped and ready. Despite appearances to the contrary, we have cause to believe that patients afflicted with this rare condition can hear and understand everything around them, so the Lieutenant and I had a nice little chat about this procedure earlier. Didn't we, Lieutenant?" Silence. "Now, Lieutenant Wilson, as I said before, I'm Dr. Moskowitz and this morning we are going to try to retrieve some of your memory. What I will do first is inject the medicine. . ."

Izzy pointed the needle that seemed huge even to him into the air, careful to keep it out of Wilson's frozen peripheral vision. Margie nodded. Her silent support was almost enough to believe he truly was capable of hitting just between the vertebrae sited between his left thumb and forefinger. He even started to push the long spinal needle forward.

The needle slightly shook. Izzy froze, kept talking in his freakishly conversational voice.

"And so we want to very carefully site the needle at the exact point of entry so that the needle is entering the spinal column and. . ." And all he could imagine was that if he jabbed now he would be watching himself create a quadriplegic with his own hands. *Morrie.*

"I can't. . ."

Just as he was ready to quit and let Peck take over, Sergeant Washington leaned closer and in his deep voice said, "Let me see just how you do that, Doc." And without the others able to observe, Washington closed his huge dark hand over Izzy's and held his hand steady as a rock and guided the needle right in. As the needle popped into the spinal column cord right on target, the Sergeant exclaimed, "Wow, perfect shot, Doc, and I actually heard that pop."

Izzy glanced over to see the Sergeant smile at him. For the rest of his life Izzy knew he would remember that singular moment of grace and kindness.

"Yes, and. . . and thank you, Sarge. And now, Lieutenant, as we inject the medicine ..." Izzy slowly pressed the plunger into the tube, dispensing the medication with exacting precision as he instructed, "Let's take just a couple of deep breaths now Lieutenant and. . .good, that's right. . ."

Wilson's face changed as if he had come back to life inside his own body. One moment he was not there and the next he was back from the far place in his mind where he had been safely residing.

"And now as that medicine takes effect you are going to feel very relaxed and comfortable and yet you will be able to hear my voice clearly and be very clear in your mind. Isn't that right, Lieutenant?"

"Yes, Dr. Moskowitz, I feel very relaxed and very clear."

"Excellent. Okay now, just getting to know each other a bit, remember I told you that I am from New York City. And you come from. . .?"

"I'm from Kansas, Doc, a Jayhawk, was in the reserves there until I graduated and got commissioned."

"Ok, Kansas, and you don't mind that I call you Kansas, do you?"

"Oh no sir, you can call me Kansas or whatever you want, just don't call me late to dinner. Especially if it's a nice, juicy steak."

The chuckles that joined Wilson's in the sterile room would have been bizarre if bizarre hadn't become the new normal. So normal that Izzy continued the conversation like they were just having a nice cook-out in the backyard while the adults enjoyed a good beer and the kids pushed each other into a pool.

"We are on the same page with that, Kansas. You know I'm a new guy here, only about a week in. What about you?"

"Oh, I just got back from R&R in Hawaii with my family, and so I am over half done, Doc."

"That's just great, were you in Honolulu?"

"Yes and then my wife and I were over in Maui for five days and then I had to leave. That part was hard. . ." Wilson's voice caught. His mouth trembled. "It was hard to say goodbye."

"I know, Kansas, I know how that feels, too. But you got past that hard part, and then you came back. What happened then?"

"I led a long range patrol out and. . . and. . ."

Wilson's breathing started to change; he was breathing hard, close to a pant.

Izzy noticed J.D. lean closer, draw a question mark with his finger.

"That is right, you were leading a long range patrol out," Izzy said, keeping his voice as gentle as possible, trying to lure Wilson back. "You led a patrol out and you were in the jungle and right now I am going to inject just little more medicine." Izzy felt Washington's hand return to steady his again—it had stopped shaking, started again. God this was so scary, never knowing when the tremor would suddenly come on, but he couldn't think about that now. He just had to do this and get it right.

The additional medicine successfully injected, Izzy continued, "Go ahead now, Kansas, you were taking the patrol out and. . .it's okay, just breathe and let the memory come to you now, it is right there."

"Yes, sir, it is almost dark and we—and we have an NVA patrol pinned down in front of us, at least I think we do, and I move us forward and it is an ambush. We are surrounded on three sides and we are getting cut down. Shit, *shit*, I have lost the radioman ...Collins, take the radio, dammit, get the radio and call in for air, right now, and it is y15 by 1.2 and. . .*yes, yes right, get the hell here now* and—and. . ."

Silence in the room, everything silent except for Wilson's agitated breathing as they all waited and waited until he suddenly cried out.

"Wait—wait! Here it comes, here comes air! But. . .oh no. No. NO. *NOOO!* It is right on top of us, I fucked up, oh God, I fucked up. . . I must have called in the wrong... They are all dead, all dead, all dead, all dead. Do you see what I have done? I am just walking around and picking up parts of them. Collins's arm and Petey's leg and boot and Jerry's head and hands and—and..."

Wilson sobbing now, sobbing with a sound that they all wanted to look away from as he wept, "They followed my orders and now they are all in pieces and all dead, all dead because of me."

Izzy had never heard such a mournful and terrible voice, not even in yesterday's hell. It was as if all the dead Wilson blamed himself for were in the room with them.

Izzy glanced at J.D.

J.D. shrugged, signaling he understood his questions were no good here. The loss of life—more specifically, Jerry's severed head and hands—was not the work of a monster, but human error. A dead end for J.D.; a very dead end for Wilson.

"You know, Kansas..." Izzy tried to remember what little he had been told about the way things worked on the ground and hoped his knowledge of the mind would compensate for any errors. "The air support people, they make mistakes too. You know it is not precise, not perfect, what they do, so it is entirely possible that it was their mistake. Remember, your radioman was down and Collins, he could have said the coordinates wrong, or the man on the other end could have heard it wrong. Come on now, Kansas. You know all that. Don't leave me now."

But he was despite the last of the injection. Wilson's face was changing again and Izzy, all of them in the room, could see Wilson leaving and going back to the place in the back of his mind where he was safe and numb and could somehow deal with the anguish of the horror of believing he had called artillery in on his own troops. Maybe back home, Izzy told himself, back in a hospital close to his family, Wilson could come back, come back little by little, to live again with the rest of the living.

"Wilson," Izzy said quickly, grasping for any remnants of Kansas that would get him back to a place where he could sink his teeth into a well-deserved steak, "Wilson, I am here and I know you can hear me, and I know you will remember what we talked about, that there is a good chance you didn't do this. You have to let yourself consider that, okay? It could have been Collins or it definitely could have been the Air or it could have been the pilot, any and all of those are real possibilities, Kansas, and you can forgive them and forgive yourself, let yourself come back and go home to your family. They need you and you can be there for them again. I know you can. But for now, Kansas, rest. Just rest."

Izzy pulled out the needle.

There was silence as they all walked out. Behind them Wilson laid in a fetal position surrounded by ghosts. His eyes stared, unblinking, from his once again frozen features, pleading forgiveness of dead people only he could see.

Life and death are one thread,
The same line viewed from different sides.
—Lao Tzu

Pink Peony in Sweet Ginger Moonlight

DARKNESS

I remember curling up as tight as I could in a little ball, like a baby inside a mother's belly, because that's how I tried to protect myself from the snakes and the monsters in the cellar my step-father put me in when I was too afraid yet to kill him.

Beating and whipping were never enough for my stepdad. I realized it was the torment he somehow enjoyed. Whippings as I say were always delayed, waited upon until he was ready, but I later could see that it was watching you squirm, beg and anticipate what was going to happen to you that he relished watching. The other end of the torment though could be more painful than the actual punishment.

The creaky old house we lived in was built late in the 1800s and there is a door outside that leads down into a cellar. A cellar is not a basement. Some other kids had basements with pine paneled walls and nice linoleum floors and ping pong tables. No, a cellar is a hole in the ground. This one went down under the house. You walked along old thick wooden planks that were sitting on pounded dirt. Then down five more steps that were creaky and now you were in the bottom of the cellar. In the summer it was chilly and musty and kind of damp smelling. In the winter it was freezing cold and wet and the packed earth felt kind of slimy. The reason I remember it so well is that I was locked up down there a lot. Especially, when I was little or maybe I just remember being more scared when I was 4 and 5 and 6. I would be put down there after punishments until bedtime and anytime when they would leave.

I guess my mom thought I was safer down there and locking me up was as good as a babysitter as far as my stepfather was concerned. He figured you couldn't get in as much mischief if it was black dark, after all you wouldn't want to move around "or the monsters and snakes will hear you and know where you are little man." Then the light bulb would go out and I would watch the filament stop glowing and then the darkness would be complete. Sometimes he would quietly wait just outside the cellar door and then suddenly bang and yell and scream, "Oh my god, here they come, they are eating me!" and I would scream and start crying for my mom ... then he would laugh and say "she's not here but the monsters are. Shhh. Be quiet or they'll get you before she hears."

So then I would cry real quietly and whimper for a long time. In a way, the crying part was better because at least it felt like something different than when the crying stopped. Because then began the fear and the endless waiting. While I was crying my eyes were closed and I could hear me crying and. . .and then when I stopped came the quiet. The dead silence of the grave like walls. I would begin to imagine the worms coming out of the walls. The rats and snakes and spiders beginning their slow slithering and creeping towards me in the absolute darkness.

Then my stomach would growl because I was hungry and I was afraid the slithering things would hear it and know where I was and come eat me. Then I tried to imagine how I would surprise the slithering things and chop them all up into little bits and stir them into one of my mom's tuna casseroles and feed it to my stepdad while I ate the leftovers he brought back from the restaurant where he had a nice dinner while I was in the cellar.

11

Izzy wasn't quite sure what to do with himself after dinner in the officer's mess. If he had received a new letter he would have gone to the beach and had another picnic instead. No letter, no picnic, but still he changed into some civilian clothes in the hope he would feel like a regular guy—not that he'd ever been a regular guy with nearly perfect recall. But while it had served him extremely well academically, he would be deeply grateful for some selective memory now.

He knew Gregg had a gift wrapped in a curse of sorts, too, an acute sense of empathy that no doubt drove him to suddenly materialize outside the villa where Izzy paced.

"Want to walk a bit through town?" Gregg asked, dressed in his civvies now, too.

"That would be great. Maybe we could discuss what we have—or really don't have—for our `assignment.'"

"Sure you don't want to go to the library again instead, do a little more research?"

Izzy groaned. "There have to be more pages of porn on the base than everything on psychiatry and psychology combined."

"At least the porn gets used a lot."

They made their way down a noisy street, past noodle vendors, and begging children. Izzy could feel his nice white Izod shirt with the little alligator on the front clinging to the sweat popping out of virtually every pore, the kind of sweat he'd never felt before in New York. Surely, they could manage in minutes at Columbia what they hadn't managed here at the crap library, which yielded little more than a worn Freedman and Kaplan Comprehensive Textbook of Psychiatry and an equally worn DSM II—*Diagnostic and Statistical Manual of Mental Disorders*, the bible for mental health professionals.

Murder, serial killing, and mutilation were not his or Gregg's areas of expertise and they had turned up virtually nothing but stuff on medical restraints, new psychotropics, brain injuries, and leftover blah-blah-blah from the Korean War.

The way things were with Gregg and J.D. made Izzy reluctant to even bring up his name, and J.D.'s response when they suggested a phone call to a couple of the top researchers or even to the FBI for consulting help, had not exactly declared them The Three Musketeers.

You two are the consultants, I told you that. I also told you that nobody is supposed to know about this and so far your best idea is to call the states and then the FBI? Why not just call in the media and see what they think about it? Come on, I read your CVs, you are supposed to both be brilliant. So. Be brilliant.

Izzy didn't feel brilliant. He felt like he would explode if he didn't unload.

"Gregg, can we talk?"

"Sure. What's up?"

"I'm worried. I feel like I'm barely hanging on here. My hands shake, have tremors. Without Sergeant Washington I could not have completed the procedure on Wilson. Sometimes I think I'm doing okay, but then I'll start shaking again. Honestly, I'm afraid something's really wrong with me. If not physically, then at least psychosomatically. It's not something I want to tell Rachel about. I don't want her to know what a mess I am. But you, I can talk to. Be straight with me. As a clinician, what are your professional thoughts?"

Gregg turned down another street, a quieter street with trees moving in the moonlight breeze off the sea. "Actually, what I think is that there is nothing wrong with you, that you are just fine, normal, doing your best like the rest of us. I feel just the same inside as you, hanging on, counting the days, thinking about going home. Your hands are just talking for you, being honest about how crazy and scary and insane this all is. . . that shooting your first day, the thing we are in with J.D., those are just some nice big frosting on the usual cake here, which is crazy enough. So I say, the future will take care of itself once you get out of here. Meanwhile, you're not nearly as much of a mess as you think. And don't worry, your hands will settle down."

Izzy let out a big breath. Gregg thought he was okay. He wasn't totally losing it after all, it just felt like that, and Gregg felt the same way and. . .that's right, his hands were being honest while the rest of him was just clenched up, pretending everything was normal when it wasn't.

"Have you got any hobbies?" Gregg asked.

"Guitar. Classical guitar." Izzy's fingers suddenly itched to let loose on the strings of the world-class, handmade concert-quality instrument he had received for his bar mitzvah. "Why?"

"Because I can tell you that the guys who make it through mentally here have something good to do—like I surf, keep a journal. It would help those hands of yours to apply them to some kind of outlet, too."

"Makes sense. Unfortunately. . ." He didn't want to get into the fit his mother had thrown when she found out he'd left his priceless guitar with his artsy, bra-burning choice in a life partner. "Rachel is keeping it for me since we decided to postpone our wedding."

"That must have been a tough decision."

"It was," Izzy lied. There hadn't been a lot of back and forth to the decision making process. Her suggestion and as usual he hadn't argued. Arguments upset his congenitally nervous stomach. "We were planning to honeymoon in Spain. I was going to take some advanced lessons while she toured the museums. Rachel's really great that way—willing to put things off to do it up right. She's an assistant curator at the Metropolitan Museum of Art."

"Nice," was all Gregg said before nodding toward a tasteful marquis down the block. "Look, there's The Racquet Club. I've heard all kinds of crazy stuff about that place. Let's go check it out and. . . no. Don't tell me. . . .."

As a turquoise 57 Chevy with a white ragtop pleated down glided beneath the long black awning that fronted The Racquet Club's entrance, Gregg staggered back several steps—

Only to surge forward and pick up his pace when one valet opened Kate's passenger door and another opened J.D.'s with a deep bow.

"She didn't return my call today." Gregg's uniquely beautiful voice sounded more like K.O. growling at a rodent. "Or yesterday. Or the day before. I am going to kill that son of a bitch J.D. He has got some nerve trying to move in on *my* territory—"

Izzy grabbed Gregg by the back of his shirt while J.D. dropped a kiss on the back of Kate's neck as they proceeded inside.

Gregg spun around, nostrils flaring, eyes flaming blue.

Izzy backed off, hands in the air. "Hey, pal, one good deed deserves another. I'm just trying to do a little damage intervention."

"What? So I can `marvel at my own magnanimous generosity' or whatever the hell Robert David advised? No. *No*. Not this time. I don't know what happened after the bastard took her home in that car that doesn't belong here but I have waited more than half my life for that woman and it'll be a cold day in hell before I let him have her."

"I understand." In truth, Izzy did not. He had never loved anyone so passionately as to be stupid with it. He cherished Rachel's letters, their history, like the touchstones to reality they were and he loved all the things she was and he wasn't. But ultimately, despite his parent's belief to the contrary, even Rachel was a logical choice.

She brought color and a sense of the avant-garde to his life. He brought other things to hers. Hell, who wanted to be married to themselves? Certainly not him.

Logic was perhaps the one thing that could save him long term. And Gregg, short term, hopefully, though that seemed doubtful given the ragged edge to his voice, demanding, "Do you really? Understand?"

"Perhaps not," Izzy slowly admitted. "But Gregg, if you would allow me to return the favor of your counsel, I highly suggest we leave before you initiate a public scene that can only end badly and will not impress Kate. That's not how you get what you've been waiting for."

Gregg's breathing reminded Izzy of Wilson confronting the dead; but then Gregg closed his eyes, took a deep breath. When he opened them again he looked at his clenched fists with the kind of regard reserved for a visitor from Mars.

"God, I'm sorry." Gregg lightly self-slapped a tanned cheek, then the other. "I don't know what got into me. Maybe this place just makes us all act crazy. I am so sorry, Izzy."

"I liked being called God better."

Gregg laughed with the jangled sound of nerves. "You MDs and those deity complexes."

"Just give us an inch and we'll demand eternity."

Attention moving to the 57 Chevy being driven off by a valet, Gregg gave a middle finger salute and called "Hey, Cyclo!" to flag down one of the little motorized cabbies with seats attached to the scooter.

"Now where?" asked Izzy, just glad to get away and fast, didn't matter what direction.

"Pawn shop," said Gregg. "Find some guitars."

✳

Kate was fully aware she had more than crossed the fashion rebel line by wearing a traditional Vietnamese aoi dai, a flowing silk dress split to the hip over slinky silk pajama pants. She also knew the combination of her upswept blonde hair and golden skin was dazzling in the graceful, white ensemble reserved for women of another culture. She had wanted to be both breathtaking and scandalous, and judging from J.D.'s response, she had scored on both counts.

They proceeded into the club where parted doors revealed a luxurious lobby with plush elegant rugs and rattan furnishings, slow moving fans and huge pink peonies with other fresh flowers that scented the air with sweet ginger. J.D. smelled even better. His cologne was subtle and understated, the smell of money well spent.

"This is so nice," sighed Kate with just the right come hither dusk in her voice, the perfect complement to their plush, intimate booth rounded in a corner. "I feel like we're sitting in the middle of a Graham Greene novel. Do you read him?"

"I read *The Quiet American*. That was enough for me. I prefer Kipling."

"Somehow that doesn't surprise me. Let me guess. . ." She fingered the two mysterious silver bracelets J.D. wore on his right wrist. "*The Jungle Book*. That would be your favorite."

His hand came down, brought hers to his mouth. It was her wrist actually, the interior of it, that he discreetly skated with his teeth. Although she was a surgical nurse and understood the marvel of human anatomy, her immediate, hot, fluid response was more a mystery than the bracelets.

Did Phillip have any idea what he was doing when he orchestrated their introduction? Surely not. Yet Phillip never, *never* did anything by accident.

"Yes," J.D. confirmed, having moved his mouth from wrist to just behind her ear. His breath tickled it, smelled like cinnamon, touched with the Gauloises they had shared en route to the club.

"The Jungle Book is my favorite. And who would be my favorite Kipling character?"

"Bagheera," she breathed out, only to inhale enough lust fueled air to qualify for a hormone spiked mickey. "The black panther."

"No." He paused, eased back, putting some distance between them. "Do you have anything for me?"

His chameleon behavior was disorienting. Kate tried to get her bearings by feigning interest elsewhere, only to see...

She squinted in the dimly lit and very large supper club, for lack of a better term.

"I think I just saw Phillip."

J.D. followed her gaze, cast his about like a minesweeper, apparently turning up nothing before returning his attention to her.

"Are you still sleeping with him?"

Kate blinked. First her eyes were playing tricks on her, now her ears. "I beg your pardon?"

"You heard me. I asked if you were still sleeping with Phillip. He would only send you here as payback for not, or a reward if you were, but his intentions would never be paternal."

"I...well, I..." Her throat was dry. She took a long sip of the *Soixante Quinzes* J.D. had ordered for her. Kate put it down, locked him in visual combat. "That is none of your business, J.D."

"Perhaps not." His attention dipped, lingered on her chest. "Yet."

Kate wasn't sure whether to throw the rest of her drink in his face or plant hers in his lap.

She finished her cocktail in silence and ordered another instead.

"We have a patient at the mission," she finally said. "We turn no one away—especially not an old friend of Dr. Donnelly. He's the mission director."

"Yes, I know. And what is the patient's name?"

Some spy she was. Kate didn't want to cough up. "Professor Nguyen," she muttered, quickly followed by an assertive, "I like him. He pioneered research in malaria here, at the Pasteur Institute."

"Yes. A credit to his profession." J.D.'s smile was enigmatic, both approving and somehow not. "Anything or anyone else I should know about?"

"Gregg left another message inviting me to the beach party they're having in a couple of days. I'm not sure I should go."

"Of course you should go—with me."

"I don't want to rub his nose in it. It's unnecessary to be unkind. Especially to Gregg."

"We'll be discreet." J.D. leaned in, confidential. "Listen, Kate, I know what Gregg means to you. I like the guy, too—and I need him."

"Why?"

"For consulting purposes on a case I'm not at liberty to discuss. And neither is he, so don't put him in a compromised position by asking questions. Understood?"

The look J.D. gave her made her stomach flutter, and not in a good way.

Kate started to challenge the dictate, but hesitated. She had a feeling of being out of her depth and, besides, Phillip could arrange to have her sent home as quickly and easily as he had gotten her here. She wasn't ready to leave. Smart girls knew when to push, when to back off.

She nodded.

"Now, about the party," J.D. continued, "I need to explore a lead and could use your help, have you spend a little girl time with Margie and Nikki, see if they might divulge anything I haven't been able to pick up about Peck."

"Why are you interested in him? It's not illegal to be a jerk."

"He's a person of interest. We'll leave it at that. Just see what you can find out about his relationship with Nikki, if he has any strange private behaviors or violent tendencies behind closed doors. That's the kind of information you can get on the Q.T. and I can't."

When she hesitated he added, "By the way, it's Hertz's birthday and Sergeant Washington is in charge of the grill."

"Is there anything you *don't* know?"

J.D. raised an eloquent brow.

The hell if she was telling him about her intimacies with Phillip. And the hell with Phillip if he thought she was sleeping with him anytime soon. It was the 60s and Kate got the whole liberation scene, but she had always felt liberated and wasn't going to be confined now by some free love movement that she considered a little stupid for its lack of foresight. Smart girls were selective. They realized they declared their own value. Two back wheels that had burned enough rubber to go bald did not command a fetching price, and while she truly loved the smell, the taste, the sweat generated by a robust romp, Katherine Lynn Morningside did not come cheap.

"Kaa," J.D. suddenly said. "The python. That would be my favorite Kipling character."

"Why am I not surprised you would best relate to a snake?"

The flash of J.D.'s smooth smile was followed by an unexpected burst of laughter. With his head tilted back, clearly exposing the scar that ran from just behind his ear to under his shirt collar it took an enormous amount of self-control not to investigate how far the scar ran.

She should run. Kate knew it with the instinctive certainty of a dog's ears quivering in response to a whistle too highly pitched for humans to hear. But she was even more certain of never forgiving herself for abandoning the human equivalent of a torqued and dangerous machine that she intended to ride like a bat out of hell with strobe lights flashing and sirens screaming full blast.

There were no Orange Julius's in Vietnam.

Just one of the things she could fall in love with here.

12

Off the coast of Nha Trang are several islands. But while Nha Trang itself is a city of culture and sophistication and commerce, the islands might as well be a thousand miles and a thousand years away....

Life passed in the same slow movement of seasons as it always had and always would, forever remaining exactly as it was before the Americans and before the French. The same fishing boats with their distinctive designs and colors, the same small village farms trading with the fishermen, they were all still here. As were the people, orienting their lives with the old calendar, the tides, the movement of fish, sun, and wind. They looked on the invading Americans as another odd and temporary form of bad weather. Something to endure until it passed.

All kinds of gear had been offloaded onto the beaches for an American style beach party, complete with a Frisbee chasing dog. Sergeant Washington was clearly in charge of the operation and if he had been Commanding General of the Army in the way he was getting this party set up, the war would have been over and won last year. As the top level professional grilling got going and the scent of BBQ sauce and sizzling steaks and big kettles of beans drifted down the beach, Izzy and Gregg wandered along the palm-rimmed sand with Margie and Nikki, K.O. trotting close with the Frisbee between her teeth. Ahead of them was a postcard scene of what old Vietnam must have been like before the wars.

"The war doesn't seem real here." Izzy's gaze was dreamlike, taking in this small fishing village where time stood still with its thatched bamboo houses and prosperous, well fed looking families. Friendly smiles accompanied friendly waves to the four of them and they waved back.

"A world away," Gregg agreed. "I'd say it's a perfect place for some music. Maybe play us a few tunes later, Izzy?"

"We'll see," he hedged, despite having parked his guitar next to Gregg's surfboard at the spot they had claimed down the beach.

"Hey, I've heard you practicing. No need to hide that kind of talent around here. A few beers and one of Sarge's best steaks, and you'll be our entertainment for the night."

"Gregg already sold us tickets." Margie, quick to back Gregg up.

"That's right," Nikki, right behind her, "so you can't get out of it now."

"More than a buck and he scalped you." Izzy grinned despite his claim as they stopped in the shade of some tall, graceful Ironwood pines looking out over the water.

They all stood quiet for a while in a companionable silence, until Margie dabbed at her eyes, any joking around having somehow segued to a somber moment.

"What's wrong, Margie?" Izzy asked.

Margie shook her head, the sun bouncing off the red hair she had piled on top like a luscious strawberry snow cone. Gregg knew it wasn't for him she was looking extra fine as she impatiently swiped at her eyes.

Izzy hesitantly put an arm around her shoulder, and that's all it took for her to let it all go.

"Izzy. . .Gregg. What are we doing? We must be sending out more and more crazy kids every week. They are like broken toys and we put a band-aid on them and send them right back out. What's going to happen to them when they get back, what about their families, what are they going to do with them? *What have we done to them? Shit. . .sorry, sorry. . .I'm sorry.* I didn't mean to lose it like this. We're here for a picnic. Who's ready for a steak and another beer? K.O. you can have part of mine, girl."

"It's okay, Margie," Gregg assured her. "You're just telling it like it is, saying everything we're all thinking every countdown day."

"That's right," Nikki agreed, even though she was there of her own volition.

K.O. whimpered and dropped the Frisbee at Margie's feet like an offering, which only made her choke on a sob.

Izzy patted Margie's shoulder, then dumbly, but sweetly, extended his beer.

"I wish I could say something to make you feel better, but I can't think of anything at all, not one thing to make me feel any better either, so here, Margie. You can have my beer."

Margie blinked, stared at him blankly a few moments. Then, she laughed. Her eyes were still a little watery, but clear and a brighter shade of hazel as she warmed them on Izzy.

"Thanks, Dr. Moskowitz, now I feel better—or at least I will when I'm in that water. Come on, let's go!"

"Uh, well, I usually don't swim or. . ."

Margie took the beer Izzy still held out and promptly shook it, playfully sprayed him with the brew.

"Come on, Nikki, tag team! Izzy's gotta get clean!" Then each of them grabbed one of Izzy's hands and took off toward the little waves, only for Izzy to kick in some speed and pull them both along with him, the three of them laughing as they plunged into the shallow end, K.O. giving chase.

Gregg watched them go. He had never seen Margie come apart like that, but if anything her mini-meltdown was overdue. Gregg knew her job was hell. She had been there about nine months, a month longer than him, and many of the patients on the unit, the psych techs too, hell, just about all of them, ended up talking to her about their personal problems. But you just couldn't listen to everyone's shit all the time and not have it take a toll, especially if you were the only female nurse at a unit, getting hit on every day by whoever was new.

And, they were always new, just like it only happened once, because you were not the oldest child of a Marine Commandant and not know how to handle presumptuous assholes. Margie could hold her own with the fresh stuff; it was seeing the suffering that she had no control over that was grinding her down.

Just then she plowed a big gush of water at Izzy, who threw it right back. Hopefully, he didn't have the letters he was always carrying in his pocket; he'd be crying worse than Margie if the pages got wet. While Gregg figured Izzy for a straight arrow kind of guy who wouldn't mess around on his fiancé, a little outside interest was a good distraction—particularly with Monday's upcoming trip to the Highlands on the pretext of routine evals at the base in Ban Me Thuot.

The med dispensing business as usual was total bullshit of course, the real purpose being to check out the troops where the Ghost Soldier story got started—and had continued to spread faster than relay runners with jungle drums.

"Monsieur, have you any new leads in zee investigation?"

Startled, Gregg spun around and shoved J.D. away. Maybe it was because he didn't have time to mentally prepare, or maybe he'd just had enough, but the gloves came off and Mister Nice Guy finally clocked out.

"What, you think that's funny?"

J.D. shrugged and for a blink he seemed slightly off-balance. Like a new comic giving stand-up a try and getting booed off-stage.

Fuck him. Gregg put it in his face. "You broke the code, man."

"Code?" J.D. stepped back, narrowed his eyes. "What code?"

"The one that says you don't mess with another guy's girl."

"But Kate says she isn't your girl."

"I don't give a damn what she says. You knew we were together when you showed up at the restaurant, and you still went after her."

"Yes," he readily admitted. "I did."

Gregg grudgingly gave J.D. points for not pushing Kate in front of the train they both knew she was equally responsible for driving, but that didn't stop him.

"Since we're clearing the air, I don't even believe there's a real investigation, it's probably just some bullshit excuse for you do some kind of drug bust on these poor freaked out kids who are getting crazy ideas—like it's a crazy idea to be here! The only 'evidence' is a bunch of gossip that feeds off fear like termites on wood, and that's all we are to the machine you work for. Termites getting dusted with Agent Orange. Admit it, Mikel. There is no psycho killer, there is just you and the government you work for fucking around with the rest of us who can't wait to get the hell out, right? Am I right?"

J.D. held up his hands, backed off. "Okay, okay, maybe there is no killer, no Boogeyman, and it's all just crap, a crazy made-up story. And you know what? I hope you're that much right. So let's just get up to the Highlands on Monday and check things out as planned, and if you're right, then I'll disappear from your radar. Okay? C'mon, let's be friends. Show me and Kate around the island." J.D. glanced down the beach and waved. Apparently some kind of signal since Kate waved back and picked up her pace. "See? Here she comes."

Gregg glared at J.D. "Let's be friends? You draft me into some kind of CIA spook show and then steal my girl, and now we are *friends?* Come on, you have got to be kidding."

"But she says she isn't your girl," J.D. reiterated, making him either the most obtuse guy Gregg had ever met or maybe he just thought being a CIA agent exempted him from the same rules regular guys like Gregg Kelly abided by. "Kate wants us to be friends. I'm trying."

"Kate knows I would give her both kidneys and my liver if she needed them, but you and me, friends?" Gregg snorted at the very idea. "My generosity does not extend that far. And by the way, if you really care about Kate, you will get off her radar, too."

Moving past Kate as she arrived, Gregg ordered himself to get some distance and his cool while he was at it—only to kick the sand, hard, when J.D. called after him, "But all I said was the Dodgers suck!"

✳

Gregg was considerably calmer after tipping a beer with some pals and toasting a few times to Hertz turning twenty-one. Blowing off some of the accumulated steam felt good but it disturbed him to have so completely gotten in J.D.'s face. That wasn't like him at all. Never in Gregg's life had he spurned an offer of friendship. Not to mention it wasn't real bright to all but insist on a duel at dawn when you didn't even know how to load a gun and the guy you slapped with a gauntlet owned the whole damn Winchester factory.

A flash of J.D. whipping Terry's pistol from his holster and taking Derek down in the split second before Derek could do the same to the rest of them had Gregg taking another long draw off his beer. *Damn.* Why did he always have to think of that when he'd rather hang onto his perfectly justified rage at all the messed up shit J.D. had unpacked along with his gear upon moving into the villa where he rarely stayed? Not that Gregg gave a crap as long as it wasn't with Kate. The whole getting off his radar thing was the surest sign Gregg had that this trip to the jungle Highlands promised the kind of outcome that would ensure J.D. stuck around.

A hypersonic blast of sound with the opening chords of "Crystal Blue Persuasion" shook the towering Ironwood pines above Gregg's head where a metallic purple and black attack helicopter hovered, then rocketed out to sea, turned, and lowered to just above the water.

The shore party went wild as the chopper slowly approached the beach, and then the crowd really went crazy as a case of Jack Daniels was thrown into the water, followed closely by what had to be over 200 pounds of rippling muscle in green shorts and a Green Bay Packers football jersey. He lifted the case and plowed into shore to a round of applause and whistles and shouted greetings as the chopper circled, then blasted away.

Gregg ran out with the cheering crowd and Nikki caught up with him, asking, "Who is that? He sure knows how to make an entrance."

"Richard Galt. Come on, I'll introduce you." Not only was Rick the coolest Special Ops Gregg had ever met, Peck wouldn't even think about messing with someone that could snap him like a twig with two fingers. He was definitely getting Nikki introduced.

Rick handed over the case to lots of eager hands and then promptly slapped Gregg on the arm, which almost knocked Gregg over.

"Hey, Rick, glad you could make it."

"Thanks for the invite, Doc. I got your message up in the Highlands and hitched a ride and here I am. And wow what a party...and *wow* who is this?"

"This is Nikki." Gregg discreetly rubbed his arm as he got Nikki signed up for some health insurance. "Nikki is the Red Cross and everything you miss about America. And Nikki, this is Captain Richard Galt, Special Ops, Lord of the Jungle."

"Just Rick, ma'am." Rick doffed his cap, revealing thick cropped black hair, cheekbones any American Indian would be proud of, and good looks straight out of Hollywood central casting set on top of a USC tailback's body. Anybody would think he was a body double for Burt Lancaster in *Apache*. "And I have to say that I'd be crazy to miss America when I'm looking at Miss America right here."

"Well, aren't you the charmer?" Nikki flirted back.

"I am trying, ma'am, I am trying."

And it was apparently working since Nikki suggested, "How about you join me and Gregg and some of our friends under the shade over there?"

"Yeah, Rick, after we grab a beer and a steak, and before you start talking about how easy we've got it and how tough you guys are that don't."

"Don't you know it," Rick ribbed him back, throwing his arm around Gregg's shoulder. "But I am not insulting my hosts, you can bet on that—and look who's here! Margie, how you doing girl? Still making sure this war is safe and sane?" Grinning broadly, Rick let go of Gregg to give Margie a little hug as she eagerly greeted him, then Rick took notice of Izzy, beside her. "And this must be the famous new guy."

"I, well. . .how did you know?"

"Your press secretary told me."

"I knew I should have changed my name before word got out I was here."

That got a good laugh, especially from Margie.

"Okay, Rowan and Martin," she said, promptly pointing them in the direction of Buckley's grill. "The good stuff's this way."

And that's where Rick hailed the King for a Day. Snagging a bottle from the case he had brought, Rick held it out to Hertz like a precious offering.

"This is just for you, kid, and let us all drink to this birthday and especially to your next one back home."

Everyone was eager to toast to that.

Like any good party this one had the rhythm of the ocean, swelling in and out with easy times, lively chatter, punctuated by bursts of laughter. Then later, as the sun dipped lower and the colors on the water deepened, things were quieting down, groups shifting, splitting off, couples necking.

Kate and J.D. had thus far kept their own touching discreet, as long as Gregg didn't count eye contact. After his little showdown with J.D., he had straightened up and acted like a big boy, didn't make anyone uncomfortable or exclude the apparent new couple from his inner circle, just kept telling himself that the cream always rose to the top and Kate would surely see he was still the crème de la crème of class acts.

He'd had lots of practice at this. He could wait J.D. out. Be there when Bond took a powder. And, just maybe it would be sooner rather than later considering the way J.D. was glad-handing Rick, clearly intent on attacking this Boogeyman case, bogus or not, by asking Rick if it would be too much of an imposition to steal some of his time in the Highlands during the evals they were coming up Monday to do at Ban Me Thuot—where Gregg was showing him and Izzy the ropes.

"Tell you what," said Rick, "you docs are putting yourselves out to make a trip to my side of the world so the least I can do is arrange the ride, something a little nicer than the usual. I'll even throw in a visit to our Special Ops camp since there's been some messed up shit I'd like to get your take on. 1100 hours at the 8th Field's LZ sound okay?"

Apparently satisfied with his latest maneuvering of a situation to his benefit, J.D. faded into the background and by the time Gregg noted his absence, he was gone and so was Kate, who had actually spent quite a bit of time hanging out with Margie and Nikki.

The two roommates were off walking the beach now.

Despite his own Heartbreak Hotel refrain, Gregg considered it a day well spent because Nikki had a big admirer in the bad ass Special Ops trainer and commando that Peck would not want to mess with.

"No way, man," Rick was saying to the group that had dwindled to Izzy, Robert David, Washington, and Gregg. "No way would I trade jobs with anybody here. Course, first of all, I love the Ops and I love my job, but you guys have one of the most heavy shit jobs around."

"That's some heavy shit coming from Special Ops," said Washington, tipping back straight from the bottle of Jack.

"No really, I thought like everybody else you were another group of REMFs, but it is one thing to go hand to hand with Charlie and a whole other thing to go at it hand to hand with our own guys turned crazy motherfucks—and have to be kind and gentle while you do it?" Rick shook his head and took a long draw on the bottle Washington handed him. "I won't ever forget when you came out last spring and helped us with Jennings."

Gregg would never forget it either. He appreciated Rick acknowledging they weren't just a bunch of REMFs—Rear Echelon Mother Fuckers—because that was a big deal coming from someone like him. A big enough deal that Gregg was suitably humble.

"No, no, no," he insisted, patting the air as Colonel Kohn did to settle things down and winning big laughs, along with a chorus of "Yes, yes, yes's" from the group, before he could finish with, "It's just what we do and you don't, Rick. Same way we could never do your job."

Rick good naturedly punched Gregg in the arm and almost knocked him over. "No, no, no yourself, Doc. Let me tell it to Izzy. I'm gonna tell it because it's a fucking legend in our unit—The day Gregg Kelly took down Jungle Man Jennings and saved him while he was at it."

And as Rick set about telling his version, Gregg sized it up next to his own. . .

13

It was a fresh day after a rain when Gregg, Robert David, Colonel Kohn, and Washington were asked to come out to the Special Ops training camp. Hertz volunteered as back up. It was unusual for any of them to get out there. Like the Special Forces, the Special Ops groups liked to take care of their own with as little outside intervention as possible; but Colonel Kohn was an old friend of the very tense major in charge, who briefed them with the assistance of his next in command, Captain Richard Galt.

"He is highly dangerous," Galt told them. "I repeat, highly dangerous. He came in last night from patrol. Seemed to be just a little messed up after he got mail and we thought oh shit, something from home, he's been here back-to-back, stayed an extra six months, mostly out on patrol and running ops. He's a good one, but he paced all night talking and yelling about his wife. Guess he got Dear Johned or something." Galt paused, shaking his head. "Anyway, just about dawn he got out his weapon and fired off a burst and then sprayed the room and cleared it out. He's still in the hootch and yelling about how he knows he's surrounded and they will not take him alive, says he will kill himself before they get him. Crazy shit like that."

"OK, got it." Colonel Kohn then assured Galt and the major, "We can handle this. Gregg's the best. He'll talk your man down and we'll back him up. Let's go now. Where is he?"

"Go?" Galt repeated. "Go? Are you kidding? This guy is fully armed, he's lethal. We're going to gas him and wanted you here to help calm him down after we get him restrained."

"If you try to gas him then he knows he is being attacked," Gregg reasoned. "And what if he gets out? The way you describe him, if he's as lethal as you say, he likely is going to take out somebody before he goes down. Give us a chance at him first, okay?"

The two Special Ops officers exchanged uncertain looks.

"He is such a good man, Major," Galt told his commander. "One of my best. And he's short. Only a few weeks left in-country. I hate to see him leave like this, but—"

"Then let us go in," Robert David insisted. "Let us take care of him if we can. Nothing on his record. Just TLTM."

Galt asked, "What's TLTM?"

"Too Long and Too Much," Gregg filled in. "Come on, just stand behind us. He knows you, right, Captain Galt?"

"Well, he did last night. But really, we should go in with weapons. Doing it your way is too risky. He could take us all out."

"No." Robert David shook his head. "No weapons."

Gregg to Galt then, "Tell him it is you and you've got friends and let us go in. Have your guys cover us just in case, but stay out of sight."

Galt looked dubiously at the major, who hesitated, then gave a curt nod.

Minutes later, they were outside a hootch and Galt was shouting, "Jennings! Jennings, it's me, Galt. I got friends with me and we are coming in. Don't shoot."

And in they went. Jennings, tall and lanky with looped cords of muscle standing out all over his body, had no shirt on, and his face, a bright red, was so contorted and agitated it looked like snakes raced under his skin. He held an M16 rifle.

"Stop it!" he screamed, waving the M16 in the air. "Stop, damn it, it is all fucked up. Everything is all fucked up!"

That's when Gregg did what he always did in this kind of situation, just slowly started walking forward, right at the person, because whether they were twenty, thirty years old, or five, he could always see that they were really just scared and hurting and the hurt is what drew him, what was drawing him now to Jennings.

"Hey," he said to him softly, "Hey, hey Sarge, slow down now, stand down, okay? We came to help. We cleared the area. It is all clear out there now, they're all gone. Nobody is out there now." Gregg had his attention, Jennings was looking at him. Gregg kept talking.

"I see you, Sarge. I see you, and it is OK."

"Bullshit!" screamed Jennings, "Bullshit! Who are you? Who are these guys with you? Spies? Motherfucking cheaters, fucking baby-killers, wifestealers. . ." Jennings stopped rambling, then suddenly yelled, "Are you ready to go? I am ready to take you out!"

"Sarge, hey Sarge, where is home?" Gregg asked, soft and calm. "Where are you from, Sarge?"

"Chicago, you fucking asshole. Chicago is my home. . .no, I ain't got a fuckin home. . .goddamn it no home, no wife, hell. . .nothing." Jennings looked around wildly while he locked and loaded a round in the M16.

"Hey, hey, hey Sarge. . .Jennings. Come on, Chi-town, talk to me. You a Cubbies or a White Sox guy, Chi-town?" A long pause as Jennings looked at Gregg from far, far away, and then—

"Cubbies, dammit."

"Well, I thought so. I thought you were a Cubbies man." Gregg took a step closer. "And who said Aparicio was better than Mr. Cub?"

Jennings blinked, his eyes focusing on Gregg. "No fucking way. Sure Aparicio can play but he can't even carry the glove of my man Ernie."

"How about the stick?" Another step closer.

"Are you crazy? You know Ernie, he hits better than any short-stop in the game and. . ."

Almost within reaching distance of Jennings, Gregg kept it going. "I'm a Dodger guy, Jennings. Dodger blue, you know? Course you know Ernie Banks beats on us like a drum, but Koufax, when he is on, he is the man."

Jennings, really looking at Gregg now, a bit of contact there, enough for Gregg to take another step closer, so close Gregg could feel the fear in him, the smell of him, the way his eyes came and went from that horrible place where his own brain was betraying him, where Jennings' thoughts were like a record skipping speeds and songs in a nauseating, sickening way, and then another little moment of contact as Jennings bellowed out:

"Koufax! Koufax was just another shit Dodger. Fergie, he is a pitcher."

"You got that right big man, Ferguson Jenkins, he can bring the ball. Hey, how bout you just hand that weapon here and we got cold brews outside, and you and me, we'll talk some baseball. Come on, Chi-town, you and me. . . ." The other guys right behind him, Gregg took his last step towards Jennings, when outside the tent:

"Okay, we got the gas and we're ready to go after him and—"

Shut up, shut up, I almost have him—

At the speed of thought Jennings' eyes went cold and far away again, and Gregg was throwing himself on Jennings, pinning the rifle against his chest, wrapping his surfer arms around hulking muscle for all he was worth, and then came the mass of Washington landing on top of them both, while Hertz raced outside to shut everyone up and Robert David came in fast with the needle, plowing it down to inject the IM benzo into Jennings—enough to drop an elephant and still Jennings was bucking and crying and screaming while the cumulative pile of five hundred pounds struggled to hold onto him, and then suddenly—

It hit. Jennings was still. They rolled off.

For a while there was only the sound of Robert David's and Washington's and Gregg's own labored breathing, and then another sound that had them looking up from the ground at what appeared to be the whole Special Ops group surrounding them.

Rick Galt was smiling, shaking his head like he couldn't believe what he saw as he began the slow clapping....

✳

"You guys were so fucking great. Like I said, it's legend," Rick concluded, having told the story that for the most part lined up with Gregg's remembrance of it. A remembrance that had Gregg happy to accept the shared bottle Rick offered as he added the best part of all. "And, you know after you evaced him, Jennings got home, even got back with his old lady. He's a training NCO now at Special Forces Fort Bragg. Not sure if you knew that, but I hear he wrote you, Gregg."

Gregg winced at the sting to the back of his throat, but it went down smooth and he had to smile. "Oh yeah, he wrote me all right. Don't know how he did it, but he had a case of Jack delivered—tasted just as good as this, maybe even better since there was a Cubs cap inside, a real one." Not wanting the night to end too soon, thanks to a little too much Jack, Gregg grabbed enough beers to pass around their little group with a shared history, worthy of a toast:

"Here's to another cold one and to good friends, old and new." Gregg pointed his bottle to Izzy, then raised it high. "But most of all, here's to Jennings, that lucky man back in the world."

"Damn straight!"

"Here, here!"

"I'll drink to that!"

Izzy picked up his guitar and went to work on "Classical Gas," proving himself amazingly dexterous, despite an impressive consumption of beer, Jack, and weed. And as the music played on, as the moon floated paper white above the crystal blue sea, for that moment they were all back in the world in that someplace called home.

✳

Peck watched from the Ironwood tree shadows, a safe distance and yet not too far away to discern the comings and goings of those he had a particular interest in watching.

This in particular would be Nikki and the retard on ethanol overdoses of testosterone.

Retard reminded him of his cousin, the poor relation who liked to say "boats, planes and women, why own 'em when you can rent a new one?"

Nikki, he would own. Or at least he would convince her she wanted to belong to him and if he didn't tire of the game she didn't know they were playing, then he might actually make good on the offering he planned to tempt her with tonight.

The entire set up was an elaborate ruse he had thoroughly enjoyed constructing.

He had the arrangements all made with a local character on this island, a self-aggrandizing little gook with a taste for American goods and a gold front tooth who called himself "Uncle Sam." Now, Uncle Sam apparently had an inordinate number of nieces who specialized in more than the usual, and while that wasn't what this paying customer was in the market for—at least not tonight—there was something else Uncle Sam had that Peck wanted.

For the equivalent for a couple of six packs and a carton of Marlboros, Peck had scored a secluded little pleasure palace which he had filled with all the bells and whistles for tonight's bit of theater. He just had to get Nikki away from Margie and the rest of the group that hadn't wanted to invite him to their precious beach party.

Well, he would show them, show them all. Donald Peck the Third had been collecting trophies since childhood and Nikki would be a splendid addition to the keepsakes in his cabinet. Besides, he had to entertain himself somehow on this tour and she was an excellent diversion.

Retard suddenly stood up, walked in Nikki's direction and that seemed to be Margie's signal to go listen to Moskowitz play his guitar. As much as Peck hated to admit it, Jew boy had some talent, at least it sounded that way from a distance.

There was a bit less of a distance from his hideout to where Nikki and Retard appeared to be saying their good-byes, but too far away for Peck to hear what was being said. Dammit. Still he could see her nodding her head and smiling and that really pissed him off. Then Retard took the hand she extended and kissed it—*oh, please, who did he think he was, Sir Fucking Galahad?* —and Nikki nodded and smiled some more, then the fucker was gone. Just took off somewhere with a wave and disappeared like he had wings.

Nikki started moving in the direction of the group. Peck seized his opportunity.

"Nikki. Psst! Nikki, over here."

Nikki gave a little start as he emerged from the shadows, laid the same hand the retard had kissed over her heart.

"Don, you just scared the dickens out of me! What are you doing here?"

"I'm here to make the other night up to you." He drew closer, slowly, not wanting to draw attention to himself and have someone intrude before he got what he came for.

Nikki crossed her arms, shook her head, but at least she kept her voice low.

"You pushed me, Don. I am not giving you a chance to do it agin—again."

Every now and then her inner hillbilly came out. Peck knew she needed some work but that was part of the game. His family would be horrified. Meanwhile he could shape and mold her like Playdough, toy with her brain while he was at it. Family/Nikki: Win-win.

"I promise it won't happen again." He bowed his head so she couldn't see his lips twitch. "Please let me make it up to you. Please?"

Now he looked up, his eyes pleading. Her own softened. Nikki always wanted to believe the best of everyone. That's what made her such an easy mark.

"I don't know. I mean, you were really ugly to me, just downright mean and—"

"And I should never drink whiskey. It has a terrible effect on me." Actually, it was the uppers on top of the booze that had gotten him agitated, but Nikki didn't know that. "I promise not to get drunk like that again. I wasn't myself, you know. Tell me you know that, Nikki."

"Well. . ."

"And tell me you'll let me make it up to you."

"We'll see, Don. Maybe we can talk later. After—"

"No, right here. Right now. I want to make this right."

He whipped out the velvet jewelry box on ready in his pocket. Good planning was essential. He had this down. Nikki gasped on cue.

"Oh no, Donny. That's too much! I can't possibly—"

"Yes, you can." He extracted the fake diamond bracelet and smoothly latched the knock-off onto her wrist. The one Retard had been an inch away from kissing. Now who was top dog? Nikki was his bitch. When he got through with her she would roll over and beg and come on call.

"I. . .it's beautiful." She held it up, flashing the paste stones in the moonlight. "No one's ever given me something so—so. . .I don't know what to say."

"Say you'll say good-night to the group and let Margie know Cinderella will not be home by midnight."

"No?"

"No." He smiled what he thought of as his ballroom dance smile—the one that dazzled silly girls and even their mothers into his charms and kept them there until he tired of them or went a little too far and had to pay someone off. "That's just the beginning, baby. You really like this island, don't you?"

"If I could, I'd stay here and never leave."

"Your wish is granted. At least for the night." He gestured toward the village. "I arranged a special place, just for us. There might even be a big wrapped box just waiting for you to open. And a little box, too. Something to go with the bracelet."

14

In the early morning after the party, alone now in her private cottage at the mission, Kate laid in bed with nothing on but a bracelet. Her clothes and sheets were strewn more like flower petals than the aftermath of a tsunami on the bamboo floor. She was limp, exhausted, still shimmering with sweat on her skin and between her thighs, and she was blissfully, ecstatically out of her mind with the residual reminders of a night that was not at all what she had expected.

She actually felt like a corny version of Audrey Hepburn in *My Fair Lady*. She could have danced all night. She still felt like she had him all over her, his taste, the scent of him. It was a very, very, *very* bad sign to wake up with this urgency to feel J.D. all over her, all over again, to keep replaying his whispers that were as sultry and suggestive as the French he spoke, the moves he made that were unlike anything she had ever experienced. *My God what he had done with those pearls....*

She felt like someone who had been going out with adolescents all her life and hadn't realized it until now. Her mother had been right. Beauty was a powerful but transient tool. Intelligence and strength is what lasted once the surface began to fade. J.D. saw more than the surface. He saw *her*. And he had let her know in the deep dark of the night that she was beautiful to him because of her imperfections, right down to the unseen scars of a botched abortion.

Gregg was one of the very few who knew about it too, but he wanted to hold someone else accountable. Why? Because Gregg thought he loved her. She knew better. What Gregg loved was an idealized version of the girl next door who never should have used him like a guinea pig in a biology class.

She never should have told J.D. about that. Never, ever should have. It was like breaking a sacred trust of a secret sin between her and Gregg who would probably make yet another excuse for her, say his rival had an unfair way of extracting information.

True enough. But she wasn't laying any blame on J.D. for what she had too easily given up. Just like Nikki while they were walking the beach, talking girl talk, with Nikki a whole lot forthcoming after just a few beers, confessing Peck had introduced her to some naughty bedroom games that involved. . .oh, she just couldn't say, and mercy her family would be so horrified if they knew, which only made such private activities all the more invitin.'

Kate slid a hand over one breast then the other, then over the belly that would probably never be able to carry a baby. Just for a moment, she felt a pang of regret. . .

But just for a moment. Raising the arms she had gripped J.D. with, she held them high and open above her head. A thin silver bracelet trickled down her left wrist and she thought of that delicate instant when he explained: *My Montagnard friendship bracelets, from the tribal people in the Central Highlands. These are very precious to me. I never take them off.*

And then he did. Just one.

Kate smiled again.

She knew how Audrey felt after dancing all night.

*

He hadn't wanted to leave and J.D. knew that was a very, very bad sign. What had transpired between him and Kate was not part of the plan. He had, in fact, stayed longer than was wise before reluctantly forcing himself away in the very early morning. He needed some time to think. About Kate, about the night, about putting on his clothes then taking them off again when she beckoned him back with a single finger. About wanting her to wear something he treasured as if it kept his skin on her somehow after he was gone in the Bermuda shorts and aloha shirt he had worn to the island party.

Now he looked like an Aussie tourist hailing down a cyclo the morning after, the sky starting to redden and purple. Riding along, he chatted in Vietnamese with the driver who had moved to the city from Can Tho down in the Delta. There were so many search and destroy actions going on down there that he had given up farming to work for his uncle in the city, doing the cyclo to make money to send for his loved ones back home.

That's when an insidious thought imposed itself upon J.D.: What would it be like to have someone he wanted to go home to?

The cyclo dropped him in the harbor area and he went directly to a familiar fishing boat and quickly arranged for a ride out to the island he sometimes called home. He loved this island and came often enough that he had rented a small house in the village from the Headman, who was like the elder or mayor of the little fishing town.

J.D. greeted the Headman and patiently sat and listened to all the local gossip with a cup of tea and shared breakfast. The Vietnamese with their ancient fears of ghosts had of course embraced the Ghost Soldier stories that had quickly made the rounds on the islands. Unfortunately the Headman had nothing solid to offer, only an echo of *"Con Quy."*

After promising to lend his assistance with a local issue, J.D. declined another cup of tea and thanked the family, then walked down to his little cottage. It looked just like any of the others on the outside. Inside, though, he kept a radio and communications setup and a Teak stereo with a tape system that ran off a generator. There was a rattan book case, a traveling typewriter and desk, a box of supplies, and a rattan rocking chair. He had a tatami mat in what passed as a "bedroom" but the hammock in the trees outside was where he liked to read in the breeze that came off the sea, and that's where he usually slept.

Changing into a bathing suit, J.D. took his mask and snorkel and fins off the wall pegs and picked up his sling spear. He walked down to the fine sandy beach and then entered the water, headed out to the reef. The diving here was extraordinary; the reef very healthy and alive with every kind of tropical fish. There were the yellow Tangs in golden clouds and then he passed by a big blue rainbow hued Parrot fish and white mouthed eels. He took a deep breath and dove lower. He wasn't really hunting for fish, he just felt calm here in the quiet blue deep. A different world with different rules where he could listen to himself insist: *you know that you cannot really have someone like Kate.*

He remembered her now as the soft, warm water caressed him, and how her skin felt on his hands, the way she smelled. He had someone once like that. . . .

He never allowed himself to say her name or even think her name because then he had to remember what had been done to her because of him. He broke his own rule that time. She paid.

Would Phillip tell Kate? No. At least J.D. didn't think so. Phillip hadn't even wanted her to be aware he was in Nha Trang the other day for a private strategy meeting. According to Phillip he had only sent her there on the pretext of doing some undercover work as a little reward for some favors she had granted him under the covers.

J.D.'s jaw clenched. He hadn't liked that. But he had been careful to appear not to care.

He remembered yet again how Kate touched his own neck, how her lips felt on his skin. The way she made him feel...it wasn't supposed to be happening this way.

Maybe he could see Kate a little, just for a little while, maybe that would be okay?

He never lied to himself and so J.D. knew he was lying now. But he so wanted to be touched by her again like that. So ... maybe it would be okay. Just for a little while.

He watched as the octopus changed color and became nearly invisible as it entered the small cave and then took its prey.

There were teachers everywhere.

J.D. moved the sling to the killing position; took a breath and dove down to the Grouper.

※

By Monday morning all the red eyes and major hangovers had pretty much subsided, though good spirits still lingered from Hertz's birthday/beach party. Izzy noticed that even Peck was whistling "Zip-a-Dee-Doo-Dah" until he, and his pet lackey Sgt. Johnson, arrived at the LZ with the rest of their small group.

Peck planted himself on one side of the landing pad with Johnson, and like the flick of a light switch, quit humming, crossed his arms. Johnson did the same.

Despite his familiarity with aberrant personalities, Izzy just couldn't get used to Peck's Jeckle/Hyde thing, and not for the first time he wondered if Peck could have anything to do with the monster they were after—presuming there was one. Gregg had his doubts.

J.D. strode to the other side of the L.Z. opposite Peck. Despite their ongoing cold war, Gregg joined J.D. and Izzy did the same as the sounds of Santana concussed the air with "Black Magic Woman" and the eye-popping *Crystal Blue Persuasion* swooped out of the sky. Landing with bullseye precision on the chopper landing pad, up close the metallic purple and black attack helicopter looked even fiercer, whipping the wind with its blades like a chain saw slicing paper at Samurai speed.

As he had at the party, Rick Galt managed to make quite the entrance. He was in full Special Ops battle mode in faded tiger fatigue pants and black tee-shirt, a camo bandana and bush hat, and with two day's growth of beard he looked like a twenty-first century pirate welcoming them aboard his Disney on acid ship.

"This is absolutely cool!" Izzy shouted above the bleating chopper blades while he and Gregg threw in their duffels. "I wish I had a camera to prove I got to ride in this thing."

"I'll send a note to your press secretary," Rick shouted back and gave him a hand up, then lent Gregg the same assist.

J.D. hopped in by himself.

Peck, at the other side entrance stayed put. Glaring at Rick, he yelled, "What the fuck is this kind of hot rod, Captain? This is not authorized transport. I will not ride in this!"

"Then I guess you can take the slow bus instead that has about five stops," Rick yelled back. "I hear they are getting the shit shelled out of them up there, so they'll probably make a couple of extra stops to pick up casualties, and be really glad to have you. Then again, with all the heavy stuff happening, you could be a casualty and never come back yourself, so good luck!"

Izzy slid a glance to Gregg and he grinned back at him as Johnson got in and extended a hand to Peck, who glowered at them all before sitting down in a huff across from J.D. Izzy couldn't help but think that he would sit anywhere but there if J.D. was looking at him like that. Not even a look really. The aviators reminded him of glossy black snake eyes, and his face was still and hard, like a hockey mask.

It was really unnerving, even more than a very first helicopter ride in something that looked like it came out of a futuristic comic book. As flashy and high-tech as it was on the outside with all its weaponry and rockets, though, the inside was as drab and utilitarian as a box. They all had seats on basically benches with web belts and most of the interior was evidently for the gunner and his huge machine gun.

Izzy could see the pilot and copilot up front nodding at whatever instructions Rick was issuing through a headset with a mouthpiece they must be using to communicate, and he wondered what Rachel would think, if she could even imagine him somehow part of a team with a Special Ops warrior and a spy. The chopper ride he would write her about. It gave him something exciting to bring to the table after Rachel's latest rundown on the Rockefeller collections being introduced at the Met, but more significantly "still hanging out down in the Village, grooving, listening to Joan Baez. Just got tickets to another concert at Fillmore East! Bonnie and Delaney, you know them?" and no he did not.

There was no getting ready or a "fasten your belts" announcement before they took off, only the ear splitting sound of Jimi Hendrix, a neck snapping lift, and they were thundering through the sky in a gunship that was rising, spinning, banking off in a shuddering turn toward the sea, and then another turn, heading towards the dark green mountains known as the Highlands.

Izzy watched the countryside roll past beneath the swaths of dark green and light green, the rubber plantations and rice paddies and rivers and small villages, where water buffalo outnumbered the crude roads below. They were climbing higher now toward the mountains and the air was much cooler. That's when Izzy realized that he was not sweating for the first time since his arrival in Vietnam, and the wind, amazing. He looked over at Gregg and smiled, and Gregg smiled and nodded back—then Gregg's mouth opened in a stunned "O" and he was frantically pointing down as they dropped and headed right for a small group of men running across a narrow dike in the paddy. They had weapons and two of the men spun around, crouched down, opening fire on the helicopter that swooped down so fast Izzy's stomach felt like it hit the ceiling while the rest of him remained paralyzed, watching in disbelief as their gunship, the one he was in, fired a rocket that just obliterated the two riflemen and then—

The Rolling Stones blasted "Jumping Jack Flash" from the huge speakers that pierced the air and the rocket ship skimmed the top of the dike toward some other men futilely running ahead while the guns opened up and then the ship was slowing and circling the carnage that had the pilots and their gunman whooping.

Izzy puked out the side of the ship. Someone handed him a green army towel.

"It's good you got to see that, Doc," Rick said close to his ear. "It's war, and that's what we do. It's what the soldiers you see every day are doing, you know?"

No, Izzy did not know, so why he nodded as if giving some tacit approval he did not know either. He was glad that no one else looked at him as he wiped vomit off his shirt and the ship climbed up into the blessedly cooler air where he silently chanted his mantra of *wake the fuck up*, in between 351 and a wake up.

At some point his hands quit talking for him and his stomach settled down, and it helped that the ship was in even cooler air high up over the Central Highlands. Rick played personal tour guide, pointing in specific directions and explaining, "Here we have a string of outposts guarding against the incursion of the VC into what's ours in South Vietnam. And over there, look over there, Izzy, that's Ban Me Thuot."

Even from the distance Izzy could see their destination was a long way from Nha Trang, which now compared to spending the war at the Plaza Hotel next to this place which looked like one big Fort surrounded by the jungle on the side of a blasted hill.

No wonder these guys called them Rear Echelon Mother Fuckers.

Rick issued some order to the pilot through his headset and rather than fly directly toward the ugly blasted hill, the chopper banked to the right and went in another direction.

"Where are we going?" Peck shrilly demanded. "The base is over there!"

"Hang onto your panties," Rick shouted back. "It's a surprise, sweetheart."

A few minutes and more than a few miles away, they circled a clearing and landed. Izzy did what everyone else did, jumping out with his own travel gear and extra Rx meds, which was no doubt different than whatever J.D. was carrying in the duffel he was the last to haul out. At Rick's wave, the chopper took off.

Two jeeps were waiting nearby, apparently part of Rick's surprise since they were parked in the middle of nowhere and he had the keys.

"Here you go, Major." He pitched one to Peck who immediately handed it to Johnson. "Feel free to go get some lunch and set up at the clinic with your side kick while I take the rest of my guests for a little tour."

"Are you fucking kidding me? Take a look around! What you see from here is what you get in this hell hole. Where in god's name are we, anyway?"

"Have you been outside the wire?" Rick motioned the rest of them into the jeep he was commandeering.

"Outside? *Outside?* Are you crazier than you already seem... what's your name again? Give me your name. I am writing you up."

"Captain Richard Galt, Special Ops. Feel free to write away. With any luck you'll get promoted to my job. But. . ." Rick looked him over, shrugged with a "meh" kind of impression and concluded, "I wouldn't count on it." He got behind his own wheel, cranked the engine.

"Wait! This is a war zone, people are out there wanting to kill us. You can't just leave us here."

"Oh yes I can, and yes I will, asshole. In fact, I think it's a great idea if you just stick around right where you are while we go sightsee and may or may not come back this way. You can wait for dark and probably get to be Officer of the Guard since we're a little short in these parts and need all the help we can get."

Rick peeled out with J.D., in the front seat next to him, laughing with glee.

Gregg chuckled, and Izzy was happy to have even some black humor to offset the earlier gunning, so he kind of chuckled, too. But he was compelled to look back anyway, guided by that part of him that he never wanted to lose touch with, but seemed to grow fainter by the day, the part of his own humanity that divided him from some gunman doing his job, and enjoying it.

Izzy noticed that Gregg glanced back, too. He was glad not to be alone in that, and Gregg nodded when their eyes caught, then shifted ahead to where J.D. and Rick sat up front, carrying on a happy conversation about something Izzy couldn't catch, but it didn't matter anyway. Those two guys were as obviously in their element as he and Gregg were not, but there they were anyway, bouncing along in the back seat as Peck and Johnson sped behind them on the crude red dirt roads, splashing through the puddles of the heavy rain that had recently fallen. The tattered base called Ban Me Thuot, so quickly left behind in the air, seemed a booming metropolis compared to the remote wilderness they were in. Izzy had grown up surrounded by streets and buildings and people. There was absolutely nothing but nothing out here except the jungle.

Izzy put his latest helicopter-Alfred Hitchcock-scenario into the section of his mind he had begun relegating all such dark things to and tried to focus on how high and green the grass was, how bright the colored flowers on the vines climbing the trees they plunged past.

Suddenly, the jeep stopped and Rick turned off the motor.

"Okay, campers, we walk from here. We'll keep it short because you have the good work to do and I'm the last person to keep you from it—trust me, that's exactly where I want you because that's where the men need you to be. But all that will still be waiting after I show you something you'll never forget. Just bring water and cameras and of course your trusty weapons in case we are swarmed by the enemy."

The last was clearly a dig at Peck, seething in the passenger seat of the jeep that had screeched to a halt behind them.

"I am not leaving this vehicle and entering this area," Peck announced as Johnson revved the engine. "This is enemy territory, for Chrissakes."

"Apparently," J.D. concurred, stroking his chin as he put his aviator snake eyes on Peck, before politely inviting, "Sure you don't care to join us, Major? After all, the only professional who knows his way around out here is with us."

"Just be back in an hour," Peck snapped, conceding ground but refusing to give up the whole farm. "If you're not, then... then..."

"Then, what?" J.D. laughed. So did Rick. "Okay, mom, if we're not back in an hour, then what?"

"I will call for support."

"Okay, fine, and do you have a secret phone in your shoe?" J.D. inquired.

"Leave me the radio," Peck demanded.

"There is no radio, you idiot," Rick informed him, signaling the way forward with his MI6 to the guests he had on board. Then as an afterthought, threw over his shoulder, "See if you can rig up two tin cans and a string. We'll see you when we see you."

15

The group left Peck and Johnson behind, arguing. Rick signaled to Gregg and was speaking to him quietly. Izzy thought he heard "Nikki" mentioned and wondered if Rick even knew about her relationship with Peck. Probably not since Rick seemed the type to confront any competition head on. As for Peck? Izzy thought about that and decided Peck would be too smart and too cowardly to confront someone physically superior to himself. Instead he would retaliate in some covert-hostile way, get some revenge that would go behind your back, not put it in your face, and be structured for maximum toxicity. That's how guys like him operated. Ugly. Sneaky. Effective.

Izzy didn't want to intrude on Gregg's and Rick's conversation, so he hung back, not too much certainly, not out here, but as he tramped along behind them he was stunned by the beauty of a kind of nature he had never thought to see.

"My god, it's like a sanctuary out here," he exclaimed to J.D., who had fallen in step beside him. "Look at the size of that tree—and, that bird that's in it, just look! And all this bamboo, the color, the size, the—"

"Okay, Tarzan," J.D. cut in, his voice very quiet but not his scary quiet voice. "Orientation number two: We are in the bush, you are entering the food chain right here, and you, with your skills, are no longer the top of the food chain. Got it?"

"Got it."

"Good. Now just remember to move a little quietly because this is not the Bronx Zoo tour, and also watch where your feet are because while you're gawking at the trees you might miss one of the twenty deadly snakes ... actually, Gregg? You might want to look up."

"Holy shit!"

The snake dangling over Gregg's head was brown with black markings, with a long, bright, flicking tongue. Gregg stood paralyzed, either too terrified to move or unsure if running would incite an attack.

Izzy's heart hammered. He wanted to run back to the jeeps but didn't dare take off solo on the barely visible animal trail they were on. So he backed up, very slowly, while J.D. drew closer to the snake, tilting his head.

"It's just a reticulated python," J.D. told them. "He's not likely to bother you unless you bother him first."

"Good call, Doc," Rick said, clearly impressed, "where'd you learn about snakes?"

"Herpetology 101," J.D. said. "Snakes are cool."

"Want me to kill it?" Rick asked. "We could have it for lunch."

At first, Izzy thought he was kidding, but when Rick reached down to his boot and unsheathed a knife, and it sure was not a nice silver steak knife like they had at Tavern on the Green, Izzy instinctively tried to stop him with a forceful, "No!"

Rick paused, frowned. "Don't move." Then he whipped the knife up and across so fast the next thing Izzy knew the knife was next to his boot pinning a snake's severed head to the ground, its tongue still flicking.

"Monocled cobra," J.D. noted, "About eight feet, looks like."

"Yep, one bite and you're good as dead." Rick reclaimed his knife from the huge hooded cobra's head, its jaws continuing to open and close in mid-air as Rick flung it from the steel tip.

"Wow Rick that was amazing." Gregg was absolutely agog. "Wow. I mean, wow."

"Just a day in the life out here, pal." Rick put a finger to his lips. "Shhh. Let's quiet down now guys and get a move on. Izzy watch your feet."

"Trust me, I'm watching, I'm watching." *Wake the fuck up. . .wake the fuck up. . .*Boy what he wouldn't give for some of his mother's matzo ball soup right now, made from scratch, the simplest of meals, and he didn't care how hot it was outside. Comfort food, comfort anything. Simple, normal, boring, everyday *please let me someday get back to all of that. . .a monocled cobra, what the hell am I doing here?*

Gregg rearranged his position to walk right behind Izzy, like he literally had his back, and J.D. was just a few steps ahead, making it look effortless as he pushed aggressively ahead while glancing back at them every so often.

Rick moved the same way, with a lithe grace, as if he was one with the soft green of the big bamboos swaying in the wind, the high grass of the meadow they were now crossing, the songs of the birds—

Rick held up his hand and signed for silence. J.D. stepped back and sank down, signaling for them to do the same. Izzy knelt in the grass, Gregg beside him, both of them too awe-struck to even blink as they watched the water show from perhaps seventy-five yards away.

Just a little below them in a hollow, where a small river broadened into a wide pool, there was a small herd of elephants. What had to be a mother elephant raised her trunk and trumpeted into the air while her baby latched on beneath her girth to nurse.

"They know we're here," J.D. whispered. His voice held the same reverence as the gaze he turned to Izzy, then back to the elephants bathing in a wide shallow pool below a picture postcard waterfall. The huge gray animals were filling their trunks and squirting water into the sunlight and making rainbows with their ponderous splashes as they rolled and played in the water.

The elephants, at some signal from the old matriarch, which J.D. pointed out to him, began to slowly move away, up the embankment and just to the right of them, and then behind the big stand of bamboo they had traversed to get here themselves.

The experience was so moving that Izzy decided it was worth it all, even the snake, to share this hallowed silence, just staring at where the elephants had passed, and then looking from one to the other, all of them understanding what such a moment meant.

Gregg was the first to break the silence and he did it gently. "Thanks," he said to Rick. "I appreciate you doing this for us. How did you know they'd be here?"

"Didn't for sure but I've seen them in this spot, about this time of day, lots of times before." Rick pointed his M16 back the way they had come and the elephants had gone. "We'd better get back. It's a little drive to Ban Me Thuot and I still want to get you out to my camp. The day's getting away from us and you know the rule."

Rick plunged ahead, and Izzy caught J.D. to ask, "What rule?"

"We own the day but Charlie rules the night. Unless you have major expertise, you do not want to be out here after dark. Rick's just taking extra precautions for our safety."

With that, J.D. caught up behind Rick and Izzy wasted no time catching up to J.D., who clearly did not need such extra precautions himself.

Gregg, however, close on Izzy's heels, was right there with him, whispering, "We came, we saw, I am so ready to go back to our nice little villa and eat a grilled cheese sandwich with some chicken noodle soup."

"Make mine with matzo balls," Izzy whispered back. "My mom makes the best chicken and matzo ball soup you ever ate in your life."

"Shhh."

J.D. didn't need to say more. The remainder of their trek through the jungle could have been five minutes or an hour. It was impossible to measure time here—

And then it stopped. The sound of sudden screaming and the crash of M16s on full automatic came from the direction of where they had left the jeeps.

Rick took off at what seemed super-human speed across the meadow screaming, "NO! NO! HOLD YOUR FIRE! NO, NO!" and J.D. was running right behind him, flying over the grass. Izzy didn't know he was capable of running so fast himself, with Gregg pumping full pistons right beside him, both of them bursting into the clearing and—

And then they were all right on top of a blasted to pieces elephant calf and his mortally wounded mother. Part of her skull was shot off and blood coursed from the wound and from her mouth, but she still extended her trunk to cover and protect the body of her little calf who bleated pitifully.

"No hope." Rick's voice caught. He shook his head. Then he fired two shots into each of the elephants. They were still now, and quiet, the blood still leaking and pooling around Izzy's feet.

"We got them!" shouted Peck as he and Johnson ran up to join them. "We got them! They were attacking us and before we could be trampled I was able to stop them both." Peck panted with excitement.

"You fucking, stupid shit." J.D. took a menacing step forward. "You fucking...piece of excrement."

"They were attacking, they work for the VC. The VC do this all the time, they train them to. . ." Peck's eyes narrowed as he realized Rick was moving in on him.

"You murdered them," Rick said coldly. He tossed aside his own gun, and advanced, fists clenching. "They are one hundred yards away from the jeeps and moving east, you asshole."

"Please, can we avoid the bad language?" Peck actually smirked, self-satisfied. "Besides, they are only animals for god's sake."

"Only animals? They're more human than you, Peck."

"Too bad I didn't know they meant that much to you, or I would have tried to kill them all."

"Say that again. Go ahead. Say it again."

The warning in Rick's voice should have stopped a freight train. But not Peck.

"It was an accident, but you know, you try taking something from me, I will take something from you, Captain—" The roll Peck had been on swerved as suddenly as the order he barked at Johnson. "Stop him, he's going to attack me!"

Foolishly, Johnson raised his arm but before he could strike, there was the distinct sound of a bone snapping and his wrist flailed impotently as Rick flipped him into the air. Before Johnson could hit ground, Rick advanced toward Peck, who dropped to his knees.

"I am an officer, you cannot— Gregg, help me. J.D., you're a doctor, get this thug away from me, please!"

J.D. clamped a hand on Rick's shoulder. "Rick, let him go, man. He's not worth it. Let us deal with our own, okay?"

The cords stood out on Rick's neck, like the veins of a horse straining in a race for the finish line, and the finish line here was to finish off Peck as completely as he had destroyed the elephants.

For what felt like eternity, Izzy didn't dare breathe. If wanting to do murder had a smell he was smelling it now; the air was so charged with blood and the thirst for more he expected to see Peck murdered right here, right now, in front of them all, with Rick's bare hands. This was personal; a gun was not personal enough.

Then Rick's body relaxed and he nodded. "You're right," he said. "You're right, He's not worth it. He's not even worth my spit." He hocked one straight into Peck's face anyway, turned on his heel, and got in the jeep.

J.D. stared at Peck in a way that prickled the skin on the back of Izzy's neck. When J.D. spoke it had the effect of an ice chisel.

"It won't be here, and it won't be today. But a storm is coming, Peck. Any time it is raining, listen for the storm."

J.D. turned away as if nothing had just transpired. "Okay, Izzy, you check Johnson's arm and get him in the jeep Major Peck will be driving now, while Gregg and I check on Rick. Five minutes and we're out of here. After all, we don't want to be trampled by VC trained elephants, do we?" A slit glance at Peck and J.D. called, "Rick, you doing okay?"

"All good," Rick called back. "I'm cool."

The ride to Ban Me Thuot was silent. Izzy sat with Gregg in the back of the Jeep that Rick drove, face stoic, eyes on what passed as a road. Glancing down again, Izzy saw the elephant blood on his boots. He wondered about J.D. He had seen the awe and joy in his eyes when they were watching the elephants, and then the absolute cold savagery when he spoke to Peck. Izzy wondered also at himself and cringed, because he really wanted Rick to hurt Peck, and if not Rick, then J.D. He wanted one of them to hurt him the way Izzy wanted to hurt him but knew he never would; he wanted them to hurt Peck the same way that bastard had hurt the elephants.

And that's when Izzy recognized what J.D. and Rick really were. Yes, a CIA agent and a Special Ops killer. But what they were and how they operated were not separate from him. They were *his* agents. Men who did for him what he wanted to do, without getting any of the blood on himself.

※

Ban Me Thuot consisted of an artillery firebase, supply base, and all the necessary military buildings like bunkered hootches, mess halls, and an air field that was not too distant from the morgue for the purposes of flying bodies in and out. The morgue and the airfield saw a lot of action. So did the extended local population of about 60,000 people in the town of Ban Me Thuot proper, with lots of prostitutes to service not only the GIs on the base itself, but the Special Forces and Special Ops Forces that spread out in every direction like a constellation of small fallen stars.

The base at Ban Me Thuot was still the muddy, red mess that Gregg remembered from his last rotation about a month ago, but lacked even a little less charm than usual as he, Izzy, and J.D. watched Peck usher Johnson into the medical clinic to get treatment, only for Peck to stop at the entrance and dramatically turn.

"You have not heard the last of this," he informed J.D. "I will be speaking to Colonel Kellogg when we return. I'm going to tell him about Galt, I'm going to tell him about you threatening me, and I'm going to tell him—"

"I think that's an excellent idea, Major. I would even go so far as to suggest that you leave early from here to tell the Colonel whatever you want. The weather looks like rain, if you know what I mean."

Peck's face visibly paled. He swiftly did an about-face and disappeared into the clinic.

"Okay, he's gone, we took care of 'our own' like we said. Now let's get out of here and do our scheduled meet-up with Rick." J.D. started walking down the cat-tracks back to the jeep that Rick had left for them.

"I thought Rick was going to kill him, like, really literally kill him," Izzy blurted. "Doesn't he even realize you probably saved his life?"

J.D. shrugged. "I was more concerned about saving Rick from the consequences. Peck would be no loss, but Galt's too good to lose."

Gregg nodded. "Good thing he doesn't know about Peck messing with Nikki or that might have pushed him over the edge. You don't think. . ."

"What?" Izzy prompted when Gregg kept shaking his head.

"I can't believe even Peck would do something so—so unbelievably sick, but. . .I'm just going to say it. Surely he wouldn't have shot the elephants as pay-back for me introducing Nikki to Rick. I mean, Peck wasn't even there to know—"

"Margie said Nikki met up with him later that night. Maybe that's what he meant by taking something. You think?"

Gregg cringed. What in god's name was Nikki thinking? As for himself, he couldn't bear the thought that his own good intentions could have resulted in something so deplorably wrong. Maybe it was to avoid a sense of guilt himself, but Gregg wanted to give Peck a pass on deliberately using the elephants to punish them. Nonetheless, "I used to think even the worst people in the world had at least one redeeming quality. Now I'm not so sure. Peck kind of fucked with that philosophy. Really bums me out."

As much as Gregg hated to admit it, even J.D. had at least one redeeming quality: the ability to scare the shit out of Peck.

"Margie told me he goes to church twice a week," Izzy offered.

"Glory be," said J.D.

"And she mentioned he does some volunteer ESL work at the big Catholic cathedral downtown to help teach the local kids some English—though it could have something to do with him getting credit towards a promotion."

"I'm telling ya, the guy's a saint." J.D. signed the cross.

"Let's see. . .oh yes, and I did see him give some money to some little girls who were begging in the street." Izzy opened his palms to Gregg as if offering the closest thing he had to a bottle of Jack. "Maybe he's not a hundred percent bad, Gregg. Just ninety-nine point five."

"Not even that if there were strings attached to his volunteer time or money." J.D. paused, as if considering a thought.

"Are you suggesting he's a child molester?" Gregg asked.

J.D. shrugged. "You guys are the shrinks, what do you think?"

Gregg and Izzy exchanged looks. "Gregg's known him longer than me. Gregg?"

Gregg gave the possibility a little thought, but just a little because even if Peck was an obnoxious, arrogant, self-serving major league asshole that needed a personality transplant, he did not readily fit the psychological profile of the disorder under discussion.

"No one offers more candy to a kid than a pedophile, it's one of the ways they lure them in, but. . ." Gregg shook his head. "Peck has major flaws, but he just doesn't give off that kind of vibe."

"And what kind of vibe would that be?" J.D. probed.

"Creepy." Gregg got into the jeep Rick had left them with; back seat, he'd let Izzy sit up front with J.D. "I could be wrong, but while Peck may definitely be bad news on women, I don't think he preys on kids."

"Don't forget elephants," Izzy added, and looked down.

Gregg knew where he was looking. He kept trying not to look at his own boots.

J.D. actually patted Izzy's shoulder and Gregg tried not to liken it to a bowl of soup extended to a starving POW—worse, a guard at the concentration camps giving him a bar of soap and telling him not to worry. Gregg hated the thought that J.D. was using Izzy's vulnerability somehow in this stinking house of horrors war, hated what that said about how his own mind was working to think a small show of compassion was so suspect it was sick. But think it Gregg did as J.D. said almost kindly:

"The elephant thing, that was bad. Unfortunately, this next thing is going to be worse."

16

Gregg looked out at the jungle as the jeep bumped along and JD and Izzy chattered away in the front seats. He had never felt this fucked up. Usually, the one thing that he prided himself on was that his mind was strong and steady with a world view of the proverbial glass half full or more. Right now that glass was running on empty. Not too surprising really. He had been in-country a long time. He was completely out of the regular routine he had established to psychically survive here with a balance of work, play, surfing, and friends.

The work was long and difficult and stressful as hell but he had been doing fine until J.D. arrived. Since then Top had been murdered in front of his eyes by Derek, Derek had been blown away, Kate had arrived, and promptly gone from the greatest thing to happen here to the worst with her involvement with Captain Hook, who had just promised the most awful thing yet was waiting at a morgue after they'd watched the bloody slaughter of a baby elephant and her mother, not to mention the snakes.

Gregg could feel his body quivering; a clear signal that he was on overload, but the recent shift in his thinking process is what bothered him the most. He could hear his own thoughts going dark side. Like when J.D. was—*or was he not?*—being kind to Izzy and his mind went to places it made him feel ill to go. *What was the matter with him?* Was he getting paranoid, turning everything J.D. did or said to double think? What was real, what was a manipulation, was anything sincere or was it all just a set up?

Gregg knew that J.D. had tried to be nice to him despite stepping over the line with Kate. But was that more soap and soup, or just an act to appease her and sucker him in? Gregg just didn't know what to think anymore, didn't trust his own judgment, or even his own thoughts that seemed to go round and round, and the more stressed he got the darker and more twisted those thoughts seemed to become. It was like having snakes in his head. *Fuck it.* He needed to get back to the ocean and some waves after they got out of here, after they found out that this was all a big load of bullshit. Then J.D. would go away and he'd be a two digit midget and on his way back home, Kate in tow with a broken heart that he would be there to mend.

God I hate the Nam. This place is so fucking my head.

No sooner had his brain produced that last bit of venom than they were pulling into the camp. The one Rick had said they were calling "Fort Apache." Specialists like Rick were great at setting up and creating these "camps" somehow overnight in the middle of nowhere. Because Special Ops apparently got whatever they wanted or needed right when they wanted it, they could go right to where it was hot and set up and operate. Pretty much like J.D. Maybe that was one reason he and Rick had hit it off so well.

"Hey, the shrinks are here!" As if it had been a week since he'd last seen them, Rick slapped J.D. some skin, then lightly slapped Gregg on the shoulder, almost knocking him over as usual. It was like the guy was made of some sort of heavy metal. Gregg had noticed the few times he played in pickup basketball games with professional athletes that their bodies were made of something far denser and harder than normal and Rick and his Special Ops guys were made out of the same material.

"Glad you could make it," Rick convivially went on, "See our little piece of paradise before we pack up again."

"Where are you headed next?" J.D. asked casually.

"That's classified but I'll fill you in anyway later. First I want you to meet a few of my men. The best of the best of the bad ass best."

Gregg knew that Rick wasn't boasting, simply stating a fact. As with the medical field there was a hierarchy of expertise and who got the most respect for their positions on the ladder. The way the totem pole worked on this end of things put Rick and his men pretty much at the top. The best of the LRRP guys who survived the training to become Rangers had a shot at the Special Forces, like the Green Berets, then the Special Ops groups operated at another elite level. They were a breed unto themselves often going out in the boonies for weeks doing recon and getting intel on the enemy. Some of them had been drawn from the Green Berets and others were darker with fuzzy affiliations to various branches of the military but most of all to the highly classified SOG. Gregg wasn't sure exactly how Rick had come up in the ranks, but in addition to leading Special Ops Groups, he trained new ones.

It really was an honor to have someone of Rick's stature usher them around, but more than anything, Gregg just wanted to go home, even if it was the villa for now. Every bone, nerve ending, and muscle in his body told him that he did not belong here. Every instinct vibrated with the knowledge that outside the perimeter here was death.

"Okay, kids," Rick said jovially, "Now that the Buckingham Palace tour is over and you've met the guard, let's get this party on the road. Oh, and before I forget—" He handed Gregg an envelope with "Nikki" printed on the front. "If you don't mind?"

"Not at all, Rick. I'll personally deliver it to her tomorrow." Gregg fleetingly wondered if the elephants had already atoned for his delivery. Then he consigned that idea with all the others that belonged in the snake pit of his brain.

Minutes later they were bouncing around in the jeep again and heading back in the direction of Ban Me Thuot, then Rick took a detour to an area Gregg had never seen before.

While Rick's Special Ops guys were fit and sharp and looked like a pretty happy bunch of mean mother fuckers, and while their Fort Apache was tidy in a roughhewn kind of way, where Rick parked the jeep and they got out, Gregg could only liken to a deeper level of Hell. One look and you knew how naïve it was to think that living in Nha Trang and working at the 99KO was really the war. They were living and working in some Disneyland Army Town, USA compared to this.

This being a vast, blasted, stinking mud hole filled with temporary fragile shells of metal and shallow holes in the ground, which were in turn filled and covered with sandbags. US GIs were actually living in this mud hole where Gregg could smell the smoke from burning cans of shit from the latrines wafting across the wasteland. The new guys in dark green jungle fatigues appeared nearly as shocked as he was to be here. The old soldiers in faded out fatigues were themselves somehow faded out, nearly spectral. Many were gaunt and wasted from stress with lesions on their skin that looked infected and inflamed. The soldiers he looked at directly just stared blankly back at him. He was a visitor. A being from another place that could come and go from the living hell they had been consigned to.

"Where are we?" Izzy posed his question in the kind of wheeze that suggested he was trying not to breathe the putrid air beyond the amount it took to keep breathing.

"We're at the firebase, Doc," Rick explained, as if that explained anything. "These poor grunts here just finished getting the shit shelled and rocketed at them for about two weeks, which we happily missed, and as you can see this place is such a goddamn puking mess all the more reason me and my guys are moving out of here two days max. We'll be setting up about twenty-five clicks north, for reasons I'm sure you'll understand."

Rick paused and his expression shifted as darkly as his demeanor. "Listen, I got the message from on high that we are after the same fucker—or fuckers—that took down some more of our guys. I was instructed to let you shrinks see the bodies first, before they got taken to the regular morgue, so we set up a temporary right here."

Rick stopped outside a battered steel Quonset surrounded by green sandbags. Gregg had a terrible premonition J.D. had not exaggerated about the "worse." His nod confirmed as much just before Rick opened the door.

The odor that whooshed out had Gregg bending over, as Izzy managed to gag out, "Oh, god, the smell."

"Yeah, well, it's a morgue," Rick said. "Come on in, and thanks for puking outside by the way, Gregg. Most people would have done it in here."

The dread crawling up Gregg's spine was one long creeping vicious tropical centipede waiting to snap its burning jaws into his brain as he forced his feet into this awful place with bright lights illuminating what looked like a storage room.

It was filled with body bags.

There was something odd here, though. The body bags were separated, with a special group of the bags laid out on several long folding tables.

These were the bags they approached.

Gregg knew he was moving in the direction Rick was going and J.D. was quickly following, but he couldn't feel his feet and there was a buzzing sound in his ears that blended with the white lights and shadows and his twisting thoughts, the black bags and stench. Like rolling drums in the background, his grinding dread escalated with each step closer, closer, to whatever was about to come.

They all gathered around one of the long tables. Gregg looked across at Izzy, silently asking if he was going to make it. Izzy nodded and Gregg could see he was holding himself together with that sort of disassociated professionalism they all had to learn to survive, while inside his guts were clenched tight.

"Now regarding that fucker—or, fuckers," Rick said. "The Ghost Soldier stories that really brought you docs here to help. . .I don't know, analyze, I guess?"

"Yeah, the Boogeyman, or whatever. Gregg thinks it's bullshit, and until Izzy and I see something to convince us otherwise, we're inclined to agree." J.D. shrugged like they just couldn't buy something baked up around a campfire, even if it had come from one that smelled more like the burning shit outside than roasted marshmallows. "One look out there and it's easy to understand how crazy stories like that get started."

"Maybe." Rick reached for the first bag and opened it. He pulled out a head, as cleanly severed as the monocled cobra's, except this one was human. It had also been scalped and the eyes were gone. "Then again, maybe not."

When the people of the world all know beauty as beauty,
There arises the recognition of ugliness
When they all know the good as good,
There arises the recognition of evil.
—Lao Tzu

Blue Fish in Love with Red Lotus

KITTENS

Maybe my stepfather should not have been too surprised when the gun went off.

When I was younger, about 7 he rented an old broken-down house. It was in town but was kind of isolated next to an old aban-doned estate. The estate house had burned down a long time ago leav-ing a burnt brick chimney, but there was a sagging garage still there with lots of old crap. Other kids would have thought it too spooky and dark and full of spiders and ghosts but not me. For a kid with no friends it was a pirate cave filled with trunks of treasure. There really were old chests of drawers and little boxes of costume jewelry. But then something better. A friend came. She was pretty scruffy and skittish but she was my friend. I took a hairbrush from my mom's room and I stole and scrounged food from the kitchen for my new friend and in about a week she was Beautiful.

I did not know she was pregnant, I just thought she seemed kind of chubby. She was so afraid of people but that was good because she never followed me home. Pretty soon I had a little nest for her with one of my old blankets and a broken cup for her food and water and with my care and feeding she looked beautiful to me even with her scars and chewed ears from all of her scraps before I took her in. Then one day there was a huge surprise. Usu-ally, whenever I got close to the garage she made her little sound, kind of a mewing squeak but today was silent and I was anxious and rushed in and there she was in her nest with 5 little kittens. Of course their eyes were shut and they just looked like little mice. They all grew so fast. They looked so different that I thought that they must have all been different kinds of cats. There was a fuzzy yellow one "Butter," and a sleek black one "Panther," and a big furry black with bright green eyes "Jade," and a striped "Tiger" and my favorite a black and white "Panda." All of these little guys were soon great fun. They would swoosh around chasing each other and tumble each other over and over and for me it was about the best time and the most friends I had ever had. In the late afternoons in the fall I would bundle up and take my own nap in the nest with them all snuggled in with me.

One day I rushed home from school. It was just after Thanksgiving and I remember because I had been taking leftovers out of the fridge for all my "friends." I decided that I would take the drumstick. Stupid, because that is easy to notice missing, but I thought nobody likes drumsticks in this family and anyway I got to the old garage with the drumstick and came running in calling out "Panda," "Butter," "Jade," and "Tiger" and they were all so happy eating the drumstick and playing with it that I did not hear a thing but there was my stepfather. He was holding Friend, the mother cat, and stroking her. I was really happy for a minute because I thought he must like her, I mean how could anybody not and she was purring and I thought maybe he will want them to move to our house and they could sleep in my room and ....he twisted her head and broke her neck and threw her against the wall so hard her head blew up in a red blob on the wall. "So the little man has his own little kitties."

"I. . .I. . .I only feed them my food, I'm sorry."

"You are sorry," he said, "and it is not your food, it is my food, you have been stealing my food and now you are going to pay for it...."

I was already crying about Friend. . .I was so used to his beatings that I just got ready for it right there....

"NO, it is not going to be that easy," he said. "Go get the shovel."

I came back with the shovel resigned to thinking I would have to dig the grave for Friend.

"I'm sorry," I begged, "please, don't hurt the kittens, it's my fault, don't hurt them..."

"I am not going to hurt the kittens, you little idiot. . .you are. You did this, you stole from me and you are going to fix it. You are going to kill every one of them with the shovel, the fast way with the sharp end or the slow way with smashing them, it's your choice ..." he took out his Zippo lighter, lit a cigarette, and then left the lighter going, "or I am going to burn them alive, you got it little

man? Kill them fast or watch them burn. Here I'll help you ... kill the one you love the most first, the others will be easier. . . ."

Maybe he was right, but I did not know that then. My hands were shaking, I was crying too hard begging for their lives that I made a mess of every one of them, one after another, after another. . .I killed Panda last.

17

When at last they lifted off, the sky was turning a darker shade of purple. Rick waved from below. J.D. waved back.

Izzy didn't feel capable of even that much. He wondered if he looked as bad as Gregg—who looked as fucked and fried as the wiped out grunts at the firebase.

Lungs still burning from doing everything possible not to inhale the rotting stench of decomposition, Izzy sucked in a big breath of fresh, cool mountain air filling the chopper. For a while he didn't move or say anything while he tried to cleanse his mind. When that became as likely as pulling a genie out of a bottle, he decided a more direct approach may better serve his own mental health, just put it on the table and purge his system with the old go-to remedy of intellectual discourse.

"Gregg? Gregg, did you ever see anything, *anything*, like we just saw in your post-doc work?"

"No, man, nothing even close. I put in my hours in a mental institution, did my rotation inside a locked ward with the criminally insane..."

Gregg trailed off. His lips visibly shook. Izzy's hands were shaking really bad but he figured after this they were entitled to chatter away so he didn't even try to hide them.

"I never liked working with the criminally insane," Izzy picked up. "I did my intern time in the hospital, right? Saw my share of bad accidents, shootings, knifings, domestic violence in the ER, you name it. But none of it comes remotely close to. . .to. . .what we saw back there was the work of a monster. A whole pack of them. Body after body after body...it was *fiendish*."

"Evil," Gregg agreed. "Like, what kind of animal could do something like that?"

"I don't know. But it has to be more than one to carve up that many. Not even Jack the Ripper could pull that off without an assist from Albert Fish."

"The Werewolf of Wisteria?" Gregg grimaced.

"One of many names. As you'll recall he was known as 'The Boogeyman,' too."

"What I mostly remember is that he liked to eat children."

They let that sit between them, the sick pathology of the mind that could be so deeply disturbing yet fascinatingly macabre. Izzy was reminded of how naïve he had been when he went into child psychiatry, as if treating kids meant a gentler, kinder type of mental hell. He had been so wrong. It was just the opposite.

"Children are the most victimized, you know," he said, and didn't know why he was even talking about it. Children had nothing to do with the mutilated remains in the body bags, but he felt so unclean it was like he had to verbally wash some of the filth out of his own mental system. "They're helpless and they're weaker. That's why the predators and most twisted seem to single them out for the worst crimes."

"I don't know how anything could be worse than the body of work we saw."

"From what we saw I wouldn't put anything past that kind of beast, demon, whatever you want to call it. Maybe he—or they eat children, too."

"Yeah."

Maybe they eat children, too. "I'm not a forensic pathologist but... judging from the bruising, blood, and swelling around the eye sockets of the first head, I suspect the eyes were taken out while the victim was still alive. Dead bodies don't respond to injuries like that."

"Why remove the eyes first?"

Gregg and Izzy looked at J.D. as if he had just walked into a room.

"For the joy of it?" Izzy guessed. "Fulfillment? A sense of power?"

"Or maybe for entertainment purposes," Gregg added. "The same way some people get off on snuff films or cock fighting."

"But why?" J.D.'s brow furrowed. "What can you tell me that I don't know? Come on, guys, I need your help here."

Izzy considered the source of the request. J.D. had pumped Derek full of bullets with the fluid precision of a professional killer.

But he had done it without emotion, without glee, more like an accountant balancing the books. Killing was just part of the job for him, not a passion.

"We all have a dark side," Gregg explained. "There's a part of the mind that is immensely stimulated by the dark and the violent—it's not a conscious choice, it's how we're hardwired as humans. That's why sadism makes great entertainment. The gladiators in Rome, they weren't warriors. They were mostly prisoners forced to fight to their death with animals or other prisoners, and the gorier the better for the crowds. Popcorn, peanuts, Crackerjacks anyone?"

"I'm afraid Gregg is right. It's part of the human psyche, even if we don't like to admit it or think about what sort of cruelties we're capable of. Though after today, there's not a lot of guess work left about that, is there?"

"If you mean the elephants, agreed. But if you're referring to what we saw at the morgue?" J.D. shrugged. "At first I wondered if it could be some good old payback, which is all about revenge, not just shits and giggles."

"Payback?" asked Gregg.

"Yes, it's a thing that happens in wars, each side escalating on their kills to terrorize the other side, but in this case, as you say, pretty creepy and over the top. Actually, after seeing the extent of the evidence, I think it's pretty clear to all of us that there is more at work here than anything as simple as payback. Or pleasure seeking."

It struck Izzy that J.D. was immune to the impact of the mutilations. Maybe that made him well suited to his job. Maybe one reason J.D. needed them was because a lack of immunity is what made him and Gregg good at theirs. Yet the difference between them was thinning and Izzy had to wonder if he would ever reclaim the sweetness of life that was as untainted as picking berries with his grandmother on a summer morning and watching them swirl into the taste of ice cream just made with his dad. Now, the images of those body bags opening squirmed around in his mind, and he remembered something his mentor, Dr. Haride, had not that long ago said:

We have a wonderful capacity to make little rooms that we can carefully set aside inside our heads and we know well before we approach those rooms that it best not to even start to go down the hallway lest we start nightmares. I warn you all that if you can avoid those rooms do so. I was once involved in a case of a man who abducted and tortured children; I will not say to you anything of what he did, only that with all of my heart I wish for the time before I saw the images of what he had done. For now I cannot rid my mind of them and I tell you it is a kind of hell to know.

Dr. Haride had warned Izzy and his small, hand-picked group of young specialists about to graduate, what the minds of both clinicians and MDs in the practice of psychiatry could hold. Even the best and strongest minds could only tolerate so much of the soul poisoning quality of the horrific work that often came within the field of child abuse, which, as it turned out, often crossed paths with the criminally insane, which was the very field he had tried to avoid.

Izzy now knew what Dr. Haride meant. He thought he did when he thanked him for such a compelling lecture. He thought he did when he worked with children who had survived unthinkable atrocities. But now that he had gazed upon the chilling hell unleashed upon those poor men in the morgue—*they were someone's children*—Izzy knew too well and he knew too much, because he knew the depth of his own capacity for cruelty.

As with the elephants, he wanted revenge on the perpetrators of those mutilated bodies. He wanted Rick to find them and send them home in body bags, too. Just clean kills, nothing too cruel or sordid, nothing like what they had seen, but whoever was capable of that was unsalvageable and the world was a better, safer place without their poisoned presence. *Listen to myself,* he thought, *"clean kills." My head is starting to twist stuff just like Gregg said it would. Instead of wishing we could cure the predator, now I want "clean kills."*

At first Izzy wasn't aware he had spoken aloud, but then J.D. asked, "What did you say?"

And Izzy knew. He might have lost his innocence but he had been instilled with guiding principles and at least he hadn't lost those yet. There was a difference between being forced into something against your will and funneling that will into a worthy cause. He had crossed that line.

"I said I want to help you." Izzy looked over at Gregg. Apparently they had been raised on some of the same "do the right thing" stuff. Gregg, maybe even more, all things considered.

"Yeah." Gregg nodded. "Me, too."

*

Upon landing at the LZ, where they had been picked up earlier that day, Gregg nearly dropped to his knees and kissed the ground. He had never been so grateful to live in Nha Trang, to sleep in an old villa and work at the 99KO, Camp McDermott included.

J.D. had arranged a waiting jeep. He threw his gear into the back and got behind the wheel.

"I could use a walk," Gregg told him. His insides were still vibrating.

"Same here." Izzy shouldered his gear.

"Then I'll see you guys. Listen, thanks a lot. I'll try to make this up to you someday." J.D. actually saluted them. "Okay, time for me to get to work."

As the jeep sped off, Gregg wondered if J.D. was really on his way to the mission to see Kate. But after the elephants and the fire-base and the morgue, he was simply too numb to think beyond some immediate means of self-comfort.

"Grilled cheese sandwich," Gregg said to Izzy.

"Chicken soup," Izzy said back. Then, "Do you ever wonder what J.D. does to relax?"

"No," Gregg said. "I don't think guys like him ever really relax."

"Even Hitler liked to paint and Fish liked to write messed up stuff when he wasn't eating kids. Everyone needs some form of sanctuary, Gregg."

"Maybe." Before Gregg could stop it, he was thrust back into the room where Rick was opening a body bag and extracting its contents with his pronouncement of, "Maybe not."

Izzy suddenly stopped on the cat tracks. "This isn't really my area of expertise, but. . ."

"What?"

"I'm just thinking of that whole awful thing with the eyes being cut out before killing the victim—I'm pretty positive about that—but it just makes me wonder if that kind of torture could be more than just for fun, or to maximize the psyops value Rick was talking about. Like, could it be the Ghost Soldier's own kind of sanctuary, or if it's a group, even some kind of cult worship—especially if the killings involve some type of ritual mutilation?"

"There's a thought," Gregg agreed.

"I know it sounds strange but. . . " Izzy held out his hands; they were no longer shaking. "For some reason it helps me to analyze. As disturbing and gruesome as all this is, laying the pieces out and trying to put everything together gives me a sense of control over the situation, even if I realize I'm feeding myself a load of crap for a false sense of security."

"Whatever works, man, I'm all for it."

They were still discussing the various possibilities while savoring a late night grilled cheese sandwich, a can of Campbell's, and a bottle of Jack when Robert David appeared in the villa's kitchen. If he noticed they immediately fell silent upon his arrival, he gave no indication, saying without preamble, "Kate called to invite us all to a little get together she's hosting at the mission come next weekend. I told her I would pass the word to Nikki and Margie since she hoped they could come, too. Oh, and Izzy, my good man, this is for you."

As Izzy did a Jack-in-the-Box to latch onto the letter Robert David extended, Gregg made a mental note NOT to forget Rick's letter to Nikki.

Robert David sniffed the air, wrinkled his patrician nose, and took a closer look at them both. "Good Lord, you two look like hell and don't smell much bettah. What happened in the Highlands today?"

"Oh, you know the usual routine," Gregg said. "Murder, mayhem, slaughter in a muddy hellhole. It is a great place the Highlands, a fun get away for anyone and everyone. Right, Izzy?"

Izzy was pressing the letter to his chest as if it might resuscitate him from the shock overload of the day. Gregg knew Izzy had a little ritual of taking his letters to the beach to open them; not so strange really since most guys considered them holier than manna from heaven. But under the circumstances, Gregg figured this was one letter that would be ripped into the second Izzy got it alone in his room.

"If I had to choose between the Highlands and this upcoming Woodstock festival Rachel's been writing me about, I'm heading back to the Highlands, no question."

"Yep," Gregg agreed, "Give me the Highlands over the Summer of Love any time, any year because I'd rather smell burning shit than those damn hippies." Gregg touched his hair and silently promised Top to get a haircut.

"Might I presume that Peck was not on his best behavior?"

"He killed some elephants," said Izzy.

"He killed some elephants, what the hell?" Robert David looked from Izzy's ravaged face to Gregg biting down hard on his lip.

"Yeah," Gregg said, sounding far away even to himself, "It was the elephants. A mother and her baby, right after we watched them play."

✳

The Boogeyman was at Camp McDermott's Court again and he wanted to play. But for now he was happy just to watch and blend in, wait his turn like everyone else while the sound of the ball, the rim, the boards, the grunts and curses mixed with the boombox music of Marvin Gaye.

The game was sanctuary. It was something pure and holy like gospel songs lifting the rafters off a church, and those who watched were like the choir whooping the players on and hoping their own game could go that high until the last shot was dropped.

Then, when it was your turn to play. When you were next. You had better be ready. This was not some game you eased into. There were at least two, three teams waiting to get in while the team that had won would continue to hold court until they were beaten and nobody wanted to give that up. The "winners" were already high, and that's where they wanted to start and keep on going. You shot for first outs and that winner would take the shot, top of the key and just nail that first jumper and the next and the next. And, then they would switch, and that's when it always happened. Some fucking white kid jumping that high and shooting that kind of shit. . .the black guys just did not believe it at first. And if that white kid could jam down a rebound, ok then he was leading whatever team he was on and they were singing, taking the game higher and they were all back home for that moment and no one could take it from them.

At least not until some asshole came along. It was late that night when he ruined the game for them all. Yes, he had a good game and he was strong and he could hit the boards and he could shoot. He seemed like just a great big good old boy trucked in from Texas. Fort Sam Houston he said, but he had a mean streak, a bad one. He had some good players with him too and they got up a little bit and started the mouthing that he took to the next level. Then Texas started with the cheap shots and little dirty hits in the stomach when guys were shooting, and deliberate bumps on the elbow. All the little crappy, crappy stuff that took away from the real game. When someone would make a nice move and come in hard for a good shot he would just knock the guy to the blacktop.

"Not cool," finally said one of the players. "Oh boo-hoo-hoo," said Texas, "so sad." He hit one and then another and another, and finally, when it was the final point and another player got ready to just drop the ball over the rim, Texas shoved him hard, right into the steel pole.

Now Texas held The Court, and the guy with the big bruise on his forehead and his nose still bleeding sat cross-legged on the ground, watching a couple more games. And whenever Texas would pass he'd say to him: "Boo-hoo."

Finally. Texas left, unaware he was being followed. And as he headed toward the MP compound the shadow behind him could only think, "Hmm figures, a fucking cop. Probably go home and spend his life enjoying busting heads and hurting anybody and everybody smaller than him."

There was a dark quiet spot ahead. The shadow hurried a little to catch up, calling "Hey, Texas."

"Yeah, what do you want asshole?"

"You hurt the game."

"Hurt the game, hurt the game you stupid fuck, I kicked ass." Texas flicked a match and lit a cigarette, blew a stream of smoke in his worst nightmare's face. "Walk away right now you little pussy—no, better, say 'boo-hoo' for me and then I won't fix your face so your mama won't want her little baby anymore."

Boogeyman chopped Texas right in the soft place in his gut. As Texas bent over, struggling to breathe, Boogeyman punched him hard, very hard, just once, right in that little place in the throat. He stood over Texas, watched him dying, trying so hard to breathe through his crushed windpipe.

"You hurt the game. Not cool."

And then he bent down and looked Texas in the eyes and smiled as he died. With a twist of his Converse he ground out the still burning cigarette, picked up what Texas had dropped, and with the amazing grace of silent wings, disappeared into the dark, hot night.

18

Two days later, J.D. had not yet resurfaced. Neither had Peck. A phone call after Wednesday morning rounds, however, had Margie waving Gregg and Izzy over to the nurse's station. Her tone was serious, hushed.

"You're both supposed to report to the HQ immediately. Apparently there is a CID colonel over there."

"What do you mean CID?" Gregg's pulse up-ticked like there was a flashing red light in the rearview mirror.

"You know, military police. Investigative unit."

"I know that, I mean what the hell do they want with me and Izzy?"

"I have no idea, but promise you won't get arrested. At least not until after the party Saturday since Nikki and I are counting on you two being our escorts to the mission."

Izzy was still smiling back at Margie when Gregg grabbed his arm. "We better see what's up."

Walking down the cat tracks, the same path they had taken Izzy's first day to meet The Emperor, Gregg noticed Izzy was not the same guy who arrived here. His walk was taller, his skin darker, his face more hard than bewildered. And, "Hey, you're not sweating as much."

"I'm not wearing any underwear either. Crotch rot is bad, you know."

"May not be as bad as what's waiting for us at HQ. Military police, that sounds serious. And Peck's not here. Maybe Rick went back and killed him."

"Or maybe something better. Maybe Rick found the killer and this whole Ghost Soldier nightmare is over."

Just the thought was enough for Gregg to feel his body slightly release inside. If this awful thing would go away and J.D. along with it, he could just count the days while convincing Kate to go home with him. Add in a good night's sleep and then he could call it perfect.

Upon entering HQ, Gregg was struck by the freshly painted walls and he wondered how Terry felt sitting at the desk that Top had commandeered. Terry raised the arm that wasn't bandaged in greeting and Gregg plowed a hand through the hippy surfer hair that still needed that damn haircut he'd promised Top to get.

"How're you doing, Terry?"

"Still working on the load of cookies Nikki brought me and I'm still around to eat them, so no complaints here." Voices rose in the direction of the CO's office. "The two of you better go on in. You're expected." Terry's smile bore little resemblance to the effusive young West Point officer the last time he allowed them past Colonel Kellogg's door.

Moments later, Gregg and Izzy entered the domain of their commanding officer.

"Shut the door," ordered Kellogg.

If a room could boil with tension, Gregg figured he and Izzy would be cooked faster than a couple of lobsters in a bubbling cauldron.

In one chair sat Peck with a smug look on his face. In another chair was a full bird colonel, his assistant standing behind him, all of them facing Kellogg who rose from his desk in a clear fury as Gregg and Izzy gingerly stepped closer.

Peck decided to stand up too. "I want to press full charges, sir, and—"

"Sit down Major and shut up. You will speak when either I or Colonel Johnson ask you to, and not before. Captain Kelly, Captain Moskowitz, thank you for coming. As for *you*—" Kellogg jabbed a finger in Peck's quickly seated direction. "This is what you have done so far. You came back from the field with some pissant complaint to your CO—that would be *me*—that you had been assaulted and threatened by a fellow officer and when your CO—again that would be *me*—told you to knock it off, you went over your CO's head to contact military police headquarters in Saigon, which has caused the head of the CID—that would be Colonel Johnson here—to come all the way to our division to find out why I cannot manage my own people which makes me look. . .well, do you see where I am going with this?"

"I do, sir," Peck responded. "But you have to understand that these people were in the company of those who were threatening me and as the ranking officer—"

Kellogg guillotined the air and politely turned his attention to Izzy and Gregg. "Doctors, do you care to weigh in here? To your knowledge was Major Peck inappropriately dealt with by either Major Mikel or Captain Galt under whatever the circumstances might have been?"

Gregg and Izzy exchanged glances. In unison they responded, "No sir."

At that point Colonel Johnson leaned close to Peck and thumped him once, squarely in the chest. "You are not the ranking anything except idiot and fuckup, Major. If I get one more call from you, or about you, I will personally see that the rest of your tour here makes a firebase look like cooking up brownies in an Easy-Bake Oven. Do you understand what I am saying?"

Peck blanched. He looked from Johnson to Kellogg, darted a furtive glance at Gregg that reminded him of, "*I'll get you my pretty and your little dog, too!*" before contritely nodding, nodding. "Yes sir, my apologies, sir, I understand. I see I have made a terrible mistake. You won't hear from me again."

Kellogg pointed to the door. "You are dismissed Peck. Just remember, if I hear one more thing about you myself from Doctors Kelly, Moskowitz, or Mikel that doesn't make me want to invite you to my daughter's wedding, you are goner than gone to wherever Colonel Johnson wishes to send you and that includes Hell."

"Thank you, sir, yes sir. Thank you." Peck all but bowed his way out.

Upon his departure Colonel Johnson beamed at Gregg and Izzy. "Doctors, Mikel tells me he is more than pleased with your performance so whatever it is that you are doing to assist him, carry on."

"Me too, sir?" interjected Kellogg.

"Yes, you carry on, too, Colonel." Johnson passed Gregg and Izzy on his way to the door where he paused to say, "Sorry to have bothered you with this."

A salute, and before they could return it, Johnson was gone.

Kellogg was still holding his salute pose when Gregg and Izzy haphazardly saluted him back and made their own exit.

Terry was taking a swig from a Milk of Magnesia bottle at Top's desk.

"Let me know if you need any meds," Izzy offered.

"Thanks, Doc Moskowitz, I'll let you know." Then to Gregg he said, "Looks like you guys have connections. That's always a good thing, right?"

Gregg had once thought so, but now? "Maybe. Maybe not."

✻

J.D. showed up Friday, butt-crack-of-dawn, at the villa. At this point he had basically dropped the ruse of coming in for rounds at the hospital and only slid in an appearance if there was something case-specific. Gregg thought it might be good news that no new reports of Ghost Soldier mangling had surfaced; their beds were just constantly occupied by damaged and deranged soldiers brought in from the field under typical circumstances.

Gregg found himself thinking about his thinking again: What did it say about his own mental health when he considered damaged and deranged young men a welcome reprieve and classified war in terms of "typical circumstances?"

He wished to God he had never walked through the door of that morgue. Sleep had once been a respite from the unrelenting suffering he witnessed daily; now he dreaded crossing the line from consciousness into the unguarded territory of sleep. The first nightmare shook him, but he passed it off as a singular event. The next night when he woke himself up shouting, he let it go too, nothing chronic to worry about.

The body needed rest but the brain needed sleep and the deprivation of it, now four nights in a row, was not pretty.

"What happened to you?" The alarm on J.D.'s usually inscrutable features made Gregg wonder if he looked even worse than the mirror had indicated before following the aroma of freshly brewed coffee into the kitchen.

"None of your damn business." Gregg knew he sounded grumpy because he was grumpy, and he completely did not care. J.D., on the other hand, apparently cared enough to pour a cup from the percolator he was manning—and fix it just right with a splash of milk and two sugars before handing it to Gregg, whose mother would have been horrified that instead of a polite "thank you" he snapped, "How do you know how I take my coffee?"

"Because I pay attention." J.D. tapped the top button of Gregg's mis-buttoned shirt. "You may want to try this again. And tie your boot strings while you're at it."

Gregg refrained from muttering "screw you" as he clomped over to the kitchen table, plunked down the mug harder than intended, and bent down to tie his boots. He was so damn tired he was ready to crawl on top of the table and go to sleep right there.

J.D. pulled up a chair next to him and tapped his fingertips together. "So, how bad are the nightmares?"

Gregg shrugged. "Bad enough."

"Can you take something to help?"

"I'm thinking about it." And he had. What Gregg hadn't expected was his own resistance to signing up for the very medication he was so liberal in dispensing. Not that he prescribed the Rxs., that end of the job went to the MDs, but as for why he was so reluctant to dip into the medicine cabinet himself...

On some level some part of him had decided that it would be like admitting the war had won. And he did not want this miserable mess of a war to beat Gregg Kelly.

"Look, Gregg, I've been thinking, too. I know we have this thing between us—"

"Kate is not a *thing*. She's a wild child with an incredibly intelligent mind and she's a woman with a sweet and generous heart that's not always so wise. I know what she looks like now, but I still see a girl with braces and a bad perm that earned her the nickname Bozo and when some bully down the street called me her little clown she knocked that bastard flat and told me to take my best shot. Tag-team, me and Kate. I loved her then. And I love her now. I will *always* love Kate. Even if she doesn't always love me back the same."

Gregg quickly put the mug to his mouth before he said more. Worse, before he choked up in front of J.D., who genuinely looked sympathetic.

God, what was the matter with him? Everything he'd said about Kate was true but his emotions and his nerves were so raw he was saying shit he would normally keep to himself, or maybe after a few beers confess to a trusted friend like Robert David or Izzy too now. But not to J.D. Telling him this, letting him in on personal territory, was like giving Intel to the enemy.

"But she does love you, Gregg." J.D.'s voice was quiet, thoughtful. Gregg half expected him to pull out a box of tissues and start taking notes, like he was the therapist sympathizing with the wreck on the couch. "She even told me she didn't deserve you. Maybe that's why she thinks I deserve a chance with her. I probably don't. Actually, I'm quite positive that I don't. But even guys like me need something good every now and then, something to remind us that certain things in life are worth living for. Whether we deserve it or not."

Even Hitler liked to paint and Fish liked to write when he wasn't eating kids. Everyone needs some form of sanctuary, Gregg.

As if the echo of Izzy's observation had summoned him, there he was, stumbling half-asleep to the coffee pot and scratching his nuts en route.

"If you look in the refrigerator there's some stuff mom sent; baloney, good cheese, grapes, and some fresh bread on the counter. Maybe you'll share with Gregg?"

Izzy spun around to their corner of the room, blinking furiously behind his horn rimmed frames.

"You scared the crap out of me! Where did you come from?"

"Hell?"

J.D. laughed like the devil that Gregg really wanted him to be. It would make things so much easier to keep him consigned to a neat little box marked with a big fat X. But no, it wasn't that easy and such complications weren't helping him keep all the snakes and worms slithering out of the gray matter lately.

"Actually, Gregg and I were just discussing Rick's opinion that our little morgue visit came compliments of the Chinese doing a psyops overachiever thing—you know, because those short guys have to compensate somehow, Napoleon complex or whatever you call it. But if it's not them, and we're dealing instead with some whacko of our own—"

"I'd say more like an entire lock down unit from what we saw." Gregg was glad to pick up the thread and switch from personal to professional dealings. "Izzy and I did consider the possibility of a cult or religious sect being the perpetrators but discounted that theory as being the least likely in this particular scenario."

Izzy schlepped to the table with his coffee and a hastily prepared tray of eats.

"Thanks for the food, J.D. That was thoughtful."

"I have no idea what came over me."

Izzy put together a sandwich and handed it to Gregg. J.D. waved away a similar offering and got down to business.

"Okay, let's hear your theories. Izzy, you start. Educate me."

"Very well." Izzy touched his temple with his forefinger, reminding Gregg of the Scarecrow launching into the Pythagorean Theorem upon receiving his brain. "As you probably know from your own training, profiling has been in order for a long time, at least since the days of Jack the Ripper in the 1880s, when the good doctors George Phillips and Thomas Bond used the crime scene evidence to make predictions about who the killer might be. The whole process about assembling crime scene evidence from victims or witnesses and survivors then results in a description or profile like age, race, sex, and physical traits such as being big or small, strong, left handed, right handed. Then there is the method and manner of killing, frequency, body mutilation or not, or staging the victims' bodies and so forth, and so Gregg and I put together something that also indicates a certain kind of personality and pathology."

"Like the Matesky case," added Gregg.

"Exactly," Izzy said. "Matesky, also known as the Mad Bomber of New York, was profiled by Dr. James Brussel, then New York's Assistant Commissioner of Mental Hygiene. He created a description that said the bomber would be a male in his 50s living in Connecticut, unmarried, foreign, self-educated, and paranoid and that he would have had a vendetta against Con Ed, the initial target in over thirty bombings between 1940 and 1956. Using that profile, the police found him. So, basically, the idea is to create a description of our killer. Personally I like Gregg's perspective over anything classical theory can come up with."

"Gregg?" J.D. prompted, looking at them both a little differently.

Gregg's inner dragon was responding to the sandwich. He wasn't typically one to show off, but if J.D. wanted theories and classroom pontifications, Gregg didn't mind unloading both barrels.

"In a nutshell, how the persona behaves before, during and after the crime event are kinds of behaviors, and behaviors are what a personality does, just as crime scenes and victims show us those behaviors. If this is just a person, not a foreign psyops team effort, then what we are seeing is someone who is able to accomplish on their own what would normally take a team of efficient killers. He would have to be extremely, extremely efficient and organized and methodical and very strong and fast and skilled. He would be a ruthless killing machine acting in a controlled, tactically organized, frenzy. Just think about that." Gregg paused for effect. "He hunts and stalks these victims who themselves are hunter stalkers on the highest order. He methodically kills them, mutilates them in various creative ways which, in his mind at least, approaches an art form. He looks to have a huge ego about who he is and what he is capable of doing to even attempt this kind of event, and from your initial information to the evidence Rick provided, he seems to be escalating the challenge in his hunts and also escalating the level of carnage, shock, and terror inflicted. However, I personally do not see one person remotely capable of sustaining all of this, so 'he' is most likely 'they.'"

"Really?" J.D. tapped his chin, clearly intrigued. "'They' as in you think the killer has an accomplice?"

"It is not entirely unheard of for a killer like this to have an accomplice or partner, but if you are looking for a psychotic killer who could be one of our own, with an accomplice scenario you would then be looking for two psychotic killers working in tandem and living in close enough proximity to plan, then execute their strategy of murdering a targeted patrol without raising suspicion. Repeatedly. What are the chances of all these factors coming together to support such a theory?" Gregg pinched his thumb and forefinger together. "About this much, if you ask me."

"Or me," Izzy agreed. "Therefore, the most logical explanation has already been offered by Rick, that this has to be a team. And this team is almost certainly a Chinese or Russian organized psyops operation that is utilizing a highly trained band of killers for a mission that it is succeeding magnificently well."

"Which also indicates that the best and most logical course of action would be for a team of highly trained experts like Rick to go after the opposing team of assailants that the evidence presented points to," Gregg concluded.

"I concur with Doctor Kelly." Izzy whipped off his glasses. "If this is one guy it is Superman. If it's one guy with an accomplice, it's Batman and Robin. And, as we all know, outside a comic book, they simply do not exist."

19

An impressive entry gate with a sweeping arch overhead announced in English and Vietnamese: Peace Mission Hospital. The turquoise Chevy convertible glided beneath the arch and continued along a long, curving drive with J.D. in the driver's seat, Nikki and Robert David squeezed into the front with him, Margie sandwiched between Gregg and Izzy in the back. All in all a very handsome group en route to a party and dressed for the occasion.

The aloha shirts with vibrant flowers that Gregg had scored for him and Izzy matched everyone's moods. Maybe especially his and Izzy's moods, Gregg thought, since J.D. had not challenged their "Ghost Soldier" analysis that got the ball out of their court and into the one where it really belonged: J.D.'s and Rick's and any other higher powers that snagged a piece of the action for covert psyops missions. Two just graduated shrinks from California and New York were more than happy to pitch in with the analysis end of things, contribute what brains and skills they possessed to extinguish a group of monsters that were going after their own guys in uniform. But—and this was a very big BUT—such assistance did not extend to further examining dismembered, decomposing remains and/or praying they made it back to the 99KO alive before getting bit by a deadly snake or witnessing a murder outside the wire.

The relief was so enormous that Gregg had not only slept through the night, he slept so peacefully and deep that he hadn't even heard his alarm.

And now, as they swept past the lawns and flowered grounds of an old French country estate, he felt not only rested but delivered from a living nightmare into a waking dream. The red tiled roofs, light blue shutters, and white stucco exteriors could have been anywhere in the South of France with the mission house proper, Matisse's home. Around the old bright red painted door were huge pots of geraniums in brilliant whites and reds. Bougainvillea plants climbed up the walls creating an effect like something out of a nine-teenth-century watercolor painting.

"It's beautiful!" Margie exclaimed, leaning even closer to Izzy and looking as sunny as her pale, yellow dress while they all piled out from J.D.'s magic carpet ride.

"Y'all are the best to let me tag along." Nikki impulsively gave J.D., Izzy, and Robert David a kiss on the cheek, then a big hug to Gregg.

"Better not let Rick see you doing that," he teased Nikki. "That is one hombre I would not want to make jealous."

"I do like him," Nikki admitted. "He treated me so nice and said such nice things in his letter it makes me wish I could see him again sooner than. . . well, I take it he's not sure since he's training some new troops and doing some kind of scouting, but he said he's work-ing on it. That's probably for the best since I'm working on a few things myself. At any rate, thanks for delivering his letter, Gregg."

"My pleasure, ma'am, my pleasure." Gregg pretended to tip his hat as he emulated Rick's initial attempt to impress her. Nikki laughed and gave him a wink. It made Gregg wonder yet again what kind of torturous childhood had twisted someone with so much going for them to get involved with anyone who didn't treat them nice. Nikki made "nice" sound special, like it was something earned rather than an intrinsic right to have.

The French doors fronting the mission opened and Kate rushed out to greet them, followed by a dapper looking middle-aged man Gregg presumed to be the mission's director Dr. Donnelly, the head surgeon who had overseen the mission for nearly two decades, and a very attractive much younger thirty-something woman who had to be Shirley, his new wife.

Gregg didn't know a lot about them, but Kate had said she deeply respected Donnelly and adored Shirley, so Gregg was really looking forward to meeting them both.

He just hadn't expected Shirley to be so young and vivacious and extraordinarily pretty. She was already taken, of course, but it was something of a relief to Gregg to have another woman command his attention for a change while Kate was in the same vicinity.

Introductions made and the guests warmly received, Shirley insisted, "While all of you make yourselves at home and see the grounds, I'll prepare some refreshments—let's say gin and tonics all around with appetizers on the veranda, in an hour?"

Upon their hearty collective approval of that, Shirley disappeared while Dr. Donnelly clapped his hands. "It is nice to have an ordered universe, isn't it? Now let's have the mandatory tour with the boring old man, along with Kate who we all know is anything but boring."

Their little troop followed Donnelly through a winding garden path, Kate bringing up the rear with whispers exchanged between her and J.D. Gregg could feel his heart literally sinking while he pretended not to notice as they approached the first of the hospital's wards. Each of the smaller buildings were separate wards in clean white stucco buildings with blue shutters and more flowers and screen doors to allow the natural flow of air. One unit was for surgery and surgical recovery, one for pediatrics, and another for obstetrics and maternity, which was where they started.

"Kate it is your show," said Dr. Donnelly, "take over the tour here, please."

Kate led them into a bright airy space and for the first time Gregg wondered if, at least professionally, she had made the right decision to come here. It was hard to believe she could be happier anywhere else in the world as she introduced the Vietnamese nursing staff and walked their visiting entourage through the maternity ward. From there she tour-guided them to the next white stucco building, where it seemed they had entered another world.

Displayed on one wall were childish paintings, many disturbing; while on another wall was a mural with rainbows, flowers, birds, and children flying through a bright sky with clouds shaped like bears and tigers and elephants.

Izzy stopped at the foot of a small bed where a boy smiled and lifted two stumps that had once been his arms. The little girl in the bed next to him had only one arm and only half of her face left. The other side was covered with burns.

Gregg walked right into the back of Izzy, deliberately bumping him. The little girl laughed.

"Oh no," Gregg said playfully, while inside he could only think, *oh god no.*

"Oh no!" The little girl repeated back to him. "Oh no!" And she laughed again.

Gregg walked into Izzy again and slapped his head, exclaiming, "Oh no!"

Now, both the kids were laughing. Izzy caught on to the game and walked ahead two steps then suddenly stopped again so Gregg bumped right into him. "Oh, no!" said Izzy this time, and both the kids were joined with two other little girls, laughing, their arms waving, no legs.

Izzy stepped, stepped, stopped one last time and when Gregg bumped into him they both fell down on the floor.

All the kids were on the edge of their beds now as Gregg rolled his eyes and conducted them in a chorus of: "Oh! No!"

"I had no idea I would get two professional circus clowns today," said Kate, with an emphasis on *clowns*. But rather than punch a bully out and invite him to do the same, Kate went down the line and named each small patient, from, "Six-year-old Diu and her sister An, and this little guy Trang is five years old. . . . "

And on she continued down the row of beds of maimed, burned, and disfigured Vietnamese children. Then up the row on the other side, the same.

Robert David grimaced. "Kate, so many."

"Yes, so many mines and napalm bombs, so little time."

J.D. picked up a ball from the floor that had rolled away from a little boy with a blanket over his legs and spun it like a Harlem Globetrotter on one finger.

He crouched down and held the spinning ball in front of the delighted boy.

Gregg heard J.D. say something in Vietnamese and the boy held out his arms. J.D. rolled the ball toward the boy and he rolled it back. Back and forth, back and forth, the game was on and even as the blanket fell away to reveal two stumps the boy's smile got bigger and bigger.

J.D. said something else in Vietnamese and the boy nodded, smiling broadly. J.D. tucked the blanket back around him and patted his head.

"What did you say to him?" Gregg asked. He had hung back, watching, while everyone else followed Kate to the next ward.

"Just that he was my little friend and I would come back to play with him."

"You actually have a nice way with kids." Gregg had to grudgingly give him that. He then thought of Kate, of the bastard who got her knocked up during her semester in France, and the consequences of a back room abortion.

"Thanks, Gregg. Plenty around here to adopt." J.D. pretended to dribble a ball and toss it into a basketball hoop.

The little girl Gregg had won over giggled and squealed, "Oh no!"

This time Gregg didn't mind that J.D. had stolen yet another girl's affections.

They quickly caught up with the rest of the group, just entering the next bright airy building. Here there were wounded men, mostly amputees, and burn victims. Several were gathered near a bandaged middle-aged man on a bed in a corner. Upon seeing the visitors their bodies stiffened and they went silent.

"These men are all doctors and my guests," Dr. Donnelly hastened to explain, then spoke some Vietnamese that caused the injured men to visibly relax before he made introductions, specifically to the man holding court.

"I'd like you to all meet my old and dear friend Professor Nguyen. The professor was one of my father's students and is a colleague in tropical medicine."

The silver haired professor had eyes of warmth and great intelligence, Gregg thought. He was very evidently a man of stature and strength in his late fifties, looking fit and robust except for the bandages around his chest.

Robert David stepped forward to shake his hand. "It is indeed a great honor to meet you, Professor. I remember well your paper on consciousness and malaria when you were with the Pasteur Institute here. Are you still with the Institute, Sir?"

The professor acknowledged the compliment with a gracious nod of his head.

"My research, I am afraid, has been interrupted of late with. . . " he gestured around at the beds filled with other Vietnamese patients, "shall we call it extended research and practice in the field? But I am so very flattered that you remember me and it is a great pleasure to meet you, Dr. Thibeaux. And you. . .and you. . . "

He shook each of their hands in turn.

Gregg noticed that Kate shifted uncomfortably, glancing at J.D. with something akin to a silent ... plea? The exchange happened so fast Gregg would have thought he imagined it, except for the subtle nod J.D. gave in return.

"Professor, could you join us for dinner later?" invited Dr. Donnelly.

"Yes, please do," insisted Robert David, equally oblivious to whatever dynamics were bouncing between Kate and J.D.

Gregg darted a glance towards Izzy. He was just as clearly oblivious to everything but Margie in her yellow sun dress, touching his arm.

The professor agreed and Kate suddenly clapped her hands, announcing, "Who's ready for those nice G and T's on the veranda that Shirley must have waiting for us?"

That was all the incentive everyone needed to move on and quick, as Kate no doubt intended, with the exception of J.D.

When he lingered, so did Gregg.

J.D. bowed respectfully then spoke to the professor in Vietnamese, their conversation short but cordial, before J.D. said in English, "The wise man bends like the bamboo in the wind."

"Yes," agreed Professor Nguyen. "As you know, war changes all."

J.D. nodded. "I hope your family is well and that your recovery here is speedy. Please extend my greetings to your eldest son."

"I will." The professor then concluded their little chat by saying, "Dr. Kelly, perhaps you will tell me more about yourself over our coffee, after dinner."

Their pleasantries done, Gregg asked J.D. after they left the room, "Do you know his family?"

"Yes. His son and I were classmates." J.D. paused, then added, "It's a good thing the mission does here, turning no one away."

And that's when Gregg realized. "His extended research in the field. . .?"

"We should all be as civilized as Colonel Nguyen. By the way, I never saw him here and neither did you."

✳

Lounging on the veranda under a lazy fan made Izzy feel as if he was on a southern plantation in a distant time. He felt so dreamlike that Dr. Donnelly's collection of Jungian works had induced him to relax back on the rattan couch and leisurely thumb through the semi-autobiographical, *Memories, Dreams, Reflections.*

He knew she was there before he looked up. Even in her fatigues Margie always smelled like honeysuckle and lemon; wearing a dress the same color, she smelled closer to heaven, which presently landed Izzy in a pleasant sort of hell.

"Jung, huh," she said, sitting right beside him, even though they had the whole couch. "And here I thought you classical guys wrote him off as a voodoo man."

"Well, uh, I. . .uh. . . " It was really hard to focus with her sitting so close and smelling so good, and if he didn't know better he'd think she might be flirting with him. Glamorous women like Margie never flirted with guys like him. Actually, he hadn't dated much beyond Rachel who was brilliant and opinionated and pretty in a Joan Baez kind of way—especially with her new straight hair and Indian headband picture—so Margie was way outside his realm of experience. Izzy could even feel himself blushing, which made him even more self-conscious and that seemed to make him start sweating all over the newest letter he had stuffed inside his shirt and— "Hey!"

Izzy rubbed the warm spot on his arm, where Margie had playfully punched him. She grinned and he found himself grinning back, then she laughed and he laughed, too.

"That was an excellent intervention. I'll have to remember that technique." Izzy commanded himself to focus on Jung, the subject at hand, and not on the urge to touch Margie's face, her neck, just anywhere he could make a tactile connection. "And yes, most of my professors would have thought him a voodoo man but personally, now that I am actually in a world of good and evil and synchronicity and waking dreams—like dream girls sitting next to me in exotic tropical settings—I think Jung may have more than a little credibility. What about you?"

"Jung totally works for me here. I've seriously thought about going over to Switzerland for a training course at the Institute once my tour of duty is up."

Izzy couldn't get over how many colors were in her hazel eyes, the brown and gold flecks competing with the most amazing shade of green. He also couldn't get over the fact he had successfully managed to get in a smooth line with a gorgeous girl who wasn't anything like Rachel. *Rachel.* Now how would he feel if she was flirting with another guy, the way he was flirting with Margie? He wouldn't like it. So no more flirting; but it was a really good feeling to talk to a beautiful woman who spoke his language and he could indulge himself that much.

"I've always wanted to go to Switzerland," he confessed, "Well, after Spain. Though I suppose choosing between the two is like 'the pendulum of the mind operating between sense and nonsense, not between right and wrong.'"

Margie threw back her head and laughed, and oh man, did she have a great neck. "You did not make that up! Jung said that."

"I know. I was just testing you."

Margie put her hand out. "Let's shake on that. You and me. Before or after Spain. Switzerland, Jungian Institute. "

Even if it was pretend Izzy knew he should say something about checking with Rachel or bringing her along, but that would spoil the moment and he had become acutely aware of how priceless an unspoiled moment like this was, and so he gripped her extended hand.

He could feel a fine tremor in his but this was different; he was enjoying the rush.

"Agreed, but only if there's snow."

"And skiing," Margie said, upping the ante.

"Ice skating," Izzy shot back.

"Snowmen," she said softly.

Izzy realized he still had her hand and his thumb had found her palm. And like a snow man he was melting because she was so close he could smell her breath, the lingering hint of lime from the cocktail they had earlier consumed. For an endless moment he thought of kissing her. She wanted him to, her eyes said so. Every instinct he possessed demanded he act on the invitation. Just a kiss, it would only be a kiss, and Rachel would never know....

But he would. Maybe it was a good thing Margie was leaving in eighty-two days. She was here and Rachel was not, and that simply wasn't fair to the fiancé who had sent him letters almost daily since he left for training camp, filled with clippings, even apartment ads, and would someday have their babies. Babies she would nurture with love and art and music; babies that wouldn't be fried from

Napalm bombs or have their faces disfigured or stumps for arms and legs. Their children would play in ball fields, not killing fields, and no matter how tempting to put his hands and his mouth all over Margie, his intellect was getting the say over his emotions. Because that's who Israel Moskowitz was raised to be, and he could not lose sight of his moral compass even if his sense of direction had never been less clear.

Izzy quickly let go of Margie's hand and tried to cover the awkward pause with a feigned cough. Margie was the first to speak.

"You know Jung also said, 'Often the hands will solve a mystery that the intellect has struggled with in vain.' Methinks you think too much, Dr. Moskowitz."

"Hey, do I hear people talking about ice skating and skiing out here?" Kate's timing was either as good or as bad as it got as she appeared with a tray of glasses and the rest of the gang on her heels. "It just so happens I have some nice hot chocolate—oh, wait, looks like someone switched trays. Any objections to champagne before dinner instead?"

A chorus of whoops went up as Kate headed for the table that had been set for their special occasion on the veranda, a lazy rattan fan overhead subtly cooling the air as the crystal flutes were lined up and the crystal liquid flowed into the glasses, bubbles rising like tiny prisms in the shafts of sunset light, piercing the cool shade.

Shirley tapped her glass, bringing Izzy back to the present and everyone into the moment. "Please, everyone." Shirley raised her glass. "May all your joys be pure joys. And all your pain champagne."

It was the perfect toast for a perfect evening that unfolded like a beautiful play in which they all had a part. Dinner was perfect. The company and coffee they shared with Professor Nguyen was perfect. The path they strolled across illuminated by the candles in paper bags that created a soft warm orange light under the stars was perfect.

And the fireworks were like the perfect exclamation point on the night as across the bay flares suddenly shot up into the sky. Perhaps it was the dreaminess of it all that made them first think it was fireworks. But then the concuss of an explosion came across the water. There were more explosions before a huge fountain of flames lit the clouds and brightened the whole night yellow and orange.

"That's the jet fuel storage at the airbase!" Robert David shouted over the whistling explosion. "*Dammit. Dr. Donnelly, Shirley, thank you—*"

"Nikki, you stay," Margie instructed, the Captain checking back in. "It's safer here."

"Margie, you should stay too," Kate hastily insisted.

"Can't. I have to go back with the guys." Margie grabbed Izzy's hand and they started running with Gregg and Robert David and J.D., all of them racing for the Chevy and whatever awaited them at the 99KO.

20

Inside the unit was bedlam. Patients were screaming and crying while corpsmen and specialists got everybody out of bed and onto the floor. Gregg rushed over to help wrestle a patient out of his restraints and down to the ground. Margie immediately jumped in to help Kohn prepare extra med shots to sedate the patients. The emergency lighting kept going on and off from parachute flares, creating a weird strobe light effect augmented by waving flashlights and bursts of yellow and red from explosion after explosion.

They were under a major rocket attack. In the midst of the screams Margie shouted, "J.D., Izzy, somebody, help us!"

Izzy was in mid-injection and saw Margie and Hertz being overpowered by the patient they were trying to wrest to the floor. Quicker than he could pull out the needle Izzy saw Margie's head rock back as she took a fist in the face. Blood gushed from her nose and upper lip but she still managed to yell, "Benadryl here stat! Stat! Come on, we are losing him—he's going to get away!"

Suddenly it was all dark, the lights completely gone. No explosions, just Margie crying, "Shit, shit, shit where is he? Where's Berrigan?" while Hertz panted, "I can't see him. I lost him. Shit, shit. . ."

Then Robert David's calm voice called out in the dark, "Corporal Berrigan, come on son, call out. I will come over to you, no one will hurt you." Silence. Robert David again, "Come on out son, call out."

More rockets exploded in answer, the momentary respite just that, a moment, and all hell broke loose again while Colonel Kohn ordered, "Down, down, get down! More incoming, get down now!"

In the dark, Izzy tried crawling over to Margie only for a flailing leg to knock his glasses off while he felt a hand grasp his foot and pull. He wanted to get the hand off of him but he didn't kick just in case it was Berrigan, the one who got loose, which would at least keep him away from Margie.

Patients were crying and screaming inside; outside there were more screams as medics and soldiers who were running for cover got hit.

And just like that, silence outside. Even the patients quieted down. The emergency lights flickered back on. Dim, but ample to see what and who was where.

"Margie?" Colonel Kohn said gently, "Margie, are you okay? I think you are going to need stitches."

There was no response. Izzy felt around for his glasses. The hand let go of his foot. He didn't look to see who had held it, just started crawling on all fours in Margie's direction, where she was on the floor and leaning up against the wall. She stared straight ahead, unblinking in the pretty lemonade yellow dress splattered red, and for a horrifying moment Izzy thought she might be dead, she was so unnaturally still.

Sergeant Washington was already there with a blanket, saying, "Cap'n? Come on girl, you okay, Sarge is right here." Still no response. Izzy crawled faster.

"She's in shock," Sergeant Washington said, lifting her up in his arms, "Stay with us here girl, you goin' to be okay."

"Sergeant, you and Bayer get her on a bed," Colonel Kohn directed. "Robert David you cut and stitch. Right away now."

"I'll do it," Izzy insisted, then adjusted his tone. "That is, I'd appreciate you letting me take care of her. If you and Robert David don't mind."

"Fine, fine," Kohn agreed. "Okay, the all clear is blowing. Let's get everybody up and in bed and settled back in and—goddamn it, now where the hell is Corporal Berrigan? Did he get out?"

Gregg and J.D. stood guard by the exit doors. "Nobody got by here," Gregg answered. He stopped. "Oh no."

Noises were coming out of the bathroom. Hertz, the nearest, got to his feet and slowly opened the door, wide enough for everyone to see Berrigan standing in the toilet. He had a fork poised near a bare light socket. The bulb that had been in it still rolled on the floor. In Berrigan's other hand was another fork. Hertz rushed in, calling over his shoulder, "I've got him—"

"NOOO!" Gregg shouted as Hertz grabbed Berrigan to pull him out of the toilet. Berrigan violently raised and lowered his right arm, stabbing right down into Hertz's skull while he jabbed the other fork into the socket, just as the juice to the whole hospital came back on, all the lights brighter than bright and all the electricity coming right down through the fork in the socket and relayed through Berrigan standing in the toilet water. Both men were shaking and dancing while blood sprayed from the fork prongs in Hertz's skull, until they both collapsed.

"Oh god, oh god, oh god," Gregg cried, racing alongside J.D. to pull out Hertz, his body still smoking on the floor. Robert David and Bayer were right behind them, grabbing Berrigan, slumped over the sink, his legs burned black.

Their attempts at CPR were futile but Gregg was still trying to resuscitate Hertz when J.D. gripped his pumping fist.

"He's gone, Gregg. Let him go."

Gregg's head fell forward and his shoulders shook.

Izzy couldn't tear his gaze away from the whole macabre tableau. He gripped Margie to him, wrapped in a blanket with blood running from her lip and nose and tears running out of her eyes and onto her party dress. Sergeant Washington gently stroked her hair, started whispering again, "You be okay, girl, you be okay. . . ."

As if from a great distance, Izzy noticed most of the other corpsmen and specialists were all staring too in a stunned silence, while some of the patients made pitiful sounds and others drew into the fetal position and covered their heads.

Bayer was openly weeping. Robert David put his arm around him and bowed his head. Colonel Kohn pulled up a chair right behind them and for a while just let his palms rest on their backs, his own head bowed, just shaking and shaking it.

When the Colonel looked up his face was weary but his voice steady.

"All right, all right now, 99KO, we have patients here, we have people to take care of—"

The door flew open and Peck just then showed up, huffing and puffing, eyes bugging out and shirt torn like he'd broken through enemy lines and dodged mortar fire to belatedly get to the unit.

"Uh, Colonel, we . . . Holy fucking Christ in hell, are they dead?" Peck backed up against the wall, his eyes riveted on the electrocuted remains.

Colonel Kohn stood up. "Take it easy, Major. We are holding on here; what is happening out there?"

"The OG grabbed me on the way in, said we might have a ground attack and HQ wants everybody not critical out and armed on the perimeter. I told him I'd deliver the orders to our unit."

Colonel Kohn shut his eyes and took a moment, then resolutely issued orders.

"Okay then, Gregg, Izzy, Bayer, and J.D., take off and get your weapons. Specialist Jackson, alert the rest of the unit in the hootch. Sergeant Washington, you and Robert David and I will secure the immediate premises and see to the patients. Peck, you call the morgue and tell them we have casualties, then get your weapon and go wherever you're needed on the perimeter, too. Let's just get through the night and pray to God we do not have a ground attack. Hold together people, hold together and get moving."

When Kohn saw Izzy hesitate, he came over and privately whispered, "I'm sorry, Izzy, but orders are orders. I have mine and now you have yours. I promise we'll take good care of her."

Reluctantly Izzy nodded. And then he did what he'd never forgive himself for not doing if there was a ground attack and there was no tomorrow: He kissed Margie. It was just beside her temple where he could taste the wet salt on her skin. He could smell the tinny scent of the blood still running from her lip and nose but what he inhaled was the memory of honeysuckle and lemons.

✳

The night was clear and calm now. No wind. The stars shone brightly, only to suddenly be obliterated by the burning orange glow of flares illuminating the whole hospital compound and casting sharp edged shadows everywhere.

Bayer was too much of a mess to be much help so J.D. paired off with him and Gregg had to admit if anyone could keep him safe it would be J.D. He and Izzy most definitely were not the guys you wanted to be with for safekeeping in the event of a ground attack.

Still dressed in their Aloha shirts they sat together side-by-side holding M16s and wearing web belts and holsters with pistols they had no idea what to do with either except for some minimal training at Fort Sam Houston. More flares lit up their faces and as if by common accord, they looked at each other again. It was like they were all they had and Gregg supposed that much was true. As true as the haunted memory they now shared of what happened in the hospital unit that had seemed like a haven after the firebase and the morgue. Not anymore. They were both wearing helmets to go with all their artillery, their party attire now covered in Hertz's and Margie's blood and dusted with the dirt from the bunker they were cowering in together.

K.O. lay next to Izzy, her head in his lap.

"She always seems to know who is the most scared and who to comfort," Izzy whispered as if the VC might hear.

And who knew? Maybe the Ghost Soldier himself was close enough to take off both their heads faster than Berrigan had stabbed a fork into Hertz's skull.

"Then she is making her first missed diagnosis of the whole war," Gregg whispered back, "because you cannot be more scared or freaked out than I am right now."

"Wanna bet? Dinner at Henri's on the loser if we make it to morning. K.O., who is most scared, me or Gregg?"

She lifted her head to lick Izzy's hand.

"See? She knows, and I will start with the white wine shrimp..." A whistling mortar made a shrill landing just outside the compound perimeter they had been sent out to guard. "I never thought, I mean ever, *ever* thought I would be doing this."

"Look on the bright side. With all the casualties coming in, even if there isn't a ground attack they'll be pulling all the medical docs into the ER in about 30 minutes and that'll at least get you out of this bunker."

"At least then I could do something I know how to do. I mean, what the hell am I doing holding this thing like I'm a commando or something?"

"You tell me. I didn't even have a BB gun growing up." Gregg stared at the rifle in his hands. "Honestly, I'd have a better chance of fending off the enemy with my surfboard."

Another mortar hit, only closer, and they both jumped.

"Gregg, could there really be a ground attack here? At the hospital?"

"Yeah, there could be. There was one during the Tet holiday last year. I'm sure you must have read about it. The NVA had planned it for months, timing it so all the Vietnamese were traveling to go home for their big new year holiday, then *boom*, the NVA hit every-where at once with everything they had. They almost took over the whole country. Hell, even Saigon got overrun. But you know all this already, right? Remember the battle at the Embassy?"

Izzy nodded, just slightly. "I remember. But, you know back home you read that stuff and it doesn't really mean anything. Even the front page of the *New York Times* can scream 'Tet Offensive, Saigon Overrun and Ground Attack!' and you never for a moment imagine that there are real people being overrun and that overrun means the Indians are running over the walls and through the fort and want to kill everyone."

Izzy took a deep breath and K.O. licked his hand again.

"I know," Gregg agreed, not even caring if Izzy had K.O. for now because at least he wasn't alone in this scary stinking hole they had no business being in. "I mean, who would even think about what it feels like to be out on a perimeter fence like this, looking into the dark where there's probably somebody who actually does know what they are doing and can cut right through or wiggle under and just come right at us? And to think just a year ago I was so worried and concerned about getting Jefferson Airplane tickets. Yeah, that was a big worry and I was interviewing for a job at Pepperdine, another big worry." He thought then of Hertz, who would never have the chance to be so self-indulgent. "You know, I really liked Hertz, a lot. He was a good, smart guy, and he was planning to go to college when he got out of here. I'm glad you were there for his birthday. He really dug your music. And I'm glad Rick gave him that bottle of Jack, too. I hope Hertz drank every drop, I hope—"

Another rocket shrieked overhead and landed somewhere on the airbase and the ground shook like an earthquake.

K.O. licked Gregg's cheek then rested her head in his lap.

"Thank you, girl," he whispered, "Thank you."

21

The stars were bright overhead, but the explosions brighter as the concuss of the rockets and mortars carried across the calm waters of the bay to the mission's veranda, where Kate, Nikki, and Shirley waited—for what, none of them were sure.

"I feel like I should be there, not here," Nikki said, nervously shaking her foot.

"There is nothing you can do really," Kate reminded her. "Except take care of yourself now so you can be there when they need you after this is over."

"I guess you're right. It's just that almost everyone I really care about is in some kind of danger over there."

Kate knew the feeling. But she refused to think of anything bad happening, especially to Gregg or J.D. Instead she asked Shirley, "Do you think there's any chance they might attack here, at the mission?"

"No." Shirley shook her head. "We have more than God on our side."

Kate realized she must be referring to their "turn no one away" policy which included Professor Nguyen. The relief Kate had felt when she realized J.D. had no intentions of turning him in had been too profound to continue pretending she could actually be some kind of informant for Phillip. The Mission was like Switzerland refusing to take sides and ratting anyone out contradicted everything the people she worked with stood for. These were good people with a purpose. They had made her start wondering about her own purpose in life.

Far off they heard a siren.

"That's the all clear," Nikki said, a sigh of relief.

"Finally," breathed Kate.

"No, not finally," Shirley corrected. "Maybe. Sometimes they stop and then wait for the all clear and once the Americans go out to get their wounded and come out of their bunkers, they attack again."

"I wish Rick was there to help them," Nikki said. "All those Viet Cong would skedaddle and quick if he and his men showed up."

Kate was happy to take that ball and run with it; anything to keep her mind off what could be happening this very moment across the bay.

"So, are you and Rick an item now?"

"Too soon to call it that, but. . ." A handwritten letter along with a snapshot of her very handsome new pen pal materialized and Nikki fanned herself with the letter while clearly mooning over the other. "Let's just say he sure does have a way with words. I wrote him right back and he even called me at the Red Cross yesterday. He's got such a dreamy voice, too, I could've listened to him talk for hours."

"Should I take that to mean that Major Peck is out of the picture?"

Nikki took a moment to answer. She traced a line on the letter she held, something that was clearly special to her. "My relationship with Don is complicated but I do realize it is unwise. He hasn't made it easy to break things off." She lifted her left wrist, flashing a bracelet.

Kate had wanted to compliment Nikki on it earlier but with Gregg around, she didn't want to risk the attention boomeranging back to her own new piece of jewelry.

"That's lovely, Nikki." Kate looked closer at the stones, the setting.

"Don said it was elegant, like me. Nobody ever called me elegant before. And no one ever gave me a diamond bracelet before—a platinum one, too! It is beautiful, isn't it? He said it came from Cartier."

Kate nodded even as she weighed the importance of telling Nikki the bracelet couldn't have possibly come from Cartier. To the untrained eye it could pass as a fine piece of jewelry. However, she detected a few tiny bubbles a real gemstone would never have, the craftsmanship was less than perfect, the platinum was almost certainly sterling silver, and the line Nikki had been fed, total bullshit.

"Really? Cartier?" Kate delicately put the possibility out for Nikki to consider. "I wouldn't have guessed that."

"I know, it's amazing, isn't it?"

Nikki clearly wasn't wanting to let go of the notion she had a Cartier bracelet. Since Kate didn't relish the idea of prying it from her dream pool, she went at it another way.

"I can see how Major Peck is making it hard to break things off when he gives you such extravagant gifts, but Nikki, is he really the man you want to be with?"

"Yes, gifts are very nice," Shirley chimed in. "But something like this suggests a more long term commitment than mere dating."

"I know you mean well, Kate." Nikki looked over at Shirley. "You too, Shirley. And yes, you are right about thinking ahead—which I've been doing a lot of lately since Don proposed. Can you believe that? I mean, look at where I come from, and then look at him. He actually said he wanted to marry me, buy me a big, fancy house once we get back to the States, and put a ring on my finger to match all the fine furniture and fancy clothes a wife befitting a man in his position should have. I don't expect either of you ladies to understand but, coming from where I do, what Major Peck has offered me is an awful lot to walk away from."

"Except?" Shirley prompted.

Nikki traced the line on Rick's letter again. Her smile was so radiant she glowed. "Like I said, Captain Galt sure does have a way with words. I feel like he respects me and women in general, in a way that Don just doesn't. Maybe it has something to do with the way they were raised, but they sure do have different choices when it comes to calling me something other than my name."

Kate waited a beat. "And what would that difference be?"

"To put it politely, it's the difference between a sweet little cat and a female dog."

That did it. "Nikki, I hate to tell you this, but that bracelet isn't—"

Before Kate could blow the whistle Dr. Donnelly rushed out of the mission, joined by a renewed onslaught of mortar blasts raining from the sky and guns going off like firecrackers across the bay. It was all mesmerizing in its own crash and burn kind of way even as he delivered the latest news.

"We already have some casualties on their way. Shirley, Kate, we need to get scrubbed up and plan on an all-nighter in surgery. Nikki, I know you aren't a nurse but—"

"I can do more than hold hands and pass out cookies." Nikki was already off the sofa. "I can give out meds, even poke somebody with a needle and stitch in an emergency as long as they don't cry when I do it."

Overhead the stars were bright. The sound of the surf on the beach followed them up the lawn and toward the wounded who would come since they turned no one away.

Water is fluid, soft, and yielding.
But water will wear away rock, which is rigid
and will not yield.
This is another paradox:
What is soft is strong.
—Lao Tzu

Bouquet and Two Oranges Together

CLEANSING

Once I killed the kittens, I felt like I would never get clean after what I did to them all, especially Panda. As you can imagine, it was a lot easier to shoot my stepfather than do that to the kittens and when I finally did kill Bert I felt a lot better, at least until I got out of juvie.

After juvie, things did not ever seem to go so well for a long time after that. I imagined like a lot of kids that if the evil stepfather or the evil stepmother were gone that everything would be great. While I was in juvie I dreamed all the time that I would get home and my mom and my sisters would think I was a hero and would be overjoyed to see me again and somehow we would live in a nice house in the old neighborhood and everybody would be happy ever after.

When you are locked up you have so much time to think about how things are going to be and I would think in just the smallest details of the welcome home cake my mom and sisters would make with gooey chocolate frosting and bright white coconut and yellow letters saying WELCOME HOME HERO. Anyway, instead they lived in a shithole, my mom had become a drunk, or maybe she always had been and now was a worse drunk and my sisters were sluts, fat sluts and they all blamed me. Somehow history had been rewritten to the point that my stepfather had been a great guy who my mom had always loved a lot, we had lived in a great house in a nice neighborhood which he had provided for us and I was a psycho who had ruined everything and was totally responsible for the loss of their great life. So you can imagine the great homecoming I got. No homecoming. Juvie let me out. Nobody came to pick me up. I took a bus home. They were all out at a movie or something.

My mom was ragging my case constantly and really I just got sick of being blamed CONSTANTLY for EVERYTHING THAT

WAS WRONG all the time. My sisters were ALWAYS SCREAM-ING at me. The house was just a stinking pisshole that no one ever cleaned up. I hated the dirt, the filth, my sisters, my mom.

One night, I thought I have got to clean this up. First we can start with painting this place. I cannot go on living like this. I did a good job. I did some careful planning which is always critical in fixing things. I got the primer stuff, I got the paint thinner to clean the brushes, I got the roller pans to put the stuff in and paint rollers, and I got the paint. Somehow I worked out a deal with Mr. Davis down at hardware to get this stuff in exchange for delivery work on weekends. Everyone was real excited about it.

Particularly me, because You know fire is a Cleansing I thought. Out of the ashes, the Phoenix and all that.

Mom's a drunk, everyone knows that and she smokes. Put some lit cigarettes in packets of matches on top of open paint thinner cans. You have to be careful doing this.

We had a gas oven. Maybe she forgot to turn off. Put some paint out on all the floors. . .

I watched from across the street. Most people do not realize that old wood frame houses are almost explosively flammable, actually they are explosive with the oven gas on. I don't think I even heard any screaming but maybe there was.

The best part was I felt good again, like when I killed Bert. Only this was better because I didn't have to go to juvie for cleaning up the dirt.

22

Nikki felt dirty. And, not from the blood and frenzied aftermath of the wounded, many of them children, which had been brought to the mission. She had come to Vietnam as an escape, only to learn you could take the girl out of the hills, but not the hills out of the girl.

She had tried to better herself by doing well enough in school to get accepted to community college, only for her daddy to scoff at the notion since all she apparently needed was a degree from The School of Hard Knocks. Well, she had countered, feeling a bit full of herself she supposed, she should already have a PhD from that particular school considering how many times she had been back-handed for daring to speak up and want more than milking cows, tending fields, and a flour sack for a Sunday best dress.

Her daddy didn't know what a PhD was, so that just made him madder. Made him even more sure she thought herself too good for the rest of them, her third cousin who wanted to marry her included, and since that was the case—*whap*—then she'd better pack her things and not show her face again until she had one of them PhDs herself.

Nikki knew she wasn't nearly as stupid as what she had been told, but she also knew attaining a PhD was beyond her mental ability and fiscal means to manage. It had taken her seven years to work her way through night school for the bachelor's degree she needed to sign up with the Red Cross to "bring a touch of home in a combat zone." She had gotten so excited upon seeing the recruitment ad, asking "Are you creative? Could you develop an interesting program on travel, holidays, sports, music, or current events? The American Red Cross needs qualified young women who are willing to serve one year overseas." Then it said among the qualifications the job required considerable ingenuity and a capacity for hard work under far less than ideal conditions.

Well heck, that made her qualified and then some, and here was the opportunity to make a yearly salary of $4800 and get paid to see the world! Then the next thing she knew, she had landed herself something even higher than a PhD: a psychiatrist whose family included a US senator that could have surely gotten him out of serving in Vietnam—only Dr. Donald Peck the Third had wanted to sign up.

Don said it was because he wanted to be valued for himself and what he could contribute to humanity rather than be constantly judged by what everyone perceived his family to be and therefore him.

She could relate to that.

He said that they were kindred spirits that way. That their families didn't understand them, but they understood each other.

Agreed again.

Don had said a lot of things that she could relate to. So when he pushed her around the first time, she told herself it was just a little accidental shove and nothing compared to what she had grown up with. The second time, though, was more than a shove. That's when she began to wonder if a psychiatrist could work other people's brains to make them believe things they shouldn't. Like when he called her a bitch and she protested, he turned it around to make her seem like a prude because he liked that kind of talk in bed.

Still, despite it all, she wanted to believe in his good intentions, even if the truth probably was that she just didn't want one more man to let her down.

Meeting Rick had made her stop and think, but Don's surprise proposal reminded her she had practical matters to consider:

Wasn't a bird in hand worth two in the bush? And who knew where anything with Rick would end up, she hardly knew him.

Nikki looked at the clock in hers and Margie's apartment, the one they had bought together at a local market and hung up over the entry door as a joke because on the hour it chimed "Cuckoo-cuckoo."

Margie said it was a reminder that once she clocked out and walked in the front door, she could be as crazy as she wanted minus the patients. She loved that clock.

But she couldn't stand Don. Margie was taking her turn working the night shift and wouldn't like it that Don was showing up without her here. She didn't want much to do with him, almost nobody did, which had a lot to do with Nikki not rebuffing his interest. She knew how it felt to be an outsider.

The Cuckoo clock signaled 8 p.m., that was 20 hundred hours in military time, and she could see why Don, despite his faults—*and didn't everyone have them?*—actually liked being in the army. He liked precision, and being a stickler for punctuality, sure enough there he was, doing a "Shave and a Haircut," right on time.

Nikki still wasn't quite sure how she was going to go about this. She opened the door anyway since, after all, she had done the inviting once the onslaught of casualties had died down.

"Baby!" he greeted her, and before she could say a word he was bending her back against a strong, supporting arm while his free hand held aloft a spray of flowers and some very fine wine he had introduced her to.

Nikki knew she should immediately break the kiss, but darn, he was an awfully good kisser and this would probably be the last one she was getting from Don. Meanwhile she used the time to consider the best approach to keep things civil.

Mad as she was for him giving her a fake piece of jewelry and claiming it real, it was still the nicest piece of jewelry anyone had ever given her before.

And could be someone had sold him a bad piece that he had paid too much for and lacked Kate's knowledge to realize he was being taken for a fool. Yes, that could definitely be.

Having decided she was going to politely return the bracelet rather than throw it in his face, Nikki broke the kiss.

"Don, we need to talk." She said it firmly, taking control of the situation before he could since he had quite a way of doing that.

"But I'd much rather make love, not war. God, you are the best thing I've seen since all hell broke loose. I've missed you so much." He was smoothly moving toward the couch, trying to take the conversation in a direction she was not going. "C'mon, baby, we can talk later. About my grandmother's ring, getting you all dolled up to meet my family, about—"

"Don, I've decided that's not a good idea." She kept her feet planted. Unlatched the bracelet, extended it. "I'm really sorry, but I shouldn't have accepted this. You should take it back and ask for a refund. Or save it and give to another girl who can properly return your affections."

"Return my affections?" His face turned beet red all of a sudden, like a light switch that got flipped. "What, are you kidding? You didn't have any trouble returning 'my affections' on the island. Or the night after that. What's gotten into you?"

Nikki instinctively backed away, closer to the door. She did not want an ugly confrontation or to put him on the defensive. That much she had learned from her backhanding daddy. She also knew that even if Don hit her in retaliation, she had to end this. She might never have one of them PhDs much less MD's herself, but she was not so stupid, or so ambitious, as to agree to marry a man she didn't really love just to shove the equivalent of a Whoopie Pie into her daddy's face by marrying up into a family who would probably hate her on sight.

When she took too long to answer the sound of exploding glass hit the cuckoo clock with such force it fell from over the door and almost hit Nikki on the head.

She surveyed the burgundy splash of wine, looking way too much like blood, all over the front door, the damaged clock at her feet, and demanded, "Why'd you do that? Margie loves that clock! And that's a waste of good wine."

"Did Galt get into you? Huh? Did he get into your pants while I was saving lives in the E.R.? I'll kill that son of a bitch, I'll—"

"No he did not, and no you won't." Nikki flung open the front door and pointed in the direction of the best decision she felt certain she had ever made. Even if she never got married, Don had just verified she was better off being a spinster than married to him or anyone like him. "You will leave now, Dr. Peck. I tried to do this nicely. You don't want to be nice. And I don't want to marry any man who lacks kindness. Or class." She shot a scathing look at the bracelet he had thrown on the floor. "Good night. And goodbye."

He stared at her with his eyes kind of wild and his breathing fast, for endless, heart-palpitating seconds. Then he kicked the clock so hard it exploded with a final "Cuck...coo" and died before he nearly took the door off its hinges with his exiting *slam*.

Nikki quickly locked the door. She shut every open window and locked those too. She didn't care how hot it got in the apartment.

Then she went and poured herself a tall, icy glass of lemonade and hit it up with a big shot of gin straight from the bottle, no jigger.

She would pray for whatever forgiveness was due for her vices or misjudgments later, but for now she was celebrating.

Major Doctor Donald Peck was out of her life, and this time for good. That called for some Elvis on the record player while she reread Rick's latest letter as proof that a bird in the bush was far better than anything from Donald Peck on her hand.

*

Izzy had never needed a letter from home more than he needed this one. In the days that had passed since the attack he had been immersed in mangled, burned bodies. He could not even imagine the additional damage and loss of life from an actual ground attack when so much was lost and beyond damaged already.

Margie would physically heal, and she was resilient, but a lot of other damage on top of more damage had been done and he hadn't been around much to lend what support he could. Mostly he'd gotten his information from Gregg who was in not such good shape himself. Even Robert David seemed to have had something vital leeched from his internal resources. The only thing that seemed to have been spared was their villa; miraculously untouched again. And the mission, but that was "sanctuary" and so Izzy supposed that didn't count on some level.

The letter from home counted. Thank god the military found a way to keep the mail trucks running since the letters were sanctuary for him and every other GI in desperate need of some assurance that there was still a place waiting for them "back in the world."

He'd been beyond exhausted until Rachel's letter arrived. Just the sight of the envelope had the effect of a B-12 shot to keep him going until he could properly enjoy his reward for being as faithful to Rachel as she had been to him.

A few times he had been too desperate to hold off for his little ritual that had expanded to reading the two previous letters to build up to the big event. Today, though, he was doing this right, making it an extra special date.

Izzy showered, shaved, even put on some cologne instead of the usual Coppertone lotion. It was a pleasant early evening at the beach when he arrived, and actually rather deserted. The peddlers and beggars had left. The mama-sans in their woven conical hats selling pineapples, the peanut man, the amazing little man who was a walking BBQ shop with his meats and skewers, he barely caught them before they all went home. Then it was just him and his favorite spot under an Ironwood pine.

Izzy cleared the area of debris, put down a clean towel for his picnic. Then he placed the last two letters on top of the new one, making the moment last.

He already knew where this would take him: in bed, jerking off; at least sometimes, okay often. He had not masturbated this much since junior high. Did war make you horny? He felt a little guilty that somehow Margie kept intruding into these steamy fantasies. He had to try to do a better job of censoring her out; she was a colleague, a friend he truly cared for, and . . . anyway he had a new letter. And he did not just tear into something so precious.

Izzy opened the oldest of the three letters. While he had tested at reading over a thousand words per minute, the letters he always read out loud, slowly, like a love song. He wanted to feel like he was really with her, listening to her talk about someone named Janis Joplin and. . .

It made him a little anxious, Izzy realized, not for the first time. Like the picture with the Indian headband, where she looked younger, happier, and this "everybody is against the war now" bothered him because she had never been political before. . .or maybe what really bothered him was it sounded like the world was changing and he was completely, absolutely out of it while the real world was going on and—

"Stop it," he ordered himself harshly. "You have to stop this right now. Deep breath."

He took several deep breaths, got his ridiculous anxiety under control, and then read on, aloud, until he got to the best part at the bottom, "My dear, sweet, brave man. I love you dearly, madly. . . "

Izzy relaxed, laughed softly at himself, moved on to the second letter, the one that had arrived before this latest. He pretended he hadn't read it countless times already and knew each word by heart.

But the new one, ah, it was a virgin letter and the two before it, foreplay.

There was a right way to do this and this was the ritual he had perfected:

He would look over the entire letter. He would look at the way her handwriting was either fast or slow, what pen had she used; he would look at the postmark, the kind of envelope, and his silly APO address where the stamps should be. Every little thing was a piece of her and it was all that he had of her here. He would smell it and sometimes there was perfume or lipstick. He would hold it then and weigh it in his hands to see if it was a big or small letter, if it contained a photograph or a news article. Sometimes she would send him things she knew he would like from the *New York Times*. Once there had been a wedding announcement of a couple they knew, another time a book review of a friend's new novel. There was news of people he had studied and worked with during his internship, appointed to positions at the New York hospitals. He especially liked the ads she circled for apartments they might like to live in someday. Sometimes there were little drawings she made or sketches from Central Park.

He had noticed this new letter was skinny, though. But even skinny letters without drawings or clippings deserved the royal treatment. He was grateful for anything.

So he opened the envelope.

There were many things soldiers all dreaded and Izzy knew what they were: A mine blowing off their legs or, even worse, their balls. Burns from the napalm or white phosphorus. Beyond that though was the "Dear John," and it was only when he was half way through reading her letter that he realized he was holding a deadly snake in his hands.

First Izzy felt cold and his hands were numb and shaking as if he was going into shock, and maybe he was because he started over from the top because he was sure, he was certain, that he did not understand what he was reading...

"We are so far apart and it is not the distance, it is that nothing is the same anymore, because we have grown in different directions." *What was she saying?* "I was in the Village with a friend and heard Bob Dylan singing 'Mr. Jones,' and I thought you are like Dr. Jones now. It's something my women's anti-war group has really helped me see." *What the hell did Bob Dylan and Mr. Jones have to do with him? And just what was she talking about. . . seeing what?* "I have started seeing a man that I feel is like a soulmate to me." Izzy looked up and out at the sea. *What the fuck is a soulmate?* "I have sent both the ring and your classical guitar back to your mother, Israel. I don't think she was too unhappy with my decision. You know she never thought we were well suited and I've come to realize on that much she was right. I'm sorry you were drafted but maybe it's not entirely a bad thing if it kept us from making a serious mistake. Please know I wish you only the best. . . . " *Best? BEST?*

"Fucking god!" he suddenly screamed. "Wish me the BEST? The BEST *what?* Have the best fucking war over there, have the best fucking time ever by yourself over there?" Izzy leaned over and puked up everything in his stomach. He could not believe how much pain he already was feeling, how betrayed and deserted. . .*what was he going to do?* He needed to get home and right now. He would talk to Colonel Kohn and say—

Say what, that just like half of all the other poor sons of a bitches over here he'd gotten a Dear John and that he was sorry to say that he had to leave immediately, had to get home to straighten all this out and he would promise to come right back as soon as he could? He just had to talk to her, had to—

He made himself finish reading the letter, forced his blurry vision onto the remainder that said: "please do not try to call me, my mind is made up. I have thought long and hard on this Israel. To everything there is a season. Now I need my space and you must accept that the engagement is over. One day you will thank me. With deep affection, Rachel."

"Affection," Izzy whispered. Then shouted, *"AFFECTION?"*

Izzy crumbled the letter in his fist. He sat in the sand. It got dark. After a time, he realized that someone was sitting next to him. It was K.O. He turned and looked into the brown eyes of the big dog. She licked the hand that still gripped Rachel's betrayal. And he wept.

And then Izzy realized someone else had come to sit on his other side.

"Dear John, huh?" J.D. passed him a joint. "Welcome again to Vietnam."

23

Izzy destroyed Rachel's letter with the burning tip of a joint and proceeded to get so stoned and wasted that he didn't remember much of the night or know how he managed to wake up in his own bed sometime the next afternoon. He had never been so irresponsible as to sleep in late and miss a class, much less rounds, but once he pried his aching eyes open from his pounding head, Izzy saw the note taped to his chest:

Take the day off. We've got you covered.

A glass of water was beside the bed. Along with a bottle of aspirin, a bottle of Jack, and a sleeve of saltine crackers.

He eventually managed to make it to the kitchen sometime before dark. There were chocolate chip cookies on the counter. He knew who was responsible for that. And he knew who had him covered at the hospital. Izzy realized then that the one person he thought he could count on at home knew nothing about loyalty or real friendship. He wondered if she had planned this all along, if she had been going out on him while he was in training, before he even got shipped over here. Maybe he was better off without Rachel and maybe he would thank her one day, but now all he felt was stupid and duped and hurt and so extremely hung over that he was grateful to have something to focus on besides the utter bleakness he felt inside because it felt a lot like the day Morrie ended up in the hospital as a quadriplegic.

Izzy looked at his arms. He looked at his legs. All he had on was a pair of boxer shorts so he could see himself pretty good if he didn't count his still blurred vision. Something had happened to the tone of his body and the color of his pale skin since he had been here and he wondered if Rachel would notice, if it would make a difference. And if it did, what would it matter anyway since she wanted her space with a soul mate that didn't remind her of Mr. Jones while she went to her women's anti-war protests and was counting the days to Woodstock?

Days, how many days?

"342 and a wake-up," muttered Izzy as he bit into a cookie.

When Gregg and Robert David quietly entered the kitchen they simply said, "How're you doing, man?"

Gregg slapped him some skin. "Margie was in for a few hours today. She asked where you were and I told her you'd been called into the ER at the hospital again but I knew you had a little something for her when you got back."

Gregg slid a nice box of chocolates next to the cookies.

Robert David followed up by depositing some cheap green, purple and gold beaded necklaces with a coveted copy of the latest Playboy magazine and said, "That will have to do until I take you to a proper Mardi Gras."

And then they gave him his space.

The next morning Izzy woke up early. He wandered down to the beach, the same place where he had read Rachel's Dear John, as if he could eradicate her betrayal by greeting a new day where the sun would soon be rising out of the South China Sea. He knew this would be the only cool whisper of breeze there would be, the only peace to be had, until he went to sleep again and woke up early tomorrow.

He was a lucky man to have such good friends in this strange, foreign place that had begun to feel more familiar than home. Izzy knew that, but he still felt like shit. Though maybe he wouldn't feel quite as shitty if he still had the letter to put up in the enlisted men's hooch on the Wall of Shame with all the rest of the Dear Johns he had been invited to join. Bayer had trekked over to the villa to issue the invitation with a big slice of lemon cream pie hijacked from the enlisted men's mess hall, saying that was Hertz's favorite and he'd want Izzy to have it.

News traveled fast in this fraternity he had never imagined joining, and for once Izzy didn't regret being in the company he was keeping instead of the company he just might be better off without. If Rachel couldn't stand by him in the short term, what kind of long term chance for happiness did they have, really?

Just then, Izzy came upon something he didn't expect. Feeling like a voyeur he softly padded over the sand and closer to the ironwood tree where J.D. moved in some sort of bizarre slow motion dance choreography.

"Take off your shoes and socks and shirt and copy me," J.D. instructed, his back still turned and a good ten feet away. "Come on, Izzy, it'll do you good."

"How did you know it's me?"

"I heard you walking and I smelled your aftershave and you are a mouth breather. So close your mouth, breathe through your nose, be quiet and copy me. We'll work on the aftershave later but for now, just shadow my moves and see what happens."

And he did. Izzy moved and he moved and he moved and for a few seconds he was not here, not anywhere, he was just present in the silent movement.

In the end, J.D. bowed out to the sea. Izzy copied that, too.

"Did you like that?" J.D. asked.

"Actually, I did. It was relaxing. What was it?"

"Something very old, called Tai Chi, something my grandfather taught me."

"You have a Chinese grandfather?" Interesting. J.D. had a unique look about him but Chinese didn't seem part of his genetic composition.

"Maybe," J.D. answered, typically cryptic, before pointing to the water. "Let's swim out and we'll work on some breathing lessons."

"I don't like to swim and besides, it's deep out there."

"It's all deep everywhere and always will be."

"Since when did you become a philosopher?"

J.D. grinned. "Since I studied to be a monk?"

"I think your sense of humor is highly underestimated, J.D."

"Who knows, maybe I'll give stand-up a try if this agent gig doesn't work out. Until then, though. . . " J.D. motioned in the direction of an in-coming chopper. "I hate to tell you this, but we have a ride coming for you, me and Gregg later this morning. Compliments of Rick again."

"*What?*" Izzy just started shaking his head no, no, no. "Uh-uh, no way. I am not going back to the Highlands, not after that last trip to see Rick and our nice little tour of the morgue."

"You and Gregg said you would help." J.D.'s voice was firm. "I took you at your word and I'm asking you to step up to the plate now."

"I'm not going back on my word J.D., but we seem to have a little difference of opinion as to what 'help' means. I can understand your need to make sense of why some psychopathic monsters might be carving up our troops. I can even understand why you possibly felt the need to drag us to a firebase in an attack helicopter to look at mutilated dead bodies to help figure that out. But Gregg and I don't need any other visible evidence to assist you in a consulting capacity."

"A consulting capacity?" J.D. repeated. "Oh, you mean like sitting around the table the other morning and discussing theories and throwing out some ideas about psychological profiles, I believe you called them."

"Exactly."

J.D. tapped his chin as if deep in thought. "Hmm. Okay, then if you don't mind humoring me, could you describe how you went about your previous consulting experience?"

"Excuse me?"

"I mean, back home, maybe you had a nice office to use, a comfortable chair, possibly even an impressive desk?"

"Yes. It was typically a pleasant academic or clinical setting. That's how most assessments are offered, or discussions conducted on whatever psychopathology is being presented by, or to, a psychiatrist."

"While you enjoy a fine coffee, perhaps."

Izzy closed his eyes and sighed deeply, imagining himself in the office overlooking Central Park with a beautiful cup of cappuccino on a beautiful modern Eames table, and sighed again, "Yes."

"Then you need to wake the fuck up, Dr. Moskowitz, because this is *not* a pleasant academic or clinical setting. This is *not* a situation that is conducive to a nice cushy chair with coffee served while you discuss or assess or psycho-whatever in a typical consulting capacity. What this *is,* is a top of the very top hierarchy of needs from the military brass that doesn't give two shits about what you or Dr. Kelly consider 'helping.' If they wanted assistance in the kind of 'consulting capacity' you're so generously offering, don't you think they'd hire Einstein if they wanted to?"

"Einstein was a physicist," Izzy muttered, toeing the sand. "And he died in 1955."

"That's not the point!" J.D. paused, lowered his voice. "Listen, I don't know what you think I'm doing when I'm not around but I can assure you that it involves getting information potentially pertinent to this case from resources less savory than your own."

Izzy suddenly felt a little belligerent. "Oh? And here I thought you were sipping *Soixante Quinzes* with Kate during happy hour. I'm sure Gregg will be relieved to know all of your time is being wisely invested elsewhere."

A muscle ticked in J.D.'s cheek. He took a deep breath and appeared to be exercising an enormous amount of control. "If I'm calling you in it's because I've exhausted all other possibilities and I have no choice but to go with what I've got to work with and right now that means responding to a request Rick made via the right channels that we pay another visit to discuss a plan he has in the works."

"Fine, he can come here and we will plan to your heart's content."

"He's training some new troops, so we go to him, not the other way around."

"Then Rick is calling the shots now, is that it?" Izzy didn't know why he was deliberately pushing J.D.'s buttons except he didn't feel like he had anything left to lose, except maybe another friend he thought he had but was no more a friend than Rachel had turned out to be if he was willing to subject him and Gregg to more trauma.

"This is why guys like me don't get to have friends like you, Moskowitz. Because then you start to think we're equals, that I owe you some kind of explanation. But that's not the way it works, it's not how I get the job done, and as to who is calling the shots, let's get it straight for sure that you and Greggy boy are not calling any."

J.D. folded his arms across his chest. Izzy knew what that defensive body language signaled. J.D. was closing out the friend he said he couldn't have.

Maybe they had never been friends. Maybe Gregg was right and J.D. was possibly a sociopath since he clearly displayed enough hallmarks for one:

Charming when necessary, even seductive.

Successful, often at the expense of others.

A natural aptitude to manipulate people and situations to his advantage.

A lack of remorse when others paid for his personal gain.

206 John Hart and Olivia Rupprecht

And he could be a stone cold killer as Izzy had witnessed their first day.

Despite the ax Gregg had to grind over Kate, Gregg had not wanted to assign J.D. to that particularly disturbing personality category—*especially* because of J.D.'s involvement with Kate. Izzy thought of how J.D. had been good to him in his own way, and he didn't want to go to that dark place of suspicion either. But neither did he want to delude himself into the possibility of friendship with someone capable of strategically using others to their benefit while emulating expressions and emotions often learned at a young age from normal people because they were usually highly intelligent and became highly accomplished actors in order to fit in when, in reality, they were not capable of real feeling or carrying the burden of a conscience.

Hell, who knew? Maybe J.D. was the Ghost Soldier by night to keep his day job safe and had no qualms about using him and Gregg as the equivalent of imprisoned gladiators to keep the top brass entertained. Izzy had never thought himself the paranoid type, but anyone who didn't have a degree of paranoia in this crazy place would be less than normal. Yay. He was paranoid. That made him normal. Amazing how the mind worked to justify just about anything.

Izzy crossed his own arms. "Did you know about this trip being set up when you found me the other night?"

"It didn't seem the best time to bring it up."

"So were you being nice to me, just to get me to agree to this?"

J.D. stared at him, hard, his eyes sharp yet dull like flint. Izzy stared straight back, refusing to give up ground. "Well?" he demanded.

"I don't have to be nice to anyone to get them to do what I need them to do," J.D. said flatly. "I expect to see you and Gregg at the LZ at 1100 hours. I'm not sure how long we'll be gone so pack accordingly."

"Anything else? Sir?"

"No. That will be all."

Izzy had gone several steps when he heard J.D. say, "Wait."

Izzy kept walking. Acknowledging any excuses or apologies from J.D. was not how it worked; not when the fury Izzy nursed had nothing on the fear already rolling like thunder through his guts.

J.D. had been right at the get-go. He needed to wake the fuck up.

*

There is nothing more fearful than fear. It has its own life, its own way of growing. It becomes stronger, ever more powerful and irresistible. Like water dripping on stone, it weakens the mind and body, insidiously eroding the spirit.

The patrol starts out well before sunset. They seem in good spirits but the too loud joking and bravado belies the underlying dread from the stories they all have heard at the base camp. The patrol has barely started their long trek toward the place where they want to set their ambush when the last sun dappled light of the evening is suddenly replaced with a wraith like mist. The night fog slithers down through the trees and the leaves begin to drip as the jungle darkens around them.

"Fuck this shit," Clay, the point man, whispers to the radioman.

"Double fuck," says the radioman. "This is goddamn Ghost Soldier weather if I ever have seen it."

"Who said Ghost Soldier, who said Ghost Soldier? Shut up, shut the fuck up."

All the way back the whole patrol is now stopped, frozen every one of them, looking blindly out into the white mist which writhes through and around the trees. Clay sees the mist move and fires and everyone opens up completely freaked.

An AK47 bursts behind them and the now fear-frenzied patrol runs forward. Clay hits the thin sharp wire strung across at neck level and is nearly beheaded, the jugular artery pumping out his life with each final beat of his heart.

His two buddies behind him see the blood spraying; see a beckoning opening in the jungle to the right, and speed up, shouting, "This way!"

The opening is too wide, too clear, but they can't think of that with that thing chasing them, no it's too beckoning, and the whole patrol is running nearly abreast when the three in the middle impale themselves into the angled razor sharp bamboo stakes set at groin level. Their agonized screams make the two men on the outside turn their heads to see and they hit the bamboo stakes angled low at ankle level and fall hard, full speed, into the sharp-ened stakes on the ground in front of them.

Their whimpering cries attract the Nightbird. It sits and cocks its head, watching as another bird alights and begins to feed on the point man's bloodless face while the impaled ones finish their slow dance of death on the stakes.

24

Crystal Blue Persuasion took a long looping diving turn and so did Izzy's stomach. The high cool air was refreshing but only sharpened his senses to the horror show of where he was going and what they were doing, though he wasn't too clear on that much yet.

Rick had not been in the flashy gunship this time to greet them and while J.D. had tried to act as if they were all buddy-buddy since meeting up at the 8th Field's LZ, Izzy and Gregg knew better. They'd had a frank discussion minus J.D. as they packed at the villa.

Izzy: *Can you believe he's taking us out there again, only this time to god knows where Rick has his camp set up?*

Gregg: *I can believe anything at this point that suits J.D.'s agenda.*

Izzy: *Do you think he's a sociopath?*

Gregg: *I don't know but if he is then we are completely expendable and if we have to be sacrificed it won't be hard to explain our disappearance in a war zone. The military will completely back him up. We're just draftees, no different in their eyes from every other grunt they throw out like trash in the field.*

Izzy: *It's hardly insurance against the worst possible, but it might be a good idea to take a page from the playbook J.D. could be working from.*

Gregg: *Agreed.*

The agreement being that sociopaths weren't the only ones who could emulate certain behaviors to successfully get what they wanted. In his and Gregg's case it was simple: out of this trip alive. Therefore, if J.D. wanted to act like they were all cool and in this together, that's how he and Gregg would pretend to play it while they watched each other's backs.

J.D., now seated across from Izzy and Gregg, smiled apologetically, as Izzy hugged his stomach. Not only was he queasy, his chest was so tight he felt like he was drowning, but Izzy smiled back as convincingly as possible as the brilliant blue helicopter finished its dive and came down perfectly on the LZ of . . . he had no idea where they were besides a deserted area where the blue shimmer of a river could be seen in the far distance.

"We're about 25 clicks North from Ban Me Thuot," J.D. explained, raising his voice over the loud bleat of the helicopter blades. "Let's go!"

So out they all jumped with their gear and J.D. waved the pilot off with a thanks and "Good hunting."

They were met by a fit looking young man in a ranger uniform with dark embroidered LT Bars on his collar.

"Welcome to Firebase Zebra, doctors."

The LT did not look or sound very welcoming. It felt like they were intruders into a very private club. Which it was. The military's Long Range Reconnaissance Patrols were highly trained and experienced men that could travel light and fast and far and deep to perform important missions. Izzy knew he and Gregg belonged in this club about as much as the LRRPs belonged where they did:

Stateside. California and New York. With private practices, nice coffees, and patients who didn't dismember LRRPs like the lieutenant here for profit, fun, or cult worship, though they had pretty much ruled that last one out.

"Captain Galt is down at the training site and said to come on over," said the Special Ops LT who proved to be an experienced guide with his monotone patter down as he walked them to their destination.

"We are remote here as you can see, but this is where some of the best LRRP training in the country takes place. We have a lot of volunteers from all over Vietnam who come specifically because of the exceptional training that results in a high kill rate and a very low casualty rate. We have about twelve LRRPs all over the country now...."

Mr. Congeniality's tutorial was along the same lines as Rick's the last time he had played host in the Highlands, so Izzy was only paying half attention when he nearly bumped into Gregg, who suddenly stopped as they came upon a scene that looked like something out of a corny Hong Kong Chinese martial arts movie.

The area was some kind of an arena. A group of ten men, armed with long wooden knives, circled around a shirtless blindfolded opponent in the middle who held a wooden staff-like sword. The first attacker came silently from behind the blindfolded man who whirled around and even before the attacker hit ground, he took out the next two attackers coming in from his left, then the two on his right were thrashed into one another and the man in the middle just completely wiped out attacker after attacker faster than Izzy's eyes could follow.

The blindfold came off and it was Rick Galt. His body was slick with sweat, every cord and muscle so accented, he looked like an illustration from an anatomy text on perfect muscle development. There was no fat. He was not overdeveloped like a body builder. On the contrary, he reminded Izzy of a jungle cat, built for speed and power.

Rick looked right at Izzy, flashed him a smile and winked.

Izzy whispered to Gregg, "Don't forget to give him Nikki's latest letter."

Gregg patted his shirt pocket. "Maybe he'll send us back with some flowers and chocolates this time."

"Your job is to kill!" Rick shouted. "Attack to kill. Do not hesitate. *Ever*. If you are going to kill, you strike hard, and strike first. What did I say?"

The circle of trainees shouted back: "Strike hard! Strike first!"

Rick dropped his staff and pointed to one of the men. "All right, Stone. You're the best of this bunch. What are you going to do? You have one enemy between you and getting home with the intel to save the patrol."

"Sir, yes, sir," Stone barked. "Strike Hard! Strike first!"

Stone yanked off his shirt and ran forward, whipping it toward Rick's eyes in an attempt to blind him while whipping the sword in a whistling arc at his legs to amputate them at the knees. It was a frighteningly fast attack.

Rick reacted as if it was all in slow motion. He grabbed the shirt at the same time he leapt high in the air and kicked Stone in the solar plexus, dropping him to his knees. Rick's elbow was at his best student's Adams apple, effectively killing him if the blow had been fully executed. Rick stopped there and pulled Stone to his feet, face still contorted as he gasped for breath while Rick threw his arm over Stone's heavily muscled shoulders.

"The shirt idea was a good surprise," Rick told the group. "Combined with the leg blow it would have been crippling. Well done, Stone, you almost had me. Good work." Then like a tiger in a circus show, Rick effortlessly leaped to a nearby platform to finish his address.

"Now listen up everybody. As promised, we are going out to get whoever is fucking with us. You've all heard the latest and we are putting a stop to this because someone has come into our territory, our hunting grounds, and there is only one top predator in this territory and it is—who?"

"Cobras!" the men shouted.

"That's right. We are the hunters here, not the hunted, and the bullshit myth of this Ghost Soldier will be done because we will find the gooks doing this, we will kill them, and we will end it. After this is over, count on a party you'll never forget, but tomorrow we pack up and head out. You will be the hunters of a hunter and we will do what?"

"Kill him!"

The rabid shouts ceased when Rick made a silencing motion and commanded, "Sergeant Oakley! You know the drill. Get them ready."

"Yes, sir!"

Rick leaped off the platform and came directly over, asking, "Well, Doctors, enjoy our version of an intervention procedure?"

Izzy wasn't sure if "enjoy" was the word. What he'd seen was amazing and unnerving. Their thirst for blood was as palpable as Rick's had been when Peck shot the elephants. Gregg gave a little nudge and Izzy remembered their pact to act the part of happy campers while they mentally dissected everyone and everything that stood between them and their safe return.

"That was, I mean, you were wearing a blindfold and they were for real attacking you full speed."

Rick laughed. "Naw, if it was real. . ."

"There'd be a lot of blood," Gregg supplied.

"That's right, a lot of blood," Rick said, laughing again. "Getting real hot, bet you're thirsty. Come on, this way." Rick led them all over to a small tent that was actually dressed up like a cantina with palm leaves and had a poncho liner over a crate for a table with a group of chairs around it. He opened a cooler and miraculously pulled out four cold beers.

Gregg extended Nikki's envelope and made the exchange.

"Well, look at that. Christmas just came early." Rick gazed at the envelope like it was the frosting on top of some delicious cake waiting inside just for him.

Izzy knew the feeling. Or, he had. At this point, Rachel could go fuck herself, or her soul mate at Woodstock, because he still had some chocolates to deliver in Nha Trang. He could not get back there soon enough, no matter how cold the beer Rick hoisted.

"Here's to dead motherfuckers and happy endings."

Everyone clinked bottles to Rick's toast and Izzy wondered if anyone else noticed J.D. was being unusually quiet. Or that Gregg's easy smile was strained even if his compliment had to be sincere.

"You are something else, man. I have never seen anything like that, not even in the movies. Tell the truth, you were eating Wheaties in the womb."

"Everybody has to keep their secrets—even shrinks, right?" Rick grinned at J.D., making Izzy wonder if Rick suspected J.D.'s doctor status was a sham.

"Especially shrinks," J.D. agreed. "All the bad things we hear, we have to keep to ourselves. Right, Gregg? Izzy?"

Izzy felt like he'd just been slammed in the solar plexus faster than Rick had decked Stone. Had J.D. planted some kind of bug in the villa to overhear conversations? Did he know that they were mulling potentially bad things about him and were feigning loyalty now? Shit. *Shit.* J.D. was a spy; of course, he probably had the whole damn villa bugged. Izzy swallowed the gulp of beer lodged in his throat. Glanced at Gregg who appeared to have a hard time swallowing, too, before they echoed: "Right. Right."

J.D. raised a brow, glanced back at Rick who seemed too preoccupied with stroking Nikki's envelope to notice any subtext between the three of them.

To see that he-man press Nikki's envelope like a prayer to his chest before laying it aside assured Izzy there was some gentleness in Rick that perhaps J.D. was incapable of possessing, and if so, they might need Rick to get them back in one piece.

"Is there something we can do to help the men before they go out tomorrow?" Izzy asked, then pointedly added, "Before we leave to go back ourselves."

"The reason I asked you to come here is because the bastards struck again and took out another patrol that included some men I personally trained. I've started noticing a pattern I'd like to talk to you guys about, how they seem to be going after the newbies, but right now my biggest concern is that everybody here is completely freaked out and pissed off. Pissed off is good," Rick stated, "But the other, that's just poison. These men look badass and they are badass, but the morale isn't where it should be. We are supposed to be the proverbial meanest motherfuckers in the valley of death and we are. *We are*. But someone's been coming into our own house here and shitting on us and it's really bad for our self-image. The taunting has to stop."

"Taunting?" Gregg prompted. "What do you mean by that?"

"We never could find our guys' bodies," Rick answered. "They took them and that's just wrong. They—or 'he'—left some heads and hands, that's all, not even enough to send them all home in a single body bag. It's like they think they can get by with this because we're not good enough to out-game them. That's taunting. Now we've got some scores to settle."

"We can help with residual anger management after your guys settle those scores," Gregg offered. "Meds, no problem either. Right, Izzy?"

"Absolutely. I can dispense meds like nobody's business. And no one is better than Gregg when it comes to talking things out."

"I do my best." Gregg was talking fast, too. "In fact, Rick, I could help your guys with some positive self-talk techniques to improve morale and performance in the field before you go out. If you wanted we could get to work on that right away so you can all get a fresh start tomorrow without us around. We know we're just extra baggage and you have a mission to accomplish."

"I'm on board with that," Izzy quickly agreed. "Then we could either come back to do our meds and therapy thing after you have your big victory party—or, better yet, the men who really need tending, you could send to the clinic and we could do better work with them there. Sound like a plan?" Izzy finished hopefully.

Rick scratched his head. "Well, 'actually,' that's not quite what I had in mind."

"No?" Something strange and prescient stitched up Izzy's spine as he looked from Rick to J.D. "No?" Izzy repeated, hating the higher pitch to his voice yet too afraid to completely care. "Then what did you have in mind?"

"For starters, I have a special surprise lined up to make amends for what happened with the elephants on your last visit. I hope that's okay."

"Absolutely," J.D. said before Izzy could react. "Then what?"

"I figured I could leave you shrinks with the Mnong—damn, there goes my surprise—while the new patrol and I finish our hunt. One day, two max. Then when we get back you could be there to help my men with any of that stress or trauma stuff after we have our victory party. So if you'd be so kind as to stick around, I would really appreciate it, and just maybe..." Rick glanced at Nikki's envelope, a dreamy smile playing at his lips. "Maybe I'll go back with you, play hooky for a few days in your nice little section of town and take my chances that Miss America will agree to go out with me."

"Sounds like an excellent plan to me," said J.D., hopping right on board. "That's really thoughtful of you, Rick. Thanks, man."

Abiding by their pact, Gregg and Izzy nodded along and pasted on amenable smiles while they made all the right noises.

"Glad you're agreeable." Rick slapped them all a high five, right down the line, then chugged back the rest of his beer before confessing, "I was worried the three of you might bail on me when we need you the most. Goddamn, I'm glad to have friends like you I can count on when the going gets tougher than even us tough guys can manage. Now, finish those brewskies so I can pay up with some proper thanks, starting with dinner and some drinks that'll knock your socks off."

25

The LRRP wound its way out through the jungle heading north. The toxic, devastating herbicide, Agent Orange, had not been sprayed in this area, and after only a mile from breaking camp they were in a primeval forest. Gregg knew from talking with Rick and other Special Ops and Forces guys and Rangers that everything they did had deep planning and extensive training involved. He was walking along with the best of the badass best, but it still didn't keep his heart from hammering so loud he felt like everyone could hear. Despite Rick's assurances of safety, Gregg knew that anything could happen out here at any time. They could stumble right into a VC patrol, although Rick had told them that they were entering Mnong territory and nothing bad happened on their lands.

Gregg supposed that made the area something of a sanctuary like the Peace Mission Hospital, but still he felt like he had somehow gotten himself into a horrible western movie and entered Apache territory after being reassured that he need not worry now about Comanches.

"Docs, could you use a water break?" Rick asked solicitously.

"Thanks, I sure could," answered J.D. despite looking as relaxed and in his element as Rick.

"A break would be great," Gregg wheezed. He was no more accustomed to the jungle than Izzy, who could hardly keep his glasses perched on his nose or the sweat out of his eyes.

They paused long enough to down some water in this place where they were surrounded on every side and even over their heads with what looked like a confusing, moving solid wall and ceiling of green with roots reaching up to trip them and blades of grass to cut them and giant green leaves full of every kind of insect just dumping on their sweating heads.

Damn, why hadn't he gotten that hair cut yet? All too soon they were back to humping it through the jungle and Gregg couldn't say for how long, just that he had a sense of the day passing and his stomach sinking. He tried not to imagine how terrifying it must be for the new troops to be sent out, how whispers would take on a different, haunting sound in this wildish place, or the impact stories like the Ghost Soldier would make when the fear factor was already so high.

He was not very successful in controlling his imagining. When they finally stopped for another break, he was almost glad for the proximity of J.D. since his presence afforded them some measure of protection—at least as long as he needed them to maintain his cover.

Crouching down next to him and Izzy, J.D. said quietly, "You're doing great. You've made it, we're there, and they are here for us."

Gregg looked around. "I don't see anything."

"Me either," said Izzy.

"Just let your eyes go soft, don't try so hard to focus and you'll see."

Gregg did as instructed and drew in a sharp breath. "Holy shit."

"Oh god, we're surrounded." Izzy frantically grabbed Gregg's arm. "We are dead."

Rick came over then and J.D. went back to his know-nothing charade.

"Hey guys, I told you not to worry. We've had company for the last hour or so, shadowing us."

"Who are they?" Gregg couldn't even blink; his eyes were glued on the natives surrounding them with guns.

"These are the Mnong warriors, my friends," Rick said with a tone of reverence. "You are looking at the lords of the forest, the elephant hunters."

❋

The Mnong warriors leading, they were all escorted along a well-used path that opened up on the banks of the Srepok River. The river, a muddy green blue, fronted the long houses built on stilts along the sandy bank. Children were happily jumping into the sparkling waters, making the shrieking sounds that kids at play make everywhere. Further down the river women were washing bright colored clothes and drying them out on the smooth stones along the banks. J.D. and several of the troops flanked Izzy and Gregg as Rick and the rest of his platoon approached the village.

A number of Mnong Elders came out to greet and welcome the obviously respected Captain Galt, who hailed them in their native tongue. They exchanged bows and good tidings in what struck Gregg as a very warm and festive affair. He noticed that J.D. responded in English when introduced, though Gregg would lay money that J.D. could speak their dialect better than Rick if he was so inclined.

The suspicion was solidified when J.D. whispered, "They're giving us a special guest house and offered to bunk Rick's guys together but Rick declined and they'll be setting up camp nearby. I don't think they'll be coming to the party tonight. Rick wants them fresh for tomorrow."

Rick clapped his hands. "Okay men, take off with Oakley and we'll join you in the morning."

"We?" Izzy repeated with alarm.

"Oh sorry, Doc." Rick guffawed at Izzy's openmouthed expression and several of the tribesmen joined in the universal language of humor. "Me and one of the top warriors here who expressed an interest, *we'll* be joining them. But if you want to come along you're welcome to join the party."

"Uh-uh, no thanks," Izzy quickly assured him. "I am perfectly happy staying in our special guest house."

Rick paused, no doubt wondering where Izzy had gotten that information prior to his dispensing of it, then let it go with a shrug. "Aw darn, and here I was hoping you'd rather go hunting with the rest of us. Of course you'd have to step things up a notch to keep pace so I guess it's just as well all you docs hang out at the Holiday Inn here and sleep off what's in store for the night with these good people."

In short, the guests from the 99th were treated to something better than any Holiday Inn Gregg had ever slept in. The interiors were shaded and cool compared to the outside. The bamboo woodwork was expertly done in a manner that allowed shade, shelter and ventilation. The place was immaculately clean and had a fresh herbal scent. They had comfy hammocks at intervals which allowed them protection from any creepy crawly creatures.

As they got settled, Rick gazed longingly at his own hammock. "Man, wish I could pack it in here with you once we call it a night— or early morning—but that wouldn't be right. If my men are sleeping outdoors, that's where I need to be too, even if it's just to catch a few Z's."

"You're an exemplary commanding officer," J.D. told him and Gregg had to agree.

"Thanks for saying that." Rick shook his head. "With so many of these attacks, good men lost, and taking my guys out when their morale is down, I don't feel so exemplary lately. Listen, I heard you guys talking up the patrol, telling them what badasses they were while you had to be sweltering in the heat that we're used to. I really appreciate that. Makes me realize what a great idea it was to invite you here when you could have just as easily begged off and stayed in Nha Trang."

Gregg and Izzy met eyes. *Not really* was the silent message shared. J.D. quickly covered the awkward pause, assuring Rick, "When Colonel Kohn passed the invitation along, we didn't think twice about accepting. It was the least we could do considering how much harder you and your guys have it, though I have to say, who would want to be in Nha Trang when we can crash here instead?"

"Yeah, this is really cool," Gregg affirmed, taking his cue. "Not just this Mnong Hotel, but the air, it's cooler, too."

"Absolutely, what Gregg and J.D. said. I just got Dear Johned by a chick who's going to this thing called Woodstock, but I'd rather be hanging here with you guys than with her if you can believe that."

"Yeah, I can believe it." Rick promptly produced some weed. "Let her put this place in her peace pipe and smoke it if she wants a real trip."

After the pipe made the first round, Gregg wondered if it was such a good idea for him and Izzy to get stoned if they needed to be on their feet. Then again, if J.D. decided they were expendable, or if they got attacked and killed by some VC once Rick left, then at least this was one helluva send off.

"So, about these Mnong that hunt elephants," Izzy coughed out, "Is it for their tusks?"

"Hell no!" Rick actually looked appalled. "The elephants are like their brothers, not animals. They capture them to be tamed because they're like the most powerful spirits of the forest so the warrior who captures and tames the most is the most powerful leader of the tribe. Legend even has it the founder of this village captured four-fucking-hundred elephants in his lifetime. Try topping that."

"Man, that's crazy." Gregg tried doing some mental math to estimate how many a year in an average lifetime but the best he could do was, "Wow. That's a lot."

"A warrior without peer," J.D. said somberly, then grinned at Rick. "Like you. All hail Rick Galt, Lord of the Jungle!"

"We aren't worthy!" Izzy and Gregg bowed in semi-supplication towards Rick's feet.

"Aw shucks, you shrinks are so good for my self-esteem, makes me want to keep you around." Inspired by their theatrics, Rick yanked open his shirt and pounded his chest.

Izzy howled. Gregg snorted smoke out his nose. J.D. called, "Oh Jane dear, what's for dinner? By the way, anyone else hungry?"

"I am," Gregg said, suddenly ravenous at the thought of food.

"Me, too," agreed Rick. "Good thing Cheeta isn't around."

"I'm so hungry I could eat an elephant!" Izzy proclaimed.

"Man, that's sick," Rick said, laughing smoke out the side of his mouth. "Let's just keep that joke between us. The guys cooking dinner might not get it and we don't want to offend our hosts."

＊

Izzy had been to some pretty impressive New York galas and restaurants and parties but he had never seen anything like the heaping platters of smoked and grilled meats, of roasted vegetables and huge baskets of tropical fruits that the Mnong village brought out in their honor. Rick had said he wanted to make up for the awful incident with the elephant shooting, and he had more than delivered.

The sweet smell of the foods mingled with the fire smoke rising up into a starry night. The villagers were dressed in their finest with gold and silver jewelry. The elders were unsurpassed in their beautifully woven black smock-like shirts with intricately woven stripes of red, yellow, blue, and green.

The leaders of the village had created a communal drinking fest with great celebration. "It's their way of making a friendship bond," Rick explained as they all sat around these large pots that reminded

Izzy of huge jars with long pipes that acted as straws that all the men were drinking from.

Gregg took another big hit and collapsed onto his back.

"Are you okay?" Izzy asked, wondering if he was anywhere near it himself.

"Man, this stuff is intense. My god. This is like draining a personal keg of beer."

"Yeah like wine infused with intoxicating plants." Izzy could feel his lips smiling a wild smile; his eyes felt like they were spinning. "I have to get the recipe to take home. They think Haight-Ashbury is psychedelic and mind altering? I have never been this high ever, ever."

Rick leaned over, grinning. "They really like you guys, all of you. They like you a lot. See? They're even bringing out the music!"

Drumming started and various sized gongs began to play, ancient and hypnotic. Rick pointed to an instrument that looked a little like a xylophone made of stone. "Can you believe? They invented that thing like 5,000 years ago. Izzy, they want you to dance. C'mon, show us how it's done."

"Ooo-kaaay!" And, somehow he managed to get to his feet, dancing and dancing and shaking his hips and entwining his arms like snakes reaching for the sky while everyone clapped, until he stumbled and fell on his ass a little too close to the fire. Scooting back to his place like a dog scratching its butt on the grass, the villagers roared with laughter and clapped even harder.

"Now they REALLY like you!" Rick said approvingly. "Too bad you didn't bring your guitar. Hey, anybody know where J.D. went?"

"He is always somewhere," Gregg mumbled. "Hopefully he found a tiger to chase him."

"Don't like the guy, huh? Why not, have something to do with that pretty missionary girl?"

Just then Izzy noticed J.D. standing. . .somewhere, he couldn't be sure how far away or how close with his eyeballs zooming in and out, but JD was outside of the party circle with one of the elders he thought Rick had said was the Headman. Izzy started to point but then J.D. and the Headman or whoever he was were out of sight, and maybe he only imagined them there anyway.

Gregg just took another liquid hit from the pipe straw going into the jar and slurred, "Have you ever finished one of these things?"

"I think they're bottomless," Rick told him, then clapped his hands like a grand sultan and said, "Let's get this dance going again, Izzy. C'mon, I'll join you!"

The night moved on, endless it seemed with a bottomless keg. As the music played faster, Izzy began to wonder if there was some kind of herbal amphetamine infused in the psychedelic brew because by some miracle, or chemical infusion, they did not all pass out as they partied all night long. J.D. rejoined them at some point, insinuating himself as discreetly as he had disappeared.

The sky was starting to lighten. There were streaks of red and purple across the water as the tropical dawn began.

Izzy thought he was hallucinating when he saw a line of elephants coming toward him. Then he was sure he was hallucinating when several pigs were slaughtered in front of his spinning eyes.

Their heads were ceremoniously cut off, and he abstractly wondered if that's how the Boogeyman-Ghost Soldier did his own whack jobs. Only, this was like something okay because it seemed respectful somehow when the pigs' heads were reverently placed like headdresses on the great lords of the jungle.

Each elephant now wore a crown of blood and a pigs head as the elders bowed before their celebrated guests.

"They want you guys to ride an elephant," Rick explained.

"But I don't want to ride an elephant," Izzy had the presence of mind to say. "Especially one that's been. . .decorated like that."

"Sorry, Doc, but you have to do it. It's an honor." Somehow Rick and J.D. were already up on their elephants and Rick was saying, "Come on, Gregg, come on up. Izzy come on, this is the chance of a lifetime. You will never do this in New York City."

Izzy knew that without having drunk what seemed like a keg of the mind altering beverage he would never have said yes to even approaching an elephant. As he walked up, though, something remarkable happened. The elephant kneeled down and looked at him. Not in his experience had a creature looked at him like this, making contact like a sentient being. The elephant was measuring him up. He could feel it.

"I only know English," he said and could have sworn the animal nodded in response. "I know you understand me. I would like to be able to ride you. May I?"

The creature reached out with its trunk. It touched his face, as gently as a mother touching a child. She scented his breath and shared her breath with him. He felt so much emotional contact and connection that he almost dropped to his knees but she caught him with her trunk and lifted him, swung him through the air and he felt as if he was flying, flying onto her back and there he was, sitting on her back and she was getting up.

And now they were all up and riding. Moving faster and faster and then running through the tropical dawn by the sparkling river with the sun and sky swirling around them while behind them he could hear the drums and gongs that seemed captured in his chest, building in intensity as they moved through the jungle at elephant level and speed. Izzy knew he was under the influence of the concoction he had been drinking, but he was absolutely sure this experience was like nothing humanly imaginable. Every sense was magnified. The thin dappled light between the darkness of overhead canopy and the colors all around were so intense he could hear them, taste them, smell them. The physical movement of the elephant was so magnificently, staggeringly huge as to be overpowering. Their trumpeting vibrated through the air and his body. The sheer enormity of power he felt with an elephant under his legs left him breathless.

He was riding the Lord of the Jungle who moved effortlessly through the trees and brush without any fear of any other creature. Izzy looked over to see Gregg and their eyes met. And in that shared gaze they knew this experience would forever be one of those that divide your life into everything that came before and then this.

26

The keening wail was the first thing to pierce Gregg's consciousness, followed by an urgent shaking of his shoulders that felt dense as lead, as heavy as the head he couldn't possibly lift.

"Get up!" It sounded like J.D.'s voice. Had to be a nightmare. "Goddammit, get up *now*."

Gregg tried to roll over and felt himself literally hoisted to his feet. His head bobbed back and forth while the shaking continued. Somewhere in the distance the wailing continued while J.D. harshly commanded, "Wake up. *Wake the fuck up!* We *have* to get out of here."

"Huh?" Gregg managed to groggily respond. Nothing seemed real.

Then Rick's voice was part of the bad dream he must be having, demanding, "Izzy, snap out of it! C'mon, Doc, here, I'll carry you. J.D. can you help drag Gregg out? Oakley, grab their gear. Careful with Izzy's glasses."

"Sir, yes sir. Good thing they at least passed out in their clothes."

"Shit, did Izzy just throw up all over himself?" J.D. again.

"Yeah but maybe not a bad thing to get some of that stuff out of his system. God, J.D. I'm glad you're not such a lightweight; thanks for the assist. We'll throw them both in the river to wake them up, get Izzy here cleaned up once we hump it the hell out of Dodge."

The familiar voices merged and mingled while Gregg had a sense of being half-carried, half-dragged out of the Holiday Inn where they had a room. But then the voices changed to a foreign language and the nightmare was worse because children were crying, women were wailing, and men shouting. The cacophony of their joined rage and confusion and fear and sorrow beat at Gregg like stones all over his aching body, then at his back as he was being moved faster and faster while the voices retreated and then—

The cool whoosh of water. Someone dunking his head in and out while he felt the warm relief of pee leaving his body. Then his stomach was heaving and everything in it was coming up his throat and out his mouth while the dunking continued.

When he opened his eyes he was laying on the jungle floor. Izzy had been deposited beside him, almost close enough to be Siamese twins joined at the arms. Gregg started to try to get up but he hurt all over and shut his eyes again, trying to get his bearings and hoping his head would stop pounding.

There was movement around him, hushed voices, but he could make out Rick saying, "What do we do with them now, J.D.? You're the doctor. I'm just an officer with a couple of dead Mnongs on my hands and a village that thinks one of my guys did it."

"Normally, I'd say give them two aspirin and tell them to call in the morning after they sleep it off, but we need to make tracks before some of those villagers decide to take matters into their own hands. I don't think anyone there is in the mood to have a civil discussion about what might have actually happened or set up some kind of trial with an investigation and a court appointed lawyer. For a minute I wondered if we were going to get out of there alive."

"Me and my guys wouldn't have let anything happen to you docs, and if they do come after us we can make that go away pretty quick, but I don't want it to come to that. I feel bad enough already the Headman and his Mrs. got taken out in their sleep." Rick made a distressed noise. "The idea that one of my guys did that is bullshit. What a mess."

"I didn't see the results but I gathered it was pretty brutal. Any thoughts on what might have happened?"

"Fuck yes. It's just another perfect fucking Chinese psyops bullshit ploy to crap morale and dump more crap on my guys. How convenient they left those US matchbooks behind from their stinking little bag of tricks."

"So you think it's got something to do with that whole crazy Ghost Soldier thing we're dealing with?"

"What else? It's so fucking obvious a blind man could see what happened—and god it makes me feel like some stupid new guy not to have seen it coming myself."

"Hindsight's always 20/20," J.D. said like some compassionate doctor would. "But I'm not sure what you're beating yourself up about. What did you miss?"

"Simple. The plan was to drop you guys off so we could go on our hunt, and frankly, I wasn't counting on having to go too far. I know the areas where they've been doing their dirty work and they've been progressively moving in this direction. And, I know what I'm looking for—I've seen the boot tracks, I've seen the shell casings, I've seen the wires and the stakes and it all points to some high level assassins who really know their shit. I also noticed there's a pattern with them going after some of the newer LRRPs, so I made sure my guys had fresh uniforms—"

"I thought these were newer trainees here."

"Yes and no. Maybe new to my unit, new to this group of Special Ops, but they've had plenty of experience, hardly new kids on the block. They definitely have more training than the troops that have been chopped up so far. But the bastards one-upped us again. Had to have followed us to the village and while we were partying they were probably setting up traps, then flushed us out by murdering the Headman and his old lady in their sleep. Man that sucks. I really liked him. Her, too. And now here we are with two passed out casualties that probably don't know how to shoot more than a hole in their own feet while those psycho Chinese bastards are probably laughing their asses off while I figure out what the hell to do next."

There was a long pause and Gregg nudged Izzy to see if he had amply revived to also be listening in on the conversation between J.D. and Rick. Izzy nudged him back.

"And you're sure it's the Chinese and not one of our guys, Rick? I hate to say it, but matchbooks from a cowboy joint in San Antonio and a Vegas nightclub does look pretty suspicious."

"What the fuck kind of question is that? Hell no!" Rick thumped something with his fist. "It's bad enough to have to try defending us to the Mnong, but I shouldn't have to do it with you or any of the CID snitches the brass probably sent to sniff our tails. The LRRP's have had a little more outside company than usual lately and I don't think for a minute any of us are part of a three hour tour. What a bunch of paranoid panty waists who think they get to call all the shots from some nice safe place with air conditioning. We're the ones getting the Ronco Veg-O-Matic slice and dice treatment in the field, and they have the gall to even suggest such a thing? Just one more reason for me to bag the bastards responsible and put an end to this once and for all."

"Sorry, Rick, sorry, man. You're right, that's not fair. It's just that as, um, shrinks we have to consider all possibilities. . . ."

J.D. trailed off and Gregg could sense his attention shifting their way. He also sensed that J.D. somehow knew they were awake and he was expecting them to back him up. Gregg did not know what J.D. was capable of but he did not want to risk retaliation. Neither did he want to risk defecating on himself. After everything he'd heard his fear factor was racing through his entrails with ample speed to crap his pants.

Gregg suddenly "came to" with a miserable groan and that much he didn't have to fake.

"God, I feel sick." Gregg leaned over and didn't have to fake dry heaving either. "Where are we? Where's the john? I gotta go."

"John?" Izzy muttered, "Who got Dear Johned? Where's Rachel?"

"Well, lookee there," Rick said with a dry laugh. "Our sleeping beauties back to join the land of the living. The toilet's the nearest bush, Doc. But I wouldn't go too far."

A strong arm helped lift Gregg from the ground and the one silver bracelet remaining on the wrist told him it was J.D. doing the lifting. Verification came in the form of a whisper next to his ear.

"I'm going to walk you out just a little bit and you're going to pretend I don't tell you anything I'm about to tell you. Nod if you've got that."

Gregg's first instinct was to grab Izzy to go with him but Rick beat him to it, pulling Izzy up and declaring, "might as well take them both to save some time. Here, put your glasses on, Doc."

Whatever J.D. had been about to say in private was exchanged for, "You guys packed the medic bag. Anything in there to help this situation?"

"We just brought the usual. Morphine, Dexedrine, Valium, and Thorazine, and some IM Benzo." Gregg groaned like he meant it, and boy did he. "Don't think that'll help the situation, though."

"I brought toilet paper," said Izzy.

"Well you sure don't want to forget something as important as that," Rick snickered and leaned Izzy against the nearest tree. "Listen, let me go just a little ahead of you to make sure there aren't any traps. J.D. maybe you could grab the goods for our m'ladies here? Back in a flash."

Rick plunged ahead and J.D. whispered, "Whatever you guys do, do *not* get out of my sight. Got that?"

At their nods, J.D. followed Rick's instructions to grab the toilet paper, giving Gregg just enough time to whisper to Izzy, "We're in trouble."

Izzy agreed with another quick nod, then signaled a zipper to his lips just as J.D. returned with the bag, and Rick emerged with an, "All clear. Found you a good bush and everything, just watch out for snakes and the usual."

Once they were at the appointed bushes, Gregg turned to J.D. and Rick, and sniffed, "A little privacy please?"

"Good god," Rick groaned, "far be it from me to insult your delicate sensibilities. Come on, J.D."

With more riding on their stolen moments than modesty, Gregg didn't waste a second dropping his pants with Izzy close enough to pass the toilet paper, at least that was the impression meant to be conveyed.

"What are we going to do?" Gregg said urgently, in a hushed whisper. "We're basically part of the patrol now and I'm not sure we can trust J.D."

"No more than he probably thinks he can trust us if he's got the villa bugged. No wonder he doesn't want us out of his sight. He's probably afraid we might rat him out to Rick."

"Yeah, Rick is maybe the best shot we have to get out of here in one piece, especially if traps have been set. I'm not sure how much J.D. knows about those things or even if it matters where we're concerned. Fuck, I just don't know."

"You guys doing okay over there?" called J.D.

"Fine!" Gregg called back. "Just give me a few, okay? I'm going as fast as I can." Then to Izzy he whispered, "I swear it's like he's got antennae or a sixth sense."

"I know, I know," Izzy muttered. "I hate being so paranoid. I. . .Oh! Fuck. I just remembered something. From last night."

"What, what is it?"

"I could be wrong. I was so messed up, I hope I'm wrong but. . .I think I saw J.D. with the Headman. Rick asked where he was and I looked and saw him off to the side, but then I looked again and he wasn't there, I—god, I hope I just imagined that. Maybe it was just part of tripping on that stuff."

"But if you weren't? I mean, Rick was with us for as long as I can remember before passing out. J.D., he comes and goes like some kind of phantom. And what about those match books? Could J.D. have planted something to implicate Rick's guys, just to get us out of there? You know he had to be planning something to make sure we didn't get left behind while Rick went after the freaks that J.D. considers his. No way would J.D. want Rick to get credit for doing the job he was sent in to do."

"Are you guys having a damn tea party or what over there?" Rick called. "Another minute and I'm coming over for some curds and whey."

Just then a spider the size of a tennis ball dropped on Gregg's forearm.

"Oh shit!" he yelped and sprang to his feet, waving his arms furiously to get the spider off.

"Careful, don't step in it," Izzy warned, and Gregg could only wildly wonder when life had gotten to a point where he didn't even care if he stepped in his own shit on a jungle floor if it got him one step closer to home.

He and Izzy had nothing solved, but time was up and, as he bent over to accept the tissue Izzy held out, Gregg finished by whispering, "If push comes to shove we could tip Rick off about J.D. maybe being with the Headman last night, but we don't know that for sure and I don't think J.D.'s going to let us out of his sight, so for now I don't know what else we do besides do whatever Rick says since this is his turf and he's probably our best means of getting the hell out of here."

"Agreed."

"Other than that"—Gregg passed the roll—"You and me, Izzy, we is all we've got."

Rick seemed to have come up with some kind of plan in their short absence, as upon emerging he clamped them both on their shoulders.

"Listen, I already had a word about this with J.D. and he understands we don't have a lot of choices at this point. We've already lost more of the day than I'm comfortable with so we need to push through as far as we can while it's still light. No offense but you guys held us up before, and you'll be holding us up now. With a bit of luck, I can get to a place I can radio in for some transport tomorrow to get you out of here but we'll need to make camp tonight. I know this is probably scary for you, especially with the possibility we're being followed—"

"Followed?" Izzy repeated, his apprehension spiking even higher. "You—you mean the Mnong? Actually, I'm not so afraid of them." They liked him, knew he hadn't killed the Headman, and Izzy would much rather take his chances with them than whatever was in the jungle at night. "Maybe Gregg and I should go back to the village."

"Sorry, but you can't go back there. None of us can. And double sorry but they aren't the ones I'm concerned about following us with you guys around. Honestly, this is worst case scenario since you docs are so obviously not one of us that you could be bait—"

"Bait?" Gregg repeated, his voice tight. "You mean...like, how?"

"I mean that the enemy doing the dirty work you've seen likes to go after weaker prey so we need to load you up with some gear, make you look like you're part of the patrol," Rick said patiently. "Then you don't look quite as much like the easy pickings you are that could further attract the guys we're playing cat and mouse with...Hmmm."

While Rick considered the merits of the ploy he seemed to have unintentionally unearthed, Izzy died a thousand deaths and judging from Gregg's grip on his arm, he was equally as terrified at the thought of being used to lure in some killers, and not just any killers.

Boogiemen liked to do it gory.

"Well, it was a thought, but I'm not about to put you shrinks in harm's way," Rick determined, and Izzy could have kissed his boots for that. "So let's get the three of you fixed up and try not to worry. You will have me and all my best guys in front and in back of you. I will not let anything happen to you out there I promise. Okay?"

Soon Izzy and Gregg were geared up in their fresh new soft round booney hats, LRRP Tiger fatigues with utility belts, flak jackets, canteens, their holsters and pistols. They each had a new M16 which Rick had reviewed for them and showed how to tape their gear down for silence and efficiency. J.D. was a good actor, pretending he didn't know any more about gearing up than they did.

"Wow Rick, I'm impressed," he said. "I didn't expect us to get a new wardrobe out here."

"Hey, I'm just a Boy Scout at heart." He raised the three finger hand sign. "Always be prepared, that's me. Now you guys just carry this stuff and the medic kits. We will hump the rest of any gear you might need. Come on, no need to worry," he assured them. "This is like a camping trip for you."

Although they were not carrying as much gear as the rest of the real LRRPs, and J.D. insisted on carrying the medic kits and canteens to lighten their load, what Izzy had on even standing in place felt like he was carrying a ton. "How far do we have to go?"

"A lot depends on you guys, Doc. But if we can manage about ten clicks out and set up by nightfall, assuming we're not being followed or closed in on, then we're gold and you'll be home this time tomorrow."

"Is there. . ." Izzy swallowed. "Is there any chance we could be ambushed while we're doing those ten clicks? Or, maybe in our sleep, like the Headman and his wife last night?"

Maybe it was just his imagination but it felt like J.D. was staring a hole through the middle of his head, like he was trying to send him some kind of message.

Probably to shut the fuck up.

"Anything's possible, Kemosabe," Rick responded as he made hand signals that caused the LRRP he commanded to make some kind of formation around him and Gregg and J.D. while Rick hitched his M16 like a baby on his hip. "But me and Tonto and the posse here, we've got you covered. Let's move!"

People in their handling of affairs often fail when they are about to succeed.
If one remains as careful at the end as he was at the beginning,
There will be no failure.
—Lao Tzu

The Blood Red Prince and Hibiscus

CUT

Sometimes success has its price. Obviously I had to move after I did my little trick with the matches and the paint, but I'm glad to say that the foster home I got sent to was not so bad at first. It was clean and they tried hard. They had to because there were 7 other kids there. Some of them not as nice as me actually, especially Robert. He took a dislike to me right away. It was mutual. He was a big dumb slow retard but strong as hell unfortunately. Once he got hold of you it was over for you. He had a reputation for hurting people. He made it hard on everybody there.

The house was almost in the country on the edge of town near a forest. The nice foster mom made a pretty great picnic to take us out to cut our own Christmas tree.

It was going to be pretty nice.

There was really only one trail to go on out there, so I knew pretty much where we were going. I think I said it before but it bears repeating: Planning ahead is good.

I put the extra axe out there in advance.

I hung back on the return.

She noticed I was missing and sent the others ahead to go home because it was getting dark.

She always kept Robert with her so he wouldn't hurt anybody.

I hit her hard in the neck with the first blow and she went down and bled out and then Robert got all bloody trying to help her, which was a lost cause and then he grabbed the axe and when she died he ran after me. I said he was slow so I had a big head start and when I caught up with the rest I screamed "Robert killed Ma. . .run, run, he's crazy!"

Everybody was afraid of him anyway and we ran into the house and locked the doors and called the police who came and found a bloody, crazy kid pounding at the doors with an axe. He was lucky they didn't shoot him. I thought they would.

He's hopefully still locked up where they sent him.

27

Gregg never thought he would gladly pay to be incarcerated, but as night fell in the jungle and Rick's LRRP patrol of seven men set up a small perimeter around them, even a lock down unit with the criminally insane seemed like a safe haven compared to the insanity of this.

Gregg knew he should feel as safe as one could possibly feel in VC jungle at night since Rick's hand selected team of killing machines was specifically put together for this mission. He did not feel safe. But he was so bone weary and hot that he started taking off his pack and bandolier and flak jacket, breathing, "God, what a relief."

Izzy began stripping down himself, groaning, "I had no idea how heavy all this gear is. I'm not wearing it anymore."

J.D. patted his own flak jacket. "Okay and good thinking, guys. Now you can stand out from all the rest of us so if the Boogeyman notices he'll say: Hey, cool they brought some Medical Services Officers this time, how interesting. Maybe I should kill the rest and capture those two. Me? I'd rather be dead."

Izzy and Gregg immediately put all their gear back on.

"So, what do we do now?" Izzy asked, dripping sweat, "Just wait for something to come out and try to get us, then you jump them?"

Rick chuckled. "Not exactly, no. We do not wait for anyone to make the first move or just hang around here like sitting ducks. Men, quietly now, remind our guests, what do we do?"

"Strike hard. Strike first."

Their subdued voices were no less powerful than their shouts volleyed at the training camp. Rick nodded his approval.

"That's right," Rick confirmed and patiently baby-walked his guests up to speed. "So, what's going to happen now is you three are going to stay put here with the guard while I do some recon. Then I am going to wire this place up like a fun house to keep you safe from any intruders while we go hunting."

"You mean you're going to leave us here while you and the patrol go after the bad guys?" Gregg knew his voice squeaked but he couldn't help it.

"No, no, not just yet," Rick assured him. "First, I'll take care of business and come back and make sure you're all tucked in, then leave my best guy to guard you shrinks once you go nighty-night. Stone, you get the honors."

"Do I?" *have to?* went unsaid as Stone's deflated expression transformed to a stoic mask with a single, sharp glance from Rick. "Sir, yes sir, my honor."

"And Stone here will also see to your dinner or anything else you need while I go do my thing now. Okay?"

Then Rick seemed to disappear before their very eyes, he was that silent and swift.

With the patrol basically surrounding them it wasn't exactly conducive to small or private talk, and despite the growl of his stomach Gregg couldn't eat a bite of the rations offered. J.D. passed a canteen but didn't say much beyond a whispered, "You two stick together. I'm going to need to leave," then appeared to be meditating on his next move, which did not include them.

Normally, Gregg would have thought this a good thing, but for J.D. to force them to join him on this journey only to throw them out on their own in enemy territory could be the equivalent of a death sentence and Gregg didn't give a rat's ass if Stone was playing babysitter.

"You fucking Benedict Arnold," he snarled under his breath. "Don't you have any sense of right and wrong? Even a small, tiny shred of human decency?"

J.D. didn't so much as shrug, just kept staring ahead, plotting whatever he was plotting until Rick returned as soundlessly as he had left.

He signaled to Stone, who signaled to his left.

"Go silent," J.D. muttered out the side of his mouth, playing interpreter.

Gregg watched the hand signals as the other men passed the message: Go silent.

Izzy gripped Gregg's arm. They were both so deeply out of their element they may as well be on the moon but at least he had Izzy to remind him he wasn't completely alone. Still it didn't alleviate a gnawing premonition so intense it was a physical sensation. Gregg felt like his feet were strapped onto a conveyor belt and everything he had experienced so far in this war was only a long hallway leading him to a door that was just now opening to reveal what war really was all about. He desperately wanted to get off the conveyor belt because in the pit of his stomach was the knowledge that once he crossed that threshold, he was never coming out of here again. *How did the grunts out here live for their 365 days with this never ending dread?*

Time passed. All quiet. They were deep into the night. Gregg actually felt his head bob with the weight of his helmet as he nodded off. He slightly jerked and saw Izzy lightly dozing, sitting next to him, his chin on his chest, helmet slightly askew. How either of them could sleep here was beyond Gregg, but given everything they had ingested the night before, and the relentless trek through the jungle that afternoon, it was probably a minor miracle they weren't comatose.

The moon cascading through the overhead tangle of trees was bright enough to slightly see a bit. Rick sent a hand signal to Stone who was a little further down the line. Then Gregg glimpsed J.D. making a signal of his own to Rick and Gregg let his head bob down again, pretending to sleep, which he was strangely fighting as he strained to eavesdrop when Rick came their way.

"Well, well," Rick whispered to J.D., "Just as I thought. Much as I like the docs, they wouldn't know a hand signal from wiping their asses with the toilet paper they brought along. Actually, Mikel, I feel a hell of a lot better with you being out here and knowing you're not one of them."

"That makes two of us, Captain."

"Care to share who sent you?"

"Let's just say a mutual friend who wants this thing to stop. I'm here to help. I saw you signal Stone to stay and guard the sleepers while you and the rest of the patrol slip out to reconnoiter. Let me go out on the perimeter with you. I can help check trip wires and," J.D. slyly chuckled. "Make the 'rounds' as it were."

"I like your style, Mikel. Tell you what, we'll leave Stone to watch after your buddies."

"They aren't really my buddies, but they have been useful so I appreciate you leaving Stone to keep an eye out for them. We may need them later."

"Gotcha. I've already told Stone where to look for the wires and where the path is to get out if necessary, so they're gold. Let's go out so I can show you if, worse case, anybody goes down. The way I have this rigged they won't, but just as back up to make sure you know how to get these guys out, and after that we can split up. If you're comfortable with that?"

"Absolutely."

J.D.'s imitation of Izzy had Rick softly laughing while Gregg wanted to pummel the shit out of J.D. for mocking Izzy and deserting them both. Then again, maybe they were safer without J.D. in case he decided they were no longer of use.

"Okay, then let's check the traps," Rick whispered with the glee of a kid embarking on an Easter egg hunt. "With any luck we'll be back with some Boogeyman heads before our two sleeping beauties wake up."

"They should wake up in time to hear the birds but not too much before." The light sound of a finger pinging the canteen was followed by J.D.'s smug assurance, "I figured they were safer with a little help from the medic bag than deciding to look for a little privacy behind a bush that might trip before Stone could warn them. The nerves they're nursing aren't healthy for them or anyone else around here."

"I say that makes you a good buddy after all—to all of us." Then Rick was already gone like the wind, chased by J.D.'s muttered, "Not really," before he was just as gone, too.

That was the last thing Gregg remembered until the ground itself seemed to be shaking him awake, followed by the shrill sound of trip flares. Either he was trapped in a vivid nightmare or the jungle was coming alive with light and sudden explosions.

If it was yet another nightmare or reality, Gregg didn't know as he grabbed Izzy and began shaking him so hard that the back of his head hit the tree they were both somehow now leaning against.

"Ouch, son of a bitch! What the hell?"

"Izzy, Izzy wake up!"

Gregg got in another two shakes before Izzy backhanded him. Gregg's head snapped back with the haphazard blow.

"Oh shit, I'm sorry! Sorry, Gregg, sorry, sorry! I didn't realize that was—"

Another flare, then more explosions that seemed to go on and on while Izzy's mouth moved and Gregg clamped his hands against the deafening Boom. . .Boom. . .*BOOM!*

Suddenly, all was quiet. Izzy's mouth quit moving. Gregg removed his muffling hands. They both looked around in the kind of raw terror and that only a really bad B movie with walking zombies could capture.

"It's over," Gregg whispered. "We're next."

"Wait." The sound of a morning bird coincided with Izzy's frantic point towards Stone, stoically sitting against a nearby tree, rifle positioned against his chest, on ready to protect the men on his watch.

Stone was a man of few words beyond "Sir, yes sir" or "Strike Hard! Strike First!" and he hadn't wanted to babysit the shrink pansies, so his lack of response to their "Psst! Hey, Stone!" was no surprise. Although Stone might be too proud to be relegated to the duty he had been assigned to, Gregg had no problem groveling in their protector's direction; or Izzy, crawling on all fours right behind him.

"Stone," Gregg whispered, shaking him, "Stone come on, wake up—"

Stone fell over, right on top of Gregg. Something wet was on Gregg now, coming from Stone, slick on Gregg's own body. Recoiling, Gregg jerked away and Stone hit the ground with a *thump.*

His throat was slit from ear to ear.

Shouts were coming towards them. Gregg fumbled with the M16 Rick had strapped onto him, tried to raise it to fire. Izzy was doing the same, crying "Shit, oh shit, how do I do this?"

Neither had time to figure it out before J.D. and Rick were both racing into the clearance, with Rick barking, "Stone! Stone!"

"Stone's dead," Gregg panted, struggling to rise on watery knees.

"What the fuck?" Rick snapped, stopping just long enough to lean down over Stone. "Oh god, shit! Not Stone, not— goddammit. I'll have to come back for him. Mikel, grab them, get them out of here. Take them the way I showed you. Only that way got it?"

"Roger, got it," said J.D.

"I'll gather the unit and you meet us at the rendezvous point I showed you."

Rick took off at light speed while Gregg and Izzy both latched onto J.D. like baby kittens onto a mama cat.

"What's happening, what's happening?" Izzy demanded, gripping J.D.'s arm.

"Stone had his throat slit." Gregg felt crazy, wiping the blood on his hands onto J.D.'s flak jacket.

"Yeah, yeah, I see that, we'll get you some therapy for it later, but right now you both have to keep it together, stay with me and we can still get out of here alive."

"But what's happening, what's—"

"I don't know, just that something's wrong. Now stay with me and run, or stay here and die. Okay? Now *Run!*"

With J.D. leading them out the same way Rick had exited, they ran down the jungle path through the eerie weird orange light of trip flares and jungle shadows greeting the first hint of morning. More flares went up and it was suddenly like a full but fleeting sun with even more dark contrasting shadows. They heard the sound of an M16 and then the sound of an AK47 and then. . .

They caught up with Rick, but he was down and bleeding. Badly. The remaining six members of his platoon came running from another direction and circled around him while Rick groaned, "Shit, I'm hit."

"Oh no, I forgot the medic bag." Izzy pumped a fist into his palm. "Dammit, dammit, I'll go back."

"No! And keep your voice down," Rick ordered, his own voice stern but low. "Mikel, grab him. We got our own medics, Doc. Oakley, got a hand?"

The entire platoon responded, assisting Rick as he struggled to get to his feet while Oakley pressed on a compress and wrapped a quick bandage around him. Blood continued to ooze past the bandage. Undeterred by the deep wound, Rick proved himself a true example of courage for the men he commanded in a sharp whisper:

"Come on, come on! Don't stop now; get the fuck after them right down there." Rick pointed north, toward an incline, with his gun. "I saw three of them in masks go that way. Get them! I'll be right behind you. Mikel, you and Oakley, take the docs west, that's the safest route, and we'll catch up once we have these fucking chinks heads on a stick. Understand everyone? We end this now and send a message that will be heard all the way to goddamn China!"

Rick's men took off as directed and immediately disappeared into the thick undergrowth, as Oakley instructed, "This way" and made tracks. Izzy hesitated.

"I'll stay here with you, give me something to stitch up the wound with—"

"Get the fuck out of here," Rick snapped. "I'm fine. Mikel, get him out of here!"

And Rick loped slowly north, well outdistanced by his men but even wounded, refusing to let them fight without him.

Oakley gestured impatiently and kept going while J.D. seemed to pause before giving Izzy a push forward. Gregg hit the ground running right behind Izzy. He still felt woozy from whatever J.D. had put in the canteen and maybe Izzy too since he was struggling to run with all the gear on. His bandolier slipped off his shoulder, slid down his legs and tripped him.

Izzy fell forward, hard. Gregg hit Izzy from behind, and J.D. ran into Gregg so they all fell like dominoes, the three of them tangled with limbs and gear on the ground. They were still getting themselves extricated to get back up and run when an explosion went off on the trail Oakley was leading them on and it was like a bad, bad flashback of one of Izzy's first nights when they ran from the villa and the soldier with no name who tried to help them got blown into a gory cartoon character where they should have been, only Izzy was too busy pissing his pants to get up and run with him.

As Oakley's arms and part of a leg sailed through the air and landed within reaching distance, Izzy tried to focus on breathing, but he did not piss his pants or vomit. Not even when a tremendous series of explosions immediately to the north went off, close enough to see pieces of bodies and limbs flying in the first blush of dawn did he do more than blink.

All was silent. There was only the call of a morning bird, the wisp of a breeze carrying the acrid stench of enough gunfire and smoke to destroy a small city. Izzy wondered how many dead there would be in Manhattan within the same perimeter of explosions. Countless, countless, and not just from the explosives, terror and hysteria would create a stampede and countless more would be dead from that; surely enough bodies to fill two hospitals.

Judging from all the body parts there would not be anyone remaining to take to the hospital.

"Can we stand yet?" Gregg asked in a voice like a flat line on a heart monitor. "Or do we just play dead and wait for the bogeymen to show up if they won?"

"You and Izzy stay here. Hide inside your helmets and don't move. I'll—what the hell? Never mind, get up."

J.D. was already up and trotting in the direction of a limping Rick Galt, holding his bleeding side with one hand, with his other a raised M16—and on the tip was a large fragment of something white that looked like part of a ghost mask.

Izzy got to his feet. Gregg, too. They ran towards Rick, who staggered then collapsed, but even as he lay there he kept the butt of his rifle to the ground, the barrel pointed skyward. The mask-like white thing lightly moved in the breeze as if it were the American flag holding the promise of freedom.

Izzy, Gregg, they picked up their pace. All around them was destruction: Blown up earth and pieces of bodies hanging from the broken plants and flaming, smoking trees. But in spite of it all there was a flicker of hope, that somehow at least one other person had survived, and that someone was a friend who just might not go home in a body bag, and pray god whatever Rick had signaled them with meant an escape from this nightmare that had sent J.D. here like some dark angel of death.

28

Rick was barely semiconscious when they got to him. J.D. immediately examined what did appear to be a portion of a shattered mask, as Izzy inspected the physical wounds and Gregg did his own kind of triage.

"Rick, Rick? We're here for you, buddy. Izzy's going to patch you up as best he can with. . .Mikel, can you go get the medic bag? We should have whatever painkillers you didn't put in our water along with a suture kit."

J.D. hesitated maybe a second then for once took his orders from Gregg. "Fine," he curtly agreed. Then no doubt needing to be top dog issued the directive: "Stay put."

As J.D. left them with Rick, Gregg noted several things:

J.D. didn't ask why they were suddenly not on a first name basis.

Nor did he bother denying his little doping trick.

And he didn't try to defend his actions by saying it was to keep them safe.

Yeah right. Gregg suspected if Rick hadn't come running with J.D. on his heels to get them out of the camp maybe his and Izzy's throats would be slit wider than the bloody gash in Rick's torso and J.D. wouldn't do more than shrug. Gregg hated jumping to such ugly conclusions but J.D. wasn't giving him much reason to think otherwise. And why? Because J.D. didn't explain himself to anyone, and that included a couple of pawns drafted into a chess match by a high level player who thrived on intrigue and subterfuge and drove a 57 Chevy when it suited his purposes to impress, rather than a jeep like the rest of the poor slobs who were counting the days to go home.

Jesus. You only had a Chevy here if this was your home.

Rick gripped Gregg's wrist and pleaded, "Forget about me, can you go see if any of my guys are still out there, if you can help them. . .if you can find more than this—this. . ." He managed to hurl away the fragment of the mask J.D. had left behind. "There were three. . .I saw three of them. . .maybe more I didn't see. Need to know we got them. Need. . .to know. . ."

"Hey, it's okay," Gregg said soothingly, glad to have someone to care for besides his completely fucked up self. "Once Mikel gets back, we'll go look, but let us tend to you first."

"Not. . .right. Captain goes down with his ship. Please. . ." Rick's voice was broken, his grip lax. "Please just do this for...me."

Gregg looked at Izzy. He gave a small nod. There was, after all, nothing they could do for Rick until J.D. got back with the medical necessities and if they could do this one thing then they had paid Rick back in some small way for quite possibly saving their lives, not to mention the lives of how many others if the Ghost Soldier/ Boogeyman psyops initiative was finally, *finally*, over.

They left Rick lying alone and went in the direction from where he had emerged. Just more body parts, more blood and bone fragments and—

"Look!" Gregg picked up more pieces to a shattered mask, then quickly found another. Suddenly he understood Rick's earlier glee of going on an Easter Egg hunt for the bloody bastards.

"I found some, too," Izzy said excitedly, ignoring the very disturbing bits of bloody body debris surrounding what he lifted from the ground. Then he really hit the jackpot with an AK47 Soviet rifle and shreds of blown apart Chinese Regular Army uniforms. "Wow, it's all here. Everything is what Rick was saying all along—which we did concur with, of course. But. . . there's just one thing that bothers me."

"What?"

Izzy shook his head, as if trying to clear it from the massive amounts of hallucinogen and whatever else they had consumed since arriving for this second trip to the Highlands, compliments of J.D. Sure, Rick had invited them but J.D. had made sure it happened.

"Oakley. He got blown up, too. We should have gotten blown up with him, right?"

"Right. Maybe not J.D., though, if he was far enough behind us."

"Rick thought it would be safe in that direction. Maybe I imagined it, but it seemed like J.D. hesitated before pushing me in Oakley's direction."

Gregg was amply paranoid himself to latch onto Izzy's train of what-if?

"You think J.D. may have wired something up without Rick knowing it?"

"I don't know what I think any more. But I can't fathom what motive J.D. would have in killing off Rick's troops."

"Yeah, even if he decided we're less dangerous being permanently quiet than just really sleepy. He drugged our water."

"*What?*" At Gregg's nod, Izzy snorted in disgust. "Why would he do that?"

"Supposedly to keep us and everybody else safer while he was doing his thing out here."

"Maybe he did some extra wiring while he was out and about."

"Yeah. Or maybe Oakley veered off from where Rick said to go, or maybe Rick thought wrong and just made a costly mistake. Who knows? Shit happens, man."

Izzy nodded. "You're right. Shit happens. And I'd rather that be the case than think J.D. had something to do with Oakley or these guys getting taken out while he used his own methods to get rid of—" Izzy lifted the remains of evidence in his hands.

Gregg couldn't dispute the fact that if the trap had been J.D.'s doing, even if his methods were morally reprehensible, the results were indisputable and that was something J.D. would consider perfectly justified. Like doping their water.

"We'd better get back before he shows up," Gregg said.

"Right, and puts us in a corner for not staying put."

J.D. beat them back after all and was lightly slapping an unconscious Rick on the cheek when they arrived, trophies of shattered masks, Chinese uniform shreds, and firearm in hand.

J.D. stopped his ministrations, such as they were, and glared at them both.

"You tampered with the crime scene?"

For a moment Gregg couldn't find his voice, but when he did, it was the low and lethal roar of an awakened dragon.

"Crime scene? *Crime scene?*" he repeated, beyond incredulous. "This whole goddamn war is a crime scene. It's criminal. And *you* are nothing but a whore for the crime bosses with enough innocent blood on your hands to burn in hell for. . .eternity is not long enough for any of you motherfuckers."

Gregg won the staring match but not the final call.

"Better not let mom hear you talking like that, Gregg, or she might wash your mouth out with soap instead of letting the babysitter take you to the boardwalk. Dr. Moskowitz, would you please do your best stitching work on Captain Galt while I radio in for help?"

Gregg was rendered speechless. Surely Kate hadn't. . .

No, he refused to believe her capable of breaking their sacred trust, especially with the bastard who had become his worst nightmare.

A nightmare with a radio. One J.D. could have used to spare him and Izzy from any and all of this, though apparently he had kept them around in case they might be of further use.

Because he was apparently still keeping them around. . .

J.D. walked in the direction of the "crime scene" and came back shortly to announce, "Pick up is on its way."

Izzy had just finished his emergency field stitching of Rick's gaping wound when Rick groggily asked, "Where are my guys? Did you find any of them you could help? Oakley. . .?"

Izzy nodded to Gregg. This was his job.

"I'm sorry Rick," he said gently. "We looked but they're. . .I'm afraid they're all gone."

"All?" The agony in Rick's voice was so visceral that Gregg had to swallow past the lump in his own throat as he solemnly nodded. "But they were my men," Rick protested. "My best men. There *must* be someone left."

Rick struggled to rise and Izzy pressed him back down.

"You need to rest until we can get you out of here and into a proper medical facility, Rick. I'm really sorry about your guys, but there's nothing you can do for them now except take care of yourself. They would want that, I'm sure."

Rick covered his face with both hands and kept shaking his head. It was hard to know how to console such a tough guy who was so broken up. When he spoke, his voice was choked.

"Okay, I want to get my guys bodies back. It's important they go back home. And," he swallowed deeply. "I've got a lot of sad letters to write. But I don't want to do it in a damned hospital. I've got some LRRP buddies near the firebase in Ban Me Thuot, so just take me there. You did a great job stitching, Doc. I'll heal up fine."

"You need antibiotics," Izzy said firmly. "And you need more medical care than what I could manage here. I cannot in good conscience allow you to return to any firebase, Rick. That's a breeding ground for infection, and enough has been lost today without you ending up in ICU or worse."

Izzy then hit Rick with the painkiller and he relaxed, confessing, "I don't like hospitals. Goes back to a bad experience I had as a kid."

Gregg had an idea but he couldn't get clearance on it. J.D., however, could and should even consider it an appealing alternative for other reasons: there was bound to be extensive debriefing for a proven Chinese psyops, plus there was the matter of all Rick's dead Special Ops guys. Messy stuff that J.D. and the military would want kept off the record. There would be fewer ears to hear outside a military hospital.

"Hey, Mikel, what do you think of taking him to the mission? He could recover and do his writing there. Kate and the Donnelly's and their staff, they'll take extra good care of him."

"Not to mention it's a good, quiet place for the soul to heal, as well," Izzy added.

Gregg expected an immediate agreement but J.D. stroked his chin and looked away, seeming to debate what should be a no-brainer.

At his curt nod, Gregg reassured Rick, "You're going to like this hospital. Kate and the Donnelly's will make you feel like you're part of the family, not in some sterile ward."

"Really?" Rick asked hopefully. "Would they really take me in?"

"They turn no one away." Izzy patted Rick on the shoulder, using his best bedside manner. "And we would come down to see you. Even bring Nikki over. Right, Gregg?"

"Absolutely. Just what the doctor ordered."

Rick smiled weakly, and Gregg wondered why it was okay for him to imitate Izzy but not J.D. As Izzy smiled along, all of them just borrowing what humor they could to offset the overload of trauma, Gregg realized it was because he wasn't doing it behind a friend's back and on top of all the other issues he had with J.D., he did not feel safe turning his back to him. A part of him wanted to trust J.D. even now, that itsy-bitsy molecule of naiveté that still wanted to believe in Santa Clause, still hoped on some desperate level that J.D. would find a way to redeem himself, that he wasn't the whore Gregg had accused him of being. That J.D. wouldn't just as easily shoot them from behind as slap them on the back and say they were all on the same team.

"I have one more favor to ask," Rick whispered. "Could you get me all my guy's dog tags?"

"I have them right here." J.D. pulled them out, dangling them on their standard issue ball chains.

When Rick reached up to touch them, J.D. held his gaze and didn't give up the tags. "I will take care of getting these back with the body bags."

"Thanks, man," Rick said.

"Strike hard. Strike first," J.D. said like a eulogy.

"Damn straight," Rick confirmed and slumped back on the ground, eyes closed.

29

Nikki opened the front door and immediately wished she had a peep hole because she sure wouldn't have opened up for Don, not after his last visit.

Too late, the door was open and there he was, down on one knee and extending flowers, a big box of chocolates with a fat red bow, and a fancy bottle of wine.

"Peace offering?" he asked, sweet as you please. "I'm willing to beg."

Nikki folded her arms. She knew she was a soft touch but not this time.

"Go away, Don."

"But if I do then I can't properly apologize for the last time I was here. I just hated the way we ended things. My behavior was deplorable, and I want us to at least be friends. Besides, I've been working on my Elvis, just for you, because you know. . ." Then he launched into, "I ain't nothin' but a hound dog—"

"Stop it!" Despite herself, Nikki smiled. She was still floating on air from her visit with Rick at the mission. And, she had to admit, she really hated the way she and Don had ended things, too, so if he just wanted to be friends. . .

Well, she didn't want him hearing through the grapevine she had an official new boyfriend. That was just plain tacky and she wanted to deserve what Rick had said when she visited him at the mission hospital today: *Kitten, you are one class act.*

They had kissed. It gave her tummy butterflies. Just remembering must be why she felt that strange fluttering in her stomach when she went against her better judgment and said, "Okay, you can come in. But just for a minute and you have to promise to behave."

"I promise." Don got up and gave her a kiss on the cheek just before sailing through the door, which he promptly shut before she could do it herself.

His breath had a strange smell, like he had tried to cover up whatever was really on it with Listerine. And he had another smell that was, um, feral. She knew that fancy word because she was educated, but her real understanding of it came from growing up where predators went after more vulnerable prey, like those weasels that killed their chickens in a coop.

She wasn't a chicken. Nikki knew underneath the cotton candy surface, she was tough. So why she had this frantic urge to run out the door Don had just shut was beyond her. Especially since he was so gentlemanly the way he went about getting them wine glasses, saying, "Let's toast to letting bygones be bygones," opening the bottle with the corkscrew, and putting her favorite Elvis 45 onto the stereo. But as "Are You Lonesome Tonight" began to play, and Don poured a big glass of red merlot for her, then him, Nikki just couldn't shake the feeling that something was not right. The feeling grew even stronger as he patted the place beside him on the couch where they had "done it" the first time and she felt kind of cheap since bad girls did and nice girls didn't. At least not in the buckle of the Bible belt where she came from.

She was a nice girl; she just regretted doing it with Don.

Reluctantly she sat, but on the chair beside the couch. Don pursed his lips into a pout, then scooted closer, leaned in. Maybe it was his eyes that didn't seem quite right. They were really dilated. And the way he smiled made her heart beat really fast.

"Why aren't you drinking your wine? It's your favorite." He tilted the glass she clenched, pushed it toward her mouth and she gulped as fast as she could to keep from choking while rivulets went down her chin and he instructed, "Come on now, drink up. A little more, yes, that's good. Here, let's have another glass."

"But I don't want another glass," she gurgled, eyeing the door and swiping the wetness from her chin.

"If I say you do, then you do. And I say"—He exchanged her glass for his and said flatly— "You do."

She tried to push the glass away and him along with it, but she only succeeded in knocking the glass to the bamboo floor and freeing up both his hands as he surged from the couch, grabbed her by the shoulders, then pushed her down, pressing her knees deep into the glass she had shattered.

Nikki tried to scream but he gripped her jaw, pressed a hard, mean kiss against her lips until she tasted blood, and when he pulled back, she still couldn't make a sound with the hand he now had at her throat. He began to lift her by it, giving her no choice but to stand or be strangled as he whispered, "You're mine. You know that, Nikki, just like you know that you can never see him again. I won't stand for it. If you understand nod your head."

She tried but it was hard with him tightening his grip into her windpipe.

"That's right, Nikki, but sweetie you humiliated me, and there is a little punishment to be paid. And you love your little punishments, don't you?"

She tried desperately to shake her head 'no' but he only laughed.

"Now, now, you know that you love your little punishments. This time though it's going to be more fun because you owe me for being bad. Then once you've paid up and we've had our fun, I will forgive you and everything will be back to where it should be. The good doctor might even still marry you so you don't have to go back to the pathetic little village you came from."

Adrenaline shot through her and Nikki shoved him away with all her might. She could feel the blood pumping past the glass shards in the knees she would get on in church once she was safe. She just had to run a few feet more, get her hand on the handle and—

She was reaching for the knob when her head snapped back and her body along with it, propelled in reverse by the hand yanking her by the hair, then the cruel other hand that spun her around and slapped her hard across the face.

"You fucking bitch," he seethed, "Get on your knees and beg."

"No!"

"I said get on your knees." He slapped her again. "Now do it."

"You're crazy! I'd rather marry my third cousin than you. Now get out before I tell Rick you put your hands on me. *Get out.*"

And as Elvis sang "Is your heart filled with pain?" Nikki's head cracked back, she lost her balance, and split her skull on the corner edge of hers and Margie's coffee table.

Peck was breathing hard as he surveyed the damage. The 45 skip, skip, skipped on the phonograph needle and Elvis kept repeating, "lonesome tonight...lonesome tonight...lonesome tonight..." while blood flowed from Nikki's head, her neck at an impossible angle.

He knew the outcome already but still he frantically checked for a pulse. "Come on Nikki, come on, don't you dare die on me," he pleaded.

Her pulse fluttered. Stopped. Her pupils were fixed. The record continued to scratch... *Lonesome tonight*...He looked around. The place was a mess... *Lonesome tonight*...Her blood was all over him...*Lonesome tonight*. He had to think...

Think.

He washed his hands, his face. Quickly cleaned himself up from the top of his head to the bottom of his boots. Left the glass she had shattered, shards still sticking out of her knees. And Nikki, who actually would have made a good doctor's wife with the right clothes and some lessons in elocution, he left her exactly as she was as he considered his options.

This was not how he meant this lesson to go. The game had gotten completely out of hand. He had come here high and drunk and furious after learning Nikki had visited the missionary hospital to see the big stupid hulk the idiot doctors had brought in yesterday.

They had humiliated him, all three of those little pricks. Just thinking about it had made him want to hurt something, so Uncle Sam had fixed him up with one of his "nieces" who didn't even fight him when he took his frustrations out on her.

No one would care what he did to a Vietnamese girl. A lot of people would care about the death of a Red Cross Dolly. MPs and CIDs would be crawling all over this place like ants at a picnic as soon as the alarm was raised.

Peck checked his watch. It wouldn't be easy to dispose of the body properly and get everything spic and span before Margie finished the night shift, but he could possibly manage it. Then again, that would only be a temporary fix since a one minute investigation would confirm Nikki hadn't gone back to her hillbilly relatives or simply disappeared overnight. No. Foul play would be presumed and he would be a top suspect.

He still had a buzz going from the amphetamines and liquor he had consumed, but it was wearing off. His heart wasn't racing as fast as it should be, that's what the uppers and carefully constructed games were for, but for once he was glad his triggers worked differently than others, enabling him to stay calm now that he had a dead Dolly on his hands and very little time to figure out a plan when he was already in trouble with the CID.

Colonel Johnson: *If I get one more call from you, or about you, I will personally see that the rest of your tour here makes a firebase look like cooking up brownies in an Easy-Bake Oven.*

Kellogg: *Just remember, if I hear one more thing about you from Doctors Kelly, Moskowitz, or Mikel that doesn't make me want to invite you to my daughter's wedding, you are goner than gone to wherever Colonel Johnson wishes to send you and that includes Hell.*

Mikel must have done or said something to get him in trouble, then Kelly and Moskowitz backed their ringleader up. They were the reason he was in trouble with the CID. They were the ones who brought the goon to the mission and that's what had really set him off, so in a big way it was their fault he had come over to teach Nikki a lesson, and that made it their fault that she was dead. Now the question was, how could he implicate them to get off the hook himself? If he could do that, then he would be spinning shit into gold.

Peck put together a hasty plan. It wasn't perfect but neither was the military system. He left Nikki exactly as she was and slipped into the remaining twilight, humming to himself, *Are you Lonesome Tonight?*

❋

It wasn't even 9 a.m. and Gregg felt like a broken record. He felt broken all over.

"We do not know where Major Mikel is," he repeated, sitting next to Izzy on the couch in the villa's living room. "I told you that. We are not his keepers and he does not tell us where he is going or when he is coming back, okay? Man, for the tenth time already."

"Keep it cool, Doctor," said the MP, standing next to the chair where the local CID agent sat across from them. The MP had his hand on his pistol.

Gregg took a deep breath. He wondered if the MP shot him in the head what in god's name would come slithering out now. He could see that these guys were stressed over the situation too, but Nikki hadn't been their friend. As for the friend who found her...

Peck had come in early and offered to relieve Margie on the unit; he had been the one to pick up Margie's call shortly thereafter. She was so hysterical not even Colonel Kohn could calm her down on the phone, as Peck raced over to see what had happened. Margie had to be sedated. The MP and CID had stopped Izzy from going to see her.

And all this before morning rounds.

The murder of a Red Cross Dolly was going to scream headlines in the States, let alone that it looked like a psycho officer went crazy and did it. These guys wanted to make an arrest right now and probably did not care who it was as long as it took some heat off of them. The local CID guy was expecting the top brass from Saigon within the hour and he was pushing hard to make progress before they arrived.

"I say again we would like to have a lawyer here for us," Izzy asserted. "This is serious and we are taking it seriously. Gregg, if need be, I'll call my dad."

The CID officer named Jamison reminded Gregg of a crocodile the way he smiled. "That all sounds good in the movies, Doc, but as the song goes 'You Are In The Army Now.' This means you will get a lawyer, an army lawyer, when we give you one so shut it about the lawyer and tell me again where you were last night, and where is Major Mikel? The boot tracks at the scene clearly match the boot tracks on your stairs. And how interesting that your own boots have the same red dirt from up in the Highlands where you say you returned from with Major Mikel. And besides the dirt there is the matter of the blood, a lot of blood, staining both of *your* boots."

"I told you it was elephant blood." Gregg repeated again.

"Right, elephant blood." Jamison looked at his notes and his crocodile grin got bigger. "Let's see, you guys were out for a jaunty safari ride to go watch elephants play in the water and got your boots bloody. You know, I have to say this is quite the fucking story you have for an alibi on those boots and I would work a little harder on it if I were you because if this Mikel comes back and has any better story, then you guys are my prime suspects, you know what I mean? So again, where were you last night?"

It dawned on Gregg that J.D. could implicate them however he wanted and the army could throw away the key. The two drafted shrinks were easily dispensable to the military. J.D. was not. This could be a convenient way to shut them up indefinitely if J.D. or the army was worried about any classified information being leaked about the latest Chinese psyops disaster they wanted kept under wraps.

"Listen, the victim is our friend and we want her killer brought to justice even more than you do," Gregg said carefully. "Our story about the elephants can be verified, even if Dr. Moskowitz and I are both a little fuzzy on everywhere we were and everything we did last night. Suffice it to say we had a couple of really bad days before hitting the town to try to forget them. But I can assure you that it did not involve brutally assaulting and murdering an innocent young woman whose welfare and safety has been very important to me."

"He's telling you the truth," Izzy interjected before Jamison could wedge the broken record question in again. "Not only that, doesn't this all strike you as a little too convenient? The individual who relieved Captain Kennedy of her duties early and answered the phone at the unit when she discovered the body has been suspected of perpetrating a previously abusive relationship upon the victim. As a result he certainly bears your scrutiny as a potential suspect."

"But he's the one who called us, Sherlock."

"Precisely!" Izzy, several steps ahead of Jamison. "Major Peck is the one who shot the elephants. He has a suspected troubled history with the victim. He has a troubled history with a lot of people, in fact, including Doctor Kelly, myself, and Major Mikel. As a fellow officer, he has access to our quarters here—he even has a room, he just never uses it. I believe you have been too easily misled to interrogate the wrong parties."

Sometimes, Gregg thought, Izzy could be too smart for his own good. Jamison looked like he was grinding nails with his teeth and wanted to crucify them both.

"For your information, I did interview Dr. Peck and he even volunteered to show me his own boots, which had no blood stains, unlike your own. He also—"

"I said HALT right there!" shouted a loud voice just outside the villa's entry. "I am drawing my weapon—get your hands up and get out of the jeep and get down on your knees."

The MP moved to the window, gestured Jamison over to have a look.

"Okay, here he is, and here comes Saigon," Jamison announced. "How nice they all arrived at the same time. Sometimes shit does work out."

The door burst open and in came two MPs holding J.D. between them while another MP with a drawn pistol cocked it at the back of J.D.'s head, and behind that MP stood the big boss of them all, Colonel Johnson.

"Good morning, sir," Jamison greeted him with a sharp salute. "I'm ready to bring these two in for more questioning with the Major you have there. I think we're dealing with some crazy sexual escapade that got out of control—"

"Jesus fucking Christ," gasped the Colonel. "The retards I get stuck with. Sit down, Captain Jamison, and please shut up and take a deep breath through the asshole you must breathe through and tell me what this is all about. Good morning Doctors Kelly and Moskowitz. Mikel, what the hell is going on?"

"I'm not completely certain myself," J.D. responded evenly. "But I'm sure the detective—Captain Jamison, I believe—will be happy to fill us in."

"Very well, then. Jamison, proceed."

"Sir, yes sir. The victim, Nikki Dalton was discovered by her room-mate, Captain Marjorie Kennedy, who then called her unit, and Major Donald Peck came to help her at the crime scene. He called us on her behalf and reported they had also found boot tracks leading out of the premises. His suspicions were raised since there also appeared to be the same sort of red dirt that could be attributed to some recent travel to the Highlands by his fellow officers here, who also knew the victim. Of course I notified Saigon then immediately went right over to the victim's residence where the scene was undisturbed. The woman was dead, with her neck broken and a large wound to the head. As reported there were boot tracks through the blood and out the door. Although the trail was not visible from there to here, it does pick up on the stairs we now have taped off—" Jamison pointed significantly to his handiwork, "and the tracks lead to Major Mikel's room where we did find the boots with blood and red Highlands dirt. The two doctors here have similar blood and dirt on their boots, which makes them also suspect."

Johnson looked at J.D., raising a brow and waiting for his reaction.

J.D. just nodded.

"Wow. Sounds like a pretty open and shut case," said Colonel Johnson. "Looks like we have an arrest right here, Jamison."

"Are you kidding me?" Izzy exclaimed. "The boots are in the closet. The bloody tracks are going up the stairs. This is like a junior high drama class set up! None of you can possibly believe this."

"Be quiet, Izzy," muttered J.D. Then to Gregg, "Tell Rick I'm sorry. And get Kate off the reservation for a few days, would you? Please?"

"Okay, cuff him," Johnson ordered, "And we'll take him back to Saigon. Put him in my jeep until we get to the LZ. Looks like we have a lynch mob out there. Jamison? Your work here is done for now. Unless you are otherwise notified, leave Doctors Kelly and Moskowitz alone."

Outside the villa stood a line of MPs and what looked like half the hospital staff that continued to gather as news had no doubt been generously and swiftly spread by Peck, standing in their midst.

As J.D. was escorted out, Peck raised his voice. "Look, there he is! I suspected him the first day he arrived here. She was a wonderful woman. I loved her. She was going to be my wife."

Gregg flipped him off. He did not know what J.D. had up his sleeve, but he was certain of two things:

One, J.D. was capable of just about anything but he had not killed Nikki; and,

Two, if Peck had anything to do with her death, Rick Galt would see to it that he dearly paid.

"We should take Margie to the mission," Izzy suggested. "She's close to having a nervous breakdown if she isn't having one already. Colonel Kohn will approve us getting her out of here, won't he?"

"I'm sure he will." Gregg glared at Peck. "And while we're there I'll have to break the news to Rick. Now I wish I hadn't even introduced them. I hope he won't be the next one to go off the deep end."

30

Izzy stood at the door of the private room the missionaries had given Rick, prudently placed at the building furthest away from where Professor Nguyen was still recovering. The beauty of the missionaries was that they turned no one away, but they knew that even if this was their sanctuary and red, yellow, black, or white, they were all precious in His sight, someone like Rick would see it differently.

Izzy didn't want to be here right now. He had left Margie on the veranda where he had almost kissed her that magical day before Hertz was killed. Even with her face stitched up she was achingly beautiful to him and he wanted to kiss her like mad. But she was too vulnerable and he couldn't desert Gregg, not while he was consoling Rick.

"She was so sweet. I asked her to be my girl just yesterday. Even before we had a real date, I knew she was the one for me." Rick accepted the tissue Gregg offered, pinched it between his eyes. "Who would ever want to hurt Nikki?"

"I have my suspicions, Rick, but I can tell you it wasn't J.D. You know we're not exactly best buds, so if I would swear he didn't do it, you know it's the truth. I don't know why he didn't speak up for himself."

"Whoever did this better pray they get locked up instead and quick." Rick crumbled the tissue in a fist that looked as lethal as his vow. "Because if I get my hands on the motherfucker first, there won't be anything left to put behind bars."

"Yeah, that would be justice." Gregg nodded sympathetically. "It wouldn't bring Nikki back but it would sure make me feel a helluva lot better."

Me too, Izzy silently agreed, and he had to wonder when two decent guys like him and Gregg had crossed the line from wanting to save humanity from itself, to this kind of disposable mentality where death was an acceptable means of eliminating the undesirables of the world. Now, he almost understood how Rick could repeatedly kill and take pride in what he felt was doing a good job. As for J.D., he just seemed indifferent to carnage and death. Even this morning he hadn't flinched when he heard about Nikki, just utilized the situation as a means to be whisked away to who knew where to better plot who knew what. Things like that made Izzy wonder if J.D. really was a sociopath who didn't have the capacity to care for Kate, or anyone else, the way Rick obviously cared for Nikki.

He was gazing at a wallet size photograph she must have given him, repeating, "I'm so sorry, kitten," and tenderly tracing her image with his fingertips when they left.

"Man, that sucked," Gregg breathed once they were outside and moving in the direction of the jeep. "How many more days, Izzy? How many days?"

"337 and a wake up. But who's counting, right? Just ask J.D."

"Yeah, how weird was that this morning? I can't believe he wanted to get arrested just to save our asses, so he must know something we don't."

"He always knows something we don't, Gregg. That's why he's the secret agent man and we're his grunts. Or we were. Not any more since—" Izzy groaned.

"What?"

"You don't think he's going to use us for something else now, do you?"

"God, I hope not. If he goes off on some tangent with this murder he was so happy to get arrested for, let's just hope like hell he'd rather work alone or break in some new guys that won't tamper with a crime scene."

Izzy hesitated before asking, "Are you afraid of him?"

"Of course not," Gregg said a little too fast.

"Not even a little?" Izzy persisted. "I mean, he could get rid of us both and make it look like an accident if he was worried we might spill something about the cover-up the military was doing on the psyops operation, even before Rick's whole troop was taken out. Besides, you know they have to be putting a spin on that."

"Sure they are," Gregg agreed as they approached the jeep. "But if J.D. really wanted to get rid of us, he had the perfect opportunity already."

"I don't think he's done with us." There it was; the suspicion that felt like a hot breath on the back of Izzy's neck. "Did you see that little wink J.D. gave us while the MPs hustled him into Colonel Johnson's car?"

"No, I was too busy watching Peck make an ass out of himself." Gregg got in the jeep and banged his head against the wheel. "Shit..shit..shit."

"My sentiments exactly. In fact, I'll bet you anything J.D. shows up in the next day, two max, and tries to pull us into his next scheme, maybe even play on our feelings for Nikki to get us on board."

Gregg responded with a full body slump against the wheel. A heavy sigh and he gestured to the veranda where Margie was curled up in a protective ball on the rattan couch, her hand vaguely waving them good-bye. "Maybe you should tell Margie you'll write her if she doesn't see you soon."

"I'll make it quick."

"Take your time."

Time was a funny thing Izzy had noticed since arriving in Vietnam. It expanded and contracted like elastic but mostly felt like being underwater while you tried not to give up whatever little oxygen was left or suck in the liquid that could drown you.

All Margie had to do was lift her soulful eyes to his and he felt her accumulated pain like a third person in the atmosphere they occupied, and still he didn't want to come up for air.

"Margie? I'm so sorry for everything I couldn't stop from happening to you."

"But you didn't do anything." She reached for his hand with shaking fingertips. "Funny, isn't it? Your hands don't shake anymore. Mine do."

"They won't always. You'll come out of this. You have to. We're meeting in Switzerland, remember?"

"Promise?"

"I promise." And as he said it, Izzy remembered another promise he had made to a fatally burned soldier who was more worried about his mother getting the news than he was about being sent home in a casket. Time. Who knew how much any of them had? Time was an illusion and he wasn't wasting a second of it now.

For once Izzy didn't think, he just let it happen. He moved to the couch and pulled Margie to him. He tenderly ran a fingertip over the stitches running from her nose to her upper lip. Ever so lightly he kissed her full on the mouth. She tasted like heaven and honeysuckle. His body responded in a way it never had with Rachel or even with his steamy fantasies where Margie was the star of his one man show.

She whimpered.

Izzy forced his mouth away. "I'm sorry. I didn't mean to hurt you."

Margie's chest began to shake and he wanted to bury his face between her breasts, lose himself in the hot naked yearning just the thought of her always provoked.

As for the thoughts he was having now, they were nothing to be proud of, not while she was in such a terrible state.

"I'm such a mess," she half laughed, half sniffled, "And you weren't hurting me. You were turning me on, you crazy guy, making me forget—"

That's as far as she got.

Izzy kissed her with enough fire to melt Switzerland and half of Norway, too.

*

As it turned out Izzy's prediction was right on the money. J.D. sleuthed his way into the villa about 1900 hours the following evening. Gregg hung up the phone and didn't waste a second on pleasantries that were no more than a thin veil separating the rivalry and distrust between them.

"Where are you going?" J.D. demanded as Gregg headed out the door for the jeep he immediately cranked up, put into gear.

"None of your damn business," was all Gregg gave up as he peeled out.

And he wasn't about to stop even if J.D. was yelling, "Wait! I need to talk to you!" and waving his arms furiously in the rearview mirror.

No, it sure as hell was not J.D.'s business that Kate had called and asked him—that's right, *him*, Gregg, not J.D.—to come to the mission. Okay, so she had asked Izzy to come too, but he wanted to see Kate alone. Her voice was strained, and the Doctah of Damage Control was In.

As Gregg drove the jeep around the winding turn and then over the bridge to the mission hospital, the thrill of anticipation mingled with the scent of flowers and fresh mown grass on warm tropic air. He could even hear the soft breeze rustling the palms in the way that always sounded to him as if it were raining. He could almost understand why Kate loved being here in a way that he never had. But she didn't belong here either. None of them did. Except, perhaps, J.D. And Rick. He was in his element in the jungle and quite happy to hunt down the enemy he was assigned to kill, which didn't necessarily translate well into hearth and home and a nice little white picket fence in Mayberry.

Once the war was over, if it was ever over, chances were that a guy like Rick would not do well unless he was sent elsewhere to do exactly what he was doing here, or at least be training new men. Otherwise, Gregg could imagine him straggling in to some VA hospital with a bottle of Jack in one hand, a loaded gun in the other.

God, he hated the things he found himself thinking.

Gregg pulled up to the front of the mission, ran a comb through his hair and wished he had splashed on some Canoe. Too late now, he took a deep breath and counted to ten before knocking on the mission's front door.

The lights were on inside, and although he knew that Robert David had come over earlier to visit Margie, it was unusually quiet as the door slightly opened, revealing just a portion of Kate's face, like she was peeking around the side.

No doubt she was being extra careful. Gregg had hugged her when he gave her the news about Nikki, and he loved the way she had held so tight to him, buried her face against his chest. But he didn't try to get her "off the reservation" for a few days as J.D. had asked because he knew she wouldn't go. And he had asked Izzy to fill her in on J.D.'s arrest because he didn't want Kate to think he was gloating. Not that it mattered now anyway since J.D. had obviously been sprung out of the slammer as quickly as he had put himself in.

Gregg opened his arms and said simply, "I am so glad to see you."

Kate put a hand up as if to signal him to stop, but he was already inside the door and reaching for her in the foyer when it registered that something was not right.

She was stiff and her eyes were wide open. In them he saw none of her usual fire. What he saw was raw fear.

"What's wrong?" Gregg asked.

The door shut quietly behind him. Turning, Gregg exhaled a huge sigh of relief.

"Rick, hey man, great to see you up and about so soon."

Rick smiled. "Fit as a fiddle. Thanks to all you fine folks. So, where's Izzy? It's like you're missing the other bookend."

"Sorry, it's just me."

"Aw, shucks. Guess we'll have to celebrate without him." Rick nodded toward the adjoining living room. "Kate? Time to rejoin our friends. After you."

Kate had yet to utter a word and the whole exchange seemed even weirder when they entered the living room and Rick said brightly, "Great timing, Doc. We were waiting for you to start the party. And here we have the whole gang gathered for a cozy time together."

Gregg looked around at all their tense and terrified, confused expressions as Rick amiably went on, "You know our hosts here, Gregg. The good Doctor Donnelly and his lovely young bride Shirley, as they say on TV, and of course straight from his Mardi Gras ball is Robert David with the enigmatic Professor Nguyen—or should we say Professor Spymaster Nguyen? And there's nurse Margie looking a little banged up, but she took a lickin' and she's still tickin'! And last but certainly not least, your very own old pal, the 'stab you in the back and leave you for the handsome J.D.,' our gal Kate."

Gregg kept blinking, trying to process what his eyes were telling him but his brain refused to register.

"Why is everyone tied up?" Everyone except Kate had their hands and feet tightly bound.

Rick moved behind the bar. "Would you like a drink? For missionaries they have an amazingly well stocked liquor cabinet."

From behind the same liquor cabinet Rick produced an AK47 and placed it on the bar. He did some swift maneuvering and emerged with a lethal looking blade in one hand, a martini glass in the other. Around his waist were grenades and a claymore mine.

Rick took a sip of whatever contents he had in the glass, then placed it on the bar in exchange for the AK47 he picked back up.

"You look surprised, Gregg. What's wrong? You invited me here, didn't you?"

"What are you doing, Rick?"

"I'm tying up loose ends, Gregg. We've got to put an end to this Boogeyman business once and for all. Speaking of, let's get you and Kate taken care of right now. I'll even tie you up together, now isn't that sweet?"

"Boogeyman," Gregg repeated. He was still unable to process the bizarre scenario but that didn't stop him from clocking in on automatic pilot. "Come on, Rick. That's over and done with. You already took care of that business, remember? You're a fucking hero, man. Oh, sorry about my language, Dr. Donnelly. Shirley."

Rick guffawed then fired a single shot from the AK47. The burst of sound exploded the silence of the room. Shirley and Kate screamed. Dr. Donnelly spastically jerked with an anguished cry. Blood spurted from his shoulder.

"Oh, sorry about my little trigger finger there, Dr. Donnelly. Shirley. But not to worry, it is just a flesh wound. Actually, a very difficult shot with this type of weapon. Another quarter of an inch and it would have taken his arm off."

Gregg moved toward Rick, speaking in his intervention voice.

"Hey, take it easy, man. Everybody loses it here, that's all. You're upset about your guys. About Nikki. But you're with friends now. Give me the gun, okay?"

"Okay, Gregg, will do."

He extended the weapon, and as Gregg reached for it an exploding sensation cracked across his face.

Gregg felt his knees buckle, hit the ground, felt blood spurting out of his nose and the surrounding area where Rick had smashed him in the face with the butt of the rifle. Kate ran to him, tried to cover him with her own body, screaming at Rick, "Don't touch him again, you monst—"

"Er. . ." Rick finished as he silenced her with a slap. "Shut up, Kate, and don't make me do that again," he advised.

Kate lunged at Rick, snarling like a mother bear protecting its cub but before Gregg could struggle to his feet Rick smacked her back down. In a matter of seconds, he had a length of cord wrapped around them, tied up as tight as a couple of turkey legs holding in the stuffing for Thanksgiving dinner.

"Barbie and Ken would be so jealous," Rick remarked, looking them over. "Well, maybe except for the mess you're making of her hair."

With that, Rick leapt through the air and flat bladed his knife across Robert David's face, and then back across Professor Nguyen's in a blurring move. They were both rigid, stunned, with blood spurting from their split open cheeks; a bone protruded from Robert David's nose. Another swipe and Dr. Donnelly's throat was nearly severed. He lurched forward into Shirley's lap and as he gurgled his life out in bubbles of blood, she began to pray, "I will fear no evil; for thou art with me. . . ."

"Pray all you want, lady, but it won't do you any good unless you've got a different god listening than I had growing up." Rick calmly went back to the bar, put down the knife, and took another sip from the martini glass. He considered the now paralyzed group, only Shirley making a sound as she quietly continued the Lord's Prayer. Rick rolled his eyes before observing, "Amazing is it not just how stunned the average civilized person is by violence. The brain kind of just slows down and stops, doesn't it?"

"Rick, stop," Gregg pleaded, willing to do anything to save Kate from a killing machine pushed over the edge. "You're hurting people, man. Let us help you. Please."

Rick looked over at Gregg like he was the slowest kid in school and was pitied by the class president wearing a lettermen jacket.

"Always the good doctor, huh, Gregg? Don't you get it? I killed those men." Rick huffed on his knuckles, polished his chest. "All of them."

Gregg shook his head, frantic to restore even a small sense of reality because Rick had to be out of his mind. "No you didn't, Rick. You did your best to save them. The boogeymen that did it, that's who you killed, the whole gang you wiped out. You were a hero. And you can still be a hero. Just put down the gun and let me help you. We're friends, remember?"

"Gregg?" It was Robert David, speaking for the first time through his slashed open cheek and ruined nose. "This isn't your friend. *He* is the Boogeyman."

31

Rick released a big, hearty guffaw. "He's figured it out, Gregg. I guess medical school guys are smarter than you other shrinks that don't get a brass plated MD on the office door."

As Rick set about stringing wire across the area where they were pinned, he pleasantly took them along like a tour guide down a well-traveled mental health ward.

"Oh, I know all about that stuff, could even be a shrink myself after all the time I've spent getting diagnosed and prescribed this and that pill like they're vitamins for the brain. Even had a few of those electroshock treatments. Actually, I kind of liked those. Not as good as getting laid, but they are mighty stimulating. Anyway, that's why I could tell right off the bat that J.D. wasn't really one of you. Boy did I have a good time playing with that crazy motherfucker. Reminds me a bit of myself."

"You are insane."

Kate's defense of J.D. felt like a cut to Gregg, and yet he would kiss that crazy motherfucker himself right now if only he had followed him here. But a glance in the rear-view mirror had assured Gregg that J.D. went into the villa instead.

"Ouch! You hurt my feelings." Rick looked pained then good-naturedly informed Kate, "Fact is, sanity is way over-rated. It's an illusion anyway. Just ask Gregg. Right, buddy? Bet you wonder if you're crazy yourself half the time, don't you?"

Gregg could feel Kate trying to move her hands that were pinned between their chests but that only seemed to make the rope tighter. He had to keep Rick talking.

"Honestly, Rick, I'd have to say at least three fourths of the time. Maybe full-on crazy after the shit you laid on us here."

"Man, you crack me up! Like I said at our little tiki hut hotel, makes me wish I could keep you shrinks around."

"Yeah, that was a great time, wasn't it? Until the next morning. I guess maybe you had something to do with that, too?"

"Oh, you betcha. Not that I much enjoyed doing the Headman and his old lady in while they were sleeping. I do like a challenge and that was easy as taking candy from a baby."

"No one offers more candy to a kid than a pedophile, it's one of the ways they lure them in. . .Peck has major flaws, but he just doesn't give off that kind of vibe."

"And what kind of vibe would that be?" J.D. wanted to know.

"Creepy."

Gregg's own words came back to him from that first visit with Rick in the Highlands, when Peck had shot the elephants. Rick had been feeding them candy from the very beginning and how easily he had lured them in. And even now, in the midst of the mission being turned into a House of Horrors, Rick didn't put out a crazy vibe. He wasn't foaming at the mouth or having his eyes roll up in his head or even remotely looking like the most obvious candidate in the room for a strait jacket.

No, he was still looking like a Burt Lancaster body double and sounding like his personable self when he added with a touch of modesty, "Excuse me for tooting my own horn, but I did think the matches were a nice touch, even if I hated giving them up."

"And why was that, Rick?"

"My, you are just full of questions tonight, aren't you, Doc?"

"Occupational hazard," Gregg said, struggling to keep his voice conversational. They were all going to die, just like the Headman and his wife. He couldn't protect Kate. It was the worst way he could possibly go.

"Anybody ever tell you that you'd make a good shrink?" Rick chuckled as he went about attaching the grenades with precision to the claymore wires.

"Apparently not good enough."

"Now, now, don't you feel too bad about not catching my hand in the cookie jar sooner. I've had lots of practice at this and I'm a very good planner. That's important, you know. Careful planning is always critical in fixing things, Gregg."

"Like the matches you hated giving up because. . .?"

"Back to that are we? Let's just say the matches were a little keepsake for a good deed, a reminder not to always just think of myself when it comes to taking out the trash. Okay, I am just about done here, not my best work, but it'll do. I will enjoy a little more chat time with you, Gregg—because I really will miss you most of all, Scarecrow—and maybe have another drink since this is some very fine vodka. But then?" Rick licked a finger and put it to the sky as if to determine the weather. "Sadly, it will look like I'm going to arrive just a little too late to avert a horrible Viet Cong atrocity, committed by this Professor guy and his little Charlie buddies."

"Come on, pal. What would Nikki say if she heard you saying stuff like this?"

Rick scratched his head, shrugged. "Dunno. But you can ask her once you get to where she's already gone."

"Did you do it? Did you kill Nikki, too?"

Rick looked offended. "Hell, no. She would be easier than the Headman. Even easier than a kitten. There's no challenge in that. If you don't believe me, you can ask her yourself shortly." He checked his watch. "Let's say in two minutes."

"But what about you, Rick?" Gregg frantically asked. "Where do you go from here? You know the CID, the CIA, they'll eventually figure it out and then they'll be hunting you down."

"Really?" Rick chuckled. "Now how did that work out for them this last time? Or the time before that? Naw, sorry Gregg, but I'm smarter than them. In fact, smarter than you, too. The way it's going to play out here is that the army's going to ask me and my new guys to hunt the Professor and company down since they took out the whole hospital, even the kids, in a bloody, horrific massacre. You know, like what happened in Hue during Tet."

Rick stepped back to review his handiwork, nodded in satisfaction, went to the bar, decided, "Maybe I'll just take the bottle to go," and picked up his gun.

At the sound of a window breaking, he whirled around and a flying shadow came soaring right at him. Rick opened fire, but J.D. was faster, hitting Rick's gun arm just before he could swing it around, and knocked the gun to the ground, where it skittered across the wood floor, inches away from a claymore wire.

J.D. was on top just for a moment before Rick flipped him over, and that's when another body came sailing through the window. Izzy had something in his hand and was dodging the struggle as he tried to get closer to Rick—Rick who freed his knife arm and swung it in a blur at J.D.'s chest. Then reaching down to his calf sheath, he whipped out another blade, and was flashing it towards Izzy's chest when Professor Nguyen threw his body over the wire, his hands and feet still bound, and took the hit for Izzy.

Rick smiled with a kind of radiant ecstasy as he impaled the professor with one hand, had a knife partially in J.D.'s chest with the other, and crowed, "Good try, kids! Now it's time to finish everything up nice and tidy. Perhaps Mikel will notice he has a souvenir to remember me by."

Izzy got up from the floor and swiped his palms together as if ridding them from dust or germs. "And perhaps, Captain Galt, you will notice a souvenir of your own. Or possibly not. The thing about violent adrenaline-oriented people is they quite often don't recognize immediate pain themselves. Say, like the Benzodiazepine needle I have jabbed in your leg?"

Rick looked down where Izzy pointed, and in a trip-hammer moment his face contorted, filled with rage. He released a diabolical roar and was trying to rip the needle out of his leg when he seemed to lose control of his muscles and slowly collapsed.

J.D. got up. He pulled out the knife embedded in his flak jacket before throwing an arm around Izzy's shoulder.

"Great job. How long will he be out?"

"At least two hours. I injected enough to take down a horse."

"Okay, cut everybody loose, and nobody touch any of this stuff. Let me disable all the explosives he has strung up. All you medical folks, get busy here taking care of each other. The professor looks really bad."

His chest wound was pulsing blood and he gasped for air. Having seen to Shirley first, Izzy sliced the bindings on Robert David and Margie so they could help work on the professor. His wheezing breath mingled with Shirley's continued utterance of the Lord's Prayer over and over her dead husband.

Kate struggled against the trusses that bound her to Gregg, her voice urgent. "The children, he said he was killing them, too. What if he already has?"

"The professor's dead," Robert David pronounced.

"Then leave him here," J.D. said briskly as he disabled the last of the claymores. "Kate's right. Who knows if he started here, or in the hospital wards. There's no telling what we might find there, but we better hurry."

J.D. flipped open a switchblade. "Excellent work, Doctor," he said quietly to Gregg, then cut the rope that bound him to Kate. Kate, who J.D. lifted up, who in turn kissed him quick and hard, full on the mouth.

It hurt more to watch than the butt of the rifle Gregg had taken to the face.

J.D. offered him a hand up. Gregg ignored it and got off his own knees and went over to Shirley whose pain had to be so much worse than his. He put a hand on her shoulder, letting her know she wasn't alone as she kept rocking back and forth while she stroked her husband's bloodless face.

"All right everybody," J.D. said to the group, "We need to clear this room and get over to the wards immediately."

"Come on," Gregg whispered to Shirley, knowing she was in shock and yet the longer she stared at the ghastly vision of her husband, the deeper she would go. "We need to check on the kids. Come on, Shirley. David would want you to do that."

She vaguely nodded and Gregg managed to extricate her from Dr. Donnelly. Margie wobbled over to lend her support as Shirley's legs gave way. Robert David seemed oblivious to his ruined nose and slashed cheek that had coagulated so the blood no longer drained as he and Izzy made for the exit.

"Just to be on the safe side," J.D. said as he hastily tied Rick's arms and legs.

They were a sad looking troop of the walking wounded doing their best to race across the lawn to the children's ward. Kate got there first and was reaching for the door when J.D. shouted, "Do NOT open that door."

With deft and knowledgeable precision J.D. scoped out the perimeter of the building, looked through windows, and quickly ascertained the situation.

"Okay, there are bodies all over the floor but the children are in their beds. He's got wires all over the place and the door is rigged to blow. Everyone get back."

They all took cover and J.D. did his magic, somehow disabling the explosives at the door, then doing the same inside before calling, "All clear. Get in here, on the double."

The place was a disaster with dead nurses and children so traumatized and damaged already, they were probably still alive because most of them didn't have all their limbs to get out of bed and trip one of the wires en route to a murdered nurse or the booby trapped exit.

They all went to work as best they could, even Shirley, covering the dead bodies to hide what the children had already seen, and then seeing to each of the kids. Gregg knew he and Robert David must look pretty scary with their injuries, but the children clung to them nonetheless.

Everyone pitched in as a unit, except for J.D. who went to check the other units and no doubt find more of the same, until a finger tapped Gregg's shoulder.

Gregg jumped. The little girl with half a face he was holding cried, "Oh! No!"

J.D. said something to her in Vietnamese and she nodded, releasing her hold around Gregg's neck.

"I hate it that kids this age can understand how quickly they have to let go," said J.D. "But I need you and Izzy with me right now for backup. I radioed in for a pick-up with our favorite chopper. They'll be here soon and I want Galt out the second they touch ground. We should have at least half an hour before the drug starts to wear off according to Izzy, but Galt's something that's not quite human and that was a rush job I did on his restraints. Like Rick said, always be prepared, right?"

J.D. did the Boy Scout three finger hand signal and Gregg had to admit the guy was good. Gregg gave a curt nod and minutes later he, Izzy, and J.D. were back at the mission house they had left, traipsing up the veranda, and reentering the foyer, then the living room where Professor Nguyen laid dead, having sacrificed himself to save Izzy and everyone else, where Doctor Donnelly was just as dead with his neck nearly severed from his head.

And where Rick Galt had been, there was only a rope.

32

The distant sound of a chopper coincided with the distinct revving of an outboard engine.

"Where the hell is he?" Gregg examined the ropes like they had come out of Houdini's magic box.

"Never mind that"—J.D. stated as he headed for the door— "we need to get to the beach, if it's not too late already."

It was. On the beach they could see a Zodiac and there was Rick standing in the bow, blowing them a kiss goodbye as the boat gunned away onto a moonlit sea.

"That bastard!" Izzy started rummaging in his pockets. "I hit him with. . . " He frowned. There were two prefilled injections in the medic bag he had grabbed when J.D. raced into the villa and said he would explain on the way to the mission. Izzy was terribly afraid he might have screwed up. "Well, where the hell can he go? He's a fugitive in a war zone in a foreign country."

J.D. laughed dryly. "This guy? He can go anywhere and disappear, live in the jungle for weeks. He can get up to the border, contract out to a warlord and have a nice cushy job doing what he does best, killing people, by next week. Probably with a big pay raise. We have to get him now. Let's go."

The chopper was getting closer as Rick sped further away. *Crystal Blue* came low, right over the water, and Izzy beat a path to the chopper when it touched down, propelled by his fear he might have used the less potent IM injection and if anyone else died by Rick's hand, it would be his fault.

"Hop in boys," said the pilot in greeting. "We gotta stop meeting this way."

J.D. issued orders to the pilot and in seconds *Crystal Blue* was lifting up, spinning, and they were flying over the water. This time there was no Jimmi Hendrix or "In-A-Gadda-Davida" blaring from the speakers, only their hot, single minded pursuit of the Zodiac.

They were lucky the moon was bright. Izzy could see the white spray from the outboard and the wake of the boat on the inky black water.

"Looks like he's heading for the river mouth just ahead," J.D. shouted over the whirring blades. "Yeah, that's exactly what he's doing so he can beach the boat and disappear in the jungle. We have to tackle him on the boat before it's too late. If he gets on land, he'll be hoping we chase him so he can have some fun. Izzy, do you still have that knife I gave you on the way?"

Izzy nodded. The sheath on his leg with the blade felt awkward but comforting on his body as J.D. laid out the plan.

"Okay, when we're close enough we're all going to jump onto the craft. While I get him subdued, Gregg, you man the boat, and Izzy hit him again with the other needle. Got it?"

"Got it," Izzy said, his jaw set while he double checked to make sure he had easy access to the syringe he probably should have delivered the first time. Any mistake that had been made was on him; he had to make this right. He didn't have the luxury of being afraid to jump out of the helicopter when J.D. gave the order.

"Now when I say 'jump'—wait! Not yet!"

Too late Izzy was out of the chopper and landing awkwardly on the Zodiac, right next to Rick, who immediately pounced. He had a hand on Izzy's throat, and just as immediately sent a message overhead with a wave: *Jump and he dies.*

Izzy could feel his eyes bulging behind his glasses, could see the chopper hovering while Gregg and J.D. hesitated. Then there was a jolt, like the boat had hit a submerged rock and Rick bounced off of him.

Izzy did not analyze. He acted on pure adrenaline and instinct and unsheathed the knife J.D. had given him, scrambled back to the other end, and madly started stabbing the inflated craft.

"You stupid fuck!" Rick screamed as the knife punctured the skin and Izzy kept stabbing and stabbing while the boat deflated.

They were close to shore and Rick jumped out while Gregg and J.D. leaped from the chopper, landing near the edge of the beach where Izzy scrambled out of the deflated Zodiac.

Rick was already running for the jungle.

"Don't lose sight of him!" J.D. yelled, going right after him, and Izzy knew if they lost this maniac any future blood spilled would be on his hands. He had to have used the wrong injection in the heat of the moment when there wasn't time to think, just act.

No time to think now, they were all on the ground running, trying to catch up to a physical force of nature. Gregg seemed to turn into a thoroughbred and sprinted past J.D., closing the gap on Rick, then flying through the air to make a pro ball tackle.

Rick spun around, kicked, and dropped Gregg with a blow that left him gasping at the jungle's edge. Rick stopped in his tracks. He grinned.

"Okay, great, we might as well have some fun now and finish off you clowns, and then I just may go back and have my way with the girls you all left behind." He laughed jovially as Izzy caught up, gasping for breath. "Now who's first? Larry, Moe or Curly?"

"Try me," said J.D. and walked straight into Rick's onslaught.

Izzy grasped the syringe and tried to track their movements, knowing if he got J.D. instead it was over for them all. He watched in the milky moonlight as the shadows of two figures whirled and spun in a choreographed like rhythm. Rick was still laughing, enjoying himself immensely, until his knife went flying out of his grip, his wrist was snapped, and he was dropped to his knees by a kind of martial arts blow to his chest even he must not have seen coming.

Izzy seized the moment.

Rick tried to get back up but fell on his back, further embedding the needle that Izzy had jabbed into his shoulder.

"Strike hard. Strike first. Isn't that right, Rick?" he asked.

Rick howled in frustration. But he couldn't move.

"Your muscles will not respond," Izzy informed him. "It's a little like curare, Rick. The medication is paralyzing your system right now. You will soon even find it hard to breathe."

"You fucking idiots," Rick gasped. "They won't take me anywhere but somewhere they can use me." He gasped again. "They can use me. But you? You're just a couple of shrinks who know too much. You're the expendables." Another gasp. "Hit me with something else...to reverse this. Not too late. I can still. . .save you. From him."

It was then that Izzy became aware of a creepy crawly feeling at the base of his neck, making his skin prickle, his hair stand on end. He looked at Gregg, kneeling beside him over Rick's fallen body, and in Gregg's eyes was a kind of primal fear that echoed Izzy's own. Like every snake in their minds had come alive.

Weapons are instruments of fear; they are not a wise man's tools.
He uses them only when he has no choice.
—Lao Tzu

Dilemma of Picking Flowers

If you flew like a Nightbird up over the water and into the dark of the jungle and then sat on a limb above a small animal trail and waited. . .

You would see the assassin. His growing uncertainty is becoming palpable. He thinks he can feel something like a conscience worming its way past the determination to do what he should do, and has done many times before. A thousand thoughts and calculations are happening in a part of his mind that is too ingrained to shut off.

The two men on their knees in front of him look like they are praying. His grandfather would simply say it is the way of the Tao. From the beginning this was the way it was supposed to end.

But then again his grandfather would also say:

The highest good is like water.
In ruling, be just.
Water gives life to the ten thousand things and does not strive.
It flows in places men reject. . .
And so it is like the Tao.

The two men kneeling are frozen. Their hearts are hammering with the urgent beat of Run through the Jungle. On the ground they see a predator. They sense another predator right behind them.

They slowly turn.

They see the gun.

"J.D.?" says the one named Izzy. His hands have begun to shake. "What are you doing?"

"Yeah, knock it off," says the one named Gregg but his voice quivers. He sees a cold glitter in the green eyes like sea glass.

The Nightbird watches as a flare shoots into the sky and explodes, bathing them in the shimmering orange light as the predator stares straight at them and wonders when he got so soft.

"Congratulations, guys," he says. "Looks like you made the team."

And the Nightbird folds its wings.

33

Gregg and Izzy walked across the cat tracks toward the 99KO. It was growing dark and Kohn had called to tell them to get over to the unit ASAP.

"So where do you think J.D. really took Galt?" They had not seen either of them in the week since the mission massacre. Gregg touched his bandaged nose. It was healing up well and so was his broken cheekbone, which looked a lot better than the running length of stitches on Robert David's face. The plastic surgeon who repaired his fine nose anticipated excellent results even if Robert David now had a terrible tendency to snore. Loudly.

"Who knows beyond someplace the government can observe him while keeping the troops and everyone else a safe distance away.'" Izzy made J.D. quote marks that reminded Gregg of the Howdy Doody grin lines Izzy got whenever he was around Margie. "I guess we're supposed to feel special that everyone else thinks he got carted out in a body bag and we know better."

"Yeah. I can't say I enjoyed lying to Robert David and Margie about that."

"It's better they don't know. Kate and Shirley, too," Izzy reminded him. "They have enough to deal with at the mission as it is." He shook his head.

Gregg wondered if he would ever get his own head back on straight. He could have sworn J.D. was ready to shoot him and Izzy both, literally in the back, before they turned around. J.D. had hesitated, then smiled as he exchanged the pistol for a flare gun and laughed in a way that reminded Gregg a little too much of Rick: charming, sincere, infectious. So completely believable you had to think that you were the crazy one, not him, when he turned out to be an accomplished actor who delivered his lines with a good dose of the truth.

Upon entering the unit, K.O. practically knocked over a cart in her enthusiasm to greet them. Colonel Kohn didn't look so enthusiastic himself as he immediately gestured them over to a private corner.

"You're both wanted for a conference over at HQ."

"What now?" Gregg asked. His stomach dropped.

Kohn signed wearily. "I'm not sure. Colonel Johnson is there with some of his superiors in the CO's office. They're waiting for the two of you. I called you here first to give you a heads up. If there's any trouble, I'm in your corner."

Izzy and Gregg hurried to their summons, pausing only as they passed the Red Cross building where a line of soldiers were still waiting to use the phone.

"It will never be the same without Nikki." Gregg tipped his head as they kept walking. "I hope to god they get who did this."

"Maybe that's what this meeting is about. CID knows it wasn't J.D."

Gregg had to admit J.D.'s decision to get arrested so Rick would think he was momentarily out of the picture was not a bad move. J.D. explained he had strong suspicions at that point about Rick, but it was mostly based on a private conversation with the Mnong Headman who had some misgivings about Rick he couldn't substantiate beyond "a bad feeling" and other circumstantial evidence—unfortunately, some of it tampered with—and J.D. thought the killer might be lured out if only given a small window of time to strike.

The problem was getting Kate out of there just in case, not to mention everyone else possibly being put in jeopardy. J.D. even had some suspicion that Rick may have murdered Nikki and was hastily working with Colonel Johnson on getting enough evidence to make an arrest at the mission, which would effectively take Rick away from the field on the pretext of another crime, even if further investigation proved he hadn't committed it. But at least it would temporarily keep him under lock and key while conclusively determining whether or not the highly decorated Captain Richard Galt was responsible for the murders of their men in the field. Further complicating the arrest of an extremely valuable Special Ops trainer was that if he was not the one doing the killing, then the field was exactly where they needed to keep him so he could help track down and eliminate the true culprit or culprits.

J.D. checked himself out of the slammer early when he made a connection between the matches from San Antonio and an MP who had come in from Fort Sam Houston, murdered just next door at Camp McDermott. This coincided with a little time off Rick decided to take right after they left the Highland's firebase morgue.

He should have used a different chopper. The pilot of *Crystal Blue* confirmed that he no sooner dropped them off than Rick radioed in a request for a pick up and drop off next door and it sort of irked the pilot he had to make two trips back to back that didn't include some action—and he wasn't talking about the kind of action that had Rick wearing a pair of Converse.

As Gregg and Izzy neared HQ, Gregg recalled, "The last time we were summoned over here Peck was responsible."

"He sure seemed to get over Nikki quick. What I don't understand is why he gets to waltz around whistling like he's going on vacation and we get called into headquarters."

"Guess we're about to find out. Wow, check out the car."

A black Cadillac limousine with dark windows was parked in the shadows near the building, about where Derek had pushed past them before getting his M16 to blow the hell out of Top.

"I still need a haircut," Gregg said thoughtfully. He ran a hand through his beachcomber blond hair as they entered HQ and approached Top's old desk. "Hey, Terry, how you doing?"

"242 and a wake-up," Terry muttered. He was already out of his seat. "I'm to escort you to the conference room immediately. You'll notice a couple of Green Berets standing guard at the door."

"Who's in there?" Izzy whispered.

Terry kept his own voice low. "Colonel Kellogg, Colonel Johnson, General Claymore from MACV headquarters in Saigon, and a very important looking gentleman in a suit who was not introduced to me."

Terry escorted them past the Green Berets standing at attention in their nylon combat boots, and there was Colonel Kellogg looking as if he was screwed into his chair at one end of the conference table, with Colonel Johnson beside him. At the other end a much decorated General paced near a man of obvious stature who stood in the shadows of the room.

The General turned his gaze on Kellogg.

"You are excused now. Remember what I told you."

*

Izzy watched Kellogg leave with his head down, looking at no one. The guards followed him out. General Claymore then deferred to the man in the suit, who stood in the furthest corner as if seeking privacy in the shadows.

His hair was thick and silvery. When he spoke his voice was high and a bit squeaky, which in no way matched his attire or his bearing as he flipped open an engraved pocket watch.

"Let's get to it, Glen." The man in the suit tapped his foot.

Maybe it was because of all the combat boots Izzy was accustomed to seeing but he noticed the tapping foot was wearing really shiny shoes.

"Have a seat, Doctors," the general instructed, indicating the chairs across from him in the glare of what looked and felt like interrogation lights. "Relax. This is just a briefing. According to J.D., you both deserve medals for what you've been through, but of course you won't get any because none of this ever happened. Now did it?"

For a moment, Izzy couldn't find his voice. He wasn't sure how they were supposed to relax when a very clear threat had been issued in the question that wasn't really a question but an order.

"No, sir," Izzy answered.

"It never happened," Gregg repeated.

"Good. Then we also understand each other that you never saw what I'm about to show you. Correct?"

"Yes, sir."

"Yes, sir."

He shoved a folder across the desk, directly in front of them. "Open it."

Izzy wasn't sure what he or Gregg were expecting but there was a picture of Rick Galt attached to some official looking military papers, then beneath those were a stack of typed pages that looked like journal entries. He was drawn to pull those out while Gregg studied the remainder of the file.

"The guy in the picture was here in 64. Jerry Prince was his name. Same deal, though. Started doing his own guys. No proof but clearly a nut job. They sent him back home to the Madigan General Psych Unit, the locked ward, then to the special unit for the criminally insane where he suddenly disappeared with his records in December of 66."

"When you say disappeared, do you mean in the conventional sense?" asked Izzy, eyeing the top page that read: KILLERS.

"Walked away. Do not ask how. 'His' body was found later, horribly burned, beyond recognition—but, with some Jerry Prince ID conveniently left intact. We just recently tracked it down with the picture."

"And when did Rick Galt arrive?" asked Gregg.

"June, 67."

"His file here says ROTC."

Colonel Johnson jumped in. "Yeah, well, apparently the real guy has been missing since that winter. Went on a ski trip. His parents thought he took off to Canada to get out of Nam after he graduated from Washington State. Instead he moved up quickly in the ranks. Great soldier, Richard Galt."

"You mean Prince actually returned here after escaping the psych unit?" Izzy couldn't keep the incredulity from his voice. Or, his eyes from racing over the headers of the typed pages he flipped through:

DARKNESS

KITTENS

CLEANSING

CUT

And then he came to the last one. It read: NOTES FROM HELL

"As Rick Galt, he did well. Highly decorated. Volunteers for all the shit. Teaches hand to hand. Highly proficient and skilled. Dedicated and deadly." Johnson snorted. "Should be on a poster."

"If you think about it, a war is a perfect place for a psychopathic killer." Gregg, pointing out what had become all too obvious.

Izzy moved the journal pages closer, so Gregg could get a look at them too.

"Absofuckinglutely," Johnson agreed. "We could use more of them if there was a way to keep them from crossing the wrong line."

"True." For the first time the shiny shoes spoke to Izzy and Gregg. "So what can you tell us, doctors, to help us better understand how a mind like this works? The information may be useful."

Gregg looked up at Izzy and shook his head, then continued to turn from one trauma and horror filled page to the next. This firsthand account of the ongoing brutalization and twisting of a child's psyche and humanity, the systematic eroding of any sense of empathy or compassion, was so disturbing that Izzy was relieved to transfer his attention to clinical theory.

"It's a mental illness," he explained. "The obsession, the fantasy, the victim, the shock, the fear, the thrill he gets from doing it in his own private, precise, and unique way. Close, from behind, feeling it. Nothing else provides the release. Only this serves him and he only serves it."

"What else?"

"He's a hunter. He loves the hunt and he loves the kill. It's actually what gets him off. The adrenaline rush is like a big drug hit." Izzy shivered, remembering the look of ecstasy on Rick's face as he impaled Professor Nguyen.

"But why our own guys?" General Claymore persisted.

"He wants to hunt the best. In a sick, twisted way he's like a bull fighter who raises and trains the best bulls in the world to be killers and then he kills them. It makes him the best. The very best killer in the world. A monster. He really is the Boogeyman."

Gregg held up a hand. "Just give me a minute here."

They all went quiet; even the shiny shoes stopped his toe tapping.

When Gregg laid down the entries, he asked, "How did you get these?"

Claymore answered. "He had some secret notes hidden away that were found after his escape, but most came out as part of his therapy at Madigan and one of the shrinks was studying his writings when the medical records disappeared. Why?"

"Because if you want to have a step-by-step construction plan on how to make a psychopath, these entries of his provide a nice blueprint for creating one: The isolation, the abandonment, the trauma of killing at a young age, a child inured to emotions against the unthinkable, then getting twisted to a point where it feels good to kill, to feel the ultimate power after you've been so powerless to defend yourself against others, against the system."

"But not everyone would turn out the same way under duplicate circumstances," Shiny shoes noted.

"Of course not. But don't ever doubt that everyone has a dark side of the brain and that's where we can all feel some excitement or pleasure in pain and killing. That's our big cultural no-no, to admit that violence and even killing is exciting. But just go to a major prize fight in Vegas. Listen to the cheers when the blood flies. And, the more brutal it becomes, the more frenzied the audience gets. Blood lust. It's in all of us. And it shames us. Well," Gregg amended, "most of us."

"Absolutely," Izzy concurred. "It wasn't that long ago that burning a witch at the stake or a public beheading was cause for a festival. Free entertainment. Come one, come all, bring the whole family and have a picnic. The fact simply is that civilization and civility is a very lovely and precious, but very thin veneer, over a twisting, brutal savagery within us all."

"And Richard Galt—or Jerry Prince—has embraced his own inner dark side. Horrifically so. The result?" Gregg tapped the typed pages. "He is a psychopath's psychopath."

A clock ticked in the background. Long moments passed before General Claymore suddenly reached over to reclaim the file. Gregg laid a hand on the entries.

"You know, I knew this guy. I even thought he was a friend. Somehow I missed it all, completely, and I would like to understand how I got so blindsided. Is there any chance I could have a Xerox copy of these to study? Or, even just the last one since I didn't read it yet?"

The general looked at the mysterious shiny shoe guy. He simply opened his watch again and said, "The request will be considered. Doctors? Until we meet again. Glen, you know what to do."

He exited the room without speaking to anyone else and Izzy could hear the steady march of the combat boots escorting him out of headquarters.

The General cleared his throat. "I will say simply that you are to have an immediate and permanent case of amnesia regarding your dealings with the individual you were assisting on a case that never existed."

"You are referring to J.D.?" Gregg asked.

"Who?" The general shook his head. "Never heard of him. You know nothing that you have learned and you know no one because, well, Doctors, you would like to go home, wouldn't you? Otherwise I can arrange a nice year's extension, then maybe another one after that. But if everyone shuts up, everyone goes home on schedule. And once you're there you still keep your mouth shut or there will be dire consequences. Go home, tell no tales. Am I clear?"

Gregg nodded. Izzy was just as mute. There was an unspoken innuendo in the general's tone that raised the fine hair on his neck. It reminded him of the creepy, crawly feeling he had at his back when they were bent over Rick and turned around to see J.D. pointing a gun at them.

The army wanted this whole thing squashed, gone, nonexistent, and the army would get its way. But, Izzy now wondered if they had somehow not gotten their way when the General snapped, "Let me hear you say it, Doctors: Go home, tell no tales."

"Go home. Tell no tales."

"Louder."

"GO HOME. TELL NO TALES."

There was a long silence. "All right, don't make me regret this. Are we on the same page?"

"Sir, yes, sir!"

Another long silence. "Dismissed."

Izzy had never managed such a sharp salute. He got out as fast as he could without running, didn't even stop to say goodbye to Terry.

Neither did Gregg.

They were both breathing hard when they got outside.

"Holy mother of—" Gregg gasped as soon as they were out of earshot of a living creature. "Did you pick up on the subtext of that shit?"

"Loud and clear. It's what he didn't say that said it all."

They looked at each other and knew: *Dead men* tell no tales.

There had been over 10,000 troops sent home in body bags in the past year alone. A great many drafted, just like them. What difference would two more casualties make, particularly if they were in on some top secret shenanigans the powers that be had a vested interest in containing?

"Do you. . ." Izzy swallowed hard, kept his voice hushed. "Do you think, just to be on the safe side, J.D. was supposed to. . .?"

"Who?" Gregg said.

"Right," Izzy agreed. "Well, we seem to be safe for now at least. But, what about everyone else?"

Kate, Shirley, Robert David, Margie, they all knew Rick was the Ghost Soldier now. They all knew J.D. worked undercover and had vanished as suddenly as he appeared. What they didn't know were the details, and the devil was in the details when it came to what the two of them knew and no one else did. The others had not seen the body bags, the proof of Rick's handiwork in the field. They did not know Rick had brutally murdered a Mnong Headman and his wife or an MP from San Antonio and no telling how many others. Or that he had escaped from a military mental ward to make a mockery of the US government's internal checks and balances or that he had been whisked away to cover it all up, as if he had never existed, but was nowhere near as dead as anyone else thought.

And *that* was the biggie. That's what made Izzy and Gregg a potential liability the others were not, whose collective silence had nonetheless been bought through other means:

The directive to Shirley and Kate was to simply go along with the story of the horrible VC massacre, a version in which Shirley's late husband was a heroic Christian martyr; otherwise, the three of them would be traitors who harbored the enemy like Professor Nguyen and their shared blame for the massacre would ensure they were incarcerated indefinitely and the mission would be closed. As for Margie and Robert David, they had careers to consider and it was clearly up to them to salvage their futures, not to do anything stupid. If anyone squealed, everyone paid. The military held them as hostage as Rick had himself.

And none of them had a fraction of the dirt to spread as the new team players did.

"They don't have the same tales to tell, Izzy. They didn't make the team." Gregg's still-healing jaw clenched as he added, "Not even Peck. He's safe, too."

34

It felt like a sugar sweet night ahead, Peck thought with a smile, as he arrived on his favorite island via a pleasant sunset boat ride on calm seas.

Uncle Sam was expecting him. Because of the whole Nikki fiasco he had waited a respectable time before scoring some action through his favorite source with nieces to spare.

His patience was about to be rewarded and handsomely. The stars were already aligned in his favor. Life at work was so much better now with that pompous Robert David Thibeaux returned stateside, then Margie shipped out just the week before which meant that Jew Moskowitz was moping around.

Best of all, though, a solid two months had passed with Mikel gone. As far as Peck knew, he was rotting away in LBJ, or better yet at cozy Ft. Leavenworth. It would almost be worth a trip to Kansas to see him behind bars. Indeed, that would be a pleasure.

But tonight he had more immediate gratification ahead of him and if that included some uppers and Jack to enhance the evening while he roughed up the girl, inside and out? That was one of the great things really about being in the military, and especially about being in Vietnam, most of the people around him were just so simple and unimaginative he could get by with just about anything, and no one would care what he did to a gook.

Uncle Sam met Peck outside the secluded hut on schedule, showed him in, simpering, "Numbah one for you GI. Numbah one, very young, very pretty."

Uncle Sam immediately bowed out the door and shut it.

Peck heard a noise like ice cubes clinking in a glass. He turned. The room was as he remembered it with a desk, a phonograph, a chair, mattress on the floor surrounded by mosquito netting, a box containing adult toys—but there was an addition he wasn't expecting.

His heart immediately raced. His breath caught. That didn't happen often, not even when Nikki died. Normally, it was the elusive high he was always after, but not like this.

"What the hell are you doing here?"

Mikel smiled. He stood beside the rattan chair, the same one Peck had urged Nikki to sit on before kneeling at her feet and delivering his Oscar-worthy proposal.

"Listen," Mikel said softly. "Outside the wind is moving in the palms. And what's that? I do believe I hear the sound of rain on the roof."

"It's raining," whispered Peck. And he realized, suddenly—it was.

"Remember, I made a promise about the rain." Mikel took another sip from his highball glass, filled with an amber liquid. "A certain headman who owes me a favor is waiting outside. I told him I had the officer responsible for killing another headman in the Highlands. I told him to bring his machete. Just not to come in until I gave him the word. And I will give him the word if you do not do exactly as I say."

"But I didn't kill a headman!"

"No, you only killed Nikki."

Peck's heart was pounding like the drums he thought he could hear outside.

"I am a United States Army Officer. You can't do anything to me."

"Oh, really?" Mikel put down his glass, casually strolled over, and delivered a sharp blow straight to Peck's solar plexus.

Peck didn't even remember falling to the floor where he squirmed in pain, trying desperately to breathe.

Mikel pulled the chair closer. Turned it around, straddled the seat. He rested his arms and chin on the chair's back, then just sat there, quietly staring down where Peck continued to writhe and gasp for air.

"You know Peck, I actually thought about this, and believe me when I tell you I really dislike having to spend any time thinking about you. However, because of what you did to Nikki, and because you are basically the biggest asshole I have ever met in my life, I decided you and I could spend some quality time together on this nice rainy night in the tropics. So, I thought up a couple of nifty, old school Asian entertainments, say the old bamboo under the nails or perhaps actually skinning your face down to your neck line, or... perhaps some things involving insects. Actually, I like the idea of all three. What about you?"

"Please, please," Peck managed to gasp out. "I'll confess. Go with you right now to Colonel Johnson. Give a full confession about Nikki. It was an accident." An accident, he might get leniency. Even better, once he got out of here he would recant it all and turn evidence against Mikel. How Mikel got out after being arrested was not the issue right now, getting out of here alive was.

"Yes," Peck repeated, his voice dripping with sincerity, "I will confess to accidentally killing her if that's what you want."

"Well that is a fine idea, Major. In fact, knowing how smart you are I came prepared." Mikel reached into his shirt pocket and produced a typed sheet of paper. "I just happened to bring along a confession—you know, anticipating your remorse and all. So, you just can sign this... come along now over to the table and have a seat and please make yourself comfortable."

Peck did as instructed. "Certainly, we can be civilized about this," he agreed. "It was a terrible mistake all around. Honestly, I just went into shock, like a panic, and then made up a stupid story. I meant no harm, believe me. I'm truly sorry you got stuck with the blame."

"Oh, that's all right, Major. No harm meant. So go ahead there and just sign and then you can make a nice hand written statement on the back about how you covered it up like you said."

Peck signed off with a flourish. "There, it's done. See? I did what you asked and now let's get right back to the unit and call the colonel and we are done with it all. Okay?"

"Okay," agreed Mikel.

Just to be sure, Peck asked, "Then we can go?"

Mikel extended his hand. "After you."

"And you will tell the Headman to leave me alone, make sure he doesn't harm me?"

"Absolutely."

As they both moved toward the door, Peck was again hit with a sharp blow that left him writhing like a beached fish gasping for air.

Again Mikel pulled up the chair and simply sat, watching. After a while he said pleasantly, "Well, sure, that takes care of things for Nikki, but. . .what about the elephants?"

"The elephants," Peck gasped, still writhing. "What about them?"

Silence.

"Okay, I'm sorry. Sorry! That was a mistake. I wish I could take it back."

It began to rain harder outside. Peck's heart had never beaten so fast. "Please, you said we could go."

Mikel was quiet for a long moment. Then he moved from the chair, went to the toy box, and returned with a very long rope made of twisted silk. "Time to get up now and put this around your neck."

"You are joking? You cannot possibly be serious."

"Get up on the chair."

"*No.*"

"Then you are saying that you prefer my Chinese entertainment options, followed by being served up to the outside company with something sharper? Oh come on, be a good sport. I'll just leave you up there until you pass out so you know how it feels to look death in the face. Consider it an exercise in empathy, Doctor, a little extended education. I know it might scare you at first—and honestly I do hope it does—but the next thing you know you'll feel like you're going under with some very nice drugs. And when you wake up, you'll be on the boat so we can pay that nice visit to Colonel Johnson. Now, what's it to be? The chair and scarf or the Headman outside who owes me a favor and has an ax to grind? Your choice."

Peck had heard that momentary asphyxiation could be stimulating. It was just a matter of Mikel not leaving him up too long. He did not trust Mikel, but neither were the present options much of a choice. At least this way there was a chance, however slim.

He climbed up and stood on the chair, hesitantly put the silk around his own neck. Mikel cinched it tight then looped the long end over the rafter. Pulled it down and then down a little more.

"Oh my, that might be a little too high. I fear I might have misled you. Can you hear the rain?"

Lightening cracked outside.

Peck had to dance on tiptoe to relieve the pressure on his neck.

Mikel secured the end he held. A nice, professional wrap job so if Peck kicked back the chair he would immediately hang himself.

Humming "Tonight" from *West Side Story*, Mikel made a show of producing some sharp bamboo, a scalpel, a few other instruments an actual MD might find useful in performing surgery.

Then he went over to the phonograph, flashed a smile. "Any favorites?"

35

Gregg got up extra early. If the wound to the balls and Dear John letters were the dreaded awfuls of RVN, then DEROS was the Holy Grail:

Date of Estimated Return from Overseas. DEROS had arrived.

He was leaving the unit today. He was already packed. Everything he was going to wear was on his bed. The shorts and tee and booney hat he had on, he would leave behind. His duffel was packed with all the gifts and souvenirs for family and friends. He had shipped the new Teac tape deck and stereo receiver, the Pioneer speakers; all the stuff everybody typically bought would greet him at home in Del Mar. He also had splurged with his last paychecks and bought through the military deal the new MG in racing green, which would be waiting along with a new life back in The World.

But today was wake up day. He had only to make it down to Saigon, spend a night, and then board a Freedom Bird, and he was gone. Goodbye to Vietnam. The weird thing was. . .Why did he feel like he was really excited but also sad and empty?

It was not anything like what he had expected.

Gregg walked alone through the scented Ironwood pines and the dawning light down to the beach and looked out at the now familiar sparkling South China Sea. He kicked off his sandals, took off his shirt, tossed aside his wallet, then walked to the water, dove in and swam out as hard as he could for a long ways. On the return, he swam on his back and watched the sky turn brighter. He sat down on the sand and waited for the sun. It was hard to imagine that in a couple of days he would be sitting on the sand in Del Mar and looking out across the waters there.

"Hey, surfer boy, you dreaming of Del Mar or Laguna?"

Gregg watched her walk toward him. She was so beautiful to him. In her cutoff jeans and T-shirt, she still could have been the girl next door. Though as fate would have it, a few years older and a head taller until he had a spurt of growth—not that it mattered because he still hadn't been able to catch up with the competition.

Seemed some things never changed.

"Come home with me," he said anyway. He would never stop trying.

"Don't start with that. . ."

"You're staying because of him, aren't you?"

"No, because of me. He has nothing to do with it."

"You're a liar and you know it."

Kate sat down beside him. They were silent, just sitting, looking out over the water. Then she nudged his shoulder and leaned close. The feel of her skin, the warmth of it, had the same impact of that day so many years ago on another beach.

He was turning thirteen. She said she wanted to give him a birthday present he would never forget, something special before another girl beat her to it because he was *her* Gregg and always would be. Besides, she was curious and knew he wouldn't tell. It would be their secret.

"Did you tell him?"

"What?"

"Don't give me that. You know what."

Kate hesitated, then shook her head. A little too adamantly.

Gregg thought she was lying but he wanted to believe her. He wanted to believe her so badly, that J.D.'s "babysitter on the board-walk" comment had just hit a spot he was overly-sensitive about and Kate hadn't divulged their private, sacred trust.

"I still wonder if you have ever fully grasped what that day did to me."

"Gregg, please, let's not get into this again. Don't make me sorry I came here so we could have a private goodbye."

"After that day," he said anyway, "I spent a lot of time looking at the picture I still carry in my wallet." He took it out, showed her the proof. "I used to look at it when I did what boys that age natu-rally do. Hell, I'm way beyond embarrassing myself, so the fact is, it's still my go-to. I looked at it when guys who could drive came to pick you up, and then while I waited in the shrubs outside to see when you got home, how long you stayed in the car, knowing all the while I wouldn't even be able to get a license until you were gone." He laughed, no mirth in it. "Knowing you let them touch you while you acted like I was some kind of kid brother. Knowing how desperately in love I was with you and I didn't have a chance. It was hell then. Still is."

"I wish I could take it back," she whispered. "I wish, I wish. What I did was wrong and I've regretted it more than you'll ever know. But Gregg, that was a long time ago and the girl you thought you fell in love with—she doesn't exist anymore. She probably never did. You've turned me into some kind of fantasy girl that I'm just not. What you fell in love with is an illusion." She put her hand over his, over the picture he held between them. "But that doesn't mean we can't always love each other. Just not the way you—"

He kissed her then, full on the mouth and with every accumulated year of longing to do it, with the fury of a boy who had been enticed then spurned, only to turn into a man who had never forgiven her for not loving him back the way he loved her.

Kate's mouth was soft, pliant, as full of sweet nectar as a cherry ripe and juicy to the tongue. He didn't even know if she was kissing him back or just letting him do it, or maybe she was still curious and wondering how he might stack up against J.D.

Gregg hated him more than ever, the bastard intruding on the moment he had dreamed of since adolescence. And so Gregg kissed Kate harder, as if he could obliterate all those years and that bastard J.D. along with them, making it just him and Kate again, together alone on a beach.

She suddenly broke away, breathing hard, and pressed his head down, against her chest.

He could hear her heart beating. He could feel his own pounding in time to the thrum of blood infusing his veins, but. . .

Like this whole strange DEROS morning that wasn't at all what he had expected while he waited an eternity for it, this wasn't the moment he had envisioned a thousand times before. Kate was kissing the top of his head, rocking him more like a child than a man she wanted to strip down and mount.

Perhaps that's why he gave up the picture so easily. Why he let her take it, kiss it, then tear it down the middle.

She tucked the side that bore his image against her heart. But before he could grab back the other half, the image of her smiling with all the innocence and mischief and sexual alchemy of a sultry

Lolita at sixteen, Kate tore it up. She threw the pieces to the wind like crematory ashes that floated up and out to the South China Sea.

"Let it go, Gregg. Let me go. You deserve better. And so do I. If you ever really had me, you wouldn't want me. And I would resent the hell out of you for knowing I could never live up to your expectations of who you think I am."

She kissed him then. Sweetly, and all too fleetingly.

"You are always my hero Gregg, always and always. Promise me you'll try to be happy."

He couldn't get a word past the constriction of his throat, so he nodded.

"And promise that you'll try to be happy for me, if I manage to find a little happiness of my own?"

She didn't wait for the affirmation he made himself give. It took amply long and enough out of him to grant, that Kate had already walked away.

Gregg watched her go, hoping she would turn back. He knew she wouldn't. But he could see her shoulders were shaking as she made her way to the mission that turned no one away.

✳

The time came to leave his last, private respite where the 99KO officers were housed. Everyone else had already left for early morning rounds when he ran up the villa stairs, then showered and for the last time in Nha Trang dressed in his faded jungle fatigues and boots.

Gregg carried his bags and gear down by the door. A jeep honked outside.

It was the new psychology specialist who had taken Hertz's place—not that anyone could take his place.

The new guy loaded up Gregg's bags, drove him to the unit.

Gregg got out at the 99KO.

As soon as he walked into the unit, it looked like the whole staff and even the night shift was still there, cheering and chanting, "Gregg, Gregg, Gregg!" as they waved a big "Bon Voyage Gregg" banner everyone had signed with notes and cards attached to it. Everyone was so happy for him, but all he felt was guilty for getting to go home and they had to stay. Why wasn't this like WWII and they could all leave together?

What a fucked way to do it.

Gregg knew he had never cared so much and so deeply for so many people. It was like the year was a hundred years spent with them.

Once the handshakes and hugs were over, once Colonel Kohn patted him on the shoulder and said, "It's been an honor and a privilege," then saluted him, then came the hard part.

"Hey, where's Izzy?"

"Apparently, some strings were pulled and Margie will be meeting him in Hawaii while you're landing back home yourself."

"What? Are you kidding? That's great!"

Even as he said it and forced a smile, Gregg felt so empty that his stomach gnawed.

A jeep honked outside. Gregg made himself salute them all, give K.O. a last pat on the head, then commanded himself to leave—

Only to see Izzy waiting in the jeep for him.

Gregg hopped in, feeling lighter than he had since receiving his draft notice, and together he and Izzy waved goodbye until they rounded a corner and saw the sign: 8th Field Hospital marking the entrance they had just exited.

For Gregg, it would be the last time.

36

The flight to Tan Son Nhut was the usual transport; a big, ugly, noisy no frills MACV. Even so, as it lumbered down the boiling hot tarmac both Gregg and Izzy slapped hands and grinned like kids on a Ferris wheel. They sat on Gregg's duffel, deafened by the huge propellers seemingly inches from their ears. There could be no hearing so they both settled in for the relatively short flight and leaned back into their own thoughts.

Izzy was eagerly anticipating the trip to Hawaii and reunion with Margie. He could hardly believe his luck in getting this special R&R arranged by J.D. through high command, disguised as a "Combat Stress Diagnosis and Treatment" training seminar at Tripler General Hospital in Honolulu. All Izzy had to do was check in, sign his name, and then have a blessed week in The World with his dream girl.

He wondered if the nightmares would go away, or at least be less intense. He knew Margie had the same problem. Gregg, too. He wondered if J.D. ever suffered from dreading to sleep. Probably not. In all Izzy's studies and dealings with others, he had never known anyone quite like J.D. In some ways he was like an elite athlete or artist who moved through the world in their own way with their own rules. However, in another way he was like an elegant kind of thug or rogue who imposed his will and rules on those around him. Even, perhaps, on Peck? His reported "suicide" and note of confession might have been good for his soul but clearly not for the remains that were rumored to have been found in Ghost Soldier shape.

From an intellectual and psychological perspective it was often hard to differentiate between J.D. and Rick. Each moved like another kind of species or predator animal in their own worlds. One apparently did the bidding of the US government in the shadows and the other was a true denizen of the shadows and dark.

Upon arriving at the air base, Izzy checked in at the BOQ and got the news that his Pan Am flight to Honolulu was leaving at midnight. He and Gregg both rode the jeep over to the processing station where Gregg would begin the usual army tedium. As Gregg handed over his papers with his orders for his DEROS, the Specialist looked up sharply.

"Captain Gregg Kelly? Eighth Field Hospital, 99KO?"

"That's right," Gregg said uneasily.

Gregg glanced at Izzy and like couples who finish each other's sentences, they knew they were thinking the same thing. Had this all been an elaborate ruse to rope them up together and send them on a fast rail to no telling where?

"You are to report right over there, sir, and the sergeant will take care of you. You're being expected, as well as your company."

Izzy and Gregg moved as a reluctant unit to the imposing Master Sergeant.

"Captain Gregg Kelly reporting."

The sergeant came to attention. "Captain Kelly, sir. Let me get your bags, sir."

"What?" Gregg asked suspiciously. "Why?"

"Why, sir, you must know that you are going out VIP, First Class, right through that door there with the admirals, bird colonels, generals, and you are all processed, sir." He glanced at Izzy's name patch. "The orders say to admit your friend here, too. Both of you go right in now." And he held open the door to what looked like a board room for a top Fortune 500 corporation.

The air conditioning was another level of coolness to match the walnut paneled walls with silk oriental scrolls, a splashing fountain, and a navy steward in white manning the bar who made them the tallest gin and tonics they had ever seen. On the buffet table was a silver tray with anything you could want from home.

"Oh man, are you kidding me?" Izzy filled his plate with lox and cream cheese and bagels while Gregg loaded up on prime rib that looked almost as delicious as what Sergeant Washington had grilled up on the beach.

"Apparently it is good to be a general or an admiral or a spook," Izzy noted as they got settled into the huge, comfy leather club chairs. "This must be the upside to making the team."

"It is definitely an excellent sendoff that I never expected from him. I wonder how he knew. . ." Gregg put down his G&T and turned suddenly serious. "It was unexpectedly hard for me to leave the 99 today and having you with me means the world. Promise me when you go back, you be careful, man, keep your ass down, no heroics, go out to the mission and look out for Kate—hell, you know all this. You know you better write me back. You're the only one that..."

"I can ever talk to," supplied Izzy.

"Yeah, don't you know it, buddy."

As they shook on always being a team, another steward in white approached the table, bearing a silver tray. On the tray was an envelope. The delivery made to its recipient, Gregg picked it up. His hands felt cold.

Gregg did as instructed on the outer envelope and did not open it until he was well on his way on the plane taking him home. He half expected the contents to self-destruct and take him out, only to be greeted by the unexpected yet again:

Dear Gregg,

I hope this letter finds you well and enjoying
the sort of ride back home that you deserve and
earned. We might not have seen eye to eye and
maybe we never will but I wanted to give you my
personal thanks for everything you have done.
I'm sure you will understand when I say that our
friend is at a "special" facility that is not on a map
and does not exist and do not be surprised if your
expertise is sought out again for a particular type
of research. To that end, I have enclosed a little
something you requested and ask that you keep as
confidential as I know I can count on you to keep
everything else.

In closing I would just like to say that this was the
most difficult assignment of my career. Not only
given the sensitivity of the issues involved, but
because it became more than a job for me. You and

Izzy taught me more than I ever expected to learn about human nature, including my own.

I wish you sanctuary and peace, Gregg. Read and enjoy. Until we meet again, I remain

Respectfully yours,
John Doe

NOTES FROM HELL

They say that war is hell. It is not. This is hell. The locked ward for the criminally insane. There are actually two locked doors at every EXIT. You need keys for both. I have one already. Every day the same walls, the same people, the same medications to slow down your brain to the pace of a snail. Medications that you can feel are altering your nervous system and destroying your speed and coordination. The blandness and sameness makes you crazier and crazier. The ones that have been here a long time are walking zombies. They shuffle along the halls, some of them actually drooling. Some wear helmets all the time because they seizure so often and are banging their heads all the time.

Oh, they are still dangerous, the walking zombies. They go off now and again and attack the staff. They mess them up pretty bad sometimes. If there is one thing crazy people and I have in common it is knowing who is dangerous. They stay away from me. The ones I know are dangerous I treat like very, very bad dogs. I always let them know where I am and never scare them or threaten them. If I have extra candy I give it to them. They remember. They remember the candy just like they remember who is mean to them. Milton managed to actually completely chew off the thumb and gouge out the eye of the tech that was mean to me before they subdued him. Only cost me a Mars bar. Old man Smith they say has bitten and disabled 5 techs in the crotch in his time here. He likes Snickers bars. He will help me get out for 3 bars when the time comes.

I am getting adept at faking the meds and hiding them to use later. I always know when a blood test is coming so can get blood levels where I need to. I got stupid once in Nam and got caught and then taken out of the war which was, as far as I was concerned, a great place. It will not happen again. I have a plan and it is a good one. It should be; I have gone over it several thousand times since I have plenty of time. I will get back again and this time I will be a new person with a new life and will develop my skills totally to another level. I know just what I want to do and what I want to be. I am highly motivated, gung ho as they say.

Everybody has a dream job says the vocational counselor and I agree with her. What can be better than a place they pay you to kill people for a living?? Almost everybody I knew over there was messed up by it. You go in there they say and all of you never comes back out. Me? I found myself. I felt better and better.

I can hardly wait to go back.

✳

Gregg carefully folded the pages and returned them to the envelope. If only he could put away the snakes in his head just as easily, he would gladly close the door and never look at any of it ever again.

Hours later, he opened his eyes, and remembered sanctuary and peace. Looking out the window, Gregg smiled.

He could see the lights of San Francisco.

EPILOGUE

If Kate had started as Audrey dancing, she now felt like Sophia Loren in some hot Italian movie. She stood in the dusky light by the tatami floor mattress, looking down at J.D. He was sleeping. His lithe brown, muscled body was naked and sprawled like a big jungle cat over the sheet. The breeze from the fan rustled his hair. His body had slick old scars scattered like some ancient swordsman's across his chest, arms, and legs. The sweat from their lovemaking was still on him. If this was what chemistry felt like then she had an all-time reference point for heat level. The last five days and nights were a blur of being entwined and sliding over each other's sweat slicked bodies and swimming and snorkeling in the South China Sea.

She went out to the hammock and pulled down the filmy mosquito netting and then lazily swung back and forth, watching the tropical dusky sky turn dark and the stars begin to come out. Kate took a deep breath. *Steady girl*, she thought, *steady*. And then she thought, *what the hell, am I talking about "Steady?"*

She was as far from steady right now as she was from San Diego County and Katherine Lynn Morningside was too far gone to care. She knew that the guy on the sheets was about as likely to be domesticated as a panther, and what he did professionally was just as dangerous. She did not know precisely how he fit in with the government beyond their liaison with Phillip, nor had she probed since J.D. had a way of eliciting information himself. At this stage, she really thought it best he not know that Phillip was the would-be father who had arranged the abortion that didn't go quite as expected.

C'est la vie. Such was life. And she had far more to be grateful for than most.

Certainly more than Shirley who had urged her to take a little time off, grab her chance at happiness while she could, because life was too fleeting to wait for assurances or second chances. *Go, go!* Shirley had waved her away, and away Kate had gone to join J.D. at his private dwellings.

There was a slight breeze coming up and Kate could hear some waves breaking on the shore. She had lit a candle before stepping outside and could see the main room's interior as if for the first time. The small desk, portable typewriter, various books, most on Asian philosophy. The paintings were Chinese brush on rice paper and some on silk with poems in elegant Chinese calligraphy. J.D. had translated their words and told her how the painting, the poem, and the interaction of those and the observer was a way of communicating deep feeling and beauty that had been developed over six thousand years.

When she asked him who had painted them, he smiled and just said, "Me. Let's go snorkeling."

Under the water was another whole wet world that was just another kind of exploring of sensuality like their lovemaking.

"Hey," he said next to the hammock. She had not even heard him move. "Are you receiving visitors in there?"

"I am," she said. "At least the kind that can behave themselves since the last time you joined me we flipped out of here like a circus act." Kate laughed.

So did J.D.

They canoodled side by side in the hammock, head to foot, looking at one another in the light from the lantern he had lit.

"Hungry?" he asked.

"Mmmmm," she said. "Yes, hungry, hungry."

"The Headman's sister is bringing over a special crispy fish, rice, and veggies. Fresh pineapple."

"I am calling the front desk and extending my stay."

"I hope so. Want to go on a river cruise?"

"Sure. Mississippi, Nile?"

"No, the Mekong." J.D. caught her wrist. The matching silver bracelet on his glinted in the moonlight. "I have a little work, combined with a family visit with my brother. He is, shall we say, a bit of a mystery?"

"Must run in the family." Kate pretended to think about it but they both already knew she couldn't resist an adventure any more than she could the lover in the hammock. "Actually, I think I would like that. A Mekong mystery. I know you have mysteries, but I did not know you had a brother."

"No one does, except you now." He kissed her then. "We leave in the morning."

The Island Dreaming

A man with outward courage dares to die;
A man with inner courage dares to live.
—Lao Tzu

ABOUT THE AUTHORS

JOHN L. HART, Ph.D. has been a practicing psychotherapist for more than forty years, starting in Vietnam where he was a psychology specialist, then studying with James Hillman and receiving his doctorate from the University of Southern California. John is an internationally respected lecturer, has been a consultant to the nation of Norway for their Fathering Project, and maintained a private practice in Los Angeles for twenty years. He is the author of *Becoming a Father* from HCI Books, co-author of *Modern Eclectic Therapy* (Springer), and was mentored by the renowned poets Robert Bly and William Stafford. John's poetry has appeared in many literary journals and magazines such as *Verve* and *Rivertalk*. He has co-authored three screenplays with veteran screenwriter P.J. Torokvei whose credits include *Caddyshack II, Guarding Tess, Back to School, Real Genius*, and many more. In addition to his professional achievements, John won the small college World Series and is in three Oregon sport halls of fame. His photography is featured in Sooke Regional Museum and his Chinese brush paintings, which appear in *There Will Be Killing*, can be found in Hawaiian art galleries. John divides his time between Hawaii and Vancouver Island, B.C., where he is Executive Director of Spirit Bear Art Farm and adjunct professor at the University of Victoria in British Columbia.

OLIVIA RUPPRECHT (aka Mallory Rush) is an award-winning, best-selling author who began her career as a novelist with Bantam Books in 1989. After seventeen published novels with extensive foreign translations from Bantam, Harlequin, and Doubleday, Olivia has gone on to manage fiction and nonfiction projects for major publishers as a copywriter, ghostwriter, book doctor, and developmental editor. She has served as editor for *NINK*, the official newsletter of the international authors' organization Novelists, Inc., and in 2009 assumed the position of Series Developer for the groundbreaking reality-based novel series from HCI Books, True Vows. Olivia's moveable feast of a desk is presently near Madison, Wisconsin.

ACKNOWLEDGMENTS

Anyone who writes stories of war knows how important support and encouragement is to getting through the darkness.

No one could have a finer or more gifted and giving co-author than Olivia Rupprecht, my writing partner.

With gratitude to our publisher, Lou Aronica, whose immediate belief and enthusiasm for this story meant everything.

My thanks to early readers and dear friends Nuala Vermeiren, Anne Algard, Sonja Kamber, Steven Smith, Berger Hareide, Nancy Gold, Nick Torokvei, and my brother Joseph Hart. Nora Tamada's and Glenna McReynold's early editorial feedback proved invaluable; Olivia and I are indebted to you both, as well as to Scott Rupprecht for going the distance. Much gratitude also to Michele Matrisciani and her father Dan, a Mekong Delta Vet whom I value for his endorsement of the authenticity and reality of the book.

My respect and gratitude to master calligrapher, artist, and teacher John Nip. And to Gerry Lopez for her art expertise, a special thanks.

I would like to especially mention the late P.J. Torokvei who loved the original story and with whom I wrote the screenplay from which this novel evolved. She provided support, dear friendship, encouragement, and SpiritBearArtFarm, the best sanctuary in the world for writing this story.

Love and gratitude to my children Kelly, Nick, and Caitlin.

A simple thank you is not enough for Andrea Jane who has been through the dark nights and brought me back and always believed.

Finally to the brave and dedicated women and the men of the 98th (KO), the Red Cross, and the mission hospitals in 1969–70 for all you did and all you gave.

– John Hart